YOUNG WOMAN IN A GARDEN

YOUNG WOMAN IN A GARDEN

STORIES

DELIA SHERMAN

Small Beer Press
Easthampton, MA

This is a work of fiction. All characters and events portrayed in this book are either fictitious or used fictitiously.

deliasherman.com

"Young Woman in a Garden" originally published in *Xanadu 2*, 1994. "The Ghost of Cwmlech Manor" originally published in *Steampunk!*, 2011. "The Red Piano" originally published in *Poe*, 2009. "The Fiddler of Bayou Teche" originally published in *Coyote Road*, 2006. "La Fée Verte" originally published in *Salon Fantastique*, 2006. "Walpurgis Afternoon" originally published in *The Magazine of Fantasy & Science Fiction*, 2005. "Land's End" originally published in *The Magazine of Fantasy & Science Fiction*, 1991. "The Parwat Ruby" originally published in *The Magazine of Fantasy & Science Fiction*, 1999. "The Fairy Cony-Catcher" originally published in *Sirens*, 1998. "Sacred Harp" originally published in *The Horns of Elfland*, 1997. "The Printer's Daughter" originally published in *Ruby Slippers, Golden Tears,x* 1995. "Nanny Peters and the Feathery Bride" originally published in *The Magazine of Fantasy & Science Fiction*, 1990. "Miss Carstairs and the Merman" originally published in *The Magazine of Fantasy & Science Fiction*, 1989. "The Maid on the Shore" originally published in *The Magazine of Fantasy & Science Fiction*, 1987.

Small Beer Press
150 Pleasant Street #306
Easthampton, MA 01027
www.smallbeerpress.com
www.weightlessbooks.com
info@smallbeerpress.com

Distributed to the trade by Consortium.

Library of Congress Cataloging-in-Publication Data

Sherman, Delia.
[Short stories. Selections]
Young woman in a garden : stories / Delia Sherman.
pages ; cm
Summary: "In her vivid and wise long anticipated first collection, Delia Sherman takes seemingly insignificant moments in the lives of artists or sailors -- the light out a window, the two strokes it takes to turn a small boat -- and finds the ghosts haunting them, the magic surrounding them"-- Provided by publisher.
ISBN 978-1-61873-091-6 (softcover) -- ISBN 978-1-61873-092-3 (ebook)
I. Title.
PS3569.H418A6 2014
813'.54--dc23

2014032402

First edition 1 2 3 4 5 6 7 8 9

Text set in Centaur. Titles in Castellar.

Printed on 30% PCR recycled paper by the Maple Press in York, PA.

CONTENTS

For Jane Yolen
With love and gratitude

YOUNG WOMAN IN A GARDEN

Beauvoisin (1839–1898)
Edouard Beauvoisin was expected to follow in the footsteps of his father, a provincial doctor. When he demonstrated a talent for drawing, however, his mother saw to it that he was provided with formal training. In 1856, Beauvoisin went to Paris, where he worked at the Académie Suisse and associated with the young artists disputing Romanticism and Classicism at the Brasserie des Martyrs. In 1868, he married the artist Céleste Rohan. He exhibited in the Salon des Refusés in 1863, and was a member of the 1874 Salon of Impressionists. In 1875 he moved to Brittany where he lived and painted until his death in 1898. He is best known for the figure studies *Young Woman in a Garden* and *Reclining Nude.*

Impressions of the Impressionists
Oxford University Press, 1970

M. Herri Tanguy
Director
Musée La Roseraie
Portrieux, Brittany
France

January 6, 1990

Monsieur:

I write to you at the suggestion of M. Rouart of the Musée d'Orsay to request permission to visit the house of M. Edouard Beauvoisin and to consult those of his personal papers that are kept there.

In pursuit of a Ph.D. degree in the history of art, I am preparing a thesis on the life and work of M. Beauvoisin, who, in my opinion, has been unfairly neglected in the history of Impressionism.

Enclosed is a letter of introduction from my adviser, Professor Boodman of the Department of Art History at the University of Massachusetts. She has advised me to tell you that I also have a personal interest in M. Beauvoisin's life, for his brother was my great-great-grandfather.

I expect to be in France from May 1 of this year, and to stay for at least two months. My visit to La Roseraie may be scheduled according to your convenience. Awaiting your answer, I have the honor to be

Your servant, Theresa Stanton

When Theresa finally found La Roseraie at the end of an unpaved, narrow road, she was tired and dusty and on the verge of being annoyed. Edouard Beauvoisin had been an Impressionist, even if only a minor Impressionist, and his house was a museum, open by appointment to the public. At home in Massachusetts, that would mean signs, postcards in the nearest village, certainly a brochure in the local tourist office with color pictures of the garden and the master's studio and a good clear map showing how to get there.

France wasn't Massachusetts, not by a long shot.

M. Tanguy hadn't met Theresa at the Portrieux station as he had promised, the local tourist office had been sketchy in its directions, and the driver of the local bus had been depressingly uncertain about where to let her off. Her feet were sore, her backpack heavy, and even after asking at the last two farmhouses she'd passed, Theresa still wasn't sure she'd found the right place. The house didn't look like a museum: gray stone, low-browed and secretive, its front door unequivocally barred, its low windows blinded with heavy white lace curtains. The gate was stiff and loud with rust. Still, there was a neat stone path leading around to the back of the house and a white sign with the word "*Jardin*" printed on it over a faded black hand pointing down the path. Under the scent of dust and greenery was a clean, sharp scent of saltwater.

Theresa hitched up her backpack, heaved open the gate, and followed the hand's gesture.

"Monet," was her first thought when she saw the garden, and then, more accurately, "Beauvoisin." Impressionist, certainly—an incandescent, carefully balanced dazzle of yellow light, clear green grass, and carmine flowers against a celestial background. Enchanted, Theresa unslung her camera and captured a couple of faintly familiar views of flower beds and sequined water before turning to the house itself.

The back door was marginally more welcoming than the front, for at least it boasted a visible bell-pull and an aged, hand-lettered sign directing the visitor to "*Sonnez,*" which Theresa did, once hopefully, once impatiently, and once again for luck. She was just thinking that she'd have to walk back to Portrieux and call M. Tanguy when the heavy door opened inward, revealing a Goyaesque old woman. Against the flat shadows of a stone passage, she was a study in black and white: long wool skirt and linen blouse, sharp eyes and finely crinkled skin.

The woman looked Theresa up and down, then made as if to shut the door in her face.

"Wait," cried Theresa, putting her hand on the warm planks. "*Arretez. S'il vous plait. Un moment.* Please!"

The woman's gaze travelled to Theresa's face. Theresa smiled charmingly.

"*Eh, bien?*" asked the woman impatiently.

Pulling her French around her, Theresa explained that she was making researches into the life and work of the famous M. Beauvoisin, that she had written in the winter for permission to see the museum, that seeing it was of the first importance to completing her work. She had received a letter from M. le Directeur, setting an appointment for today.

The woman raised her chin suspiciously. Her smile growing rigid, Theresa juggled camera and bag, dug out the letter, and handed it over. The woman examined it front and back, then returned it with an eloquent gesture of shoulders, head, and neck that conveyed her utter indifference to Theresa's work, her interest in Edouard Beauvoisin, and her charm.

"*Fermé,*" she said, and suited the action to the word.

"*Parent,*" said Theresa rather desperately. "*Je suis de la famille de M. Beauvoisin.*"

From the far end of the shadowy passage, a soft, deep voice spoke in accented English. "Of course you are, my dear. A great-grand niece, I believe. Luna," she shifted to French, "surely you remember the letter from M. le Directeur about our little American relative?" And in English again. "Please to come through. I am Madame Beauvoisin."

In 1874, Céleste's mother died, leaving La Roseraie to her only child. There was some talk of selling the house to satisfy the couple's immediate financial embarrassments, but the elder Mme Beauvoisin came to the rescue once again with a gift of 20,000 francs. After paying off his debts, Beauvoisin decided that Paris was just too expensive, and moved with Céleste to Portrieux in the spring of 1875.

"I have taken some of my mother's gift and put it towards transforming the ancient dairy of La Roseraie into a studio," he wrote Manet. "Ah, solitude! You cannot imagine how I crave it, after the constant sociability of Paris. I realize now that the cafés affected me like absinthe: stimulating and full of visions, but death to the body and damnation to the soul."

In the early years of what his letters to Manet humorously refer to as his "exile," Beauvoisin travelled often to Paris, and begged his old friends to come and stay with him. After 1879, however, he became something of a recluse, terminating his trips to Paris and discouraging visits, even from the Manets. He spent the last twenty years of his life a virtual hermit, painting the subjects that were dearest to him: the sea, his garden, the fleets of fishing boats that sailed daily out and back from the harbor of Portrieux.

The argument has been made[6] that Beauvoisin had never been as clannish as others among the Impressionists—Renoir and Monet, for example, who regularly set up their easels and painted the same scene side by side. Certainly Beauvoisin seemed unusually reluctant to paint his friends and family. His single portrait of his wife, executed not long after their marriage, is one of his poorest canvases: stiff, awkwardly posed, and uncharacteristically muddy in color. "Mme Beauvoisin takes exception to my treatment of her dress," he complained in a letter to Manet, "or the shadow of the chair, or the balance of the composition. God save me from the notions of women who think themselves artists!"

In 1877, the Beauvoisins took a holiday in Spain, and there met a young woman named Luz Gascó, who became Edouard's favorite—indeed his only—model. The several nude studies of her, together with the affectionate intimacy of *Young Woman in a Garden* leaves little doubt as to the nature of their relationship, even in the absence of documentary evidence. Luz came to live with the Beauvoisins at La Roseraie in 1878, and remained there even after Beauvoisin's death in 1898. She inherited the house and land from Mme Beauvoisin and died in 1914, just after the outbreak of the First World War.

Lydia Chopin. *Lives Lived in Shadow: Edouard and Céleste Beauvoisin.*
Apollo. Winter, 1989.

The garden of La Roseraie extended through a series of terraced beds down to the water's edge and up into the house itself by way of a bank of uncurtained French doors in the parlor. When Theresa first followed her hostess into the room, her impression was of blinding light and color and of flowers everywhere—scattered on the chairs and sofas, strewn underfoot, heaped on every flat surface, vining across the walls. The air was somnolent with peonies and roses and bee song.

"A lovely room."

"It has been kept just as it was in the time of Beauvoisin, though I fear the fabrics have faded sadly. You may recognize the sofa from *Young Woman Reading* and *Reclining Nude,* also the view down the terrace."

The flowers on the sofa were pillows, printed or needlepointed with huge, blowsy, ambiguous blooms. Those pillows had formed a textural contrast to the model's flat black gown in *Young Woman Reading* and sounded a sensual, almost erotic note in *Reclining Nude.* As Theresa touched one almost reverently—it had supported the model's head—the unquiet colors of the room settled in place around it, and she saw that there were indeed flowers everywhere. Real petals had blown in from the terrace to brighten the faded woven flowers of the carpet, and the walls and chairs were covered in competing chintzes to provide a background for the plain burgundy velvet sofa, the wooden easel, and the portrait over the mantel of a child dressed in white.

"Céleste," said Mme Beauvoisin. "Céleste Yvonne Léna Rohan, painted at the age of six by some Academician—I cannot at the moment recollect his name, although M. Rohan was as proud of securing his services as if he'd been Ingres himself. She hated it."

"How could you possibly. . . ." Theresa's question trailed off at the amusement in Mme Beauvoisin's face.

"Family legend. The portrait is certainly very stiff and finished, and Céleste grew to be a disciple of Morisot and Manet. Taste in aesthetic matters develops very young, do you not agree?"

"I do," said Theresa. "At any rate, I've loved the Impressionists since I was a child. I wouldn't blame her for hating the portrait. It's technically accomplished, yes, but it says nothing about its subject except that she was blonde and played the violin."

"That violin!" Mme Beauvoisin shook her head, ruefully amused. "Mme Rohan's castle in Spain. The very sight of it was a torture to Céleste. And her hair darkened as she grew older, so you see the portrait tells you nothing. This, on the other hand, tells all."

She led Theresa to a small painting hung by the door. "Luz Gascó," she said. "Painted in 1879."

Liquid, animal eyes gleamed at Theresa from the canvas, their gaze at once inviting and promising, intimate as a kiss. Theresa glanced aside at Mme Beauvoisin, who was studying the portrait, her head tilted to one side, her wrinkled lips smoothed by a slight smile. Feeling unaccountably embarrassed, Theresa frowned at the painting with self-conscious professionalism. It was, she thought, an oil study of the model's head for Beauvoisin's most famous painting, *Young Woman in a Garden.* The face was tilted up to the observer and partially shadowed. The brushwork was loose and free, the boundaries between the model's hair and the background blurred, the molding of her features suggested rather than represented.

"A remarkable portrait," Theresa said. "She seems very . . . alive."

"Indeed," said Mme Beauvoisin. "And very beautiful." She turned abruptly and, gesturing Theresa to a chair, arranged herself on the sofa opposite. The afternoon light fell across her shoulder, highlighting her white hair, the pale rose pinned in the bosom of her high-necked dress, her hands folded on her lap. Her fingers were knotted and swollen with arthritis. Theresa wondered how old she was and why M. Tanguy had said nothing of a caretaker in his letter to her.

"Your work?" prompted Mme Beauvoisin gently.

Theresa pulled herself up and launched into what she thought of as her dissertation spiel: neglected artist, brilliant technique, relatively small ouvre, social isolation, mysterious ménage. "What I keep coming back to," she said, "is his isolation. He hardly ever went to Paris after 1879, and even before that he didn't go on those group painting trips the other Impressionists loved so much. He never shared a studio even though he was so short of money, or let anyone watch him paint. And yet his letters to Manet suggest that he wasn't a natural recluse—anything but."

"Thus Luz Gascó?" asked Mme Beauvoisin.

"I'm sorry?"

"Luz Gascó. Perhaps you think she was the cause of Beauvoisin's—how shall I say?—Beauvoisin's retreat from society?"

Theresa gave a little bounce in her chair. "That's just it, you see. No one really knows. There are a lot of assumptions, especially by *male* historians, but no one really knows. What I'm looking for is evidence one way or the other. At first I thought she couldn't have been . . ." She hesitated, suddenly self-conscious.

"Yes?" The low voice was blandly polite, yet Theresa felt herself teased, or perhaps tested. It annoyed her, and her answer came a little more sharply than necessary.

"Beauvoisin's mistress." Mme Beauvoisin raised her brows and Theresa shrugged apologetically. "There's not much known about Céleste, but nothing suggests that she was particularly meek or downtrodden. I don't think she'd have allowed Luz to live here all those years, much less left the house to her, if she knew she was . . . involved with her husband."

"Perhaps she knew and did not concern herself." Mme Beauvoisin offered this consideringly.

"I hadn't thought of that," said Theresa. "I'd need proof, though. I'm not interested in speculation, theory, or even in a juicy story. I'm interested in the truth."

Mme Beauvoisin's smile said that she found Theresa very young, very charming. "Yes," she said slowly. "I believe you are." Her voice grew brisker. "Beauvoisin's papers are in some disorder, you understand. Your search may take you some weeks, and Portrieux is far to travel twice a day. It would please me if you would accept the hospitality of La Roseraie."

Theresa closed her eyes. It was a graduate student's dream come true, to be invited into her subject's home, to touch and use his things, to live his life. Mme Beauvoisin, misinterpreting the gesture, said, "Please stay. This project—Beauvoisin's papers—it is of great importance to us, to Luna and to me. We feel that you are well suited to the task."

To emphasize her words, she laid her twisted hand on Theresa's arm. The gesture brought her face into the sun, which leached her eyes and skin to transparency and made a glory of her silvered hair. Theresa stared at her, entranced.

"Thank you," she said. "I would be honored."

Young Woman in a Garden (Luz at La Roseraie) 1879
Edouard Beauvoisin's artistic reputation rests on this portrait of his Spanish mistress, Luz Gascó, seated in the garden of La Roseraie. As in *Reclining Nude,* the composition is arranged around a figure that seems to be the painting's source of light as well as its visual focus. Luz sits with her face and body in shade and her feet and hands in bright sunlight. Yet the precision with which her shadowy figure is rendered, the delicate modeling of the face, and the suggestion of light shining down through the leaves onto the dark hair draw the viewer's eye up and away from the brightly-lit foreground. The brushwork of the white blouse is especially masterly, the coarse texture of the linen suggested with a scumble of pale pink, violet, and gray.

"The Unknown Impressionists"
Exhibition Catalogue
Museum of Fine Arts, Boston, MA

"This is the studio."

Mme Beauvoisin laid her hand on the blue-painted door, hesitated, then stepped aside. "Please," she said, and gave Theresa a courteous nod.

Heart tripping over itself with excitement, Theresa pushed open the door and stepped into Beauvoisin's studio. The room was shuttered, black as midnight; she knocked over a chair, which fell with an echoing clatter.

"I fear the trustees have hardly troubled themselves to unlock the door since they came into possession of the property," said Mme Beauvoisin apologetically. "And Luna and I have little occasion to come here." Theresa heard her shoe heels tapping across the flagstone floor. A creak, a bang, and weak sunlight struggled over a clutter of easels, canvases, trunks and boxes, chairs, stools, and small tables disposed around a round stove and a shabby sofa. *The French sure are peculiar,* Theresa thought. *What a way to run a museum!*

Mme Beauvoisin had taken up a brush and was standing before one of the easels in the attitude of a painter interrupted at work. For a moment, Theresa thought she saw a canvas on the easel, an oil sketch of a seated figure. An unknown Beauvoisin? As she stepped forward to look, an ancient swag of cobweb broke and showered her head with flies and powdery dust. She sneezed convulsively.

"God bless you," said Mme Beauvoisin, laying the brush on the empty easel. "Luna brings a broom. Pah! What filth! Beauvoisin must quiver in his tomb, such an orderly man as he was!"

Soon the old woman arrived with the promised broom, a pail of water, and a settled expression of grim disapproval. She poked at the cobwebs with the broom, glared at Theresa, then began to sweep with concentrated ferocity, raising little puffs of dust as she went and muttering to herself, witch-like.

"So young," she said. "Too young. Too full of ideas. Too much like Edouard, *enfin.*"

Theresa bit her lip, caught between curiosity and irritation. Curiosity won. "How am I like him, Luna?" she asked. "And how can you know? He's been dead almost a hundred years."

The old woman straightened and turned, her face creased deep with fury. "Luna!" she snarled. "Who has given you the right to call me Luna? I am not a servant, to be addressed without respect."

"You're not? I mean, of course not. I beg your pardon, Madame . . . ?" And Theresa looked a wild appeal to Mme Beauvoisin, who said, "The fault is entirely mine, Mlle Stanton, for not introducing you sooner. Mlle Gascó is my companion."

Theresa laughed nervously, as at an incomprehensible joke. "You're kidding," she said. "Gascó? But that was the model's name, Luz's name. I don't understand. Who are you, anyway?"

Mme Beauvoisin shrugged dismissively. "There is nothing to understand. We are Beauvoisin's heirs. And the contents of this studio are our inheritance, which is yours also. Come and look." With a theatrical flourish, she indicated a cabinet built along the back wall. "Open it," she said. "The doors are beyond my strength."

Theresa looked from Mme Beauvoisin to Mlle Gascó and back again. Every scholar knows that coincidences happen, that people leave things to their relatives, that reality is sometimes unbelievably strange. And this was what she had come for, after all, to open the cabinet, to recover all the mysteries and illuminate the shadows of Beauvoisin's life. Perhaps this Mlle Gascó was his illegitimate granddaughter. Perhaps both women were playing some elaborate and obscure game. In any case, it wasn't any of her business. Her business was with the cabinet and its contents.

The door was warped, and Theresa had to struggle with it for a good while before it creaked stiffly open on a cold stench of mildew and the shadowy forms of dispatch boxes neatly arranged on long shelves. Theresa sighed happily. Here they were, Beauvoisin's papers, a scholar's treasure trove, her ticket to a degree, a career, a profession. And they were all hers. She reached out both hands and gathered in the nearest box. As the damp cardboard yielded to her fingers, she felt a sudden panic that the papers would be mildewed into illegibility. But the papers were wrapped in oilcloth and perfectly dry.

Reverently, Theresa lifted out a packet of letters, tied with black tape. The top one was folded so that some of the text showed. Having just spent a month working with Beauvoisin's letters to Manet at the Bibliothèque Nationale, she immediately recognized his hand, tiny and angular and blessedly legible. Theresa slipped the letter free from the packet and opened it. *I have met,* she read, *a dozen other young artists in the identical state of fearful ecstasy as I, feeling great things about Art and Beauty which we are half-shy of expressing, yet must express or die.*

"Thérèse." Mme Beauvoisin sounded amused. "First we must clean this place. Then you may read Beauvoisin's words with more comfort and less danger of covering them with smuts."

Theresa became aware that she was holding the precious letter in an unforgivably dirty hand. "Oh," she said, chagrined. "I'm so sorry. I *know* better than this."

"It is the excitement of discovery." Mme Beauvoisin took the letter from her and rubbed lightly at the corner with her apron. "See, it comes clean, all save a little shadow that may easily be overlooked." She folded the letter, slipped it back into the packet, returned it to the box, and tucked the oilcloth over it.

"Today, the preparation of the canvas," she said. "Tomorrow, you may begin the sketch."

Edouard Beauvoisin had indeed been an orderly man. The letters were parceled up by year, in order of receipt, and labeled. Turning over Manet's half of their long correspondence, Theresa briefly regretted her choice of research topic. Manet's was a magic name, a name to conjure up publishers and job offers, fame and what passed for fortune among art historians. But Manet, who had been documented, described, and analyzed by every art historian worth his pince-nez, could never be hers. Beauvoisin was hers.

Theresa sorted out all the business papers, the bills for paint and canvas, the notes from obscure friends. What was left was what she gleefully called the good stuff: a handful of love notes written by Céleste Rohan over the two years Beauvoisin had courted her, three boxes of letters from his mother, and two boxes of his answers, which must have been returned to him at her death.

It took Theresa a week to work through the letters, a week of long hours reading in the studio and short, awkward meals eaten in the kitchen with Mme Beauvoisin and Luna. It was odd. In the house and garden, they were everywhere, present as the sea-smell, forever on the way to some domestic task or other, yet never too busy to inquire politely and extensively after her progress. Or at least Mme Beauvoisin was never too busy. Luna mostly glared at her, hoped she wasn't wasting her time, warned her not to go picking the flowers or walking on the grass. It didn't take long for Theresa to decide that she didn't like Luna.

She did, however, like Edouard Beauvoisin. In the studio, Theresa could lose herself in Beauvoisin's world of artists and models. The letters to his mother from his early years in Paris painted an intriguing portrait of an intelligent, passionate, and, above all, naive young man whose most profound desire was to capture and define Beauty in charcoal and oils. He wrote of poses and technical problems and what his teacher M. Couture had said about his life studies, reaffirming in each letter his intention *to draw and draw and draw until every line breathes the essence of the thing itself.* A little over a year later, he was speaking less of line and more of color; the name Couture disappeared from his letters, to be replaced by Manet, Degas, Duranty, and the brothers Goncourt. By 1860, he had quit the École des Beaux Arts and registered to copy the Old Masters at the Louvre. A year later, he met Céleste Rohan at the house of Berthe Morisot's sister, Edma Pontillon:

> *She is like a Raphael Madonna, tall and slender and pale, and divinely unconscious of her own beauty. She said very little at dinner, but afterwards in the garden with Morisot conversed with me an hour or more. I learned then that she is thoughtful and full of spirit, loves Art and Nature, and is herself something of an artist, with a number of watercolors and oil sketches to her credit that, according to Morisot, show considerable promise.*

Three months later, he announced to his mother that Mlle Rohan had accepted his offer of hand and heart. Mme Beauvoisin the elder said everything that was proper, although a note of worry did creep through in her final lines:

I am a little concerned about her painting. To be sure, painting is an amiable accomplishment in a young girl, but you must be careful, in your joy at finding a soul-mate, not to foster useless ambitions in her breast. I'm sure you both agree that a wife must have no other profession than seeing to the comfort of her husband, particularly when her husband is an artist and entirely unable to see to his own.

When she read this, Theresa snorted. Perhaps her mother-in-law was why Céleste, like Edma Morisot and dozens of other lady artists, had laid down her brush when she married. Judging from her few surviving canvases, she'd been a talented painter, if too indebted to the style of Berthe Morisot. Now, if Céleste had just written to her future husband about painting or ambition or women's role in marriage, Theresa would have an easy chapter on the repression of women artists in nineteenth-century France.

It was with high hopes that Theresa opened the small bundle of Céleste's correspondence. She soon discovered that, however full of wit and spirit Céleste may have been in conversation, on paper she was terse and dull. Her letters were limited to a few scrawled lines of family news, expressions of gratitude for books her fiancé had recommended, and a few shy declarations of maidenly affection. The only signs of her personality were the occasional vivid sketches with which she illustrated her notes: a seal pup sunning itself on the rocks at the mouth of the bay; a cow peering thoughtfully in through the dairy window.

Theresa folded Céleste's letters away, tied the tape neatly around them, and sighed. She was beginning to feel discouraged. No wonder there'd been so little written on Edouard Beauvoisin. No wonder his studio was neglected, his museum unmarked, his only curators an eccentric pair of elderly women. There had been dozens of competent but uninspired followers of the Impressionists who once or twice in the course of their lives had managed to paint great pictures. The only thing that set Edouard Beauvoisin apart from them was the mystery of Luz Gascó, and as Theresa read his dutiful letters to his mother, she found that she just could not believe that the man who had written them could bring his mistress to live with his wife. More importantly, she found herself disbelieving that he could ever have painted *Young Woman in a Garden.* Yet there it incontrovertibly was, hanging in the Museum of Fine Arts, signed "Edouard Beauvoisin, 1879," clear as print and authenticated five ways from Sunday.

A breeze stirred the papers scattered across the worktable. Under the ever-present tang of the sea, Theresa smelled lilies of the valley. She propped her hands on her chin and looked out into the garden. A pretty day, she thought, and a pretty view. It might make a picture, were there anything to balance the window frame and the mass of the linden tree in the left foreground. Oh, there was the rose bed, but it wasn't enough. Then a figure stepped into the scene, bent to the roses, clipped a bloom, laid it in the basket dangling from her elbow: Gascó, a red shawl tied Spaniard-wise aross her white morning gown, her wild black hair escaping from its pins and springing around her face as she stooped. Her presence focused the composition, turned it into an interesting statement of light and tension.

Don't move, Theresa thought. For God's sake, Gascó, don't move. Squinting at the scene, she opened a drawer with a practiced jerk and felt for the sketchbook, which was not on top, where it should be, where it always was. Irritated, she tore her eyes from Gascó to look for it. Lying in the drawer was a child's *cahier,* marbled black and white, with a plain white label pasted on its cover and marked "May-June 1898" in a tiny, angular, blessedly legible hand.

"Out of place," she murmured angrily, then, "This is *it,*" without any clear idea of what she meant by either statement.

Theresa swallowed, aware that something unimaginably significant had happened, was happening, that she was trembling and sweating with painful excitement. Carefully, she wiped her hands on her jeans, lifted the *cahier* from its wooden tomb, opened it to its last entry: June 5, 1898. The hand was scratchier, more sprawled than in his letters, the effect, perhaps, of the wasting disease that would kill him in July.

> *The Arrangement. A pity my death must void it. How well it has served us over the years, and how happily! At least, C. has seemed happy; for L.'s discontents, there has never been any answer, except to leave and make other arrangements of her own. Twenty years of flying into rages, sinking into sulks, refusing to stand thus and so or to hold a pose not to her liking, hating Brittany, the cold, the damp, the gray sea. And still she stays. Is it the Arrangement that binds her, or her beloved garden?* Young Woman in a Garden: Luz at La Roseraie. *If I have a fear of dying, it is that I must be remembered for that painting. God's judgment on our Arrangement, Maman would have said, had she known of it. When I come to make my last Confession, soon, oh, very soon now, I will beg forgiveness for deceiving her. It is my only regret.*

By dusk, Theresa had read the notebook through and begun to search for its fellows. That there had to be more notebooks was as clear as Monet's palette: the first entry began in mid-sentence, for one thing, and no man talks to himself so fluently without years of practice. They wouldn't be hidden; Beauvoisin hadn't been a secretive man. Tidy-minded. Self-contained. Conservative. He stored them somewhere, Theresa thought. Somewhere here. She looked around the darkening studio. Maybe it would be clearer to her in the morning. It would certainly be lighter.

Out in the garden, Theresa felt the depression of the past weeks release her like a hand opening. *A discovery! A real discovery!* What difference did it make whether Beauvoisin had painted two good paintings or a dozen? There was a mystery about him, and she, Theresa Stanton, was on the verge of uncovering it. She wanted to babble and sing and go out drinking to celebrate. But her friends were three thousand miles away, and all she had was Mme Beauvoisin. And Luna. Always Luna.

Theresa's quick steps slowed. What was her hurry, after all? Her news would keep, and the garden was so lovely in the failing light, with the white pebble path luminous under her feet, the evening air blue and warm and scented with lilies.

In the parlor, an oil lamp laid its golden hand upon the two women sitting companionably together on the velvet sofa, their heads bent to their invisible tasks. The soft play of light and shadow varnished their hair and skin with youth. Theresa struggled with a momentary and inexplicable sense of déjà vu, then, suddenly embarrassed, cleared her throat. "I found a notebook today," she announced into the silence. "Beauvoisin's private journal."

Luna's head came up, startled and alert. Theresa caught a liquid flash as she glanced at her, then at Mme Beauvoisin.

"A journal?" asked Mme Beauvoisin blandly. "Ah. I might have guessed he would have kept a journal. You must be very pleased—such documents are important to scholars. Come. Pour yourself a brandy to celebrate—the bottle is on the sideboard—and sit and tell us of your great discovery."

As Theresa obediently crossed the room and unstopped the decanter, she heard a furious whisper. "*Mierda!*"

"Hush, Luna." Mme Beauvoisin's tone was happy, almost gleeful. "We agreed. Whatever she finds, she may use. It is her right."

"I withdraw my agreement. I know nothing of these journals. Who can tell what he may have written?"

A deep and affectionate sigh. "Oh, Luna. Still so suspicious?"

"Not suspicious. Wise. The little American, she is of Edouard's blood and also Edouard's soul. I have seen him in her eyes."

Theresa set down the decanter and came back into the lamplight. "Wait a minute. I don't understand. Of course I have the right to use the journals. M. Tanguy promised me full access to all

Beauvoisin's papers. And he didn't say anything about you. Where is he anyway?"

Mme Beauvoisin's dark, faded eyes held hers for a moment. "Please, do not discommode yourself," she said. "Sit and tell us what you have found."

Hesitant under Luna's hot and disapproving gaze, Theresa perched herself on the edge of a chair and did as she was told.

"I'd no idea he was so passionate," she said at last. "In his letters, although he speaks of passion, he's always so moderate about expressing it."

"Moderate!" Luna's laugh was a scornful snort. "Hear the girl! *Madre de Dios!*"

"Hush, Luna. Please continue."

"That's all. I didn't really learn much, except that he knew in June that he was dying. One interesting thing was his references to an Arrangement—that's with a capital A—and how he'd never told his *maman* about it." Excitement rose in her again. "I have to find the rest of the journals!"

Mme Beauvoisin smiled at her. "Tomorrow. You will find them, I'm sure of it."

"Céleste," said Luna warningly.

"Hush, my dear."

Theresa retired, as always, before her elderly companions. As polite as Mme Beauvoisin was, she always felt uncomfortable in the parlor, as if her presence there were an intrusion, a threat, a necessary evil. Which, she told herself firmly, in a way, it was. The two women had been living here alone for Heaven only knew how long. It was only natural that they'd feel put out by her being there. It was silly of her to resent her exclusion from their charmed circle. And yet, tonight especially, she did.

Theresa curled up in a chair by the window, tucked the duvet around her legs, and considered the problem of Edouard's notebooks. A full moon washed the pale roses and the white paths with silver. In her mind, Theresa followed Edouard down one of those luminous paths to the studio, sitting at his desk, pulling his current notebook from the right-hand drawer and re-reading his last entry only to discover that he'd barely one page left. He shook his head, rose, went to the cabinet, opened one of the long drawers where he kept his paints and pigments neatly arranged in shallow wooden trays. Carefully, he lifted one tray, slipped a new marbled *cahier* from under it, returned to his desk, and began to write.

When Theresa opened her eyes, the garden was cool in a pale golden dawn. Her neck was in agony, her legs were hopelessly cramped, but she was elated. The notebooks were in the cabinet under the paint trays—they just had to be!

Twenty minutes later, she was in the studio herself, with the paint trays stacked on the floor, gloating over layers of black-and-white marbled *cahiers.*

There were more than a hundred of them, she discovered, distributed over four drawers and forty-two years, from Beauvoisin's first trip to Paris in 1856 to his death in 1898. Theresa took out five or six of them at random and paged through them as she had paged through books as a child, stopping to read passages that caught her eye. Not entirely professional, perhaps. But thoroughly satisfying.

April 20, 1875
Paris is so full of bad paintings, I can't begin to describe them. I know C.'s would enjoy some modest success, but she will not agree. One of Mlle Morisot's canvases has sold for a thousand francs—a seascape not so half as pretty as the one C. painted at La Roseraie last month. I compliment her often on her work, and am somewhat distressed that she does not return the courtesy, from love of the artist if not from admiration of his work. But

then C. has never understood my theory of light and evanescence, and will not agree with my principles of composition.

Theresa closed the notebook with a snap, unreasonably disappointed with Beauvoisin for his blindness to the structures of his society. Surely he must have known, as Céleste obviously knew, that men were professionals and women were amateurs, unless they were honorary men like Berthe Morisot and Mary Cassatt? Poor Céleste, Theresa thought, and poor Edouard. What had they seen in one another?

Over the next few days, Theresa chased the answer to that question through the pages of Edouard's journals, skipping from one C. to the next, composing a sketch-portrait of a very strange marriage. That Beauvoisin had loved Céleste was clear. That he had loved her as a wife was less so. He spoke of her as a travelling companion, a hostess, a housekeeper. A sister, Theresa thought suddenly, reading how Céleste had arranged the details of their trip to Spain in the winter of 1877. She's like the maiden sister keeping house for her brilliant brother. And Edouard, he was a man who saved all his passion for his art, at any rate until he went to Spain and met Luz Gascó.

I have made some sketches of a woman we met in the Prado—a respectable woman and tolerably educated, although fallen on evil times. She has quite the most beautiful skin I have seen—white as new cream and so fine that she seems to glow of her own light, like a lamp draped with heavy silk. Such bones! And her hair and eyes, like black marble polished and by some miracle brought to life and made supple. C. saw her first, and effected an introduction. She is a joy to paint, and not expensive . . . .

Eagerly, Theresa skimmed through the next months for further references to the beautiful *señorita.* Had Edouard fallen in love at last? He certainly wrote as if he had—long, poetic descriptions of her skin, her hair, her form, her luminous, living presence. At the same time, he spoke fearfully of her temper, her unaccountable moods, her uncontrollable "gypsy nature." In the end, however, simple painterly covetousness won out and he invited Gascó to spend the summer at La Roseraie.

> *May 6, 1878*
> *Luz Gascó expected tomorrow. C., having vacated the blue chamber for her, complains of having nowhere to paint. Perhaps I'll build an extension to my studio. Gascó is a great deal to ask of a wife, after all, even though C. knows better than any other how unlikely my admiration is to overstep propriety. As a model, Gascó is perfection. As a woman, she is like a wild cat, ready to hiss and scratch for no reason. Yet that skin! Those eyes! I despair of capturing them and ache to make the attempt.*
>
> Fishing Boats *not going well. The boats are wooden and the water also. I shall try Gascó in the foreground to unbalance the composition. . . .*

How violently the presence of Luz Gascó unbalanced the nicely calculated composition of Edouard Beauvoisin's life became clearer to Theresa the more she read. She hardly felt excluded now from her hostesses' circle, eager as she was to get back to the studio and to Edouard, for whom she was feeling more and more sympathy. Pre-Gascó, his days had unfolded methodically: work, walks with Céleste, drives to the village, letter-writing, notebook-keeping, sketching—each allotted its proper time and space, regular as mealtimes. *G. rises at noon,* he mourned a week into her visit. *She breaks pose because she has seen a bird in the garden or wants to smell a flower. She is utterly impossible. Yet she transforms the world around her.*

Imperceptibly, the summer visit extended into autumn and the autumn into winter as Beauvoisin planned and painted canvas after canvas, experimenting with composition, technique, pigment. By the spring of 1879, there was talk of Gascó's staying. By summer, she was a fixture, and Beauvoisin was beside himself with huge, indefinite emotions and ambitions, all of them arranged, like his canvases, around the dynamic figure of Luz Gascó. Then came July, and a page blank save for one line:

July 6, 1879
Luz in the parlor. Ah, Céleste!

A puzzling entry, marked as if for easy reference with a scrap of cheap paper folded in four. Theresa picked it up and carefully smoothed it open—not carefully enough, however, to keep the brittle paper from tearing along its creases. She saw dark lines—a charcoal sketch—and her heart went cold in panic. What have I done? she thought. What have I destroyed?

With a trembling hand, she arranged the four pieces on the table. The image was a reclining woman, her face turned away under an upflung arm, her bodice unbuttoned to the waist and her chemise loosened and folded open. A scarf of dark curls draped her throat and breast, veiling and exposing her nakedness. The sketch was intimate, more tender than erotic, a lover's mirror.

Theresa put her hands over her eyes. She'd torn the sketch; she didn't need to cry over it too. Spilt milk, she told herself severely. M. Rouart would know how to restore it. And she should be happy she'd found it, overjoyed to have such dramatic proof of Beauvoisin's carnal passion for his Spanish model. So why did she feel regretful, sad, disappointed and so terribly, overwhelmingly angry?

A shadow fell across the page. A gnarled, nail-bitten forefinger traced the charcoaled line of the subject's hair.

"Ah," said Luna softly. "I wondered what had become of this."

Theresa clenched her own hands in her lap, appalled by the emotion that rose in her at the sound of that hoarse, slightly lisping voice. Luna was certainly irritating. But this was not irritation Theresa felt. It was rage.

"A beautiful piece, is it not?" The four torn pieces were not perfectly aligned: the woman seemed broken at the waist; her left arm, lying across her hips, was dismembered at the elbow. Luna coaxed her back together with delicate touches. "A pity that my own beauty may not be so easily repaired."

Surprised, Theresa looked up at Luna's turtle face. She'd never imagined Luna young, let alone beautiful. Yet now she saw that her bones were finely turned under her leathery skin and her eyes were unfaded and bright black as a mouse's. A vaguely familiar face, and an interesting one, now that Theresa came to study it. Something might be made of it, against a background of flowers, or the garden wall.

Luna straightened, regarding Theresa with profound disgust. "You're his to the bone," she said. "You see what you need to see, not what is there. I told her a stranger would have been better."

Theresa's fury had subsided, leaving only bewilderment behind. She rubbed her eyes wearily. "I'm sorry," she said. "I don't understand. Do you know something about this sketch?"

The old woman's mouth quirked angrily. "What I know of this sketch," she spat, "is that it was not meant for your eyes." And with a haughty lift of her chin, she turned and left the studio.

Was Mlle Gascó crazy, or senile, or just incredibly mean? Theresa wondered, watching her hobble across the bright prospect of the garden like an arthritic crow. Surely she couldn't actually know anything about that sketch—why, it had been hidden for over a hundred years. For a moment, the garden dimmed, as though a cloud had come over the sun, and then Theresa's eyes strayed to the notebook open before her. A sunbeam dazzled the single sentence to blankness. She moved the notebook out of the glare and turned the page.

The next entry was dated the 14th of July and spoke of Bastille Day celebrations in Lorient and a family outing with Céleste and Gascó, all very ordinary except that Beauvoisin's prose was less colorful than usual. Something was going on. But Theresa had already known that. Beauvoisin had grown immensely as a painter over the summer of 1879, and had also cut himself off from the men who had been his closest friends. She was already familiar with the sharp note he'd written Manet denying that he had grown reclusive, only very hard at work and somewhat distracted, he hinted, by domestic tension: "For two women to reside under one roof is far from restful," he had written, and "Céleste and I have both begun paintings of Gascó—not, alas, the same pose."

Theresa flipped back to July 6. *Luz in the parlor. Ah, Céleste!* Such melodrama was not like Beauvoisin, nor was a week's silence, nor the brief, lifeless chronicles of daily events that occupied him during the month of August. Theresa sighed. Real life is often melodramatic, and extreme emotion mute. Something had happened on July 6, something that had changed Beauvoisin's life and art.

In any case, late in 1879 Beauvoisin had begun to develop a new style, a lighter, more brilliant palette, a more painterly technique that broke definitively from the line-obsessed training of his youth. Reading the entries for the fall of '79 and the winter of '80, Theresa learned that he had developed his prose style as well, in long disquisitions on light and composition, life and art. He gave up all accounts of ordinary events in favor of long essays on the beauty of the ephemeral: a young girl, a budding flower, a spring morning, a perfect understanding between man and woman. He became obsessed with a need to capture even the most abstract of emotions on canvas: betrayal, joy, contentment, estrangement.

I have set G. a pose I flatter myself expresses most perfectly that moment of suspension between betrayal and remorse. She is to the left of the central plane, a little higher than is comfortable, crowded into a box defined by the straight back of her chair and the arm of the sofa. Her body twists left, her face is without expression, her eyes are fixed on the viewer. The conceit pleases G. more than C., of course, G. being the greater cynic. But C. agrees that the composition is out of the ordinary way and we all have great hopes of it at the next Salon. Our Arrangement will answer very well, I think.

Reading such entries—which often ran to ten or fifteen closely-written pages—Theresa began to wonder when Beauvoisin found time to paint the pictures he had so lovingly and thoughtfully planned. It was no wonder, she thought, that *Interior* and *Woman at a Window* seemed so theoretical, so contrived. She was not surprised to read that they had not brought as much as *Young Woman in a Garden* or *Reclining Nude,* painted two years later and described briefly as *a figure study of G. on the parlor sofa, oddly lighted. Pure whim, and not an idea anywhere in it. C. likes it, though, and so does G.; have allowed myself to be overborne.*

June had laid out its palette in days of Prussian blue, clear green, and yellow. In the early part of the month, when Theresa had been reading the letters, the clouds flooded the sky with a gray and white wash that suppressed shadow and compressed perspective like a Japanese print. After she found the notebooks, however, all the days seemed saturated with light and static as a still life.

Theresa spent her time reading Beauvoisin's journals, leaving the studio only to eat a silent meal alone in the kitchen, to wander through the garden or, in the evenings, to go down to the seawall where she would watch the sun set in Turneresque glories of carmine and gold. Once, seeing the light, like Danae's shower, spilling its golden seed into the sea, Theresa felt her hand twitch with the desire to paint the scene, to capture the evanescent moment in oil and make it immortal.

What am I thinking of? she wondered briefly. I can't paint. It must be Edouard rubbing off on me. Or the isolation. I need to get out of here for a couple days, go back to Paris, see M. Rouart about the sketch, maybe let him take me out to dinner, talk to someone real for a change. But the next day found her in the studio and the next evening by the seawall, weeping with the beauty of the light and her own inadequate abilities.

As June shaded into July, Theresa abandoned the notebooks and began to sketch the pictures she saw around her in the studio and garden. Insensible of sacrilege, she took up Beauvoisin's pastel chalks and charcoal pencils and applied herself to the problem of reproducing her impressions of the way the flowers shimmered under the noonday sun and how the filtered light reflected from the studio's whitewashed walls.

At first, she'd look at the untrained scrawls and blotches she'd produced and tear them to confetti in an ecstasy of disgust. But as the clear still days unfolded, she paid less and less attention to what she'd done, focusing only on the need of the moment, to balance mass and shape, light and shade. She hardly saw Mme Beauvoisin and Luna, though she was dimly aware that they were about—in the parlor, in the garden, walking arm in arm across her field of vision: figures in the landscape, motifs in the composition. Day bled into day with scarcely a signpost to mark the end of one or the beginning of the next, so that she sketched and read in a timeless, seamless present, without past, without future, without real purpose.

So it was with no clear sense of time or place that Theresa walked into the studio one day and realized that she had left her sketchbook in the parlor. Tiresome, she thought to herself. But there was that study she'd been working on, the one of the stone wall. She'd just have to go back to the house and get it.

The transition from hall to parlor was always blinding, particularly in the afternoon, when the sun slanted through the French doors straight into entering eyes. That is perhaps why Theresa thought at first that the room was empty, and then that someone had left a large canvas propped against the sofa, a painting of two women in an interior.

It was an interesting composition, the details blurred by the bright backlight, the white dress of the figure on the sofa glimmering against the deep burgundy cushions, the full black skirts of the figure curled on the floor beside her like a pool of ink spilled on the flowery carpet. Both figures were intent on a paper the woman on the sofa held on her up-drawn knees. Her companion's torso was turned into the sofa, her arms wreathed loosely around her waist.

What a lovely picture they make together, Theresa thought. I wonder I never thought of posing them so. It's a pity Céleste will not let me paint her.

Céleste laid the sketch aside, took Gascó's hand, and carried it to her lips. Her gaze met Theresa's.

"Edouard," she said.

Theresa's cheeks heated; her heart began a slow, deep, painful beating that turned her dizzy. She put her hand on the doorframe to steady herself just as Gascó surged up from floor and turned, magnificent in her rage and beauty, to confront the intruder. Her face shone from the thundercloud of her hair, its graceful planes sharpened and defined by the contemptuous curve of her red mouth, and the wide, proud defiance of her onyx eyes. Edouard released the doorframe and helplessly reached out his hand to her.

"Be a man, Edouard!" Gascó all but spat. "Don't look like that. I knew this must come. It would have come sooner had you been less blind. No," as Edouard winced, "I beg your pardon. It was not necessary to say that. Or the other. But you must not weep."

Céleste had swung her legs to the floor and laid the sketch on the sofa back on top of the piled cushions. She looked composed, if a little pale, and her voice was even when she said, "Sit down, Luna. He has no intention of weeping. No, get us some brandy. We must talk, and we'd all be the better for something to steady us."

"Talk?" said Edouard. "What is there for us to say to one another?"

Gascó swept to the sideboard, poured brandy into three snifters, and handed them around, meeting Edouard's eyes defiantly when she put his into his hand.

"Drink, Edouard," said Céleste gently. "And why don't you sit down?"

He shook his head, but took a careful sip of his brandy. The liquor burned his throat.

"Doubtless you want us to leave La Roseraie," said Céleste into a long silence.

"Oh, no, my heart," said Gascó. "I'll not run away like some criminal. This house is yours. If anyone is to leave, it must be Beauvoisin."

"In law," said Edouard mildly, "the house is mine. I will not leave it. Nor will you, Céleste. You are my wife." His voice faltered. "I don't want you to leave. I want things as they were before."

"With your model your wife's lover, and you as blind as a mole?"

Edouard set down his half-finished brandy and pinched the bridge of his nose. "That was not kind, Gascó. But then, I have always known that you are not kind."

"No. I am honest. And I see what is there to be seen. It is you who must leave, Edouard."

"And ruin us all?" Céleste sounded both annoyed and amused. "You cannot be thinking, my love. We may find some compromise, some way of saving Edouard's face and our reputations, some way of living together."

"Never!" said Gascó. "I will not. You cannot ask it of me."

"My Claire de Lune. My Luna." Céleste reached for Gascó's hand and pulled her down on the sofa. "You do love me, do you not? Then you will help me. Edouard loves me too: we all love one another, do we not? Edouard. Come sit with us."

Edouard set down his brandy snifter. Céleste was holding her hand to him, smiling affectionately. He stepped forward, took the hand, allowed it and the smile to draw him down beside her. At the edge of his vision, he saw the paper slide behind the cushions and turned to retrieve it. Céleste's grip tightened on his hand.

"Never mind, my dear," she said. "Now. Surely we can come to some agreement, some arrangement that will satisfy all of us?"

The taste in Theresa's mouth said she'd been asleep. The tickle in her throat said the sofa was terribly dusty, and her nose said there had been mice in it, perhaps still were. The cushions were threadbare, the needlework pillows moth-eaten into woolen lace.

Without thinking what she was doing, Theresa scattered them broadcast and burrowed her hand down between sofa back and seat, grimacing a bit as she thought of the mice, grinning triumphantly as she touched a piece of paper. Carefully, she drew it out, creased and mildewed as it was, and smoothed it on her knees.

A few scrawled lines of text with a sketch beneath them. The hand was not Edouard's. Nor was the sketch, though a dozen art historians would have staked their government grants that the style was his. The image was an early version of *Young Woman in a Garden,* a sketch of Gascó sitting against a tree with her hands around her knees, her pointed chin raised to display the long curve of her neck. Her hair was loose on her shoulders. Her blouse was open at the throat. She was laughing.

Trembling, Theresa read the note:

> My Claire de Lune:
> How wicked I feel, how abandoned, writing you like this, where anyone could read how I love you, my *maja.* I want to write about your neck and breasts and hair—oh, your hair like black silk across my body. But the only words that come to my mind are stale when they are not comic, and I'd not have you laugh at me. So here is my memory of yesterday afternoon, and your place in it, and in my heart always.
>
> Céleste

Theresa closed her eyes, opened them again. The room she sat in was gloomy, musty, and falling into ruin, very different from the bright, comfortably shabby parlor she remembered. One of the French doors was ajar; afternoon sun spilled through it, reflecting from a thousand swirling dust-motes, raising the ghosts of flowers from the faded carpet. Out in the garden, a bird whistled. Theresa went to the door, looked out over a wilderness of weedy paths and rosebushes grown into a thorny, woody tangle.

Céleste's letter to Luz Gascó crackled in her hand, reassuringly solid. There was clearly a lot of work to be done.

THE GHOST OF CWMLECH MANOR

There was a ghost at Cwmlech Manor.

Everybody knew it, although nobody had seen her, not with their own eyes, for years and years.

"Ghosts have to abide by the rules," I remember Mrs. Bando the housekeeper explaining as she poured us out a cup of tea at the manor's great oak kitchen table. She'd been parlormaid at the manor when Mam was a kitchen maid there. Fast friends they were, and fast friends they'd stayed, even when Mam left domestic service to marry. Mrs. Bando was my godmother and we went to her most Sunday afternoons.

I was ten or thereabouts and I was mad for wonders. Da had told me of the new clockwork motor that was going to change everything from the mining of coal to the herding of sheep. Above all things, I liked to hear about horseless carriages and self-powered mechanicals, but I'd settle for ghosts at a pinch.

So, "How do ghosts know the rules?" I asked. "Is there a ghost school, think you, on the other side?"

Mam laughed and said there was never such a child for asking questions that had no answer. She'd wager I'd ask the same of the ghost myself, if I saw her.

"And so I would, Mam. But first I'd ask her where she'd hid the treasure."

"And she'd likely disappear on the spot," Mrs. Bando scolded. "That knowledge is for Cwmlech ears only, look you. Not that it's needed, may the dear Lord be thanked."

Sir Owen indeed had treasure of his own, with a big house in London and any number of mechanicals and horseless carriages at his beck and call. It was generally agreed that it was no fault of his that the roof of Cwmlech Manor was all in holes and the beetle had gotten into the library paneling, but only the miserly ways of his factor, who would not part with so much as a farthing bit for the maintenance of a house his master did not care for.

Which made me think very much the less of Sir Owen Cwmlech, for Cwmlech Manor was the most beautiful house on the Welsh Borders. I loved everything about it from its peaked slate roofs and tiny-paned windows to the peacocks caterwauling in its yew trees. Best of all, I loved the story that went with it—very romantic, and a girl as the hero—a rare enough thing in romantic tales, where the young girls always act like ninnies and end up dead of a broken heart as often as not.

Mistress Angharad Cwmlech of Cwmlech Manor was not a ninny. When she was only seventeen, the Civil War broke out, and her father and brothers, Royalists to a man, left home to join the King's army, leaving Mistress Cwmlech safe, they thought, at home. But in 1642 the Parliamentarians invaded the Borders, whereupon Mistress Cwmlech hid her jewels, as well her father's strongbox and the family plate, dating, some of it, from the days of Edward II and very precious.

The night the Roundheads broke into the manor, they found her on the stairs, clad in her nightdress, armed with her grandfather's sword. They slew her where she stood, but not a gold coin did they find or a silver spoon, though they turned the house upside down with looking.

It was a sad homecoming her brothers had, I was thinking, to find their sister dead and in her silent grave with the family wealth safely—and permanently—hidden away.

Her portrait hung in the great hall over the mantel where her grandfather's swords had once hung. It must have been painted not long before her death—a portrait of a solemn young woman, her dark hair curling over her temples like a spaniel's ears and her gown like a flowered silk tea cozy all trimmed with lace and ribbon-knots. A sapphire sparkled on her bosom, brilliants at her neck and ears, and on her finger, a great square ruby set in gold. There is pity, I always thought, that her ghost must appear barefoot and clad in her nightshift instead of in that grand flowered gown.

I would have liked to see her, nightdress and all.

But I did not, and life jogged on between school and Mam's kitchen, where I learned to cook and bake, and Da's forge, where I learned the properties of metal and listened to him talk of the wonderful machines he'd invent, did he only have the gold. On Sundays, Mrs. Bando told me stories of the parties and hunting meets of Sir Owen's youth, with dancing in the Long Gallery and dinners in the Great Hall for fifty or more.

Sometimes I thought I could hear an echo of their feet, but Mrs. Bando said it was only rats.

Still, I felt that Cwmlech Manor slept lightly, biding its time until its master returned and brought it back to life. But he did not come, and he did not come, and then, when I was fifteen, he died.

A bright autumn morning it was, warm as September often is, when Mrs. Bando knocked on the door in her apron with her round, comfortable face all blubbered with weeping. She'd not drawn a breath before Mam had her by the fire with a cup of milky tea in her hand.

"There then, Susan Bando," she said, brisk and kind. "Tell us what's amiss. You look as if you've seen the Cwmlech ghost."

Mrs. Bando took a gulp of tea. "In a manner of speaking, I have. The House of Cwmlech is laid in the dirt, look you. Sir Owen's fortune is dead, and his fortune all gambled away. The house in London is sold to pay his creditors and the manor's to be shut up and all the staff turned away. And what will I do for employment, at my age?" And she began to weep again while Mam patted her hand.

Me, I ran out of our house, down the lane, and across the stone bridge and spent the afternoon in the formal garden, weeping while the peacocks grieved among the pines for Cwmlech Manor, that was now dying.

As autumn wore on, I wondered more and more why Mistress Cwmlech did not appear and reveal where she'd hidden the treasure. Surely the ruinous state of the place must be as much a grief to her as to me. Was she lingering in the empty house, waiting for someone to come and hear her? Must that someone be a Cwmlech of Cwmlech Manor? Or could it be anyone with a will to see her and the wit to hear her?

Could it be me?

One Sunday after Chapel, I collected crowbar, magnet, and candle, determined to settle the question. Within an hour, I stood in the Great Hall with a torn petticoat and a bruised elbow, watching the shadows tremble in the candlelight. It was November, and the house cold and damp as a slate cavern. I slunk from room to room, past sheet-shrouded tables and presses and dressers and chairs and curtains furry with dust drawn tight across the windows. A perfect haven for ghosts it looked, and filthy to break my heart—and surely Mistress Cwmlech's as well. But though I stood on the very step where she was slain and called her name three times aloud, she did not appear to me.

I did not venture inside again, but the softer weather of spring brought me back to sit in the overgrown gardens when I could snatch an hour from my chores. There's dreams I had boiling in me, beyond the dreams of my friends, who were all for a husband and a little house and babies on the hearth. After many tears, I'd more or less accepted the hard fact that a blacksmith's daughter with no education beyond the village school could never be an engineer. So I cheered myself with my ability to play any wind instrument put into my hand, though I'd only a recorder to practice on, and it the property of the chapel.

Practice I did that summer, in the gardens of Cwmlech Manor, to set the peacocks screaming, and dreamed of somehow acquiring a mechanical that could play the piano and performing with it before Queen Victoria herself. Such dreams, however foolish in the village, seemed perfectly reasonable at Cwmlech Manor.

Summer passed, and autumn came on, with cold rain and food to put by for winter; my practicing and my visits to Cwmlech fell away to nothing. Sixteen I was now, with my hair coiled up and skirts down to my boot tops and little time to dream. I'd enough to do getting through my chores without fretting after what could not be or thinking about an old ghost who could not be bothered to save her own house. Mam said I was growing up. I felt that I was dying.

One bright morning in early spring, a mighty roaring and coughing in the lane shattered the calm like a mirror. Upstairs I was, sweeping, so a clear view I had, looking down from the front bedroom window, of a horseless carriage driving down by the lane.

I'd not have been more astonished to see Queen Victoria herself.

I knew all about horseless carriages, mind. The inventor of the Patent Steam Carriage was a Welshman, and all the best carriages were made in Blaenarvon, down in the Valley. But a horseless carriage was costly to buy and costly to keep. Hereabouts, only Mr. Iestyn Thomas who owned the wool mill drove a horseless carriage.

And here was a pair of them, black smoke belching from their smokestacks: a traveling coach followed by a closed wain, heading toward Cwmlech Manor.

Without thinking whether it was a good idea or a bad one, I dropped my broom and hotfooted after, ducking through the gap in the hedge just as the traveling coach drove under the stone arch and into the weed-clogged courtyard.

Loud enough to raise the dead it was, with the peacocks screaming and the engines clattering and the wheels of the wain crunching on the gravel drive. I slipped behind the west wing and peeked out through the branches of a shaggy yew just in time to see the coach door open and a man climb out.

I was too far to see him clearly, only that he was dressed in a brown tweed suit, with a scarlet muffler wound around his neck and hanging down behind and before. He looked around the yard, the sun flashing from the lenses that covered his eyes, then raised an instrument to his lips and commenced to play.

There was no tune in it, just notes running fast as water over rocks in spring. It made my ears ache to hear it; I would have run away, except that the back of the wain opened and a ramp rolled out to the ground. And down that ramp, to my joy and delight, trundled a dozen mechanicals.

I recognized them at once from Da's journals: Porter models, designed to fetch and carry, a polished metal canister with a battery bolted on behind like a knapsack and a ball at the top fitted with glass oculars. They ran on treads—much better than the wheels of older models, which slid on sand and stuck in the mud. Anglepoise arms hefted crates and boxes as though they were filled with feathers. Some had been modified with extra arms, and were those *legs* on that one there?

The notes that were not music fell silent. "Hullo," said a diffident voice. "Can I help you? I am Arthur Cwmlech, Sir Arthur now, I suppose."

In my fascination I had drifted all the way from the hedge to the yard, and was standing not a stone's throw from the young man with the pipe. Who was, apparently, the new Baronet of Cwmlech. And me in a dusty old apron, my hair raveling down my back and my boots caked with mud.

If the earth had opened up and swallowed me where I stood, I would have been well content.

I curtsied, blushing hot as fire. "Tacy Gof I am, daughter of William Gof the Smith. Be welcome to the home of your fathers, Sir Arthur."

He blinked. "Thank you," he said. "It's not much to look at, is it?"

To my mind, he had no right to complain of the state of the house. Thin as a rake he was, with knobby wrists and sandy hair straggling over the collar of his shirt, which would have been the better for a wash and an iron.

"Closed up too long it is, that's all," I said, with knives in, "and no one to look after it. A new roof is all it needs, and the ivy cut back, to be the most beautiful house on the Borders."

Solemn as a judge, he gave the house a second look, long and considering, then back to me. "I say, do you cook?"

It was my turn to blink. "What?"

"I need a housekeeper," he said, all business. "But she'd need to cook as well. No mechanical can produce an edible meal, and while I can subsist on sandwiches, I'd rather not."

I goggled, not knowing if he was in earnest or only teasing, or how I felt about it in either case.

"You'd be perfect," he went on. "You love the house and you know what it needs to make it fit to live in. Best of all, you're not afraid of mechanicals. At least I don't think you are. Are you?" he ended anxiously.

I put up my chin. "A smith's daughter, me. I am familiar with mechanicals from my cradle." Only pictures, but no need to tell him that.

"Well." He smiled, and I realized he was not so much older than I. "That's settled then."

"It is not," I protested. "I have not said I will do it, and even if I do, the choice is not mine to make."

"Whose, then?"

"My da and mam," I said. "And they will never say yes."

He thrust his pipe into his pocket, made a dive into the coach, fetched out a bowler hat, and crammed it onto his head. "Lead on."

"Where?" I asked stupidly.

"Your house, of course. I want to speak to your parents."

Mam was dead against it. Not a word did she say, but I read her thoughts clear as print in the banging of the kettle and the rattling of the crockery as she scrambled together a tea worthy to set before the new baronet. I was a girl, he was a young, unmarried man, people would talk, and likely they would have something to talk about.

"Seventeen she is, come midsummer," she said. "And not trained in running a great house. You had better send to Knighton for Mrs. Bando, who was housekeeper for Sir Owen."

Sir Arthur looked mulish. "I'm sure Mrs. Bando is an excellent housekeeper, Mrs. Gof. But can you answer for her willingness to work in a house staffed chiefly by mechanicals?"

"Mechanicals?" Mam's eyes narrowed. "My daughter, alone in that great crumbling house with a green boy and a few machines, is it? Begging your pardon, sir, if I give offense, but that is not a proper household for any woman to work in."

I was ready to sink with shame. Sir Arthur put up his chin a little. "I'm not a boy, Mrs. Gof," he said with dignity. "I'm nearly twenty, with a degree in mechanical engineering from London Polytechnic. Still, I take your point. Tacy will live at home and come in days to cook and supervise the mechanicals in bringing the house into better repair."

He stood. "Thank you for the tea. The Welsh cakes were excellent. Now, if I may have a word with your husband?"

"More than a word it will take," Mam said, "before Mr. Gof will agree to such foolishness." But off to the forge we went nevertheless, where Sir Arthur went straight as a magnet to the steam hammer that was Da's newest invention. In next to no time, they'd taken it apart to admire, talking nineteen to the dozen.

I knew my fate was sealed.

Not that I objected, mind. Being housekeeper to Sir Arthur meant working in Cwmlech Manor, surrounded by mechanicals and horseless carriages, and money of my own—a step up, I thought, from sweeping floors under Mam's eye. Sir Arthur engaged Da, too, to help to turn the stables into a workshop and build a forge.

Before he left, Sir Arthur laid two golden coins in my palm. "You'll need to lay in provisions," he said. "See if you can procure a hen or two. I like a fresh egg for breakfast."

Next morning, Da and I packed our pony trap full of food and drink. I climbed up beside him and Mam thrust a cackling wicker cage into my hands.

"My two best hens for Sir Arthur's eggs, and see they're well housed. There's work you'll have and plenty, my little one, settling the kitchen fit to cook in. I'll just set the bread to rise and come help you."

Over night I'd had time to recall the state of the place last time I'd seen it. I was prepared for a shock when I opened the kitchen door. And a shock I got, though not the one I'd looked for. The floor was scrubbed, the table freshly sanded, and a fire crackled merrily on a new-swept hearth. As Da and I stood gaping upon the threshold, a silver-skinned mechanical rolled out of the pantry.

"Oh, you beauty," Da breathed.

"Isn't she?" Sir Arthur appeared, with the shadow of a sandy beard on his cheeks, grinning like an urchin. "This is the kitchen maid. I call her Betty."

There followed a highly technical discussion of Betty's inward workings and abilities and a pipe studded with silver keys, with the promise of a lesson as soon as he found the time. Then he carried Da off to look at the stable, leaving me with the pipe in my hand, bags and baskets everywhere, the hens cackling irritably, and Betty by the pantry door, still and gleaming.

Fitting the pipe between my lips, I blew softly. A bit like a recorder it was to play, with a nice, bright tone. I tried a scale in C, up and down, and then the first phrase of "The Ash Grove."

Betty whirred, swiveled her head, waved her arms aimlessly, and jerked forward. I dropped the pipe just as she was on the point of crushing the hens under her treads.

And that is how Mam found us: me with my two hands over my mouth and the pipe on the floor and Betty frozen and the hens squawking fit to cross your eyes.

Mam closed her lips like a seam, picked up the hens, and carried them outside. When she got back, there is a word or two she had to say, about responsibility and God's creatures and rushing into things willy-nilly. But Mam's scolds never lasted long, and soon we were cooking companionably side by side, just as we did at home.

"And what's the use," she asked, "of that great clumsy machine by there?"

"That is the kitchen maid," I said. "Betty. There is all sorts of things she can do—once I learn how to use *that* properly." I cocked my chin at the pipe, which I'd stuck on the mantel.

"Kitchen maid, is it?" Mam spluttered—disgust or laughter, I could not tell—and fetched flour for the crust of a savory pie. When it was mixed and rolled out, she laid down the pin, wiped her hands on her apron, went to the dresser, got out one of Mrs. Bando's ample blue pinafores and a ruffled white cap. She set the cap on Betty's polished metal head and tied the pinafore around her body with the strings crossed all tidy, then gave a nod.

"Not so bad," she said. "With clothes on. But a godless monster nonetheless. A good thing Susan Bando is not here to see such a thing in her kitchen. I hope and pray, Tacy my little one, you will not regret this choice."

"Do you pass me those carrots, Mam," I said, "and stop your fretting."

When Da came in and saw Betty, he laughed until I thought he'd choke. Then he pulled a pipe from his own pocket and sent Betty rolling back into her pantry with an uncouth flight of notes.

"This pipe is Sir Arthur's own invention, look you," he said, proud as a cock robin. "A great advance on the old box-and-button system it is, all done with sound waves. Not easy to use, look you—all morning I've been, learning to make them come and go. But clever."

I wanted a lesson right then and there, but Da said Sir Arthur would be wanting his dinner and I must find a clean table for him to eat it on. Mam read me a lecture on keeping my eyes lowered and my tongue between my teeth, and then they were off and I was alone, with a savory pie in the oven perfuming the air, ready to begin my life as the housekeeper of Cwmlech Manor.

A ruined manor is beautiful to look at, and full of mystery and dreams to wander in. But to make fit for human habitation a house where foxes have denned and mice bred their generations is another pair of shoes.

Had I a notion of being mistress of a fleet of mechanicals, with nothing to do but stand by playing a pipe while they worked, I soon learned better. First, Betty was my only helper. Second, her treads would not climb steps, so ramps must be built and winches set to hoist her from floor to floor. Third, I could not learn to command her to do any task more complicated than scrub a floor or polish a table.

Like speaking Chinese it was, with alphabet and sounds and grammar all against sense, a note for every movement, tied to the keys and not to the ear. Da, who could not tell one note from another, was handier with the pipe than I. It drove me nearly mad, with my ear telling me one thing and Sir Arthur's diagrams telling me another. And my pride in shreds to think I could not master something that should be so simple. Still, the work had to be done, and if I could not make Betty wash windows, I must do it myself, with Ianto Evans from the village to sweep the chimneys and nail new slates over the holes in the roof and mend the furniture where the damp had rotted the joints.

For the first month, Sir Arthur slept in the stable on a straw mattress. He took his noon meal there too, out of a basket. His dinners he ate in the kitchen, with a cloth on the table and good china and silver cutlery to honor his title and his position. Not that he seemed to care where he ate, nor if the plates were chipped or the forks tin, but ate what I put before him without once lifting his eyes from his book.

Fed up I was to overflowing, and ready to quit except for what Mam would say and the coins I put by each week in a box under my bed. But I stuck to it.

For whatever I might think of the baronet, I loved his house. And as I labored to clean the newest wing of the house and make fit for human habitation, I felt it come alive again under my busy hands.

Finally, one rainy June evening, when Sir Arthur came in to his dinner, I led him up the kitchen stairs and down a corridor to the morning room.

In silence he took in the oak paneling all glowing with polish, the table laid with linen and china and silver, and a fire on the hearth to take the damp from the air. I stood behind him, with needles pricking to know what he thought, half-angry already with knowing he'd say nothing. And then he turned, with a smile like a lamp and his eyes bright as peacock feathers under his thick lenses.

"It looks like home," he said. "Thank you, Tacy."

I blushed and curtsied and pulled out a chair for him to sit on, and then I served his dinner, each course brought up on a tray, all proper as Mam had taught me. Even Sir Arthur seemed to feel the difference. If he read as he ate, he looked up as I brought every course. And when I brought up a currant tart with cream to pour over, he put down his book and smiled at me.

"You've done well, Tacy, with only Betty to help you."

My pride flashed up like dry tinder. "Betty to help me, is it?" I said with heat. "It was Ianto Evans swept the chimney, look you, and I who did the rest. There's worse than useless that old pipe is."

Sir Arthur raised his brows, the picture of astonishment. "Useless?" he said. "How useless?"

I wished my pride had held its tongue, but too late now. His right it was to ask questions, and my duty to answer them. Which I did as meek as Mam could wish, standing with my hands folded under my apron. After a while, he sent me for a pot of coffee, a notebook and a pencil, and then again for a second cup. Before long, I was sipping at the horrid, bitter stuff, writing out music staves and scales. Telling him about intervals I was when he leapt up, grabbed my hand, hauled me down to the kitchen, and thrust my pipe into my hand.

"Summon Betty," he ordered.

Halting and self-conscious, I did that.

"Play 'The Ash Grove,'" he said. And I did. And Betty spun and lurched and staggered until I could not play for laughing. Sir Arthur laughed too, and wrung my hand as though he'd pump water from my mouth, then ran off with his notebook and my pipe to the stables.

As soon as Sir Arthur had puzzled out how to make a mechanical dance to a proper tune, he took the Porters apart, and set about rewiring them. That time was heaven for me, with Sir Arthur pulling me from the west wing, where I was evicting spiders and wood pigeons and rats from the corners and walls, to play old tunes to the mechanicals.

And then, at the end of June, a cart arrived at Cwmlech Manor, with a long wooden crate in the back.

Sir Arthur organized the unloading with anxious care, he and Da tootling away unharmoniously while the mechanicals hoisted the crate and carried it into the workshop like a funeral procession with no corpse. I'd vegetables boiling for a potch, but I pulled the pot off the stove and went to watch the unpacking.

"Go to your work, now, Tacy my little one," Da said when he saw me. "This is none of your affair."

"If that's a new mechanical," I said, "I'd dearly love to see it."

Sir Arthur laughed. "Much better than that, Tacy. This will be the future of mechanicals. And I shall be its father."

He lifted the lid and pulled back the wood shavings. I took my breath sharp and shallow, for it might have been a dead youth lying there and not a mechanical at all. The head was the shape of a human skull, with neat ears and a slender nose and fine-cut lips and oval lids over the eyes. Face and body were covered, eerily, with close-grained leather, creamy-pale as pearl.

"I bought it from a Frenchman," Sir Arthur said as he rummaged through the shavings. "It's only a toy now, a kind of super-sophisticated doll that can stand and walk. When I make it speak and understand as well, it will be a humanatron, and the science of mechanicals will have entered a new phase."

Over his head, Da and I exchanged a look of understanding and laughter mixed. It had not taken us long to learn that Sir Arthur Cwmlech was like a butterfly, flitting restlessly from idea to idea. Yet in some things, you might set your watch by him. Dinner he ate at six of the clock exactly, and he took always coffee to drink afterwards, never tea, and with his sweet, not after.

My seventeenth birthday came and went. Sir Arthur abandoned the Porters half-rewired to read books on sonics and the human auditory system and fill reams of foolscap with drawings and diagrams. He never set foot in the village. He never went to church nor chapel, nor did he call upon his neighbors. Da and old Dai Philips the Post excepted, not a mortal man crossed the threshold of Cwmlech Manor from week's end to week's end. You may imagine my astonishment, therefore, when I heard, one evening as I carried him his coffee, a woman's voice in the morning room.

In a rage of fury she was, too, demanding he look at her. Now, a lady might have left them to fight it out in private. A servant, however, must deliver the coffee, though she'd better be quick.

When I entered, I saw Sir Arthur reading peacefully over the bones of his chop, as though there were no girl beside him, fists on hips and the insults rolling from her like water from a spout. Near my age she was and wearing nothing but a nightdress with a soft grey bedgown thrown over it. Then I saw the long dark stain under her left breast and my brain caught up with my eyes, and I knew that at last I looked upon the ghostly Mistress Angharad Cwmlech of Cwmlech Manor.

Sir Arthur roused himself from his book. "Ah, coffee!" he said. "And is that gingerbread I smell?"

Mistress Cwmlech fisted her hands in her disheveled hair and fairly howled. I dropped the tray on the table with a clatter.

Sir Arthur peered at me curiously, his spectacles glittering in the candlelight. "What's wrong? Did you see a rat? I heard them squeaking a moment ago."

"It was not a rat, Sir Arthur."

"You relieve my mind. I've nothing against rodents in their place, but their place is not my parlor, don't you agree?"

Mistress Cwmlech made a rude gesture, surprising a snort of laughter from me so that Sir Arthur asked, a little stiffly, what ailed me.

"I beg pardon, sir," I stammered. "It's only I've remembered I left a pot on the stove—"

And I fled, followed by the ghost's bright laughter.

A gulf as wide as the Severn there is, between the wanting to see a ghost and the seeing it. But Mam always said there was no shock could not be cushioned by sweet, strong tea. In the kitchen, I poured myself a cup, added plenty of milk and sugar, and sat in Mrs. Bando's rocking chair to drink it.

Thus fortified, I hardly even started when the ghost appeared on the settle. Her arms were clasped about her knees, which were drawn up with her pointed chin resting upon them, and her dark eyes burned upon me.

"Good evening," she said.

I could see the tea towels I'd spread on the settle faintly through her skirts. "G—g—g." I took a gulp of tea to damp my mouth and tried again. "Good evening to you, Miss."

"There," she said, with triumph. "I knew you could see me. Beginning to feel like a window I was, and me the toast of four counties. In my day. . . ." She sighed. "Ah, but it is not my day, is it? Of your kindness, wench—what year is it?"

I pulled myself together. "1861, Miss."

"1861. I had not thought it was so long. Still, I would expect a better welcome from my own descendent, look you."

Sad she sounded, and perhaps a little frightened. "The Sight is not given to everyone, Miss," I said gently. "Sir Arthur is a good man, though, and very clever."

"He's too clever to believe in ghosts," she said, recovering. "There is pity he's the one Cwmlech in upwards of two hundred years with a need to hear what I have to tell."

I sat upright. "The Cwmlech Treasure?"

"What know you of the Cwmlech Treasure, girl?"

"Only what legend says," I admitted. "There's romantic, Miss, to defend your home with your grandfather's sword."

Mistress Angharad Cwmlech laughed, with broken glass in it. "Romantic, is it? Well, it was not romantic to live through, I will tell you so much for nothing. Not," with a rueful glance at her blood-stained skirts, "that I did live through it."

Shamed I was, and thrown into such confusion that I offered her a cup of tea along with my apologies. She laughed, a real laugh this time, and said her mama had been a great believer in the healing property of tea. So I told her about Mam and she said to call her Mistress Angharad, and I was feeling quite easy with her until she demanded to be told about the mechanicals, which she called "those foul and unnatural creatures infesting my stables."

Recognizing an order, I did my best to obey. I explained about clockwork and soundwaves and then I called Betty out of her pantry. A bad idea, that. For when Betty trundled into the kitchen, Mistress Angharad vanished abruptly, reappearing some minutes later in a pale and tattered state.

"Sorry," I said, and piped Betty back to her pantry with "The Bishop of Bangor's Jig."

"Mark my words," Mistress Angharad said. "That soulless *thing* will be the ruin of the House of Cwmlech."

"If Sir Arthur cannot hear you," I said shyly. "Do you tell me where the treasure is hid, and I will pass the word on to him."

"And he would believe you, of course," she said, her scorn thick as paint. "And drop all his precious experiments and maybe knock holes in the walls besides."

I bristled. "He might, if I put it to him properly."

"Maybe," the ghost said, "and maybe not. In any case, I cannot tell you where I hid the treasure, were I ever so willing. Your ears could not hear the words."

"Show me, then."

She shrugged mistily. "There are rules and restrictions upon ghosts as there are upon young ladies of gentle birth. Given my choice, I'd be neither."

Past eleven it was, and Mam waiting for me come in before she locked the door. I wracked my tired brain. "Can you not invent a riddling rhyme, then? Leave a trail of clues?"

"No and no. Only to Sir Arthur may I reveal the hiding place . . ."

"And Sir Arthur doesn't believe in ghosts," I finished for her. "Or the treasure, come to that."

"I wish I need not tell him anything," she said peevishly. "Great blind old fool that he is. But tell him I must. I'll not know a moment's peace until the House of Cwmlech is safe and sound."

So began Mistress Angharad Cwmlech's ghostly siege upon the doorless tower of Sir Arthur's indifference.

There is not much a ghost can do to affect the waking world, but what she could, she did. She blew in his ear, ruffled his hair, pinched his arm, spilled his coffee, knocked his food from his plate. The result of her hauntings was no more than a wry remark about drafts or fleas or clumsiness, at which she'd howl and rail and curse like a mad thing. Sometimes it was all I could do not to laugh.

This had been going on for perhaps a month, when Sir Arthur told me, after I'd brought up his coffee one chilly evening in July, with the rain coming down outside in knives and forks, that three gentlemen were coming to dine with him on Saturday.

"These gentlemen, sir," I said, mild as milk. "Will they be staying the night?"

"Yes. Is there a problem?"

Mistress Angharad, hovering by the hearth, giggled.

I put my lips together and sighed. "Perhaps you did not know, sir, there's no mattress in any bedchamber save your own, nor a whole sheet to make it up with. And while you may be happy to take mutton pie in the morning room, there's shame to serve no better to your guests, and they come all the way from London."

"Oh!" he said. "I hadn't thought. Can't have Mr. Gotobed sleeping on straw, either—he'd take offense, and that would never do. These guests are important, Tacy. What are we to do?"

I was tempted to take a page from Mistress Angharad's book just then, and tell him what I thought of inviting guests without notice. But, as Mam was always telling me, he was the Tenth Baronet Cwmlech and I was Tacy Gof the smith's daughter. Friendly we might be, but it was not a friendship to survive plain speaking, however justified. "We must do what we can, Sir Arthur," I said, dry as sand. "Buy mattresses for one thing, and cloth for curtains. Bedlinen of course, and wool coverlets that can double as blankets and—"

"Oh, damn," Sir Arthur said, with feeling. "I hadn't thought—Oh, *damn*. You must buy what you see fit, of course, but please remember that I am ruined."

"Ruined?" I echoed blankly. "But the carriages and the mechanicals. . . ."

"Are all my fortune, Tacy. With work and luck all will be restored, and you may bring Cwmlech Manor back to its full glory. But first I must secure a patent on the new pipe and find someone to manufacture it for general use."

He might have been speaking of flying to the moon, so hopeless did he sound.

"Come now," I said. "That should be easy enough for a man clever enough to invent it in the first place. Da will help you, I'm sure. As for your guests, you may leave their entertainment in my hands."

His smile was clouded with worry, but it warmed me nonetheless. "Thank you, Tacy. I have every confidence in *you,* at least."

Which is a heady thing for a girl just past her seventeenth birthday to hear. As I cleaned the kitchen, I chattered of lists and plans to Mistress Angharad until she lost her temper.

"It is dull you are, bleating about roasts and beds like an old ewe. Have you not asked yourself who these gentlemen are and what they're after, out in the damp wilds of the Borders when the London Season is at its height? Lombard Street to a China orange, they're up to nothing good."

"All the more reason to be thinking of roasts and beds," I said shortly.

Mistress Angharad wailed to curl my toes and disappeared.

After that, I had far more important things to think about than a sulky spirit. Hercules himself could not have made Cwmlech Manor fit for company in three days' time, so I went down to Mam's and begged her help.

If Da's genius was to beat dead iron into usefulness, Mam's was to settle a house into order and beauty. She began at Cwmlech by going to Mr. Thomas at the wool mill and Mrs. Wynn the Shop and charming goods from them in exchange for a letter of patronage to hang on the wall, saying that Sir Arthur of Cwmlech of Cwmlech Manor did business here and no other place. Then she summoned all the good women of Cwmlech village, who tucked up their sleeves and descended on the manor with mops and brooms and buckets. They worked like bees in a meadow, until the windows were all draped in good Welsh wool and the bedlinen white and fragrant with lavender and flowers on the chests and the wood in the dining room all rubbed soft and glowing.

On the Saturday morning, Mam came with me to the manor to help cook and wait upon the guests.

"There is funny gentlemen they are," she said when she came from showing them to their chambers. "Rat's eyes and bull's necks, no servants and next to no luggage. No manners, neither—not so much as a smile or thanks, only a sharp warning not to meddle with their things. Were they not Sir Arthur's guests, I would not willingly give them to eat."

Which was strong speaking for Mam. It made me think of Mistress Angharad and how I'd missed seeing her these past days, sharp tongue and all, and how I wished to hear her opinion of the men who would sleep at Cwmlech Manor this night.

So you may judge my joy when I carried Mam's leek soup in to dinner that evening, to see Mistress Angharad hovering at the sideboard, bloody and dishevelled as ever.

I smiled at her; she frowned back. "Eyes open and mouth shut, girl," she ordered. "Here's mischief abroad."

Which I might have guessed for myself, so smug were the guests, like cats at a mousehole, and so figdety was Sir Arthur, like the mouse they watched. Two of them were large and broad, very thick in their beards and necks and narrow in their eyes; the third was thinner and clean-shaven, but no more handsome for that, with his mouth as tight as a letterbox and his eyes hard as ball bearings.

"A fine, large workshop, Sir Arthur," Clean-cheeks said, picking up his spoon. "A pity nothing useful has come out of it."

One of the roughs said, "Don't forget the pipe, Mr. Gotobed."

Mr. Gotobed smiled thinly. "I do not forget the pipe, Mr. Brown."

Sir Arthur nudged his cutlery straight. "It's very nearly ready, Mr. Gotobed. Just a few details about the interface. . . ."

"Interface?" The second rough found this funny. "Them things got no face at all, if you ask me."

And then the tureen was empty, and I must run downstairs again to fetch the fish course. When I returned with the baked grayling, Mr. Gotobed and his friends had scraped their plates clean, Sir Arthur's soup was untouched, and Mistress Angharad was scowling blackly.

"I know Cwmlech Manor is haunted," Mr. Gotobed was saying. "There is a whole chapter on the subject in *The Haunted Houses of Great Britain.* Your resident ghost is precisely why Mr. Whitney wants to buy it. He has a great affinity for the supernatural, does Mr. Whitney of Pittsburgh, America. By his own account, some of his best friends are ghosts."

"Then I'm afraid he must be disappointed," Sir Arthur said. "You will be paid in full."

Mr. Gotobed smiled. "Yes," he said. "I will. One way or another. Mr. Whitney is very excited. I believe he intends to install a swimming bath in the Great Hall."

Mistress Angharad reached for a candlestick. Another time, her look of fury when her hand passed through it might have made me laugh, but I was too furious myself for mirth. Sir Arthur's hands clenched against the table. "A year's grace is all I ask, Mr. Gotobed."

"A year! It will take that long for the patent office to read your application, and another for them to decide upon it. I'm sorry, Sir Arthur. A manor in the hand is worth any number of inventions in, er, the bush. Pay me in full on the first of September or Cwmlech Manor is mine, as per our contract. Excellent fish, by the way. Did you catch it yourself?"

How I got through the rest of the meal without cracking a plate over Mr. Gotobed's head, I do not know. Lucky that Mam was busy with her cooking. My face was a children's ABC to her and I did not want her knowing that Sir Arthur had pledged Cwmlech Manor. She'd small patience with debtors, and she'd think him no better than his father when the poor boy was only a lamb adrift in a world of wolves like Mr. Gotobed.

The uncomfortable dinner wore on, with only Mr. Gotobed and his roughs eating Mam's good food and Mistress Angharad cursing impotently and Sir Arthur growing more and more white and pinched about the nose. When I took up the cloth at last and put the decanters on the table, he stood up. "I have some rather pressing business to attend to," he said. "Enjoy your port, gentlemen."

And then he went into his bedroom across the landing and shut the door.

I wanted to knock and give him a few words of comfort. But Mam was waiting downstairs with all the cleaning up, and I could think of no comfortable words to say.

Mam and I were to sleep at Cwmlech Manor to be handy to cook the guests' breakfast in the morning. When the kitchen was tidy, we settled by the fire to drink a cup of tea, too weary to speak. So low was I, I hardly started when Mistress Angharad said, "Tacy! I have news!" right in my ear.

Mam shivered. ""There's a wicked old draft in by here."

"Worse when you're tired," I said. "Go in to bed, Mam. I'll see to locking up."

She gaped fit to split her cheeks and went off without argument for once, which was a blessing, since Mistress Angharad was already talking.

"Listening I was, as they drank Sir Arthur's port. It's all a trick, look you. The manor is sold already, to the rich American who likes ghosts and swimming baths. And Tacy, that blackguard will wreck Sir Arthur's workshop tonight, in case he might sell his machines and pay his debt!"

I clutched my cooling tea, half-sick with rage and entirely awake. "Will we tell Sir Arthur?"

"Sir Arthur!" she said with scorn. "Meek as a maiden aunt all through dinner, and off to cower in his bed as soon as the cloth was lifted. No. If anyone is to save Cwmlech Manor, it must be the two of us."

"Right." I put down my tea. "To the stable, us. And pray we're not too late."

Pausing only to light the lantern, we crept out of the kitchen and across the yard to the stable, the moon sailing high and pale in a wrack of cloud above us. Within, all was black save for the sullen glow of the forge fire. The flickering lantern drew little sparks of light from the dials and gears and polished metal of Sir Arthur's machines and tools. The air smelled like pitch and coal and machine oil.

"The dragon's lair," Mistress Angharad said, full of bravado. "Is that the virgin sacrifice?"

I followed the faint glow of her pointing finger to a table set like a bier under a bank of lights, and the figure upon it draped with an old linen sheet.

"That," I said, "is Sir Arthur's expensive French automaton. Will you look?" I picked my way carefully through the chaos of strange machines and gear-strewn tables and reached for the sheet. "Only an old mechanical it is, see?"

In truth, it looked eerie enough, bald and still and deathly pale. Mistress Angharad stroked its cheek with a misty finger. "There's beautiful it is," she said, with wonder.

I touched the key in its neck. "Still, only a mechanical doll, simpler than the simplest automaton." Without thought, almost without my will, my fingers turned the key, feeling the spring coil tight as I wound.

Mistress Angharad turned her head. "Douse the lantern," she hissed.

Heart beating like one of Da's hammers, I blew out the candle and ducked down behind the table. The door flew open with a crack of splintering wood and Mr. Gotobed and his two thugs rushed in, waving crowbars.

I cursed my tired brain, drew my pipe from my apron pocket and played the first tune that came to mind, which was "Rali Twm Sion"—a good rousing tune to instruct the mechanicals to break down walls.

Someone shouted—I think it was Mr. Brown. Then the air was filled with whirring gears and thumping treads and grunts and bad language and the clang and screech of metal against metal.

"Sons of pigs!" Mistress Anghard screeched. "Break their bones like matchsticks I would, could I only touch them!"

From the corner of my eye, I saw her hovering, cloud-like, over the automaton. Then she said, "I am going to break a great rule. If it means the end of me, then I will at least have tried. Good-bye, Tacy. You have been a good friend to Cwmlech, and a friend to me as well." And then she disappeared.

Though tears pricked my eyes, I went on playing "Rali Twn Sion" as though my life depended on it—until the French automaton twitched and thrashed and sat up on the table, when the pipe dropped from my hands grown suddenly nerveless.

The mechanicals froze, of course. The French automaton, however, swung off the table and staggered toward the noise of iron crunching against polished metal. Not to be outdone by a toy, I snatched up the first heavy tool I laid my hand on and ran, yelling to tear my throat, toward a shadowy figure whose shaven cheeks showed ghostly in the gloom.

Swinging my makeshift weapon high, I hit on the arm—as much by luck as design. He swore and dropped the bar. I was about to hit him again when Sir Arthur's lights flared into blinding life overhead and Sir Arthur's pipe brought the mechanicals to purposeful life.

Quick as thinking, they seized Mr. Gotobed and Mr. Brown and held them while the automaton who was Mistress Angharad picked up the third thug and slammed him bodily against the wall.

Sir Arthur came running up to me, his eyes wild behind his spectacles. "Tacy! What the devil is going on here? Are you hurt?"

I hefted my weapon—a hammer, it was. "Not a bit of it. But I think I may have broken Mr. Gotobed's arm. Earned it he has, twice over, the mess he's made of things."

Side by side, we surveyed the workshop then. Like a battlefield it was, with oil stains in the place of blood. Not a mechanical but was dented, and more than one stood armless or headless and dull-eyed, its motive force gone. Not a machine but bore smashed dials and broken levers. Most pathetic, the French automaton lay sprawled like a puppet whose strings have been cut, one arm at a strange angle and the leather torn over its shoulder to show the metal underneath.

Sir Arthur pinched the bridge of his nose. "It's ruined," he said, very low. "They're all ruined. And there's no money left—not enough to repair them, anyway. I'll have to sell it all as scrap, and that won't bring enough to keep Cwmlech Manor on."

It hurt my heart to hear him say so. "What about the Treasure?"

He shook his head. "That's a legend, Tacy, like the ghost—just a local variant of a common folk tale. No. I am my father's son, a gambler and a wastrel. Mr. Whitney will have Cwmlech Manor after all."

"Do not lose hope, Sir Arthur, my little one," I said. "Do you lock those bad men into the tack room while I make a pot of tea. And then we will talk about what to do."

When I returned with the tea tray, Mr. Gotobed and his rogues were nowhere to be seen. Two chairs had been set by the forge fire, which was blazing brightly, and the automaton back upon its table with Sir Arthur beside it, nibbling on his thumbnail.

I poured two cups with sugar and milk, took one for myself and carried the other to him. He thanked me absently and set down his cup untasted. I breathed in the fragrant steam, but found no comfort in it. Abandoning my tea, I set myself to search grimly among the tools and glass and pieces of metal on the floor. Like looking for a needle in a haystack it was, but I persisted, and turned up Mistress Angharad's key at last under one of the broken machines.

"Here," I said, thrusting it into Sir Arthur's hand. "Maybe it's just run down she is, and not ruined at all. Do you wind her and we'll find out."

Muttering something about putting a sticking plaster on a mortal wound, he inserted the key, turned it until it would turn no more, and then withdrew it.

The eyelids opened slowly and the head turned stiffly towards us. Sir Arthur whooped with joy, but my heart sank; for the eyes were only brown glass, bright and expressionless. Mistress Angharad was gone.

And then the finely-carved mouth quirked up at the corners and one brown eye winked at me

"A legend, am I?" said Mistress Angharad Cwmlech of Cwmlech Manor. "There's a fine thing to say to your great-aunt, boy, when she is on the point of pulling your chestnuts from the fire."

It would be pleasant to write that Sir Arthur took Mistress Angharad's haunting of the French automaton in his stride, or that Mistress Angharad led Sir Arthur to the treasure without delay. But that would not be truthful.

Truthfully, then. Sir Arthur was convinced that the shock of losing Cwmlech Manor had driven him mad, and Mistress Angharad had a thing or two to say about people who were too clever to believe their own eyes. I was ready to shut them up in the workshop to debate their separate philosophies until one or the other of them ran down.

"Whist the both of you," I said at last. "Sir Arthur, there's no harm in hearing what Mistress Angharad has to say, do you believe in ghosts or not. It can be no more a waste of time than arguing about it all night."

"I'll speak," Lady Angharad said. "If he'll listen."

Sir Arthur shrugged wearily. "I'll listen."

The Cwmlech Treasure was hidden in a priest's hole, tucked all cozy into the side of the chimney in the Long Gallery. In the reign of Harry VIII, masons had known their business, for the door fit so neatly into the stonework that we could not see it, even when Mistress Angharad traced its outline. Nor could all our prodding and pushing on the secret latch stir it so much as a hair's breadth.

"It's rusted shut," Sir Arthur said, rubbing a stubbed finger. "The wall will have to be knocked down, I expect."

Mistress Angharad put fists on her hips. Very odd it was to see her familiar gestures performed by a doll, especially one clad in an old sheet. It had been worse, though, without the sheet. Mute and inert, an automaton is simply unclothed. When it speaks to you in a friend's voice, however, it is suddenly naked, and must be covered.

"Heaven send me patience," she said now. "Here is nothing that a man with an oil can and a chisel and a grain of sense cannot sort out."

"I'll fetch Da, then," I said. "But first, breakfast and coffee, or we'll be asleep where we stand. And Mam must be wondering what's become of me."

Indeed, Mam was in the kitchen, steeling herself to go upstairs and see whether Sir Arthur had been murdered in his bed and I stolen by Mr. Gotobed for immoral purposes. The truth, strange as it was, set her mind at ease, though she had a word to say about Mistress Angharad's bedsheet. Automaton or not, she was the daughter of a Baronet, Mam said. She must come down by our house to be decently clothed, and explain things to Da while she was about it.

High morning it was before we gathered in the Long Gallery, Da with his tools, Mam with the tea tray, and Mistress Angharad in my best Sunday costume with the triple row of braiding on the skirt and my Sunday bonnet covering her bald head.

Da chipped and pried and oiled and coaxed the door open at last amid a great cloud of dust that set us all coughing like geese. When it settled, we were confronted with a low opening into a darkness like the nethermost pits of Hell, which breathed forth a dank odor of ancient drains and wet stone.

Da looked at Sir Arthur, who bit his lip and looked at me.

"God's bones!" Mistress Angharad cried and, snatching up the lantern, set her foot on the steep stone stair that plunged down behind the chimney.

Sir Arthur, shame faced, followed after, with me and Da behind him, feeling our way along the slick stone wall, taking our breath short in the musty air.

It could not have been far, but the dark made the stair lengthen until we might have been in the bowels of the earth. It ended in a stone room furnished with a narrow bed and three banded boxes, all spotted with mold and rust. Da's crowbar made short work of the locks. He lifted the lids one by one and then we looked upon the fabled Treasure of Cwmlech.

A great deal of it there was, to be sure, but not beautiful nor rich to the eye. There were chargers and candlesticks and ewers and bowls, all gone black with tarnish. Even the gold coins in their strongbox and Mistress Angharad's jewels were dull and plain with time and dirt.

Mistress Angharad picked a ring out of the muddle and rubbed it on the skirt of my Sunday costume, revealing a flat-cut stone that winked and glowed like fire in the lantern-light.

"What think you of your variant folk tale now?" she asked Sir Arthur.

He laughed, free and frank. "I see I shall have to speak better of folk tales in the future."

All I recall of the rest of that day was the steady stream of police and masons and men from the village come to deal with the consequences of the night's adventures. When Sir Arthur sat down to dinner in his parlor at last, Mr. Gotobed and his thugs were locked up tight as you please in the magistrate's coal cellar and the treasure had been carried piecemeal from the priest's hole and put in the old tack room with Ianto Evans and two others to guard it. Mam cooked the dinner, and served it, too, for I was in my bed at home, asleep until old Mrs. Phillips's rooster woke me next morning, to walk to the manor in the soft dawn as usual, as if my world had not been turned upside down.

First thing I saw when I came in the kitchen was Mistress Angharad, sitting on the settle in my Sunday costume.

"Good morning, Tacy," she said.

A weight dropped from me I had not known I carried. I whooped joyfully and threw my arms around her. Like hugging a dress form it was, but I did not mind.

"This is a greeting after a long parting, Tacy my little one," she said, laughing. "Only yesterday it was you saw me."

"And did not think to see you again. Is it not a rule of ghosts, to disappear when their task on earth is done?"

The automaton's face was not expressive, and yet I would swear Mistress Angharad looked sly. "Yet here I am."

I sat back on my heels. "Is it giving eternity the slip you are, then? The truth now."

"The truth?" She shrugged stiffly. "I am as surprised as you. Perhaps there's no eternal rule about a ghost that haunts a machine. Perhaps I am outside all rules now, and can make my own for a change. Perhaps"—she rose from the settle and began her favorite pacing—"I can wear what I like and go where I will. Would you like to be trained as a mechanic, Tacy, and be my lady's maid to keep me wound and oiled?"

"If you are no longer a lady," I said, with a chill that surprised even me, "you will not need a lady's maid. I would prefer to train as an engineer, but if I must be a servant, I'd rather be a housekeeper with a great house to run, than a mechanic, which is only a scullery maid with an oilcan."

A man's laugh startled us both. "Well said, Tacy," said Sir Arthur from the kitchen door where he'd been listening. "Only I have in mind to make your mother housekeeper, if she will do it, with a gaggle of housemaids under her to keep the place tidy. You I need to design a voice for my humanatron. You will learn engineering. Which means I must command tutors and books from London. And new tools and a new automaton from France, of course. Perhaps more than one. I suppose I must write my lawyers first, and finish work on the pipe. And the foundation needs work, the masons say." He sighed. "There's so much to do, I do not know where to begin."

"Breakfast first," I said. "And then we'll talk about the rest."

There is a ghost in Cwmlech Manor.

She may be seen by anyone who writes a letter that interests her. Mr. Whitney came all the way from Pittsburgh to talk to her. He stayed a month and Sir Arthur persuaded him to invest in the humanatron.

She travels often, accompanied by her mechanic and sometimes by me, when I can spare the time from my engineering studies and my experiments. Last summer, we went to London and Sir Arthur presented us to Queen Victoria, who shook our hands and said she had never spoken to a ghost before, or a female engineer, and that she was delightfully amused.

THE RED PIANO

My university colleagues think of me as a calm woman. Whatever's going on, they say, I can be counted on to keep my head, to make plans, to calculate the cost and consequences, and then to act. If they also say that I live too much in my head, that I lack passion and, perhaps, compassion, that is the price I must pay for being one of those still waters that runs deep and perhaps a little cold.

It's not that I don't have friends. In graduate school, there were men who like to debate with me over endless cups of coffee and too-sweet muffins in smoky little cafés near the university. My discipline was archaeology, my area of concentration the burial customs of long-dead societies, my obsession the notion of a corporeal afterlife, rich with exotic foods and elaborate furniture, jewels and art and books and servants to wait upon the deceased as they had in life. Wherever they began, all conversations circled back to the same ever-fascinating questions: whether such preparations reflected some post-mortem reality, or whether all the elaborated pomp of preservation and entombment were nothing but a glorified whistling in the dark of eternity.

In the course of these debates, I gained a reputation for an intensity of focus that discouraged my café companions from seeking more intimate bonds of friendship or romance. I did not mind; my own silent communion with dead worlds and languages gave me intimacy enough.

Thanks to my attention to my studies, I throve in my field, finally rising in my thirties to the position of a full professor of archeology at a prominent university situated in a great city. Armed with the income this position offered me and a comfortable sum left to me by a great-aunt, I set out to look for a house to buy.

It was not an easy quest. In a city of apartment buildings and bland new construction, a detached dwelling of historical interest and aesthetic character is not easy to come by. At last, my Realtor showed me an old stable that had been renovated as a townhouse late in the last century by an eccentric developer. It had sat on the market for some time before going to an equally eccentric ballerina, recently retired from the stage. After she had suffered a crippling accident on the circular iron staircase, the stable came back on the market, where it had remained ever since.

The Realtor showed me this property with some reluctance, evincing considerable surprise when I told him that I would take it. Like a man in the grip of leprosy obsessively checking each limb for infections, he pointed out the inconvenient kitchen, the Pompeian master bath, the unfinished roof deck with its unpromising view of a back alley and the sheer brick sides of the adjoining houses, and, worst of all, the grand piano that was attached to the sale and could not, by deed, be destroyed or removed from its position in the darkly paneled living room. Enchanted with the very eccentricities that had scuttled all previous negotiations, I made my offer, arranged for a mortgage, and hired a lawyer to draw up the papers.

I well remember the day I took possession. I'd thought my Realtor the kind of small, dark, narrow man who shivers on even the hottest days. But as he handed me the key to the front door, he stopped shivering and smiled the first genuine smile I'd seen on his face.

"Here you are, Dr. Waters," he said. "I sure hope you know what you're getting into."

I thought this an odd thing to say, but I was too dazed with legal complexities to comment on his choice of words. Not that it would have done any good. Once the papers were signed, my fate was sealed.

I have said my new house was flanked by larger houses—two mansions of ancient aspect and noble proportions that had shared, in their vanished youth, the stable I now called home. One of these had been refurbished, renovated, and repurposed to a glossy fare-thee-well, losing much of its character in the process. The other was infinitely more charming. There was a vagueness about its soot-streaked brownstone facade and clouded windows, an aura of fogs and mists that spoke of gaslight and the clop of horses' hooves on cobblestones, as if it somehow occupied an ancient lacuna in the roar and clatter of the modern city.

Accustomed as I am to keeping to myself and mindful of the ancient urban habit of never acknowledging that one has neighbors at all, I did not knock on either door. I moved into my stable, arranged my books and my great-aunt's antique furniture, my Egyptian canopic jars and Roman armbands, my Columbian breastplates and Hellenic funerary steles in the wide wooden spaces where the horses of my neighbors' predecessors had drowsed and fed.

I also had the piano tuned. It was of a manufacture unknown to me, an unusual instrument made of close-grained wood stained a deep, oxblood red, its keys fashioned of a uniform polished ebony. Its tone was resonant and full, more akin to an organ than the tinkling parlor uprights I had played as a girl. It was intricately carved with a myriad of identical faces clustered around its legs and above its pedals and around the music stand. I had lost all interest in practicing the piano when I discovered archeology. But I could not feel settled in my new home until I had not only dusted and waxed all the many whorls and complexities of its ornamentation, but also restored its inner workings to their original state.

In short, I did my utmost to set my stamp on the piano. Yet it continued to unsettle me. Waking in the small hours of the night, grading papers or reading or laboring over my comprehensive analysis of the Egyptian Book of the Dead, I sometimes fancied that I heard it playing a melancholy and meditative concerto. More than once I crept downstairs, my heart in my throat and a sturdy brass candlestick in my hand, intent on surprising the midnight musician. On each occasion, I found the living room empty and dark, the piano silent. After a month or more of increasingly disturbed and sleepless nights, I formed the idea that the sounds haunting me must come from the house next door, the house whose antique air had so enchanted me. I decided to break the habit of years and introduce myself to my neighbor with the intention of asking him to remove his piano from the wall it must share with my study, or failing that, to confine his playing to daylight hours.

Accordingly, on my return next day from a seminar in reading papyri, I mounted the six steps of the ancient brownstone and tugged the rusted bell-pull hanging beside the banded oaken door. Deep within the house, a bell tolled, followed by a listening silence. Again I rang, determined to rouse the inhabitants, from sleep if need be, as they had so often roused me. The echoes of the third and last ring had not yet died away when the door opened.

My first impression of Roderick Hawthorne was that he was very beautiful. He was tall, over six feet, and slender as a reed, with long, prominent bones. His forehead was broad and domed under an unruly mass of bronze-dark curls like chrysanthemum petals that rioted over his head and down his long and hollow jaw in an equally unruly beard. His nose was Egyptian in the spring of its nostrils, pure Greek in its high-arched bridge; his eyes were large and dark and liquid behind round gold-rimmed spectacles. His gaze, mildly startled at first, sharpened when it fell upon me, rendering me sufficiently self-conscious that I hardly knew how to begin my complaint.

"Your piano," I said at last, and was startled when he laughed. He had a laugh as beautiful as his person, deep and musical as an organ's Vox Humana. Then he said, "At its old tricks again, is it?" and I was lost. His voice was oboe and recorder, warm milk and honey. I could have listened to that voice reading the phone book with undiminished pleasure and attention. He spoke again: "Do come in, Miss. . . ?"

I realized that I was staring at him with my mouth ajar, more like a cinema fan in the presence of a celluloid celebrity than a professor of archeology at a major American university. "It's Doctor, actually. Dr. Arantxa Waters."

"Dr. Waters." He held out a long hand, the fingers pale and smooth as marble, delicately veined with blue. Cold as marble, too, when I laid my own within it. "I am Roderick Hawthorne," he said. "Welcome to Hawthorne House."

The interior of Hawthorne House was as untouched by the modern world as its exterior. The walls were hung with richly figured papers and the windows with draperies of velvet and brocade in crimson, ultramarine, and the mossy green of a forest floor. The furniture was massive, dark, ornamented with every kind of bird and fruit and animal known to the carver's art. Precious carpets covered the floors, and precious objects crowded every surface not claimed by piles of books. Everything was illuminated by the soft yellow glow of gaslights hissing behind etched glass shades. It would have been perfect, if it hadn't been for the dust and neglect that lay over it all like a pall. Still, I complimented him on the beauty of his home with complete sincerity.

"Do you like it?" he asked, a touch anxiously. "It's gone woefully to seed, I'm afraid, since my wife's death. I suppose I could hire a housekeeper, but the truth is, I hardly notice the mess. And I do value my privacy."

I felt an unaccustomed color climb my cheeks, shame and irritation combined. "I shall conclude my business quickly," I said, and explained that his piano playing at night was disturbing my studies. As

I spoke, it seemed to me that the intensity of his gaze grew ever more concentrated, so that I could almost imagine my blush rather ignited by the fire of his eye than by my own self-consciousness.

"I understand," he said when I fell silent. "Although I am somewhat at a loss as to the remedy. Come, see for yourself."

He led me from the parlor, where we had been talking, up a wide and sweeping staircase to the floor above, where he turned away from the direction in which my own house and its study lay, into a room across the landing, illuminated, like the parlor, by gas and oil lamps. The soft golden light showed me a formal music room, furnished with a gilded floor-harp and a cello as well as a brocade sofa, a gallery of shadowy pictures under much-smeared glass—and a piano, the precise twin of mine, down to the carved heads and the unusual deep crimson stain.

"As you can see," he said as I stared at the piano, "the sound of my playing is unlikely to carry across the landing and through two brick walls to disturb you in your study. But I do believe that you have been so disturbed." Observing my look of bewilderment, he gestured toward the sofa. "Sit down, please, and I shall tell you the story.

"You have noticed, of course, that our pianos are a matched pair. Your piano was, in fact, made for the wife of the Hawthorne who built Hawthorne House, not long after she entered it as a bride. In this very room they played duets until her untimely death caused him, in the extremity of his grief, to banish her piano to the stable."

Feeling I should make some observation, I said, "A very natural response, under the circumstances."

"Oh no," Hawthorne said seriously, "he was quite mad. And went madder with time. A sane man might have given the piano to charity or sold it or even caused it to be destroyed. The founder of Hawthorne House had his lawyers draw up an addition to the deed preventing the piano from being moved from the stable or destroyed, in perpetuity, no matter who might come to own the stable or what might be done to it."

"Your ancestor does seem to have been a trifle eccentric," I said. "But it was a romantic and morbid age."

His large, bright eyes dwelt on my face. "You are very understanding," he murmured, his voice thrilling in my ear.

"Not at all," I said briskly. "Is there more to the story?"

He seemed to collect himself. "Very little of substance. Yet, a piano with such a history is likely to attract rumors as a corpse attracts worms. Most pertinent of these is that, under certain circumstances, it plays in sympathy with its mate."

"And do you believe in such rumors?

"I believe in everything," Roderick Hawthorne said. Shrugging away his melancholy, he turned a hospitable smile on me. "As long as you are here, will you take a glass of sherry, and hear me play?"

It was clear from his nervous hands, his febrile eye, the urgent note in his plangent voice, that Roderick Hawthorne was utterly convinced that the music I was hearing was the result of a species of supernatural possession. I myself place little credence in ghosts and hauntings, yet the charms of his person and his voice were such that I accepted both sherry and invitation and sat upon the sofa while he laid his beautiful pale hands upon the red piano's ebony keys and began to play.

How shall I describe Roderick Hawthorne's playing? I am, as I have said, a woman whose passions are primarily intellectual, whose reason is better developed than her emotions. My host's music delved into the unplumbed depths of my psyche and brought up strange jewels. The nut-sweet sherry blended with salt tears as I wept unashamedly, drunk on music and the deep rumble of my host, humming as he played.

Afterwards, we sat in the parlor with warm lamplight playing across Chinese urns and Renaissances bronzes and talked of a subject precious to us both: the wide range of humanity's response to the ineluctable fact of death. By the time I left him, long after midnight, I was well on my way to a state I had never before experienced and was hardly able to identify. I was infatuated.

In taking leave of me, Roderick proposed that I call upon him soon. "I have no telephone," he said. "Nor do I often leave my house. I would not like to think that my eccentricity might prevent the deepening of a promising friendship."

Even in the face of such clear encouragement, I waited almost a week before calling on him again. Out of his presence, I found myself as disquieted by his oddities as charmed by his beauty. I was reasonably sure that the use of gas for household lighting was against all current city building codes. And his superstitious belief in the haunted bonds between our twin pianos and the supernatural origin of the sounds I heard, combined with the fact that he himself was (I presumed) recently widowed and not yet recovered from his loss, made me reluctant to further the acquaintance. Still, there was his playing, and the intoxication of conversation with one whose obsessions so perfectly complemented my own. And there was my piano, singing softly at the edge of my hearing in the deep of the night, reminding me of the emotions I had experienced hearing him play its mate, and could experience again, if only I should take the trouble to go next door.

Unable at last to resist any longer, I put aside my reservations, rang the rusty bell, and saw again his large, mild eyes, his sweet mouth nested like a baby bird in the riot of his beard, felt his cold, smooth hand press my own, heard his voice like an oboe welcoming me, questioning me, talking, talking, talking with delight of all the things that were closest to my heart.

On this second visit, it seemed to me that the house was cleaner than it had been when I'd first seen it—the hangings brighter, the air clearer. The change was most apparent in the music room, where the piano gleamed a deep crimson and candlelight sparkled off the new-polished glass of the gallery of pictures. When Roderick began to play, I rose from the sofa to examine them.

They were sketches, in pencil or charcoal, of a female figure surrounded by shadowed and threatening shapes. Sometimes she fled across a gothic landscape; more often she sat in intricately rendered interiors that I recognized at once as my host's parlor and music room, alone save for demonic shapes that menaced her from the shadows. The figure bore only the faintest resemblance to an actual woman, being slender to the point of emaciation, overburdened with dark curly hair inclined to dishevelment, and possessed of eyes stretched in an extremity of terror. It was not until I came upon a head and shoulders portrait, that I realized, with a feeling of considerable shock, that the face gazing out so anxiously from the gilded frame was, when seen in relative repose, very like mine. Had I allowed my hair to grow out of the neat crop I had adopted to tame its natural wildness, lost twenty pounds or so, and assumed clothing over a century out of fashion, there would have been no appreciable difference between us.

Behind me, the music modulated into a melancholy mode. "The first Mrs. Hawthorne," Roderick said. "Drawn not long before her death, by her husband. The others were drawn later. He became obsessed by the idea that demons had sucked the life from her. There are boxes full of such sketches in the attic."

"They seem a very gloomy subject for a music room," I commented.

"They have always been here," he said simply. "I do not choose to move them."

"And your own wife," I asked diffidently. "Have you any pictures of her?"

Under Roderick's long, pale fingers, the ebony keys of the red piano danced and flickered in an unquiet Mazurka. "My wife," he said precisely, "died some while ago. She, too, was pale, with dark eyes and dark hair. Isabella Lorenzo, who last owned your stable, was of similar coloring. So are you."

For a moment, I was both frightened and repelled by the intensity of his gaze over the crimson-stained music stand, the throb and tremor of his beautiful voice. I felt that I had intruded unpardonably upon a grief too terrible and private for my eyes. Embarrassed almost beyond bearing, I was on the point of quitting his music room and his house, never to return. But then he smiled, and the tune beneath his fingers grew bright and gay and light. "But all that is past now, lovely Arantxa," he said softly, "and has nothing to do with you and me."

Foolishly, I believed him.

The subject of Roderick's lost wife did not arise again between us, as fearful to me as it must have been painful to him. Nor did I learn anything more of the history of the first Mrs. Hawthorne, my long dead doppelganger. These shadows on his past did nothing to decrease my fascination with him, which only grew more intense as the year faded toward winter.

Over the next weeks, I came by insensible degrees to spend almost every evening in his company. I always went to him; he would not venture even so far from his house as my adjacent stable. No stranger to the terrors that acute agoraphobia can visit on a sensitive spirit, I did not press him, but returned his hospitality by providing our nightly dinners. An unenthusiastic cook, I provided take-out from one of the local restaurants, but I will never forget the first time I descended to his kitchen in search of a teapot and hot water, only to discover that the stove was wood-fed, the water pumped by hand into the sink, and the milk kept in an icebox chilled by an actual block of ice.

"It has always been that way," he said when I came up again, defeated by the primitive technology. "I do not choose to change it."

On subsequent visits, I found the stove had been lit and water pumped ready in the kettle for our nightly cup of tea. Indeed, Roderick showed himself unfailingly solicitous of my comfort. When I complained that I was too tired, on returning home late each night, to keep up with my work, he gave me the room across the hall from the music room as a study. There I would sit, lapped in fur and velvet against the chill, grading papers by gaslight while the glorious waves of Roderick's music washed over my senses. Often, emotion so overcame me that I would have granted him whatever he might ask, even to those intimacies I could hardly bring myself to contemplate. But every night, when the great clock at the foot of the steps chimed midnight, he would lower the keyboard cover, wish me goodnight, and escort me to the door.

I soon became aware of an inconvenient lack of energy. At first I blamed my growing enervation on too little sleep and the extreme stimulation of Roderick's conversation and music. I confided my state to Roderick, who insisted that I leave at eleven, so that I might retire earlier. "For now that I've found you, Arantxa, I cannot do without you. I might have sunk into melancholy altogether, and my house with me, had it not been for you."

Indeed, both Roderick and his house had improved since I'd first seen them. Someone had cleaned and dusted, washed and polished everything to the well-cared-for glow that bespeaks a truly dedicated housekeeper. When I asked where he'd unearthed such a jewel, he smiled and turned the subject. I got more sleep, and for a time, felt a little better. But my classes remained a struggle to prepare and my students a constant irritation.

Early in the spring semester, my department chair called me into his office. He was concerned about my health, he said. I seemed languid, forgetful of meetings and deadlines. There had been complaints. It was all very troubling. To silence him, I made an appointment with a doctor at the University Health Services, who subjected me to a series of annoying and expensive tests, and in the end confessed himself no wiser than when he started. He diagnosed me with non-typical chronic fatigue, and prescribed a stimulant.

Roderick laughed when he heard this diagnosis. "Chronic fatigue? Nonsense. You possess more vitality than any woman I have known." He took my hand and raised it to his lips. "Dear Arantxa," he murmured, his breath warm on my knuckles. "So strong, so utterly alive. You must know that I adore you. Will you marry me?"

My heart stuttered in my breast with fear or passion—I hardly knew which. His bright and fixed gaze filled my mind and my senses, leaving room for nothing else. Words of acceptance trembled on my lips, but were checked at the last moment by inborn caution.

"You overwhelm me, Roderick," I said shakily. "I have never thought of marriage. You must give me time to consider your proposal."

Releasing my hand, Roderick shrank back into his chair. "You do not love me as I love you," he said, his oboe-like voice clouded with disappointment.

I leaned forward, and for the first time, touched his softly curling beard. "I might," I said truthfully. "I don't know. I need to think what to do."

He nodded, his beard sliding under my fingers. "Then you shall think. But please—think quickly."

That night, he played the red piano with unsurpassed passion. I lay on the music room sofa overwhelmed with sound, my arm flung over my eyes to hide my slow, helpless tears. Of course I loved him. I had never found anyone who listened to me as he did, looked at me with such hunger. Why then did I hesitate? In my extreme perturbation, I could hardly find the energy to rise from the sofa, and was forced to accept his arm to support me to the door. "Are you well?" he asked anxiously. "Shall I help you home?"

Knowing what the offer must have cost him, I was deeply moved. "My goodness," I said, forcing a light tone through my deadly fatigue. "Do I look that bad? No, I'll be fine by myself."

"I will see you tomorrow, then," he said, and for the first time, laid his lips against mine. His kiss, both passionate and cold, excited my nerves, lending me the strength to traverse the short distance to my own door.

I slept fitfully that night. Whenever I fell asleep, I was haunted by a groaning, as of pain unbearable, echoing up the spiral stairs. I would wake with a start and lie quivering in the darkness, ears straining to hear past the beating of my heart. The next day passed in a kind of stupor. I could barely totter down to the kitchen to boil water for tea and recruit faltering nature with soup and toast. By evening, I was simultaneously exhausted and restless beyond bearing. Which was, perhaps, why I found myself sitting on the piano bench.

I had not come near the piano in some time. As I sat before it, I noticed that the little carved faces were familiar. I knew that domed brow, that coolly sensual mouth in its nest of hyacinthine curls. My exhaustion was such that I saw nothing odd in finding Roderick's visage carved upon his ancestor's piano. It only inspired in me a desire to touch him, speak to him, draw comfort from him. Impulsively, I raised the cover, lifted my hands to the ebony keys and ran my fingers from treble to bass. If I was far too weak to drag myself to him, perhaps I could touch him through our linked instruments.

Tentatively, I embarked upon a simple song I had learned as a girl. Though I stumbled at first, sense memory soon took over. My fingers began to move as of their own accord, progressing from the song into a nocturne, and then into improvisation. As I played, I forgot my fatigue, my undone work, even Roderick and his proposal. The music I made lifted me into a realm of beautiful abstraction, spirit without substance, clean and pure and bright. When at last I stopped playing, it was a little after midnight. Strangely, I felt better—tired certainly, but not exhausted. My mind was clearer than it had been for months.

That night I slept soundly, never stirring until early afternoon, when I rose well-rested and able to eat a proper meal and do some real work. When I looked up from my papers at last, it was far too late to go to Roderick's. Wanting to recapture that feeling of perfect communion, I sat down once again at the red piano, and rose some hours later, strong, refreshed, and as sure as I could be that I loved Roderick Hawthorne and wanted to be his wife.

The next afternoon, I dressed myself with more than usual care. I brushed out my hair, which had grown during my illness, into a dark cloud that made my face more delicate and white in contrast. I put on a dress I had not worn since college—black velvet cut tight to my hips, the skirt full and sweeping below. I clasped my mother's pearls around my neck, and thus bedecked, once again rang the bell of Hawthorne House.

No sooner had my hand fallen from the pull than the door opened on a haggard figure I hardly recognized. Roderick Hawthorne's hair was uncombed, his collar unbuttoned, his cheeks gaunt and his eyes reddened. "Arantxa!" he exclaimed. "I have not slept or eaten in two days, waiting for your answer, fearing what it must be when you did not return."

My heart contracted with pity. "Oh, my dear." He smiled at the endearment, the first I'd ever used. "I could not come. I was so tired. And I did need to think."

"My poor angel. Of course. I'm glad you're better. And you are here now. It is yes, isn't it? Your answer?"

Something in his voice—satisfaction? Triumph?—stifled my agreement on my lips. I smiled, but said nothing.

Dinner was a depressing meal. The dining room was cold, the fire sullen and low, the food indifferent. Both of us avoided the subject most pressingly on our minds, every other topic of conversation an unexpected minefield of references to love or matrimony. At length, we rose from an unaccustomed silence.

"I will not plead for myself," he said. "Perhaps you will let my music plead for me." He took my hand; his was colder than ice. As we walked from the dining room to the music room, I noticed that the whole house was cold, neglected, dusty, as though none had swept or polished or built a fire there for weeks rather than the two days I'd been absent. As Roderick hurried me up the stairs, fear grew in my breast. On the threshold of the music room, I hesitated, searching for some way to excuse myself from a situation grown suddenly intolerable, but Roderick's cold hand grasped mine more tightly, drawing me inexorably toward the red piano and down onto the bench beside him.

The carved faces peered at me from the music stand. It was the first time I had seen them close up, but I was not astonished to discover that they were as like the first Mrs. Hawthorne, like me, as the faces on my piano were like Roderick. In a flash, I understood everything. It utterly defied rational belief, but I could not afford the luxury of disbelief. My very life depended on acting quickly.

I took a deep, calming breath and smiled deliberately into his face. Roderick Hawthorne smiled back, predatory as a wolf, then released me, rubbed his long hands together, and flexed his fingers. He disposed them gently on the ebony keys, and prepared to play me to utter dissolution.

Before he could sound a single note, I seized the heavy wooden cover and slammed it shut on his fingers with all my force.

He screamed like a wild animal, a scream with a snarl in it, rage and pain mingled. Springing to my feet, I ran from the music room, snatching up my cumbersome skirts. Weak and in pain, he was still stronger than I, infinitely older and wise in the terrible sorcery that had animated him so far beyond his natural span of years. If I fell into his hands, I knew I could not escape him a second time. I ran headlong down the stairs, resisting the impulse to look behind me, knowing he must follow me, clumsy with pain, utterly determined to catch me and drain me of my strength and my life.

Tearing open the door, I stumbled into the open air a step ahead of him, and down the stoop into the alley. I knew now that his life must be intimately intertwined with the house he had inhabited for so long. He might not be able to step over the threshold; then again, he might. I could not afford to take the chance.

In the light of a single lamp, my living room seemed calm and homelike. I clicked on the overhead, and there was the red piano, squatting beside the stair, oversized, over-decorated, garish, out of place among the beautiful simplicities of my collections.

A scream of rage at the end of the alley sent me flying to the box I kept under the stairs. Screwdriver, hammer, pliers, wire cutter—inadequate tools for the task ahead, but all I had at my disposal. I splintered the ebony keys and the music stand with the hammer. An inhuman howling came from the alley. I moved on to the carved faces on the legs and case and something heavy began to slam against my front door, causing it to quiver in the frame. Furiously I hammered at the carved wood, squinting against the splinters stinging my cheeks and chest.

With a great crack, the door burst inward. I looked up, and there was Roderick Hawthorne, framed in darkness, his face stark in the electric glare. If I had harbored any lingering doubts as to the uncanny nature of the night's events, I did so no longer. His face was scored and bleeding, his beard ragged and clotted with gore, his eye a bloody ruin, his mouth swollen and misshapen. I glanced down at my hammer, half expecting to see it smeared with blood. In that moment of inattention, he sprang toward me, gabbling wildly, his beautiful voice raw and ruined, his beautiful hands bruised, swollen, bleeding, reaching for me, for the broken piano keys.

Snatching up the wire cutters, I thrust open the piano lid and applied myself to the strings. One by one I clipped them, in spite of Roderick's howling and wailing, in spite of his hands clawing at my shoulders as he tried in vain to prevent me from severing his heart strings. As I worked my way down to the bass register, the howling stopped, and I felt only a weak pawing at my ankles. And then there was nothing.

When I completed my task, I turned and saw what I had done. For a moment, a horror lay on my rug, the red and white and black ruin of the man I had loved. And then his flesh deliquesced in an accelerated process of decay as unnatural as his protracted life. A deep groan sounded, as of crumbling masonry and walls, and then my world was rocked with the slow collapse of Hawthorne House, falling in on itself like a house of cards, dissolving, like its master, into featureless dust and rubble.

I was rescued from the wreckage by my neighbor on the other side. He gave me strong coffee laced with rum and chocolate chip cookies for shock and called the police and the fire department. He is neither beautiful nor mysterious, and he made his fortune writing code for a computer game I had never even heard of. He prefers klezmer music to opera and *South Park* to the Romantics. He reads science fiction and plays video games. We were married in the spring, right after final exams, and moved uptown to an apartment in a modern tower with square white rooms and views across the river. We have no piano, no harp, not even a guitar. But sometimes in the deep of winter, when the dark comes early and the wind shrills at the bedroom window, I think I can hear an echo of the red piano.

THE FIDDLER OF BAYOU TECHE

Come here, cher, and I tell you a story.

One time there is a girl. Her skin and hair are white like the feathers of a white egret and her eyes are pink like a possum's nose. When she is a baby, the loup-garous find her floating on the bayou in an old pirogue and take her to Tante Eulalie.

Tante Eulalie does not howl and grow hair on her body when the moon is full like the loup-garous. But she hides in the swamp same as they do, and they are all friends together. She takes piquons out of the loup-garous' feet and bullets out of their hairy shoulders, and doses their rheumatism and their mange. In return, the loup-garous build her a cabin out of cypress and palmetto leaves and bring her rice and indigo dye from town. On moonlit nights, she plays her fiddle at the loup-garous' ball. The loup-garous love Tante Eulalie, but the girl loves her most of all.

Yes, the girl is me. Who else around here has white skin and hair and pink eyes, eh? Hush now, and listen.

Tante Eulalie was like my mother, her. She name me Cadence and tell me stories—all the stories I tell you, cher. When we sit spinning or weaving, she tell me about when she was a young girl, living with her pap and her good maman and her six brothers and three sisters near the little town of Pierreville. She tell me about her cousin Belda Guidry, the prettiest girl in the parish.

Now, when Belda is fifteen, there are twenty young men all crazy to marry her. She can't make up her mind, her, so her old pap make a test for the young men, to see which will make the best son-in-law. He make them plow the swamp and sow it with dried chilies and bring them to harvest. And when they done that, they have to catch the oldest, meanest 'gator in Bayou Teche and make a gumbo out of him.

I thought Tante Eulalie was making it all up out of her head, but she swore it was true. It was Ganelon Fuselier who won Belda, and Tante Eulalie was godmother to their second child, Denise.

Ganie cheated, of course. Nobody can pass a test like that without cheating some. Seemed to me like cheating was a way of life in Pierreville. The wonder was how the folks that were getting cheated never learned to be less trustful. I thought if I ever went to Pierreville, and Ganie Fuselier or Old Savoie tell me the sky is blue, I'd go outside and check. And if Murderes Petitpas came knocking at my door, I'd slip out the back.

Tante Eulalie's best stories were about Young Murderes Petitpas. He was like the grasshopper because he'd always rather fiddle than work, though 'Dres was too smart to get caught out in the cold. How smart was he? Well, I tell you the story of 'Dres and the Fiddle, and you judge for yourself.

Once there's this old man, see, called Old Boudreaux. He has a fiddle, and this fiddle is the sweetest fiddle anybody ever hear. His old pap make it himself, back in eighteen-something, and when Old Boudreaux play, the dead get up and dance. Now, Young 'Dres thinks it's a shame that the best fiddler in St. Mary's parish—that is, Young 'Dres himself—shouldn't have the best fiddle—that is, Old Boudreaux's pap's fiddle. So Young 'Dres goes to Old Boudreaux and he says, "Old Boudreaux, I'm afraid for your soul."

Old Boudreaux says: "What you talking about, boy?"

Young 'Dres says: "Last night when you were playing 'Jolie Blonde,' I see a little red devil creep out of the f-holes and commence to dancing on your fingerboard. The faster he dance, the faster you play, and he laugh like mad and wave his forked tail so I was scared half to death."

"Go to bed, 'Dres Petitpas," says Old Boudreaux. "I don't believe that for a minute."

"It's as true as I'm standing here," says Young 'Dres. "I got the second sight, me, so I see things other people don't."

"Hmpf," says Old Boudreaux, and starts back in the house.

"Wait," says Young 'Dres. "You bring your fiddle here, and I go prove it to you."

Of course, Old Boudreaux say no. But Young 'Dres got a way with him, and everybody know Old Boudreaux ain't got no more sense than a possum. So Old Boudreaux fetches his fiddle and goes to hand it to Young 'Dres. But Young 'Dres is wringing his bandana and moaning. "Mother Mary preserve me!" he says. "Can't you see its red eyes twinkling in the f-holes? Can't you smell the sulfur? You got to exercise that devil, Old Boudreaux, or you go fiddle yourself right down to hell."

Old Boudreaux nearly drop his fiddle, he so scared. He don't dare look in the f-holes, but he don't have to, because as soon as Young 'Dres name that devil, there's a terrible stink of sulfur everywhere.

"Holy Mother save me!" Old Boudreaux cry. "My fiddle is possessed! What am I going to do, 'Dres Petitpas? I don't want to fiddle myself down to hell."

"Well, I go tell you, Old Boudreaux, but you ain't going to like it."

"I'll like it, I promise. Just tell me what to do!"

"You give the fiddle to me, and I exercise that devil for you."

Old Boudreaux so scared, he hand his pap's fiddle right over to Young 'Dres. What's more, he tell him to keep it, because Old

Boudreaux never go touch it again without thinking he smell sulfur. And that's how 'Dres Petitpas get the sweetest fiddle in the parish for nothing more than the cost of the bandana he crush the rotten egg in that make Old Boudreaux believe his fiddle is haunted.

Yes, that Young 'Dres made me laugh, him. But Tante Eulalie shook her head and said, "You go ahead and laugh, 'tit chou. Just remember that people like 'Dres Petitpas are better to hear about than have dealings with, eh? You ever meet a bon rien like that—all smiling and full of big talk—you run as fast and as far as you can go."

That was Tante Eulalie. Always looking out for me, teaching me what I need to know to live in the world. By the time I could walk, I knew to keep out of the sun and stay away from traps and logs with eyes. When I got older, Tante Eulalie taught me to spin cotton and weave cloth and dye it blue with indigo. She taught me how to make medicine from peppergrass and elderberry bark and prickly pear leaves, and some little magic gris-gris for dirty wounds and warts and aching joints. Best of all, she taught me how to dance.

Tante Eulalie loved to play the fiddle, and she played most nights after supper was cleared away. The music she played was bouncing music, swaying music, twirl around until you fall music, and when I was very little, that's what I did. Then Tante Eulalie took me to the loup-garous' ball, where I learned the two-step and the waltz.

I took to dancing like a mallard to open water. Once I learned the steps, I danced all the time. I danced with the loup-garous and I danced by myself. I danced when I swept and I danced when I cooked. I danced to Tante Eulalie's fiddling and I danced to the fiddling of the crickets. Tante Eulalie laughed at me—said I'd wear myself out. But I didn't.

Then came a winter when the leaves were blasted with cold and ice skimmed the surface of the bayou. Long about Advent-time, Tante Eulalie caught a cough. I made her prickly pear leaf syrup and willow bark tea for the fever, and hung a gris-gris for strength around her neck. But it didn't do no good. At the dark of the year, she asked me to bring out the cypress wood box from under her bed. I opened it for her, and she pulled out three pieces of lace and a gold ring and put them in my hand.

"These are all I have to leave you," she said. "These, and my fiddle. I hope you find good use for them someday."

Not long after, the Bon Dieu called her. She went to Him and her friends the loup-garous buried her under the big live oak behind the cabin and howled her funeral mass. I was sixteen years old now, more or less, and that was the end of my girlhood.

It was the end of my dancing, too, for a time. When I saw Tante Eulalie's fiddle lying silent across her cane-bottomed chair, I fell into sadness like a deep river. I lay in a nest of nutria skins next the fire and I watched the flames burn low and thought how nobody would know or notice if I lived or died.

Some time pass, I don't know how much, and then somebody knocks at the door. I don't answer, but he comes in anyway. It is Ulysse, the youngest of the loup-garous. I like Ulysse. He is quiet and skinny and he brings me peanut butter and white bread in a printed paper wrapper, and when we dance at the loup-garous' ball, everybody stops and watches us. Still, I wish he would go away.

Ulysse sniffs around a little, then digs me out of my nest and gives me a shake. "You in a bad way, chère," he says. "If Tante Eulalie see how you carry on, she pass you one big slap, for sure."

"Good," I say. "I like that fine. At least she be here to slap me."

Not much Ulysse can say to that, I think, and maybe he will go away now and let me be sad by myself. But he has another idea, him. He sniffs around again and starts to clucking like an old hen. "This place worse than a hog pen," he says. "Tante Eulalie see the state her cabin is in, she die all over again." He picks her fiddle and bow up off her chair. "Where she keep these at?"

To see Ulysse holding Tante Eulalie's fiddle gives me the first real feeling I have since it seems like forever. I get mad, me, so mad I go right up to Ulysse, who is bigger than me by a head, who has wild, dark hair and long teeth and sharp nails even when the moon is dark, and I hit him in the stomach.

"Tiens, chère! What is this? Why you hit your friend Ulysse?"

"Why? Because you touch Tante Eulalie's fiddle. Put it down, you, or I make you."

"Put it up, then," he says, "instead of curling up like a crawfish in winter."

I take the fiddle like it was an egg, and hang it on its hook over Tante Eulalie's bed. And then I start to cry, with Ulysse holding my shoulders and licking my hair like a wolf licks her cub till I am calm again.

After that, I clean the cabin and make myself a gumbo. I string Tante Eulalie's big loom with thread she spun and dyed, and I weave a length of pale blue cloth. The water rises to the edge of the porch and the nights get shorter. I set lines to catch fish, and make my garden with the seeds Tante Eulalie saved. The loup-garous still knock on my door, and I treat them for mange and rheumatism and broken bones, as Tante Eulalie always did. But I don't dance at their balls. I take my pirogue out at sunset and paddle between the big cypress trees and listen to the frogs sing of love and the roaring of the 'gators as they fight for their mates.

One night, paddling far from home, I see lights that are not the pale feu follets that dance in the swamp at night. They are yellow lights, lantern lights, and they tell me I have come to a farm. I am a little afraid, for Tante Eulalie used to warn me about letting people see me.

"You know how ducks carry on when a strange bird land in their water?" she says. "The good people of Pierreville, they see that white hair and those pink eyes, and they peck at you till there's nothing left but two, three white feathers."

I do not want to be pecked, so I start to paddle away.

And then I hear the music.

I turn back with a sweep of my paddle and drift clear. I see a wharf and a cabin and an outhouse and a hog pen, and a big barn built on high ground away from the water. The barn doors are open, and they spill yellow light out over a pack of buggies and horses and even cars—the only cars I've seen outside the magazines Ulysse sometimes brings. I don't care about them, though, for I am caught by the fiddle music that spills out brighter than the lantern light, brighter than anything in the world since Tante Eulalie left it.

I paddle toward the music like a moth to a lit candle, not caring that fire burns and ducks peck and the people of Pierreville don't like strangers. But I am not stupid like Old Boudreaux. I am careful to hide my pirogue behind a buttonbush and I don't come out in the open. I stalk the music like a bobcat, softly, softly, and I find a place behind the barn where I think nobody will come. And then I dance. I dance the two-step with my brown striped shawl, tears wet on my face because Tante Eulalie is dead, because I am dancing alone in the dark, because the fiddle is crying and I cannot help but cry, too.

The moon rises, the crickets go to bed. The fiddler plays and I dance as if the dawn will never come. I guess I keep dancing when the music stops, because next thing I know, there's a shout behind me. When I open my eyes, the sky is pale and gray and there's a knot of men behind the barn with their mouths gaping like black holes in their faces.

One of them steps forward. He is tall, broad-shouldered, and thick, and he wears a wide-brimmed hat pulled down low over his eyes, glittering in its shadow like the eyes of a snake in a hole. I throw my shawl around my shoulders and turn to run.

As soon as I move, all the men gasp and step back. I think that a little fear makes ducks mean, but a lot of fear makes them run. I give a hoot like a swamp owl, hold my shawl out like wings, and scoot low and fast into the cypress grove.

Behind me, there is shouting and lights bobbing here and there like lightning bugs. I creep to my pirogue and paddle away quiet as a watersnake, keeping to the shadows. I am very pleased with myself, me. I think the men of Pierreville are as stupid as Old Boudreaux to be frightened by a small girl in a striped shawl. Maybe soon I will go and hear the music again.

Next night, Ulysse comes knocking at my door. He sits down at the table and I give him coffee and then I go to my wheel and set it spinning.

"I hear tell of a thing," says Ulysse over the whirr of the wheel. "It make me think."

I smile a little. "Think?" I say. "That *is* a piece of news. You tell your friends? Old Placide, he be surprised."

Ulysse shakes his head. "This is serious, Cadence. Up and down the bayou, everybody is talking about the haunt that bust up the Doucet fais-do-do."

I look down at the pale brown thread running though my fingers, fine and even as Tante Eulalie's. "There weren't no haunts at the Doucet fais-do-do, Ulysse."

"The Doucets say different. They say they see a girl turn into a swamp owl and fly away. What you say to that, hien?"

"I say they drink too much beer, them."

He brings his heavy black eyebrows together. "Why you go forget everything Tante Eulalie tell you, Cadence, and make a nine-days' wonder with your foolishness?"

"Don't scold, Ulysse. The people of Pierreville for sure got more important things to talk about than me."

"Maybe so, maybe not," Ulysse says darkly. "What you doing at the Doucets'?"

"Dancing," I say, still teasing. "Who is the fiddler, Ulysse? He play mighty fine."

Ulysse is still not smiling. "He is a bon rien, Cadence, a bad man. Shake hands with Murderes Petitpas, you go count your fingers after."

I almost let the wheel stop, I'm so surprised. "You go to bed, Ulysse. Tante Eulalie make 'Dres Petitpas up out of her head."

"He real, all right. Everybody say he sell his soul to the devil so he can play better than any human man. Then he fiddle the devil out of hell and keep him dancing all day and night until his hoofs split in two and the devil give 'Dres his soul back so he can stop dancing. 'Dres Petitpas is the big bull on the hill, and mean, mean. You stay away from him, you."

I maybe like Ulysse, but I don't like him telling me what to do—Ulysse, who eats rabbits raw and howls at the moon when it's full. I pinch the thread too tight and it breaks in two.

"Eh, Cadence," he says, "you going to hit me again? Ain't going to change what I say, but go ahead if it make you feel better."

I don't hit him, but I am maybe not very kind to him, and he leaves looking like a beaten dog. I hear howling, later, that I think is Ulysse, and I am a little sorry, but not too much.

Still, I do not go out again to dance. Not because Ulysse tell me, but because I am not a couyon like Old Boudreaux.

Two, maybe three nights after, I hear a thump against my porch and the sounds of somebody tying up a pirogue and climbing out. Not Ulysse—somebody heavier. Old Placide, maybe. I am already up and looking for my jar of fly blister for his rheumatism when there's a knock on the door.

I open it. I do not see Old Placide. I see a big man with a belly like a barrel, a big-brimmed hat, and a heavy black mustache. I try to shut the door, but 'Dres Petitpas shoves it back easy, and walks past me like he was at home. Then he sits down at my table with his hat pulled down to his snake-bright eyes and his hands spread on his thighs.

"Hey there, chère," he says, and smiles real broad. His teeth are yellow and flat.

I stand by the door, thinking whether I will run away or not. Running away is maybe safer, but then 'Dres Petitpas is alone in my cabin, and I don't want that.

He eyes me like he knows just what I'm thinking. "I go tell you a story. You stand by the door if you want, but I think you be more comfortable sitting down."

I hate to do anything he say, but I hate worse looking foolish. I close the door and sit by the fire with my hands on my lap. I do not give him coffee.

"Well," he says, "this is the way it is. I am a good fiddler, me, maybe the best fiddler on the bayous. Maybe the best fiddler in the world. Ain't nobody in St. Mary's parish can dance or court or marry or christen a baby without me. But St. Mary's parish is a small place, eh? I am too big for St. Mary's. I have an idea to go to New Orleans, fiddle on the radio, make my fortune, buy a white house with columns on the front."

He lifts his hands, his fingers square at the tips, his nails trimmed short and black with dirt, and he laughs. It is not a good laugh.

"You maybe don't know, little swamp owl girl, these hands are like gold. I fiddle the devil out of hell once and I fiddle him down again. I will make those cuyons in New Orleans lie down and lick my bare feets."

He glances at me for a reaction, but I just sit there. Tante Eulalie is right. Close to, 'Dres Petitpas is not funny at all. He wants what he wants, and he don't care what he has to do to get it. He can't trick me, because I know what he is. What he go do, I wonder, when he finds that out?

As if he hears my thoughts, 'Dres Petitpas frowns. He looks around the cabin, and his eyes light on Tante Eulalie's fiddle on the wall. He gets up and goes to it, takes it down from its hook, and runs his thumb over the strings. They twang dully. "Good thing you loosen the strings," he says. "Keep the neck from warping, eh? Nice little fiddle. You play?"

I don't remember getting up, but I am standing with my hands twisted in my skirts. "No," I say as lightly as I can. "Stupid old thing. I don't know why I don't throw it into the bayou."

"You won't mind if I tune her, then." He brings the fiddle to the table and starts to tighten the strings. I sit down again. "One day," he says, picking up the story. "One day, my five sons Clopha and Aristile and 'Tit Paul and Louis and Télémaque come to me. Clopha is in love, him, and he want my blessing to marry Marie Eymard.

"Now, I got nothing against marriage. My wife Octavie and me been married together twenty-two years, still in love like two doves. My sons are good boys, smart boys. Clopha read anything you put in front of him—writing, printing, it don't matter. And young Louis add up numbers fast as I can play my fiddle. But they got no sense about women. So I tell Clopha that I will choose a wife for him, if he want one. And when the time comes, I'll choose wives for the other boys, too. Wives are too important a matter to be left to young men.

"'My foot!' Clopha say. 'I go marry Marie without your blessing, then.'

"'You go do more than that,' I tell him. 'You go marry with my curse. Remember, I got the devil on a string. My curse is something to fear. And you see if Marie Eymard go marry together with you when she find out you don't bring her so much as a stick of furniture or a woven blanket or a chicken to start life with.'

"Well, you think that be the end of it. But my sons are hard-headed boys. They argue this way and that. And then I have an idea, me, how I can shut their mouths for once and all. I offer my sons a bet."

He stops and holds the fiddle up to his ear and plucks the strings in turn, listening intently. "Better," he says. He lays the fiddle on the table, pulls a lump of rosin from his pocket, and goes to work on the bow.

"The bet," he says, "is this. I will fiddle and my sons will dance. If I stop fiddling before they all stop dancing, I go bless their marriages and play at their weddings. If not, Clopha and Louis come to New Orleans with me to read anything that needs to be read, and Aristile, 'Tit Paul, and Télémaque go tend the shrimp boats and help Octavie with the hogs and the chickens and the cotton."

'Dres Petitpas grins under his moustache. "It is a good bet I make, eh? I cannot lose.

"My sons go off behind the hog pen and talk for a while, and when they come back, they tell me that they will take my bet—on two conditions. One, they will dance one after another, so I must fiddle out five in a row. Two, I will provide a partner for them—one partner, who must dance as long as I fiddle.

"Now I am proud of my five sons, because this show they are smart as well as strong. They know I can play the sun up and down the sky. They know I can play until the cows come home and long after the chickens come to roost. They know nobody human can dance as long as I can play." He looks away from the bow and straight at me. "They don't know you."

I turn my head away. I don't know how long I can dance. All night, for sure, then paddle home after and dance in the cabin while I do my chores. Maybe the next night, too. I might could do what I guess 'Dres Petitpas wants. But I won't. I won't show my face to the people of Pierreville, my white face and pink eyes and white, white hair. I won't go among the ducks and risk their pecking—not for anybody and for sure not for 'Dres Petitpas.

"I see you at the Doucet fais-do-do," he says. "I see you dance like a leaf in the wind, like no human girl I ever seen. I go to a man I know, a hairy, sharp-tooth man, and he tell me about a little swamp owl girl dances all night long at the loup-garous' ball. I think this girl go make a good partner for my boys. What you say, hien? You come dance with my five strong sons?"

My heart is sick inside me, but I can't be angry at the loup-garou who betrayed me. 'Dres Petitpas is a hard man to say no to. But I do. I say, "No."

"I don't ask you to dance for nothing," 'Dres Petitpas coaxes me. "I go give you land to raise cotton on and a mule to plow it with."

"No."

"You greedy girl, you," he says, like it's a compliment. "How you like to marry one of my sons, then? Any one you like. Then you be important lady, nobody dare call you swamp owl girl or little white slug."

I jump up and go for him, so angry the blood burns like ice in my veins. I stop when I see he's holding Tante Eulalie's fiddle over his head by the neck.

"Listen, chère. You don't help me, I take this fiddle and make kindling out of it, and I break that loom and that wheel, and then I burn this cabin to ash. What you say, chère: yes or no? Say 'yes' now, and we have a bargain. You help me win my bet and I give you land and a mule and a husband to keep you warm. That is not so bad a bargain, hien?"

It sticks in my throat, but I have no choice. "Yes," I say.

"That's good," Murderes Petitpas says, and he tucks Tante Eulalie's fiddle under his chin and draws the bow across the strings. It sounds a note, strong and sweet. "The contest is set for Saturday night—three nights from now. We start after supper, end when the boys get tired. Make a real fais-do-do, eh? Put the children down to sleep?" He laughs with the fiddle, a skip of notes. "Might could take two, three days. You understand?"

I understand very well, but I can't help trying to find a way out. "I do not know if I can dance for three days and nights."

"I say you can, and I say you will. I got your fiddle, me."

"I cannot dance in the sun."

A discord sounds across the strings. "Little white slug don't like sun, eh? No matter. We make the dance in Doucet's barn. You know where it at already." Tante Eulalie's fiddle mocks me with one of the tunes he played that night. Despite myself, my feet begin to move, and he laughs. "You a dancing fool, chère. I win my bet, my sons learn who's boss, and I go be a rich man on the radio."

He's fiddling as he speaks and moving toward the door. I'm dancing because I can't help it, with tears of rage stinging the back of my nose and blurring my eyes. I don't let them fall till he's gone, though. I have that much pride.

The rest of that night is black, black, and the next two days, too. There are knocks at my door, but I do not answer them. I am too busy thinking how I will make Murderes Petitpas sorry he mess with me. I take my piece of blue cloth off the loom and sew a dancing dress for myself, with Tante Eulalie's lace to the neck and cuffs. Early the third morning, I make a gris-gris with Tante Eulalie's gold ring. I sleep and wash myself and put on the dress and braid my hair in a tail down my back and hang the gris-gris around my neck. Then I get in my pirogue and paddle through the maze of the swamp to the warm lights of the Doucet's farm.

It is very strange to tie my pirogue to the wharf and walk up to the barn in the open. Under my feet, the dirt is warm and smooth, and the air smells of flowers and spices and cooking meat. The barn doors are open and the lantern light shines yellow on the long tables set up outside and the good people of Pierreville swarming around with plates and forks, scooping jambalaya and gumbo, dirty rice and fried okra, red beans and grits from the dishes and pots.

At first they don't see me and then they do, and all the gumbo ya-ya of talk stops dead. I walk toward them through a quiet like the swamp at sunset. My heart beats so hard under my blue dress that I think everybody must see it, but I keep my chin up. The people are afraid, too. I can smell it on them, see it in their flickering eyes that will not meet mine, hear it in their whispers: Haunt. Devil. Look at her eyes—like fireballs. Unnatural.

A woman steps in front of me. She is wiry and faded, with white-streaked hair in stiff curls around her ears and a flowery dress made up of store-bought calico. "I am Octavie Petitpas," she says, her voice tight with fear. "You come to dance with my sons?"

I see 'Dres Petitpas grinning his yellow-tooth grin over her head. "Yes, ma'am."

"Your partner's here, boys," 'Dres Petitpas shouts. "Time to dance!"

The fiddler turns to five men standing in an uneven line—his five sons. The first must be Clopha the reader, thin as his father is wide, with lines of worry across his forehead. Aristile and 'Tit Paul are big like their father, with trapped, angry eyes. Louis is a little older than me, with a mustache thin as winter grass. Télémaque is still a boy, all knees and elbows.

I walk up to Clopha and hold out my hand. He looks at it, then takes it with a sigh. His hand is cold as deep water.

We all troop into the Doucets' barn, Clopha and me and 'Dres and every soul from St. Mary's parish who can find a place to stand. 'Dres climbs up on a trestle table, swings his fiddle to his shoulder, and starts to play "Jolie Blonde." He's grinning under his black mustache and stamping with his foot: he's having a good time, if nobody else is.

Clopha and I start to dance. I know right away that he will not last long. He has already lost the bet in his heart, him, already lost his Marie, who I can see watching us, her hands to her mouth and tears wetting her cheeks like a heavy rain. It is hard work dancing with Clopha. I think his father tricks him so often that he is like Old Boudreaux, who doesn't know how to win. This makes Clopha heavy and slow. I have to set the pace, change directions, twirl under his lax arm without help or signal. He plods through five, six, seven tunes, and then he stumbles and falls to his knees, shaking his head heavily until Marie Eymard comes and helps him up with a glare that would burn me black, if it could.

Then it is Aristile's turn.

Aristile is strong, him, and he is on fire to beat me. My head barely reaches his heart, and he crushes me to him as if to smother me. Half the time, I'm dancing on tiptoe. The other, I'm thrown here and there by his powerful arms, my shoulders aching as he puts me through my paces like a mule. It's wrestling, not dancing, but I dance with wolves, me, and I am stronger than I look. Six songs, seven, eight, nine, and then the tunes all run together under our flying feet. I do not even notice that Aristile has fallen until I find myself dancing alone. Then I blink at the sun pouring in through the barn door while two men carry Aristile to a long bench along the wall. I see a girl in pink kneel beside him with a cup and a cloth for his red face, and then I go up to 'Tit Paul and the music carries us away.

'Tit Paul is even more angry than his brother, and bigger and taller. He cheats. When we spin, he loosens his grip on my waist and wrist, hoping to send me flying into the crowd. I cling to him like a crab, me, pinching his shirt, his cuff, his thick, sweaty wrist. The dance is a war between us, each song a battle, even the waltzes. I win them all, and also the war, when 'Tit Paul trips over his own dragging feet and falls full length in the dust, barrel chest heaving, teeth bared like a mink.

I feel no pity for him. I think some day 'Tit Paul will find a way to shove his father's curse back into his throat.

The music doesn't stop, so I don't either, two-stepping alone as men carry 'Tit Paul to the bench where he, too, is comforted by a dark-haired girl. Through the barn doors, I see that it is dark again outside. I have danced, as 'Dres Petitpas has fiddled, for a night and a day. I am a little tired.

I dance up to Louis and hold out my hand.

Louis, who understands numbers, dances carefully, making me do all the work of turning, twisting, threading the needles he makes with his arms. From time to time, he speeds up suddenly, stumbles in my way so I must skip to keep from falling, throws me off balance whenever he can. After a time, his father sees what he's up to and shouts at him, and the spirit goes out of Louis like water draining out the hole in a bucket. There is a girl to give him water and soft words when he falls, too, a thin child with her hair in braids. I feel no pity for Louis, either, who is sly enough to beat his father at his own game when he's older.

It's light again by now, and I have danced for two nights and a day. I feel that my body is not my own but tied by the ears to Murderes Petitpas's fiddle bow. As long as he plays, I will dance, though my feet bleed into the barn floor and my eyes sting with the dust. 'Dres launches into "La Two-Step Petitpas," and I dance up to Télémaque who is still a child, and all I think when I hold out my hand is how glad I am Octavie gave her husband no more sons.

Télémaque, like me, is stronger than he looks. He has watched me dance with his four brothers, and he has learned that I cannot be tripped and I cannot be flung. He gives me a sad, sweet smile and limps as he dances, like he's a poor cripple boy I'd be ashamed to beat. I think it is a trick lower than any of Louis's, and I turn my face from him and let myself be lost in the stream of music. The bow of 'Dres Petitpas lifts my feet; his fingers guide my arms; his notes swirl me up and down and around as a paddle swirls the waters of the bayou. Around me, I feel something like a thunderstorm building, clouds piling, uneasy with lightning, the air growing thicker and thicker until I gasp for breath, dancing in the middle of the Doucets' barn with Télémaque limp at my bleeding feet and Murderes Petitpas triumphant on his table and his neighbors around us, growling and muttering.

"The last one down!" he crows. "What you say now, Octavie?"

Octavie Petitpas steps out from the boiling cloud of people, and if she looked worn before, now she looks gray as death.

"I say you are a fine fiddler, Murderes Petitpas. There ain't a man in the whole of Louisiana, maybe even the world, could do what you done. Or would want to."

"I am a fine fiddler," 'Dres says. "Still, I can't win my bet without my little owl girl, eh?" He waves his bow arm toward the five brothers sitting on the bench with their gray-faced sweethearts. "There they are, girl. Take your pick, you. Any one you want for your husband, and land and a mule, just like I promised. Murderes Petitpas, he keep his word, hien?"

I touch Tante Eulalie's lace at my neck for luck, and the little bulge of the gris-gris hanging between my breasts and I say, "I do not want your land or your mule, 'Dres Petitpas. I do not want to marry any of your five sons. They have sweethearts of their own, them, nice Cajun girls with black eyes and rosy cheeks who will give them nice black-eyed babies."

An astonished wind of whispers blows through the crowd.

I go on. "I make you a bet now, Murderes Petitpas. I bet I can dance longer than you can. Dance with me, and if I win, you will give your blessing on your sons' marriages and return what you stole from me."

His eyes narrow under his broad-brimmed hat, and his fingers grip the neck of his fiddle. "No," he says. "I make no more bets, me. I have what I want. I will not dance with you."

"If you do not dance, Murderes Petitpas, everybody will think you are afraid of a little white-skin, pink-eye swamp girl, with her bare feets all bloody. What you afraid of, hien? You, who fiddle the devil out of hell and back down again?"

"I ain't afraid," says 'Dres through his flat yellow teeth. "I just ain't interested. You don't want to marry together with one of my sons, you go away back to the swamp. We got no further business together."

Louis gets to his feet and limps up beside me. "I say you do, Pap. If you win, you get my word I don't go run away first chance I see."

"And my word I don't go with him," says Télémaque, joining him.

Aristile comes up on the other side of me. "And mine."

"And mine," says 'Tit Paul.

"And you got my word not to make your life a living hell for taking my sons from me out of pure cussedness," says Octavie.

'Dres Petitpas looks down on the pack of us. His face is red as fire and his eyes glow hot as coals. "I see you boys still got some learning to do. I take your bet, swamp owl girl. You bring up a fiddler to play for us, and I dance the sun around again."

Everybody get real quiet, and Octavie says, "'Dres, you know there ain't no other fiddler in St. Mary's Parish."

"That's it, then. I don't dance without music. The bet's off."

Someone in the crowd laughs. I'd laugh myself if this was a story I was hearing, about Young 'Dres Petitpas and how he owns all the music in St. Mary's Parish.

Then another voice speaks out of the crowd. "I will play for this dance," says my friend Ulysse.

I spin around to see him in a store-bought suit, with his wild, black hair all slicked down with oil, looking innocent as a puppy in a basket.

"I have an accordion," he says, and gives me a sharp-toothed smile, and I know, just then, that I love him.

Another man turns up with a washboard and a spoon, and he and Ulysse jump up on the table as 'Dres Petitpas climbs down. Ulysse strikes up a tune I've heard a thousand times: "T'es Petite et T'es Mignonne," which is Tante Eulalie's special tune for me. It gives my weary feet courage, and I dance up to Murderes Petitpas and take hold of his hand.

That is when the good people of Pierreville discover that Murderes Petitpas cannot dance. He has two left feet and he can't keep time, and he may know what a Window or a Cajun Cuddle or a Windmill looks like from above, but he for sure doesn't know how to do them. We stumble and fumble this way and that around the floor while the storm breaks at last in a gale of laughter. I am laughing, too, in spite of the pain in my feet, like dancing on nails or needles. I don't care if he falls first or I do. I've won already, me. The good people of Pierreville have seen 'Dres Petitpas for what he is. His sons will marry whoever they want, and he will not dare say a word against it.

Scree, scraw goes the accordion; thunk-whoosh goes the washboard, with Ulysse's hoarse voice wailing above it all, and I'm dancing like the midges above the water at dusk, with 'Dres stumbling after me.

Somehow my feet don't hurt so much now, and my legs are light, and I enjoy myself. It is still dark outside the barn when 'Dres falls to his knees and bends his head.

As the accordion wheezes into silence, Octavie runs to her husband and puts her arms around his shoulders. His sons are kissing their sweethearts, and everybody's talking and fetching more food and slapping Ulysse and the washboard player on the back and pretending that I don't exist.

I step up to Octavie and I say, "Miz Petitpas, I'll take my fiddle now, my Tante Eulalie's fiddle your husband took from me."

She looks up and says, "Eulalie? Old Eulalie Favrot, that run away to the swamp? You kin to Eulalie Favrot?"

I nod. "Tante Eulalie take me in when I'm a baby, raise me like her own."

Octavie stands up and waves to an ancient lady in a faded homespun dress. "Tante Belda, you come here. This here's Eulalie Favrot's girl she raised. What you think of that?"

The ancient lady brought her face, wrinkled as wet cloth, right up to my lace collar so she can squint at it better. "That 'Lalie's wedding lace," she says. "I know it anywhere, me. How she keeping, girl?"

"She catch a cough this winter and die," I say.

"I sure am sorry to hear that," the ancient lady says. "'Lalie is my cousin, godmother to my girl, Denise. She marry Hercule Favrot back in the 'teens sometime. Poor Hercule. He lose his shrimp boat and his nets to 'Dres Petitpas because of some couyon bet they make. Hercule take to drink, him, beat 'Lalie half to death. One morning she find him floating in the duck pond, dead as a gutted fish. 'Lalie go away after the funeral, nobody know where. She never have no children."

"She have me," I say. "Can I have her fiddle back now?"

Someone brings me a plate of food while I wait, but I am too tired to eat. My legs shake and my feet burn and sting. I think maybe I should sit down, but I can't move my legs, and how will I get home before light? I feel tears rising in my eyes, and then there is an arm around my waist and a voice in my ear.

"Cadence, chère," Ulysse says. "Miz Petitpas bring your fiddle. Take it, you, and I carry you home to sleep."

The plate disappears from my hands and Tante Eulalie's fiddle and bow appear in its place. Ulysse picks me up in his arms like I'm a little child, and I put my head against the tight weave of his store-bought suit and let him carry me out of the Doucets' barn.

The moon's getting low, and there's a chill in the air says dawn isn't far away. Ulysse sets me in my pirogue, crawls in after, casts off, and starts to paddle. I see the Doucets' wharf get small behind us, and the people of Pierreville standing there, watching us go. The ancient lady that once was the prettiest girl in the parish waves her handkerchief to us as we slip among the cypress trees and the lights of the farm disappear behind Spanish moss and leaves.

We do not speak as we glide through the waterways. The music echoes in my ears, accordion and washboard and fiddle all together as they play them at the loup-garous' ball. I hum a little, quietly. The sun rises and Ulysse throws me his jacket to put over my head. When we get to my cabin, Ulysse carries me and my fiddle inside and closes the door.

Not long after, we are married together, Ulysse and me, with Tante Eulalie's gold ring. We still live in the swamp, but we visit Pierreville to hear the gossip and go to a fais-do-do now and then. Ulysse always brings his accordion and plays if they ask him. But I keep my dancing for the loup-garous' ball and for my husband in our own cabin. We dance to the music of our voices singing and the fiddling of our eldest daughter, 'Tit 'Lalie.

And Murderes Petitpas?

Old 'Dres Petitpas fiddles no more, him. He says he fiddle himself dry in those two days and two nights. He won't go out into the swamp either, but sits on his front porch and sorts eggs from Octavie's chickens and tells his grandchildren big stories about what a fine fiddler he used to be. Aristile has Old Boudreaux's fiddle now, and you can hear him playing with his wife's brother and two cousins on the radio. But Aristile Petitpas ain't the only fiddler in St. Mary's Parish, not by a long shot. There's plenty of fiddlers around these days, and singers and accordion players and guitar players. They play Cajun and zydeco, waltzes and two-steps and the new jitterbugs, and they play them real fine. But there's none them can fiddle the devil out of hell, like 'Dres Petitpas did one time.

LA FÉE VERTE

Winter 1868

When Victorine was a young whore in the house of Mme Boulard, her most intimate friend was a girl called La Fée Verte.

Victorine was sixteen when she came to Mme Boulard's, and La Fée Verte some five years older. Men who admired the poetry of Baudelaire and Verlaine adored La Fée Verte, for she was exquisitely thin, with the bones showing at her wrist and her dark eyes huge and bruised in her narrow face. But her chief beauty was her pale, fine skin, white almost to opalescence. Embracing her was like embracing absinthe made flesh.

Every evening, Victorine and La Fée Verte would sit in Mme Boulard's elegant parlor with Madame, her little pug dog, and the other girls of the establishment, waiting. In the early part of the evening, while the clients were at dinner, there was plenty of time for card-playing, for gossip and a little apéritif, for reading aloud and lounging on a sofa with your head in your friend's lap, talking about clothes and clients and, perhaps, falling in love.

Among the other girls, La Fée Verte had the reputation of holding herself aloof, of considering herself too good for her company. She spoke to no one save her clients, and possibly Mme Boulard. Certainly no one spoke to her. The life of the brothel simply flowed around her, like water around a rock. Victorine was therefore astonished when La Fée Verte approached her one winter's evening and sat beside her on the red velvet sofa. Her green kimono fell open over her bony frame and her voice was low-pitched and a little rough—pleasant to hear, but subtly disturbing.

Her first words were more disturbing still.

"You were thirteen, a student at the convent when your grandmother died. She was your stepfather's mother, no blood kin of yours, but she stood between you and your stepfather's anger, and so you loved her—the more dearly for your mother's having died when you were a child. You rode to her funeral in a closed carriage with her youngest son, your step-uncle."

Victorine gaped at her, moving, with each phrase, from incredulity to fury to wonder. It was true, every word. But how could she know? Victorine had not told the story to anyone. How did she dare? Victorine had never so much as smiled at her.

La Fée Verte went on: "I smell old straw and damp, tobacco and spirits. I see your uncle's eyes—very dark and set deep as wells in a broad, bearded face. He is sweating as he looks at you, and fiddling in his lap. When you look away for shame, he put his hands upon you."

Victorine was half poised to fly, but somehow not flying, half-inclined to object, but listening all the same, waiting to hear what La Fée Verte would say next.

"He takes your virginity hastily, as the carriage judders along the rutted lanes. He is done by the time it enters the cemetery. I see it stopping near your grandmother's grave, the coachman climbing down from his perch, opening the door. Your uncle, flushed with his exertions, straightens his frock coat and descends. He turns and offers you his hand. It is gloved in black—perfectly correct in every way, save for the glistening stains upon the tips of the fingers. I can see it at this moment, that stained glove, that careless hand."

As La Fée Verte spoke, Victorine watched mesmerized as her hands sketched pictures in the air and her eyes glowed like lamps. She looked like a magician conjuring up a vision of time past, unbearably sad and yet somehow unbearably beautiful. When she paused in the tale, her great dark eyes were luminous with tears. Victorine's own eyes filled in sympathy—for her own young self, certainly, but also for the wonder of hearing her story so transformed.

"You will not go to him," La Fée Verte went on. "Your uncle, impatient or ashamed, turns away, and you slip from the carriage and flee, stumbling in your thin slippers on the cemetery's stony paths, away from your grandmother's grave, from your uncle, from the convent and all you have known."

Then La Fée Verte allowed her tears to overflow and trickle, crystalline, down her narrow cheeks. Enchanted, Victorine wiped them away and licked their bitter salt from her fingers. She was inebriated; she was enchanted. She was in love.

That night, after the last client had been waved on his way, after the gas had been extinguished and the front door locked, she lay in La Fée Verte's bed, the pair of them nested like exotic birds in down and white linen. La Fée Verte's dark head lay on Victorine's shoulder and La Fée Verte's dusky voice spun enchantment into Victorine's ear. That night, and many nights thereafter, Victorine fell asleep to the sound of her lover's stories. Sometimes La Fée Verte spoke of Victorine's childhood, sometimes of her first lover in Paris: a poet with white skin and a dirty shirt. He had poured absinthe on her thighs and licked them clean, then sent her, perfumed with sex and anise, to sell herself in cafés for the price of a ream of paper.

These stories, even more than the caresses that accompanied them, simultaneously excited Victorine and laid a balm to her bruised soul. The sordid details of her past and present receded before La Fée Verte's romantic revisions. Little by little, Victorine came to depend on them, as a drunkard depends on his spirits, to mediate between her and her life. Night after night, Victorine drank power from her lover's mouth and caressed tales of luxury from between her thighs. Her waking hours passed as if in a dream. She submitted to her clients with a disdainful air, as if they'd paid to please her. Intrigued, they dubbed her la Reine, proud queen of whores, and courted her with silk handkerchiefs, kidskin gloves, and rare perfumes. For the first time since she fled her uncle's carriage, Victorine was happy.

Spring, 1869

That April, a new client came to Mme Boulard's, a writer of novels in the vein of M. Jules Verne. He was a handsome man with a chestnut mustache and fine, wavy hair falling over a wide, pale brow. Bohemian though he was, he bought La Fée Verte's services—which did not come cheap—two or three hours a week.

At first, Victorine was indifferent. This writer of novels was a client like other clients, no more threat to her dream-world than the morning sun. Then he began to occupy La Fée Verte for entire evenings, not leaving until the brothel closed at four in the morning and La Fée Verte was too exhausted to speak. Without her accustomed anodyne, Victorine grew restless, spiteful, capricious. Her clients complained. Mme Boulard fined her a night's takings. La Fée Verte turned impatiently from her questions and then from her caresses. At last, wild with jealousy, Victorine stole to the peephole with which every room was furnished to see for herself what the novelist and La Fée Verte meant to each other.

Late as it was, the lamp beside the bed was lit. La Fée Verte was propped against the pillows with a shawl around her shoulders and a glass of opalescent liquid in her hand. The novelist lay beside her, his head dark on the pillow. An innocent enough scene. But Victorine could hear her lover's husky voice rising and falling in a familiar, seductive cadence.

"The moon is harsh and barren," La Fée Verte told the novelist, "cold rock and dust. A man walks there, armed and helmed from head to foot against its barrenness. He plants a flag in the dust, scarlet and blue and white, marching in rows of stripes and little stars. How like a man, to erect a flag, and call the moon his own. I would go just to gaze upon the earth filling half the sky and the stars bright and steady—there is no air on the moon to make them twinkle—and then I'd come away and tell no one."

The novelist murmured something, sleepily, and La Fée Verte laughed, low and amused. "I am no witch, to walk where there is no air to breathe and the heat of the sun dissipates into an infinite chill. Nevertheless I have seen it, and the vehicle that might carry a man so high. It is shaped like a spider, with delicate legs."

The novelist gave a shout of pleasure, leapt from the bed, fetched his notebook and his pen and began to scribble. Victorine returned to her cold bed and wept.

Such a state of affairs, given Victorine's nature and the spring's unseasonable warmth, could not last forever. One May night, pretending a call of nature, Victorine left the salon, stole a carving knife from the kitchen, and burst into the room where La Fée Verte and her bourgeois bohemian were reaching a more conventional climax. It was a most exciting scene: the novelist heaving and grunting, La Fée Verte moaning, Victorine weeping and waving the knife, the other whores crowded at the door, shrieking bloody murder. The novelist suffered a small scratch on his buttock, La Fée Verte a slightly deeper one on the outside of her hip. In the morning she was gone, leaving blood-stained sheets and her green silk kimono with a piece of paper pinned to it bearing Victorine's name and nothing more.

—

Summer 1869 – Winter 1870

Respectable women disappointed in love go into a decline or take poison, or at the very least weep day and night until the pain of their betrayal has been washed from their hearts. Victorine ripped the green kimono from neck to hem, broke a chamber pot and an erotic Sèvres grouping, screamed and ranted, and then, to all appearances, recovered. She did not forget her lost love or cease to yearn for her, but she was a practical woman. Pining would bring her nothing but ridicule, likely a beating, certainly a heavy fine, and she already owed Mme Boulard more than she could easily repay.

At the turn of the year, Victorine's luck changed. A young banker of solid means and stolid disposition fell under the spell of Victorine's beauty and vivacity. Charmed by his generosity, she smiled on him, and the affair prospered. By late spring, he had grown sufficiently fond to pay off Victorine's debt to Mme Boulard and install her as his mistress in a charming apartment in a building he owned on the fashionable rue Chaptal.

After the conventual life of a brothel, Victorine found freedom very sweet. Victorine's banker, who paid nothing for the apartment, could afford to be generous with clothes and furs and jewels—sapphires and emeralds, mostly, to set off her blue eyes and red hair. She attended the Opéra and the theatre on his arm and ate at the Café Anglais on the Boulevard des Italiens. They walked in the Tuileries and drove in the Bois de Boulogne. Victorine lived like a lady that spring, and counted herself happy.

June 1870

So Victorine buried all thoughts of La Fée Verte as deep in new pleasures and gowns and jewels as her banker's purse would allow. It was not so deep a grave that Victorine did not dream of her at night, or find her heart hammering at the sight of any black-haired woman with a thin, pale face. Nor could she bear to part with the torn green kimono, which she kept at the bottom of her wardrobe. The pain was bearable, however, and every day Victorine told herself that it was growing less.

But Nemesis is as soft-footed as a cat stalking a bird, as inexorable, as unexpected. One day, her banker brought her a book, newly published, which claimed to be a true account of the appearance of the Moon's surface and man's first steps upon it, to be taken far in an unspecified future. The banker read a chapter of it aloud to Victorine after dinner, laughing over the rank absurdity of the descriptions and the extreme aridity of the subject and style. She laughed with him. But next morning, when he'd left, she gave it to her maid with instructions to burn it.

Some two or three weeks later, Victorine was not altogether astonished to see La Fée Verte seated in a café on the Boulevard des Italiens. It seemed inevitable, somehow: first the book, then the woman to fall into her path. All Paris was out in the cafés and bistros, taking what little air could be found in the stifling heat, drinking coffee and absinthe and cheap red wine. Why not La Fée Verte?

She had grown, if anything, more wraith-like since quitting Mme Boulard's, her skin white as salt under her smart hat, her narrow body sheathed in a tight green walking dress and her wild black hair confined in a snood. She was alone, and on the table in front of her was all the paraphernalia of absinthe: tall glass of jade green liquor, carafe of water, dish of sugar cubes, pierced silver spoon.

Victorine passed the café without pausing, but stopped at the jeweler's shop beside it and pretended an interest in the baubles displayed in the window, her heart beating so she was almost sick with it. Having seen La Fée Verte, she must speak to her. But what would she say? Would she scold her for her faithlessness? Inquire after her lover? Admire her gown? No. It was impossible.

Having sensibly decided to let sleeping dogs lie, Victorine turned from the sparkling display and swept back to the café, where, having tempered her absinthe with water and sugar, La Fée Verte was lifting the resulting opaline liquid to her lips. There was a glass of champagne on the table, too, its surface foaming as if it had just that moment been poured.

Victorine gestured at the wine. "You are expecting someone."

"I am expecting you. Please, sit down."

Victorine sat. She could not have continued standing with that rough, sweet voice drawing ice along her nerves.

"You are sleek as a cat fed on cream," La Fée Verte said. "Your lover adores you, but you are not in love with him."

"I have been in love," Victorine said. "I found it very painful."

La Fée Verte smiled, very like the cat she'd described. "It is much better to be loved," she agreed. "Which you are, which you will always be. You are made to be loved. It is your destiny."

Victorine's temper, never very biddable, slipped from her control. "Are you setting up for a fortune-teller now?" she sneered. "It's a pity the future, as outlined in your lover's novel, appears so dull and unconvincing. I hope he still loves you, now that you've make him the laughingstock of Paris. Your stories used to be much more artistic."

La Fée Verte made a little movement with her gloved hand, as of brushing aside an insect. "Those stories are of the past," she said. "Me, I have no past. My present is a series of photographs, stiff and without color. My future stares at me with tiger's eyes." She held Victorine's gaze until Victorine looked away, and then she said, "Go back to your banker. Forget you have seen me."

Victorine picked up her champagne and sipped it. She would have liked to throw the wine at La Fée Verte's head, or herself at La Fée Verte's narrow feet. But the past months had taught her something of self-control. She took money from her purse, laid it on the table, and rose. "My destiny and my heart are mine to dispose of as I please," she said. "I will not forget you simply because you tell me to."

La Fée Verte smiled. "Au revoir, then. I fear we will meet again."

July–August 1870

La Fée Verte's prophecy did not immediately come to pass, possibly because Victorine avoided the neighborhood of the café where she'd seen La Fée Verte in case she might be living nearby. It was time, Victorine told herself, to concentrate on distracting her banker, who was much occupied with business as the General Assembly of France herded the weak-willed Emperor Napoleon III toward a war with Prussia. Kaiser Wilhelm was getting above himself, the reasoning ran, annexing here and meddling there, putting forward his own nephew as a candidate for the vacant Spanish throne.

"How stupid does he think we are?" the banker raged, pacing Victorine's charming salon and scattering cigar ashes on the Aubusson. "If Leopold becomes King of Spain, France will be surrounded by Hohenzollerns on every side and it will only be a matter of time before you'll be hearing German spoken on the Champs-Élysées."

"I hear it now," Victorine pointed out. "And Italian and a great deal of English. I prefer Italian—it is much more pleasing to the ear. Which reminds me: *La Bohème* is being sung at the Opéra tonight. If you wait a moment while I dress, we should be in time for the third act."

Victorine was not a woman who concerned herself with politics. It was her fixed opinion that each member of the government was duller than the next, and none of them, save perhaps the empress, who set the fashion, had anything to do with her. She did her best to ignore the Emperor's declaration of war on July 16 and the bellicose frenzy that followed it. When her banker spoke to her of generals and battles, she answered him with courtesans and opera singers. When he wanted to go to the Hôtel de Ville to hear the orators, she made him go to the Eldorado to hear the divine Thérèsa singing of love. When he called her a barbarian, she laughed at him and began to think of finding herself a more amusing protector. Men admired her; several of the banker's friends had made her half-joking offers she'd half-jokingly turned aside. Any one of them would be hers for a smile and a nod. But none of them appealed to her, and the banker continued generous, so she put off choosing. She had plenty of time.

One Sunday in late August, Victorine's banker proposed a drive. Victorine put on a high-crowned hat with a cockade of feathers and they drove down the Champs-Élysées with the rest of fashionable Paris, headed toward the Bois de Boulogne, where the sky was clearer than within the city walls and the air was scented with leaves and grass.

As they entered the park, Victorine heard an unpleasant noise as of a building being torn down. The noise grew louder, and before long the carriage drew even with a group of men wearing scarlet trousers and military kepis, chopping down trees.

The banker required his driver to stop. Victorine gaped at the men, sweating amid clouds of dust, and at the shambles of trampled grass, tree trunks, and stumps they left in their wake. "Who are these men?" she demanded. "What are they doing?"

"They are volunteers for the new Mobile Guard, and they are clearing the Bois." He turned to her. "Victorine, the time has come for you to look about yourself. The Prussians are marching west. If Strasbourg falls, they will be at Paris within a month. Soon there will be soldiers quartered here, and herds of oxen and sheep. Soon every green thing you see will be taken within the walls to feed or warm Paris. If the Prussians besiege us, we will know hunger and fear, perhaps death."

Victorine raised her eyes to her lover's pink, stern face. "What have these things to do with me? I cannot stop them."

He made an impatient noise. "Victorine, you are impossible. There's a time of hardship coming, a time of sacrifice. Pleasure will be forced to bow to duty, and I must say I think that France will be the better for it."

She had always known his mouth to be too small, but now it struck her for the first time as ridiculous, all pursed up like a sucking infant's under his inadequate moustache.

"I see," she said. "What do you intend to do?"

"My duty."

For all her vanity, Victorine was not a stupid woman. She had no need of La Fée Verte to foresee what was coming next. "I understand completely," she said. "And what of my apartment?"

He blinked as one awakened from a dream. "You may stay until you find a new one."

"And my furniture?"

The question, or perhaps her attitude, displeased him. "The furniture," he said tightly, "is mine."

"My clothes? My jewels? Are they yours also?"

He shrugged. "Those, you may keep. As souvenirs of happier times."

"Of happier times. Of course." Really, she could not look at his mouth any longer. Beyond him, a tall chestnut tree swayed and toppled to the ground with a resounding crack, like thunder. The banker started; Victorine did not. "Well, that's clear enough." She put out her hand to him. "Good-bye."

He frowned. "I hadn't intended. . . I'd thought a farewell dinner, one last night together."

"With duty calling you? Surely not," Victorine said. He had not taken her hand; she patted his sweating cheek. "Adieu, my friend. Do not trouble yourself to call. I will be occupied with moving. And duty is a jealous mistress."

She climbed down from the carriage and walked briskly back along the path. She was not afraid. She was young, she was beautiful, and she had La Fée Verte's word that it was her destiny to be loved.

September, 1870

Victorine's new apartment was a little way from the grand boulevards, on the rue de la Tour, near the Montmartre abattoir. It was small—three rooms only—but still charming. When it came to the point, none of the admiring gentlemen had been willing to offer her the lease on a furnished house of her own, not with times so troubled. She had sent them all about their business, renting and furnishing the place herself on the proceeds from an emerald necklace and a sapphire brooch. She moved on September 3. When evening came, she looked about her at the chaos of half-unpacked trunks and boxes, put on a smart hat, and went out in search of something to eat, leaving her maid to deal with the mess alone.

Although it was dinnertime, everyone seemed to be out in the streets—grim-faced men, for the most part, too intent on their business to see her, much less make way for her. Passing a newspaper kiosk, she was jostled unmercifully, stepped upon, pushed almost into the gutter. A waving hand knocked her hat awry. Gruff voices battered at her ears.

"Have you heard? The emperor is dead!"

"Not dead, idiot. Captured. It's bad enough."

"I heard dead, and he's the idiot, not me."

"Good riddance to him."

"The Prussians have defeated MacMahon. Strasbourg has fallen."

"Long live Trochu!"

The Devil take Trochu, Victorine thought, clutching purse and muff. A thick shoe came down heavily on her foot. She squealed with pain and was ignored. When she finally found a suitable restaurant, her hat was over her ear, and she was limping.

The Veau d'Or was small, twelve tables perhaps, with lace curtains at the windows and one rather elderly waiter. What made it different from a thousand other such establishments was its clientèle, which seemed to consist largely of women dressed in colors a little brighter and hats a little more daring than was quite respectable, gossiping from table to table in an easy camaraderie that reminded Victorine at once of Mme Boulard's salon.

The conversations dropped at Victorine's entrance, and the elderly waiter moved forward, shaking his head.

"We are complete, madame," he said.

Presented with an opportunity to vent her ill temper, Victorine seized it with relief. "You should be grateful, monsieur, that I am sufficiently exhausted to honor your establishment with my custom." She sent a disdainful glance around the room. "Me, I am accustomed to the company of a better class of tarts."

This speech elicited some indignant exclamations, some laughter, and an invitation from a dumpling-like blonde in electric blue to share her corner table.

"You certainly have an opinion of yourself," she said, as Victorine sat down, "for a woman wearing such a hat as that. What happened to it?"

Victorine removed the hat and examined it. The feather was broken and the ribbons crushed. "Men," she said, making the word a curse.

The blonde sighed agreement. "A decent woman isn't safe in the streets these days. What do you think of the news?"

Victorine looked up from the ruin of her hat. "News? Oh, the emperor."

"The emperor, the Prussians, the war. All of it."

"I think it is terrible," Victorine said, "if it means cutting down the Bois de Boulogne and stepping on helpless women. My foot is broken—I'm sure of it."

"One does not walk on a broken foot," the blonde said reasonably. "Don't spit at me, you little cat—I'm trying to be friends. Everyone needs friends. There's hard times ahead."

"Hard times be damned," Victorine said airily. "I don't expect they will make a difference, not to us. Men desire pleasure in hard times, too."

The blonde laughed. "Possibly; possibly not. We'll find out soon enough which of us is right." She poured some wine into Victorine's glass. "If you're not too proud for a word of advice from a common tart, I suggest you take the veal. It's the specialty of the house, and if it comes to a siege, we won't be able to get it any more."

"Already I am bored by this siege," Victorine said.

"Agreed," said the blonde. "We will talk of men, instead."

That night, Victorine drank a glass of absinthe on her way home. It wasn't a vice she usually indulged in, finding the bitterness of the wormwood too intense and the resulting lightheadedness too unsettling. Tonight, she drank it down like medicine. When she got home, she dug the green kimono out of her wardrobe and fell into bed with it clasped in her arms, her head floating in an opalescent mist.

Her sleep was restless, her dreams both vivid and strange. Her banker appeared, his baby mouth obscene in a goat's long face, and disappeared, bloodily, into a tiger's maw. A monkey wore grey gloves, except it was not a monkey at all, but a pig, beyond whose trotters the fingers of the gloves flapped like fringe. It bowed, grinning piggily, to the dream-presence that was Victorine, who curtsied deeply in return. When she rose, the tiger blinked golden eyes at her. She laid her hand upon his striped head; he purred like the rolling of distant thunder and kneaded his great paws against her thighs. She felt only pleasure from his touch, but when she looked at her skirts, they hung in bloody rags. Then it seemed she rode the tiger through the streets of Paris, or perhaps it was an open carriage she rode, or perhaps she was gliding bodily above the pavement, trailing draperies like the swirling opalescence of water suspended in a glass of absinthe.

She slept heavily at last, and was finally awakened at noon by a group of drunks singing the Marseillaise at full voice on the street under her window. She struggled out of bed and pulled back the curtains, prepared to empty her chamber pot over them. Seeing her, they cried out "Vive la République," and saluted, clearly as drunk on patriotic sentiment as on wine. Victorine was not entirely without feeling for her country, so she stayed her hand.

France was a Republic again.

Victorine considered this fact as her maid dressed her and pinned up her hair. If the drunkards were anything to judge by, the change of government had not changed a man's natural reaction to the sight of a shapely woman in a nightgown. She would walk to the Tuileries, buy an ice cream, and find someone with a full purse to help her celebrate the new Republic in style.

It was a warm day, grey and soft as mouse fur. The streets were full of workers in smocks and gentlemen in top hats, waving greenery and tricolor flags with democratic zeal. Spontaneous choruses of "Vive la République!" exploded around Victorine at intervals. Victorine bought a patriotic red carnation from a flower seller on the steps of Notre Dame de Lorette, and pinned it to her bosom. As she walked down the crowded streets, her heart beat harder, her cheeks heated; she felt the press of strange bodies around her as the most intense of pleasures. Soon she was laughing aloud and shouting with the rest: *Vive la République!*

At last, she reached the gate of the Tuileries. A man thrust a branch in her face as she passed through. "This is it!" he cried blissfully. "Down with the emperor! Vive la République!"

He was a soldier, young, passably good-looking in his little round kepi and gold-braided epaulets. Victorine turned the full force of her smile at him. "Vive la République," she answered, and brushed his fingers with hers as she took the branch.

He didn't seem to notice.

For the blink of an eye, Victorine was filled with a rage as absolute as it was unexpected. And then it was gone, taking her patriotic fervor with it. Suddenly, the pressure of the crowd seemed intolerable to her, the shouting an assault. She clung to the iron railings of the high fence and fanned herself with her handkerchief while she caught her breath and surveyed the seething mass of humanity overflowing the wide promenade. Her view of the palace was obstructed by top hats and cloth caps, smart hats and shabby bonnets and checked shawls. By standing on tiptoe, she could just see a stream of people swarming up the steps like revelers eager to see the latest opera. La République had moved quickly, she thought. The N's and imperial wreaths had been pried from the façade or shrouded with newspapers or scarlet sheets, giving the palace a blotched and raddled look. And above the gaping door, someone had chalked the words UNDER THE PROTECTION OF THE CITIZENS on the black marble.

Thinking that she was a citizen as much as anyone else, Victorine put away her handkerchief, took a firm hold on her bag, and launched herself into the current that flowed, erratically but inevitably, toward the forbidden palace where the emperor and his foreign wife had lived so long in imperial splendor.

The current bore her up a flight of shallow steps, the press around her growing, if possible, even denser as the door compacted the flow. She stepped over the threshold, passing a young infantryman who held out his shako and shouted with the raucous monotony of a street vendor: "For the French wounded! For the French wounded!" Impulsively, Victorine fished a coin from her bag, dropped it into his shako, and smiled up into his sweating face. He nodded once, gravely, and then she was in the foyer of the Imperial Palace of the Tuileries.

It was magnificent. Victorine, who had a taste for excess, worshipped every splendid inch of it, from the goddesses painted on the ceiling, to the scintillating lusters on the chandeliers, the mirrors and gold leaf everywhere, and the great, sweeping staircase, designed to be seen on. She pressed forward, determined to show herself upon it.

There must have been a hundred people on the staircase, mounting and descending, gawking over the rail. As she looked upward, Victorine saw only one woman, standing still as a rock in the waterfall of sightseers. Her hair was dark under her green hat, and her profile, when she turned her head, was angular. Victorine's blood recognized La Fée Verte before her mind did, racing to her face and away again, so that she swayed as she stood.

A hand, beautifully gloved in grey leather, gripped her elbow and Victorine became aware of a gentleman in top hat and a beautifully tailored coat, carrying a gold-headed cane. "Mademoiselle is faint?" he inquired.

Victorine shook her head and sprang up the steps so heedlessly that she caught her toe on the riser. The solicitous gentleman, who had not moved from her side, caught her as she stumbled.

"If you will permit?" he asked rhetorically. Then he slipped one arm around her waist, shouting for everyone to make way, and piloted her firmly out of the palace without paying the slightest heed to her protestations that she was very well, that she'd left a friend on the stair and wished to be reunited with her.

The solicitous gentleman was plumper than Victorine liked, and his hair, when he removed his tall glossy hat, was woefully sparse. But he bore her off to the Georges V for coffee and pastries and then he bought her a diamond aigrette and a little carnelian cat with emerald eyes and agreed that it was a great pity that an exquisite creature like herself should be in exile on the rue de la Tour. What could Victorine do? She took the luck that fate had sent her and gave the gentleman to understand that his gifts were an acceptable prelude to a more serious arrangement. One thing led to another, and a week later, she and her maid were installed in an apartment off the Champs-Élysées, with her name on the lease and furniture that was hers to keep or sell as it pleased her.

It was not a bad bargain. The solicitous gentleman wasn't as good-looking as the banker and his love-making was uninspired. But, besides being very rich, he was as devoted to amusement as even Victorine could wish.

"Why should I worry about the Prussians?" he said. "I have my days to fill. Let everyone else worry about the Prussians if it amuses them. It is of more concern to me whether M. Gaultier beats me to that charming bronze we saw yesterday."

Still, the Prussians, or rather the threat of the Prussians, was increasingly hard to ignore. Victorine and her solicitous gentleman made their way to the antiquaries and the rare bookshops through platoons of National Guardsmen marching purposefully from one place to another and ranks of newly-inducted Mobile Guards learning to turn right in unison. She could not set foot outside the door without being enthusiastically admired by the soldiers camped along the Champs, and the horses stabled there made pleasure-drives to the Bois de Boulogne (or what was left of it) all but impossible. Evenings weren't what they had been, with theatres closing left and right as the timid fled the anticipated discomforts of a siege. The Comédie Française and the Opéra remained open, though, and the public balls and the cafés-concerts were frequented by those without the means to fly. However tenuously, Paris remained Paris, even in the face of war.

One night, Victorine and her solicitous gentleman went strolling along the boulevard de Clichy. Among the faded notices of past performances that fluttered like bats' wings in the wind, crisp, new posters announced the coming night's pleasures.

"Look, ma belle," the gentleman exclaimed, stopping in front of a kiosk. "A mentalist! How original! And such a provocative name. We really must go see her."

Victorine looked at the poster he indicated. It was painted red and black, impossible to ignore:

The Salon du Diable presents
La Fée Verte!
The mists of time part for her. The secrets of the future are unveiled.
Séance at nine and midnight.
La Fée Verte!

Tears sprang, stinging, to Victorine's eyes. Through their sparkling veil, she saw a white bed and a room lit only by dying embers. Her palm tingled as if cupped over the small, soft mound of La Fée Verte's breast; she drew a quick breath. "It sounds very silly," she said weakly. "Besides, who has ever heard of the Salon du Diable?"

"All the more reason to go. It can be an adventure, and well worth it, if this Fée Verte is any good. If she's terrible, it will still make a good story."

Victorine shrugged and acquiesced. It was clearly fate that had placed that poster where her protector would notice it, and fate that he had found it appealing, just as it was fate that Victorine would once more suffer the torment of seeing La Fée Verte without being able to speak to her. Just as well, really, after the fiasco on the Champs-Élysées. At least this time, Victorine would hear her voice.

The Salon du Diable was nearly as hot as the abode of its putative owner, crowded with thirsty sinners, its only illumination a half-a-dozen gaslights, turned down low. A waiter dressed as a devil in jacket and horns of red felt showed them to a table near the curtained platform that served as a stage. Victorine, as was her habit, asked for champagne. In honor of the entertainer, her protector ordered absinthe. When it came, she watched him balance the sugar cube on the pierced spoon and slowly pour a measure of water over it into the virulent green liquor. The sugared water swirled into the absinthe, disturbing its depths, transforming it, drop by drop, into smoky, shifting opal.

The solicitous gentleman lifted the tall glass. "La fée verte!" he proposed.

"La Fée Verte," Victorine echoed obediently, and as if at her call, a stout man in a red cape and horns like the waiter's appeared before the worn plush curtain and began his introduction.

La Fée Verte, he informed the audience, was the granddaughter of one of the last known fairies in France, who had fallen in love with a mortal and given birth to a son, the father of the woman they were about to see. By virtue of her fairy blood, La Fée Verte was able to see through the impenetrable curtains of time and space as though they were clear glass. La Fée Verte was a visionary, and the stories she told—whether of past, present, or future—were as true as death.

There was an eager murmur from the audience. The devil of ceremonies stepped aside, pulling the faded plush curtain with him, to reveal a woman sitting alone on the stage. She was veiled from head to toe all in pale, gauzy green, but Victorine knew her at once.

Thin white hands emerged from the veil and cast it back like a green mist. Dark eyes shone upon the audience like stars at the back of a cave. Her mouth was painted scarlet and her unbound hair was a black smoke around her head and shoulders.

Silence stretched to the breaking point as La Fée Verte stared at the audience and the audience stared at her. And then, just as Victorine's strained attention was on the point of shattering, the thin red lips opened and La Fée Verte began to speak.

"I will not speak of war, or victory or defeat, suffering or glory. Visions, however ardently desired, do not come for the asking. Instead, I will speak of building.

"There's a lot of building going on in Paris these days—enough work for everyone, thanks to le bon Baron and his pretty plans. Not all Germans are bad, eh? The pay's pretty good, too, if it can buy a beer at the Salon du Diable. There's a builder in the audience now, a mason. There are, in fact, two masons, twice that number of carpenters, a layer of roof-slates, and a handful of floor-finishers."

The audience murmured, puzzled at the tack she'd taken. The men at the next table exchanged startled glances—the carpenters, Victorine guessed, or the floor-finishers.

"My vision, though, is for the mason. He's got stone dust in his blood, this mason. His very bones are granite. His father was a mason, and his father's father and his father's father's father, and so on, as far back as I can see. Stand up, M. le Maçon. Don't be shy. You know I'm talking about you."

The audience peered around the room, looking to see if anyone would rise. In one corner, there was a hubbub of encouraging voices, and finally, a man stood up, a flat cap over one eye and a blue kerchief around his throat. "I am a mason, mademoiselle" he said. "You're right enough about my pa. Don't know about *his* pa, though. He could have been a train conductor, for all I know. He's not talked about in the family."

"That," said La Fée Verte, "was your grandmother's grief, poor woman, and your grandfather's shame."

The mason scowled. "Easy enough for you to say, mademoiselle, not knowing a damn thing about me."

"Tell me," La Fée Verte inquired sweetly. "How are things on the rue Mouffetard? Don't worry: your little blonde's cough is not tuberculosis. She'll be better soon." The mason threw up his hands in a clear gesture of surrender and sat down. A laugh swept the audience. They were impressed. Victorine smiled to herself.

La Fée Verte folded her hands demurely in her green silk lap. "Your grandfather," she said gently, "was indeed a mason, a layer of stones like you, monsieur. Men of your blood have shaped steps and grilles, window frames and decorations in every building in Paris. Why, men of your blood worked on Nôtre Dame, father and son growing old each in his turn in the service of Maurice de Sully."

The voice was even rougher than Victorine remembered it, the language as simple and undecorated as the story she told. La Fée Verte did not posture and gesture and lift her eyes to heaven, and yet Victorine was convinced that, were she to close her eyes, she'd see Nôtre Dame as it once was, half built and swarming with the men who labored to complete it. But she preferred to watch La Fée Verte's thin, sensuous lips telling about it.

La Fée Verte dropped her voice to a sibylline murmur that somehow could be heard in every corner of the room. "I see a man with shoulders like a bull, dressed in long stockings and a tunic and a leather apron. The tunic might have been red once and the stockings ochre, but they're faded now with washing and stone dust. He takes up his chisel and his hammer in his broad, hard hands flecked with scars, and he begins his daily prayer. *Tap*-tap, *tap*-tap. *Pa*-ter *Nos*-ter. *A*-ve *Ma*-ri-*a*. Each blow of his hammer, each chip of stone, is a bead in the rosary he tells, every hour of every working day. His prayers, unlike yours and mine, are still visible. They decorate the towers of Nôtre Dame, almost as eternal as the God they praise.

"That was your ancestor, M. le Maçon," La Fée Verte said, returning to a conversational tone. "Shall I tell you of your son?"

The mason, enchanted, nodded.

"It's not so far from now, as the march of time goes. Long enough for you to marry your blonde, and to father children and watch them grow and take up professions. Thirty years, I make it, or a little less: 1887. The president of France will decree a great exposition to take place in 1889—like the Exposition of 1867, but far grander. Eighteen eighty-nine is the threshold of a new century, after all, and what can be grander than that? As an entrance arch, he will commission a monument like none seen before anywhere in the world. And your son, monsieur, your son will build it.

"I see him, monsieur, blond and slight, taking after his mother's family, with a leather harness around his waist. He climbs to his work, high above the street—higher than the towers of Nôtre Dame, higher than you can imagine. His tools are not yours: red-hot iron rivets, tin buckets, tongs, iron-headed mallets. His faith is in the engineer whose vision he executes, in the maker of his tools, his scaffolds and screens and guardrails: in man's ingenuity, not God's mercy."

She fell silent, and it seemed to Victorine that she had finished. The mason thought so too, and was unsatisfied. "My son, he won't be a mason, then?"

"Your son will work in iron," La Fée Verte answered. "And yet your line will not falter, nor the stone dust leach from your blood as it flows through the ages."

Her voice rang with prophecy as she spoke, not so much loud as sonorous, like a church bell tolling. When the last echo had died away, she smiled, a sweet curve of her scarlet lips, and said, shy as a girl, "That is all I see, monsieur. Are you answered?"

The mason wiped his hands over his eyes and, rising, bowed to her, whereupon the audience roared its approval of La Fée Verte's vision and the mason's response, indeed of the whole performance and of the Salon du Diable for having provided it. Victorine clapped until her palms stung through her tight kid gloves.

The solicitous gentleman drained his absinthe and called for another. "To La Fée Verte," he said, raising the opal liquid high. "The most accomplished fraud in Paris. She must be half mad to invent all that guff, but damn me if I've ever heard anything like her voice."

Victorine's over wrought nerves exploded in a surge of anger. She rose to her feet, snatched the glass from the gentleman's hand, and poured the contents over his glossy head. While he gasped and groped for his handkerchief, she gathered up her bag and her wrap and swept out of Le Salon du Diable in a tempest of silks, dropping a coin into the bowl by the door as she went.

The next day, the gentleman was at Victorine's door with flowers and a blue velvet jewel case and a note demanding that she receive him at once. The concierge sent up the note and the gifts, and Victorine sent them back again, retaining only the jewel case as a parting souvenir. She did not send a note of her own, since there was nothing to say except that she could no longer bear the sight of him. She listened to him curse her from the foot of the stairs, and watched him storm down the street when the concierge complained of the noise. Her only regret was not having broken with him before he took her to the Salon du Diable.

In late September, the hard times foretold by the blonde in the Veau d'Or came to Paris.

A city under the threat of siege is not, Victorine discovered, a good place to find a protector. Top-hatted gentlemen still strolled the grand boulevards, but they remained stubbornly blind to Victorine's saucy hats, graceful form, and flashing eyes. They huddled on street corners and in cafés, talking of the impossibility of continued Prussian victory, of the threat of starvation that transformed the buying of humble canned meat into a patriotic act. Her cheeks aching from unregarded smiles, Victorine began to hate the very sound of the words "siege," "Prussian," "Republic." She began to feel that Bismarck and the displaced emperor, along with the quarrelsome Generals Gambetta and Trochu, were personally conspiring to keep her from her livelihood. Really, among them, they were turning Paris into a dull place, where nobody had time or taste for pleasure.

A less determined woman might have retired for the duration, but not Victorine. Every day, she put on her finest toilettes and walked, head held high under the daring hats, through the military camp that Paris was fast becoming. Not only the Champs-Élysées, but all the public gardens, squares, and boulevards were transformed into military camps or stables or sections of the vast open market that had sprung up to cater to the soldiers' needs. Along streets where once only the most expensive trinkets were sold, Victorine passed makeshift stalls selling kepis and epaulets and gold braid, ramrods and powder pouches and water bottles, sword-canes and bayonet-proof leather chest protectors. And everywhere were soldiers, throwing dice and playing cards among clusters of little grey tents, who called out as she passed: "Eh, sweetheart! How about a little tumble for a guy about to die for his country?"

It was very discouraging.

One day at the end of September, Victorine directed her steps toward the heights of the Trocadéro, where idle Parisians and resident foreigners had taken to airing themselves on fine days. They would train their spyglasses on the horizon and examine errant puffs of smoke and fleeing peasants like ancient Roman priests examining the entrails of a sacrifice, after which they gossiped and flirted as usual. A few days earlier, Victorine had encountered an English gentleman with a sand-colored moustache of whom she had great hopes. As she climbed the hill above the Champs de Mars, she heard the drums measuring the drills of the Mobile Guards.

At the summit of the hill, fashionable civilians promenaded to and fro. Not seeing her English gentleman, Victorine joined the crowd surrounding the enterprising bourgeois who sold peeps through his long brass telescope at a franc a look. A clutch of English ladies exclaimed incomprehensibly as she pushed past them; a fat gentleman in a round hat moved aside gallantly to give her room. She cast him a distracted smile, handed the enterprising bourgeois a coin, and stooped to look through the eyepiece. The distant prospect of misty landscape snapped closer, bringing into clear focus a cloud of dark smoke roiling over a stand of trees.

"That used to be a village," the enterprising bourgeois informed her. "The Prussians fired it this morning—or maybe we did, to deny the Prussians the pleasure." The telescope jerked away from the smoke. "If you're lucky, you should be able to see the refugees on their way to Paris."

A cart, piled high with furniture, a woman with her hair tied up in a kerchief struggling along beside it, lugging a bulging basket in each hand and a third strapped to her back. A couple of goats and a black dog and a child riding in a handcart pushed by a young boy. "Time's up," the enterprising bourgeois said.

Victorine clung to the telescope, her heart pounding. The smoke, the cart, the woman with her bundles, the children, the dog, were fleeing a real danger. Suddenly, Victorine was afraid, deathly afraid of being caught in Paris when the Prussians came. She must get out while there was still time, sell her jewels, buy a horse and carriage, travel south to Nice or Marseilles. She'd find La Fée Verte, and they could leave at once. Surely, if she went to the Place Clichy, she'd see her there, waiting for Victorine to rescue her. But she'd have to hurry.

As quickly as Victorine had thrust to the front of the crowd, so quickly did she thrust out again, discommoding the English ladies, who looked down their long noses at her. No doubt they thought her drunk or mad. She only thought them in the way. In her hurry, she stepped on a stone, twisted her ankle, and fell gracelessly to the ground.

The English ladies twittered. The gentleman in the round hat asked her, in vile French, how she went, and offered her his hand. She allowed him to pull her to her feet, only to collapse with a cry of pain. The ladies twittered again, on a more sympathetic note. Then the crowd fell back a little, and a masculine voice inquired courteously whether mademoiselle were ill.

Victorine lifted her eyes to the newcomer, who was hunkered down beside her, his broad, open brow furrowed with polite concern.

The gold braid on his sleeves proclaimed him an officer, and the gold ring on his finger suggested wealth.

"It is very silly," she said breathlessly, "but I have twisted my ankle and cannot stand."

"If mademoiselle will allow?" He folded her skirt away from her foot, took the scarlet boot into his hand, and bent it gently back and forth. Victorine hissed through her teeth.

"Not broken, I think," he said. "Still, I'm no doctor." Without asking permission, he put one arm around her back, the other under her knees, and lifted her from the ground with a little jerk of effort. As he carried her downhill to the surgeon's tent, she studied him. Under a chestnut-brown moustache, his mouth was firm and well shaped, and his nose was high-bridged and aristocratic. She could do worse.

He glanced down, caught her staring. Victorine smiled into his eyes (they, too, were chestnut-brown) and was gratified to see him blush. And then they were in the surgeon's tent and her scarlet boot was being cut away. It hurt terribly. The surgeon anointed her foot with arnica and bound it tightly, making silly jokes as he worked about gangrene and amputation. She bore it all with such a gallant gaiety that the officer insisted on seeing her home and carrying her to her bed, where she soon demonstrated that a sprained ankle need not prevent a woman from showing her gratitude to a man who had richly deserved it.

October, 1870

It was a strange affair, at once casual and absorbing, conducted in the interstices of siege and civil unrest. The officer was a colonel in the National Guard, a man of wealth and some influence. His great passion was military history. His natural posture—in politics, in love—was moderation. He viewed the Monarchists on the Right and the Communards on the Left with an impartial contempt. He did not pretend that his liaison with Victorine was a grand passion, but cheerfully paid the rent on her apartment and bought her a new pair of scarlet boots and a case of canned meat, with promises of jewels and gowns after the Prussians were defeated. He explained about Trochu and Bismarck, and expected her to be interested. He told her all the military gossip and took her to ride on the peripheral railway and to see the cannons installed on the hills of Paris.

The weather was extraordinarily bright. "God loves the Prussians," the officer said, rather sourly, and it certainly seemed to be true. With the sky soft and blue as June, no rain slowed the Prussian advance or clogged the wheels of their caissons or the hooves of their horses with mud. They marched until they were just out of the range of the Parisian cannons, and there they sat, enjoying the wine from the cellars of captured country houses and fighting skirmishes in the deserted streets of burned-out villages. By October 15, they had the city completely surrounded. The Siege of Paris had begun.

The generals sent out their troops in cautious sallies, testing the Prussians but never seriously challenging them. Victorine's colonel, wild with impatience at the shilly-shallying of his superiors, had a thousand plans for sorties and full-scale counter-attacks. He detailed them to Victorine after they'd made love, all among the bedclothes, with the sheets heaped into fortifications, a pillow representing the butte of Montmartre, and a handful of hazelnuts for soldiers.

"Paris will never stand a long siege," he explained to her. "Oh, we've food enough, but there is no organized plan to distribute it. There is nothing really organized at all. None of those blustering ninnies in charge can see beyond the end of his nose. It's all very well to speak of the honor of France and the nobility of the French, but abstractions do not win wars. Soldiers in the field, deployed by generals who are not afraid to make decisions, that's what wins wars."

He was very beautiful when he said these things, his frank, handsome face ablaze with earnestness. Watching him, Victorine very nearly loved him. At other times, she liked him very well. He was a man who knew how to live. To fight the general gloom, he gave dinner parties to which he invited military men and men of business for an evening of food, wine, and female companionship. Wives were not invited.

There was something dreamlike about those dinners, eaten as the autumn wind sharpened and the citizens of Paris tightened their belts. In a patriotic gesture, the room was lit not by gas, but by branches of candles, whose golden light called gleams from the porcelain dishes, the heavy silver cutlery, the thin crystal glasses filled with citrine or ruby liquid. The gentlemen laughed and talked, their elbows on the napery, their cigars glowing red as tigers' eyes. Perched among them like exotic birds, the women, gowned in their bare-shouldered best, encouraged the gentlemen to talk with smiles and nods. On the table, a half-eaten tarte, a basket of fruit. On the sideboard, the remains of two roast chickens—two!—a dish of beans with almonds, another of potatoes. Such a scene belonged more properly to last month, last year, two years ago, when the Empire was strong and elegant pleasures as common as the rich men to buy them. Sitting at the table, slightly drunk, Victorine felt herself lost in one of La Fée Verte's visions, where past, present, and future exist as one.

Outside the colonel's private dining room, however, life was a waking nightmare. The garbage carts had nowhere to go, so that Victorine must pick her way around stinking hills of ordure on every street corner. Cholera and smallpox flourished among the poor. The plump blonde of the Veau d'Or died in the epidemic, as did the elderly waiter and a good proportion of the regulars. Food grew scarce. Worm-eaten cabbages went for three francs apiece. Rat pie appeared on the menu at Maxim's, and lapdogs went in fear of their lives. The French wounded lay in rattling carriages and carts, muddy men held together with bloody bandages, their shocked eyes turned inward, their pale lips closed on their pain, being carted to cobbled-together hospitals to heal or die. Victorine turned her eyes from them, glad she'd given a coin to the young infantryman that day she saw La Fée Verte in the Tuileries.

And through and over it all, the cannons roared.

French cannon, Prussian cannon, shelling St. Denis, shelling Boulogne, shelling empty fields and ravaged woodlands. As they were the nearest, the French cannon were naturally the loudest. Victorine's colonel prided himself on knowing each cannon by the timbre and resonance of its voice as it fired, its snoring or strident or dull or ear-shattering *BOOM.* In a flight of whimsy one stolen afternoon, lying in his arms in a rented room near the Port St. Cloud, Victorine gave them names and made up characters for them: Gigi of the light, flirtatious bark on Mortemain, Philippe of the angry bellow at the Trocadéro.

October wore on, and the siege with it. A population accustomed to a steady diet of news from the outside world and fresh food from the provinces began to understand what it was like to live without either. The lack of food was bad enough, but everyone had expected that—this was war, after all, one must expect to go hungry. But the lack of news was hard to bear. Conflicting rumors ran through the streets like warring plagues, carried by the skinny street rats who hawked newspapers on the boulevards. In the absence of news, gossip, prejudice, and flummery filled their pages. Victorine collected the most outrageous for her colonel's amusement: the generals planned to release the poxed whores of the Hôpital St. Lazare to serve the Prussian army; the Prussian lines had been stormed by a herd of a thousand patriotic oxen.

The colonel began to speak of love. Victorine was becoming as necessary to him, he said, as food and drink. Victorine, to whom he was indeed food and drink, held his chestnut head to her white breast and allowed him to understand that she loved him in return.

Searching for a misplaced corset, her maid turned up the ripped green kimono and inquired what Mademoiselle would like done with it.

"Burn it," said Victorine. "No, don't. Mend it, if you can, and pack it away somewhere. This is not a time to waste good silk."

That evening, Victorine and her colonel strolled along the Seine together, comfortably arm in arm. The cannon had fallen to a distant Prussian rumbling, easily ignored. Waiters hurried to and fro with trays on which the glasses of absinthe glowed like emeralds. The light was failing. Victorine looked out over the water, expecting to see the blue veil of dusk drifting down over Nôtre Dame.

The veil was stained with blood.

For a moment, Victorine thought her eyes were at fault. She blinked and rubbed them with a gloved hand, but when she looked again, the evening sky was still a dirty scarlet—nothing like a sunset, nothing like anything natural Victorine had ever seen. The very air shimmered red. All along the quai came cries of awe and fear.

"The Forest of Bondy is burning," Victorine heard a man say and, "An experiment with light on Montmartre," said another, his voice trembling with the hope that his words were true. In her ear, the colonel murmured reassuringly, "Don't be afraid, my love. It's only the aurora borealis."

Victorine was not comforted. She was no longer a child to hide in pretty stories. She knew an omen when she saw one. This one, she feared, promised fire and death. She prayed it did not promise her own. Paris might survive triumphantly into a new century, and the mason and his blonde might survive to see its glories, but nothing in La Fée Verte's vision had promised that Victorine, or even La Fée Verte, would be there with them.

The red light endured for only a few hours, but some atmospheric disturbance cast a strange and transparent radiance over the next few days, so that every street, every passer-by took on the particularity of a photograph. The unnatural light troubled Victorine. She would have liked to be diverted with kisses, but her colonel was much occupied just now. He wrote her to say he did not know when he'd be able to see her again—a week or two at most, but who could tell? It was a matter of national importance—nothing less would keep him from her bed. He enclosed a pair of fine kidskin gloves, a heavy purse, a rope of pearls, and a history of Napoleon's early campaigns.

It was all very unsatisfying. Other women in Victorine's half-widowed state volunteered to nurse the French wounded, or made bandages, or took to their beds with Bibles and rosaries, or even a case of wine. Victorine, in whom unhappiness bred restlessness, went out and walked the streets.

From morning until far past sunset, Victorine wandered through Paris, driven by she knew not what. She walked through the tent cities, past stalls where canteen girls in tri-colored jackets ladled out soup, past shuttered butcher shops and greengrocers where women shivered on the sidewalk, waiting for a single rusty cabbage or a fist-sized piece of doubtful meat. But should she catch sight of a woman dressed in green or a woman whose skin seemed paler than was usual, she always followed her for a street or two, until she saw her face.

She did not fully realize what she was doing until she found herself touching a woman on the arm so that she would turn. The woman, who was carrying a packet wrapped in butcher's paper, turned on her, frightened and furious.

"What are you doing?" she snapped. "Trying to rob me?"

"I beg your pardon," Victorine said stiffly. "I took you for a friend."

"No friend of yours, my girl. Now run away before I call a policeman."

Shaking, Victorine fled to a café, where she bought a glass of spirits and drank it down as if the thin, acid stuff would burn La Fée Verte from her mind and body. It did not. Trying not to think of her was still thinking of her; refusing to search for her was still searching.

On the morning of October 31, rumors of the fall of Metz came to Paris. The people revolted. Trochu cowered in the Hôtel de Ville while a mob gathered outside, shouting for his resignation. Victorine, blundering into the edges of the riot, turned hastily north and plunged into the winding maze of the Marais. Close behind the Banque de France, she came to a square she'd never seen before. It was a square like a thousand others, with a lady's haberdasher and a hairdresser, an apartment building and a café all facing a stone pedestal supporting the statue of a dashing mounted soldier. A crowd had gathered around the statue, men and women of the people for the most part, filthy and pinched and blue-faced with cold and hunger. Raised a little above them on the pedestal's base were a fat man in a filthy scarlet cloak and a woman, painfully thin and motionless under a long and tattered veil of green gauze.

The fat man, who was not as fat as he had been, was nearing the end of his patter. The crowd was unimpressed. There were a few catcalls. A horse turd, thrown from the edge of the crowd, splattered against the statue's granite base. Then La Fée Verte unveiled herself, and the crowd fell silent.

The weeks since Victorine had seen her on the stage of the Salon du Diable had not been kind to her. The dark eyes were sunken, the body little more than bone draped in skin and a walking-dress of muddy green wool. She looked like a mad woman: half starved, pitiful. Victorine's eyes filled and her pulse sped. She yearned to go to her, but shyness kept her back. If she was meant to speak to La Fée Verte, she thought, there would be a sign. In the meantime, she could at least listen.

"I am a seer," La Fée Verte said, the word taking on a new and dangerous resonance in her mouth. "I see the past, the present, the future. I see things that are hidden, and I see the true meaning of things that are not. I see truth, and I see falsehoods tricked out as truth." She paused, titled her head. "Which would you like to hear?"

Puzzled, the crowd muttered to itself. A woman shouted, "We hear enough lies from Trochu. Give us the truth!"

"Look at her," a skeptic said. "She's even hungrier than I am. What's the good of a prophetess who can't foresee her next meal?"

"My next meal will be bread and milk in a Sèvres bowl," La Fée Verte answered tranquilly. "Yours, my brave one, will be potage—of a sort. The water will have a vegetable in it, at any rate."

The crowd, encouraged, laughed and called out questions.

"Is my husband coming home tonight?"

"My friend Jean, will he pay me back my three sous?"

"Will Paris fall?"

"No," said La Fée Verte. "Yes, if you remind him. As for Paris, it is not such a simple matter as yes and no. Shall I tell you what I see?"

Shouts of "No!" and "Yes!" and more horse turds, one of which spattered her green skirt. Unruffled, she went on, her husky voice somehow piercing the crowd's rowdiness.

"I see prosperity and peace," she said, "like a castle in a fairy-tale that promises that you will live happily ever after."

More grumbling from the crowd: "What's she talking about?"; "I don't understand her"; and a woman's joyful shout—"We're all going to be rich!"

"I did not say that," La Fée Verte said. "The cholera, the cold, the hunger, will all get worse before it gets better. The hard times aren't over yet."

There was angry muttering, a few catcalls: "We ain't paying to hear what we already know, bitch!"

"You ain't paying me at all," La Fée Verte answered mockingly. "Anyone may see the near future—it's all around us. No, what you want to know is the distant future. Well, as you've asked for the truth, the truth is that the road to that peaceful and prosperous castle is swarming with Germans. Germans and Germans and Germans. You'll shoot them and kill them by the thousands and for a while they'll seem to give up and go away. But then they'll rise again and come at you, again and again."

Before La Fée Verte had finished, "Dirty foreigner!" a woman shrieked, and several voices chorused, "Spy, spy! German spy!" Someone threw a stone at her. It missed La Fée Verte and bounced from the pedestal behind her with a sharp crack. La Fée Verte ignored it, just as she ignored the crowd's shouting and the fat man's clutching hands trying to pull her away.

It was the sign. Victorine waded into the melee, elbows flailing, screaming like a cannonball in flight. There was no thought in her head except to reach her love and carry her, if possible, away from this place and to Victorine's home, where she belonged.

"I see them in scarlet," La Fée Verte shouted above the noise. "I see them in grey. I see them in black, with peaked caps on their heads, marching like wooden dolls, stiff-legged, inexorable, shooting shop-girls and clerks and tavernkeepers, without pity, without cause."

Victorine reached La Fée Verte at about the same time as the second stone and caught her as she staggered and fell, the blood running bright from a cut on her cheek. The weight of her, slight as it was, overbalanced them both. A stone struck Victorine in the back; she jerked and swore, and her vision sparkled and faded as though she were about to faint.

"Don't be afraid," the husky voice said in her ear. "They're only shadows. They can't hurt you."

Her back muscles sore and burning, Victorine would have disagreed. But La Fée Verte laid a bony finger across her lips. "Hush," she said. "Be still and look."

It was the same square, no doubt of that, although the café at the corner had a different name and a different front, and the boxes in the windows of the apartment opposite were bright with spring flowers. Victorine and La Fée Verte were still surrounded by a crowd, but the crowd didn't seem to be aware of the existence of the two women huddled at the statue's base. Every eye was on something passing in the street beyond, some procession that commanded the crowd's attention and its silence. The men looked familiar enough, in dark coats and trousers, bareheaded or with flat caps pulled over their cropped hair. But the women—ah, the women were another thing. Their dresses were the flimsy, printed cotton of a child's shirt or a summer blouse, their skirts short enough to expose their naked legs almost to the knee, their hair cut short and dressed in ugly rolls.

Wondering, Victorine looked down at La Fée Verte, who smiled at her, intimate and complicit. "You see? Help me up," she murmured. As Victorine rose, lifting the thin woman with her, she jostled a woman in a scarf with a market basket on her arm. The woman moved aside, eyes still riveted on the procession beyond, and Victorine, raised above the crowd on the statue's base, followed her gaze.

There were soldiers, as La Fée Verte had said: lines of them in dark uniforms and high, glossy boots, marching stiff-legged through the square toward the rue de Rivoli. There seemed to be no end to them, each one the mirror of the next, scarlet armbands flashing as they swung their left arms. A vehicle like an open carriage came into view, horseless, propelled apparently by magic, with black-coated men seated in it, proud and hard-faced under peaked caps. Over their heads, banners bearing a contorted black cross against a white and scarlet ground rippled in the wind. And then from the sky came a buzzing like a thousand hives of bees, as loud as thunder but more continuous. Victorine looked up, and saw a thing she hardly knew how to apprehend. It was like a bird, but enormously bigger, with wings that blotted out the light, and a body shaped like a cigar.

If this was vision, Victorine wanted none of it. She put her hands over her eyes, releasing La Fée Verte's hand that she had not even been aware of holding. The buzzing roar ceased as if a door had been closed, and the tramp of marching feet. She heard shouting, and a man's voice screaming with hysterical joy:

"The Republic has fallen!" he shrieked. "Long live the Commune! To the Hôtel de Ville!"

The fickle crowd took up the chant: "To the Hôtel de Ville! To the Hôtel de Ville!" And so chanting, they moved away from the statue, their voices gradually growing fainter and more confused with distance.

When Victorine dared look again, the square was all but empty. The fat man was gone, and most of the crowd. A woman lingered, comfortingly attired in a long grey skirt, a tight brown jacket with a greasy shawl over it, and a battered black hat rammed over a straggling bun.

"Better take her out of here, dear," she said to Victorine. "I don't care, but if any of those madmen come back this way, they'll be wanting her blood."

That night, Victorine had her maid stand in line for a precious cup of milk, heated it up over her bedroom fire and poured it over some pieces of stale bread torn up into a Sèvres bowl.

La Fée Verte, clean and wrapped in her old green kimono, accepted the dish with murmured thanks. She spooned up a bit, ate it, put the spoon back in the plate. "And your colonel?" she asked. "What will you tell him?"

"You can be my sister," Victorine said gaily. "He doesn't know I don't have one, and under the circumstances, he can hardly ask me to throw you out. You can sleep in the kitchen when he spends the night."

"Yes," La Fée Verte said after a moment. "I will sleep in the kitchen. It will not be for long. We. . . ."

"No," said Victorine forcefully. "I don't want to hear. I don't care if we're to be ruled by a republic or a commune or a king or an emperor, French or German. I don't care if the streets run with blood. All I care is that we are here together now, just at this moment, and that we will stay here together, and be happy."

She was kneeling at La Fée Verte's feet, not touching her for fear of upsetting the bread and milk, looking hopefully into the ravaged face. La Fée Verte touched her cheek very gently and smiled.

"You are right," she said. "We are together. It is enough."

She fell silent, and the tears overflowed her great, bruised eyes and trickled down her cheeks. They were no longer crystalline—they were just tears. But when Victorine licked them from her fingers, it seemed to her that they tasted sweet.

WALPURGIS AFTERNOON

The big thing about the new people moving into the old Pratt place at Number 400 was that they got away with it at all. Our neighborhood is big on historical integrity. The newest house on the block was built in 1910, and you can't even change the paint scheme your house without recourse to preservation committee studies and zoning board hearings. Over the years, the Pratt place had generated a tedious number of such hearings—I'd even been to some of the more recent ones. Old Mrs. Pratt had let it go pretty much to seed, and when she passed away, there was trouble about clearing the title so it could be sold, and then it burned down.

Naturally a bunch of developers went after the land—a three-acre property in a professional neighborhood twenty minutes from downtown is something like a Holy Grail to developers. But their lawyers couldn't get the title cleared either, and the end of it was that the old Pratt place never did get built on. By the time Geoff and I moved next door, it was an empty lot where the neighborhood kids played Bad Guys and Good Guys after school and the neighborhood cats preyed on an endless supply of mice and voles. I'm not talking eyesore, here; just a big shady plot of land overgrown with bamboo, rhododendrons, wildly rambling roses, and some nice old trees, most notably an immensely ancient copper beech big enough to dwarf any normal-sized house.

It certainly dwarfs ours.

Last spring, all that changed overnight. Literally. When Geoff and I turned in, we lived next door to an empty lot. When we got up, we didn't. I have to tell you, it came as quite a shock first thing on a Monday morning, and I wasn't even the one who discovered it. Geoff was.

Geoff's the designated keeper of the window because he insists on sleeping with it open and I hate getting up into a draft. Actually, I hate getting up, period. It's a blessing, really, that Geoff can't boil water without burning it, or I'd never be up before ten. As it is, I eke out every second of warm unconsciousness I can while Geoff shuffles across the floor and thunks down the sash and takes his shower. On that particular morning, his shuffle ended not with a thunk, but with a gasp.

"Holy shit," he said.

I sat up in bed and groped for my robe. When we were in grad school, Geoff had quite a mouth on him, but fatherhood and two decades of college teaching have toned him down a lot. These days, he usually keeps his swearing for Supreme Court decisions and departmental politics.

"Get up, Evie. You gotta see this."

So I got up and went to the window, and there it was, big as life and twice as natural, a real *Victorian Homes* centerfold, set back from the street and just the right size to balance the copper beech. Red tile roof, golden brown clapboards, miles of scarlet-and-gold gingerbread draped over dozens of eaves, balconies, and dormers. A witch's hat tower, a wrap around porch, and a massive carriage house. With a cupola on it. Nothing succeeds like excess, I always say.

I like to think of myself as a fairly sensible woman. I don't imagine things, I face facts, I hadn't gotten hysterical when my fourteen-year-old daughter asked me about birth control. Surely there was some perfectly rational explanation for this phenomenon. All I had to do was think of it.

"It's an hallucination," I said. "Victorian houses don't go up over night. People do have hallucinations. We're having an hallucination. QED."

"It's not a hallucination," Geoff said.

Geoff teaches intellectual history at the university and tends to disagree, on principle, with everything everyone says. Someone says the sky is blue, he says it isn't. And then he explains why. "This has none of the earmarks of a hallucination," he went on. "We aren't in a heightened emotional state, not expecting a miracle, not drugged, not part of a mob, not starving, not sense-deprived. Besides, there's a clothesline in the yard with laundry hanging on it. Nobody hallucinates long underwear."

I looked where he was pointing, and sure enough, a pair of scarlet longjohns was kicking and waving from an umbrella drying rack, along with a couple pairs of women's panties, two oxford-cloth shirts hung up by their collars, and a gold-and-black print caftan. There was also what was arguably the most beautifully designed perennial bed I'd ever seen basking in the early morning sun. As I was squinting at the delphiniums, a side door opened and a woman came out with a wicker clothes basket propped on her hip. She was wearing shorts and a t-shirt, had fairish hair pulled back in a bushy tail, and struck me as being a little long in the tooth to be going barefoot and braless.

"Nice legs," said Geoff.

I snapped down the window. "Pull the shades before you get in the shower," I said. "It looks to me like our new neighbors get a nice, clear shot of our bathroom from their third floor."

In our neighborhood, we pride ourselves on minding our own business and not each others'—live and let live, as long as you keep your dog, your kids, and your lawn under control. If you don't, someone calls you or drops you a note, and if that doesn't make you straighten up and fly right, well, you're likely to get a call from the Town Council about that extension you neglected to get a variance for. Needless to say, the house at Number 400 fell way outside all our usual coping mechanisms. If some contractor had shown up at dawn with bulldozers and two-by-fours, I could have called the police or our Councilwoman or someone and got an injunction. How do you get an injunction against a physical impossibility?

The first phone call came at about eight-thirty: Susan Morrison, whose back yard abuts the Pratt place.

"Reality check time," said Susan. "Do we have new neighbors or do we not?"

"Looks like it to me," I said.

Silence. Then she sighed. "Yeah. So. Can Kimmy sit for Jason Friday night?"

Typical. If you can't deal with it, pretend it doesn't exist, like when one couple down the street got the bright idea of turning their front lawn into a wildflower meadow. The trouble is, a Victorian mansion is a lot harder to ignore than even the wildest meadow. The phone rang all morning with hysterical calls from women who hadn't spoken to us since Geoff's brief tenure as president of the neighborhood association.

After several fruitless sessions of what's-the-world-coming-to, I turned on the machine and went out to the garden to put in the beans. Planting them in May was pushing it, but I needed the therapy. For me, gardening's the most soothing activity on earth. When you plant a bean, you get a bean, not an azalea or a cabbage. When you see that bean covered with icky little orange things, you know they're Mexican bean beetle larvae and go for the pyrethrum. Or you do if you're paying attention. It always astonishes me how oblivious even the garden club ladies can be to a plant's needs and preferences. Sure, there are nasty surprises, like the winter that the mice ate all the Apricot Beauty tulip bulbs. But mostly you know where you are with a garden. If you put in the work, you'll get satisfaction out, which is more than can be said of marriages or careers.

This time, though, digging and raking and planting failed to work their usual magic. Every time I glanced up, there was Number 400, serene and comfortable, the shrubs established and the paint chipping just a little around the windows, exactly as if it had been there forever instead of less than twelve hours.

I'm not big on the inexplicable. Fantasy makes me nervous. In fact, fiction makes me nervous. I like facts and plenty of them. That's why I wanted to be a botanist. I wanted to know everything there was to know about how plants worked, why azaleas like acid soil and peonies like wood ash and how you might be able to get them to grow next to each other. I even went to graduate school and took organic chemistry. Then I met Geoff, fell in love, and traded in my PhD for an MRS, with a minor in Mommy. None of these events (except possibly falling in love with Geoff) fundamentally shook my allegiance to provable, palpable facts. The house next door was palpable, all right, but it shouldn't have been. By the time Kim got home from school that afternoon, I had a headache from trying to figure out how it got to be there.

Kim is my daughter. She reads fantasy, likes animals a lot more than she likes people, and is a big fan of *Buffy the Vampire Slayer*. Because of Kim, we have two dogs (Spike and Willow), a cockatiel (Frodo), and a lop-eared Belgian rabbit (Big Bad), plus the overflow of semi-wild cats (Balin, Dwalin, Bifur, and Bombur) from the Pratt place, all of which she feeds and looks after with truly astonishing dedication.

Three-thirty on the nose, the screen door slammed and Kim careened into the kitchen with Spike and Willow bouncing ecstatically around her feet.

"Whaddya think of the new house, Mom? Who do you think lives there? Do they have pets?"

I laid out her after-school sliced apple and cheese and answered the question I could answer. "There's at least one woman—she was hanging out laundry this morning. No sign of pets, but it's early days yet."

"Isn't it just the coolest thing in the universe, Mom? Real magic, right next door. Just like *Buffy*."

"Without the vampires, I hope. Kim, you know magic doesn't really exist. There's probably a perfectly simple explanation for all of this."

"But, *Mom!*"

"But nothing. You need to call Mrs. Morrison. She wants to know if you can sit for Jason on Friday night. And Big Bad's looking shaggy. He needs to be brushed."

That was Monday.

Tuesday morning, our street looked like the expressway at rush hour. It's a miracle there wasn't an accident. Everybody in town must have driven by, slowing down as they passed Number 400 and craning out the car window. Things quieted down in the middle of the day when everyone was at work, but come 4:30 or so, the joggers started and the walkers and more cars. About 6:00, the police pulled up in front of Number 400, at which point everyone stopped pretending to be nonchalant and held their breath. Two cops disappeared inside, came out again a few minutes later, and left without talking to anybody. They were holding cookies and looking bewildered.

On Wednesday, the traffic let up. Kim found a kitten (Hermione) in the wildflower garden and Geoff came home full of the latest in a series of personality conflicts with his department head, which gave everyone something other than Number 400 to talk about over dinner.

Thursday, Lucille Flint baked one of her coffee cakes and went over to do the Welcome Wagon thing.

Lucille's our local Good Neighbor. Someone moves in, has a baby, marries, dies, and there's Lucille, Johnny-on-the-spot with a coffee cake in her hands and the proper Hallmark sentiment on her lips. Lucille has the time for this kind of thing because she doesn't have a regular job. All right, neither do I, but I write a gardener's advice column for the local paper, so I'm not exactly idle. There's the garden, too. Besides, I'm not the kind of person who likes sitting around other people's kitchens drinking watery instant and listening to the stories of their lives. Lucille is.

Anyway. Thursday morning, I researched the diseases of roses for my column. I'm lucky with roses. Mine never come down with black spot, and the Japanese beetles prefer Susan Morrison's yard to mine. Weeds, however, are not so obliging. When I'd finished Googling "powdery mildew," I went out to tackle the rosebed.

Usually, I don't mind weeding. My mind wanders, my hands get dirty. I can almost feel my plants settling deeper into the soil as I root out the competition. But my rosebed is on the property line between us and the Pratt place. What if the house disappeared again, or someone came out and wanted to chat? I'm not big into chatting. On the other hand, there was shepherd's purse in the rose bed, and shepherd's purse can be a real wild Indian once you let it get established, so I gritted my teeth, grabbed my Cape Cod weeder, and got down to it.

Just as I was starting to relax, I heard footsteps passing on the walk and pushed the rose canes aside just in time to see Lucille Flint climbing the stone steps to Number 400. I watched her ring the doorbell, but I didn't see who answered because I ducked down behind a bushy Gloire de Dijon. If Lucille doesn't care who knows she's a busybody, that's her business.

After twenty-five minutes, I'd weeded and cultivated those roses to a fare-thee-well and was backing out when I heard the screen door, followed by Lucille telling someone how *lovely* their home was, and thanks again for the *scrumptious* pie.

I caught her up under the copper beech.

"Evie dear, you're all out of breath," she said. "My, that's a nasty tear in your shirt."

"Come in, Lucille," I said. "Have a cup of coffee."

She followed me inside without comment and accepted a cup of microwaved coffee and a slice of date-and-nut cake.

She took a bite, coughed a little, and grabbed for the coffee.

"It is pretty awful, isn't it?" I said apologetically. "I baked it last week for some PTA thing at Kim's school and forgot to take it."

"Never mind. I'm full of cherry pie from next door. " She leaned over the stale cake and lowered her voice. "The cherries were *fresh,* Evie."

My mouth dropped open. "Fresh cherries? In May? You're kidding."

Lucille nodded, satisfied at my reaction. "Nope. There was a bowl of them on the table, leaves and all. What's more, there was corn on the draining board. Fresh corn. In the husk. With the silk still on it."

"No!"

"Yes." Lucille sat back and took another sip of coffee. "Mind you, there could be a perfectly ordinary explanation. Ophelia's a horticulturist, after all. Maybe she's got greenhouses out back. Goodness knows there's room enough for several."

I shook my head. "I've never heard of corn growing in a greenhouse."

"And I've never heard of a house appearing in an empty lot overnight," Lucille said tartly. "About that, there's nothing I can tell you. They're not exactly forthcoming, if you know what I mean."

I was impressed. I knew how hard it was to avoid answering Lucille's questions, even about the most personal things. She just kind of picked at you, in the nicest possible way, until you unraveled. It's one of the reasons I didn't hang out with her much.

"So, who are they?"

"Rachel Abrams and Ophelia Canderel. I think they're lesbians. They feel like family together, and you can take it from me, they're not sisters."

Fine. We're a liberal suburb, we can cope with lesbians. "Children?"

Lucille shrugged. "I don't know. There were drawings on the fridge, but no toys."

"Inconclusive evidence," I agreed. "What did you talk about?"

She made a face. "Pie crust. The Perkins's wildflower meadow. They like it. Burney." Burney was Lucille's husband, an unpleasant old fart who disapproved of everything in the world except his equally unpleasant terrier, Homer. "Electricians. They want a fixture put up in the front hall. Then Rachel tried to tell me about her work in artificial intelligence, but I couldn't understand a word she said."

From where I was sitting, I had an excellent view of Number 400's wisteria-covered carriage house, its double doors ajar on an awe-inspiring array of garden tackle. "Artificial intelligence must pay well," I said.

Lucille shrugged. "There has to be family money somewhere. You ought to see the front hall, not to mention the kitchen. It looks like something out of a magazine."

"What are they doing here?"

"That's the forty-thousand-dollar question, isn't it?"

We drained the cold dregs of our coffee, contemplating the mystery of why a horticulturist and an artificial intelligence wonk would choose our quiet, tree-lined suburb to park their house in. It seemed a more solvable mystery than how they'd transported it there in the first place.

Lucille took off to make Burney his noontime franks and beans and I tried to get my column roughed out. But I couldn't settle to my computer, not with that Victorian enigma sitting on the other side of my rose bed. Every once in a while, I'd see a shadow passing behind a window or hear a door bang. I gave up trying to make the disposal of diseased foliage interesting and went out to poke around in the garden. I was elbow-deep in the viburnum, pruning out deadwood, when I heard someone calling.

It was a woman, standing on the other side of my roses. She was big, solidly curved, and dressed in bright flowered overalls. Her hair was braided with shiny gold ribbon into dozens of tiny plaits tied off with little metal beads. Her skin was a deep matte brown, like antique mahogany. Despite the overalls, she was astonishingly beautiful.

I dropped the pruning shears. "Damn," I said. "Sorry," I said. "You surprised me." I felt my cheeks heat. The woman smiled at me serenely and beckoned.

I don't like new people and I don't like being put on the spot, but I've got my pride. I picked up my pruning shears, untangled myself from the viburnum, and marched across the lawn to meet my new neighbor.

She said her name was Ophelia Canderel, and she'd been admiring my garden. Would I like to see hers?

I certainly would.

If I'd met Ophelia at a party, I'd have been totally tongue-tied. She was beautiful, she was big, and frankly, there just aren't enough people of color in our neighborhood for me to have gotten over my liberal nervousness around them. This particular woman of color, however, spoke fluent Universal Gardener and her garden was a gardener's garden, full of horticultural experiments and puzzles and stuff to talk about. Within about three minutes, she was asking my advice about the gnarly brown larvae infesting her bee balm, and I was filling her in on the peculiarities of our local microclimate. By the time we'd inspected every flower and shrub in the front yard, I was more comfortable with her than I was with any of the local garden club ladies. We were alike, Ophelia and I.

We were discussing the care and feeding of peonies in an acid soil when Ophelia said, "Come see my shrubbery."

Usually when I hear the word "shrubbery," I think of a semi-formal arrangement of rhodies and azaleas, lilacs and viburnum, with a potentilla perhaps, or a butterfly bush for late summer color. The bed should be deep enough to give everything room to spread and there should be a statue in it, or maybe a sundial. Neat, but not anal—that's what you should aim for in a shrubbery.

Ophelia sure had the not-anal part down. The shrubs didn't merely spread, they rioted. And what with the trees and the orchids and the ferns and the vines, I couldn't begin to judge the border's depth. The hibiscus and the bamboo were OK, although I wouldn't have risked them myself. But to plant bougainvillea and poinsettias, coconut palms and frangipani this far north was simply tempting fate. And the statue! I'd never seen anything remotely like it, not outside of a museum, anyway. No head to speak of, breasts like footballs, a belly like a watermelon, and a phallus like an overgrown zucchini, the whole thing weathered with the rains of a thousand years or more.

I glanced at Ophelia. "Impressive," I said.

She turned a critical eye on it. "You don't think it's too much? Rachel says it is, but she's a minimalist. This is my little bit of home, and I love it."

"It's a lot," I admitted. Accuracy prompted me to add, "It suits you."

I still didn't understand how Ophelia had gotten a tropical rain-forest to flourish in a temperate climate.

I was trying to find a nice way to ask her about it when she said, "You're a real find, Evie. Rachel's working, or I'd call her to come down. She really wants to meet you."

"Next time," I said, wondering what on earth I'd find to say to a specialist on artificial intelligence. "Um. Does Rachel garden?"

Ophelia laughed. "No way—her talent is not for living things. But I made a garden for her. Would you like to see it?"

I was only dying to, although I couldn't help wondering what kind of exotica I was letting myself in for. A desertscape? Tundra? Curiosity won. "Sure," I said. "Lead on."

We stopped on the way to visit the vegetable garden. It looked fairly ordinary, although the tomatoes were more August than May, and the beans more late June. I didn't see any corn and I didn't see any greenhouses. After a brief sidebar on insecticidal soaps, Ophelia led me behind the carriage house. The unmistakable sound of quacking fell on my ears.

"We aren't zoned for ducks," I said, startled.

"We are," said Ophelia. "Now. How do you like Rachel's garden?"

A prospect of brown reeds with a silvery river meandering through it stretched through where the Morrisons' back yard ought to be, all the way to a boundless expanse of ocean. In the marsh it was April, with a crisp salt wind blowing back from the water and ruffling the brown reeds and the white-flowering shad and the pale green feathery sweetfern. Mallards splashed and dabbled along the meander. A solitary great egret stood among the reeds, the fringes of its white courting shawl blowing around one black and knobbly leg. As I watched, openmouthed, the egret unfurled its other leg from its breast feathers, trod at the reeds, and lowered its golden bill to feed.

I got home late. Kim was in the basement with the animals and the chicken I was planning to make for dinner was still in the freezer. Thanking heaven for modern technology, I defrosted the chicken in the microwave, chopped veggies, seasoned, mixed, and got the whole mess in the oven just as Geoff walked in the door. He wasn't happy about eating forty-five minutes late, but he was mostly over it by bedtime.

That was Thursday.

Friday, I saw Ophelia and Rachel pulling out of their driveway in one of those old cars that has huge fenders and a running board. They returned after lunch, the backseat full of groceries. They and the groceries disappeared through the kitchen door, and there was no further sign of them until late afternoon, when Rachel opened one of the quarter-round windows in the attic and energetically shook the dust out of a small patterned carpet.

On Saturday, the invitation arrived.

It stood out among the flyers, book orders, bills, and requests for money that usually came through our mail slot, a five-by-eight silvery-blue envelope that smelled faintly of sandalwood. It was addressed to The Gordon Family in a precise italic hand.

I opened it and read:

Rachel Esther Abrams and Ophelia Desirée Candarel
Request the Honor of your Presence
At the
Celebration of their Marriage.
Sunday, May 24 at 3 p.m.
There will be refreshments before and after the Ceremony.

I was still staring at it when the doorbell rang. It was Lucille, looking fit to burst, holding an invitation just like mine.

"Come in, Lucille. There's plenty of coffee left."

I don't think I'd ever seen Lucille in such a state. You'd think someone had invited her to parade naked down Main Street at noon.

"Well, write and tell them you can't come," I said. "They're just being neighborly, for Pete's sake. It's not like they can't get married if you're not there."

"I know. It's just. . . . It puts me in a funny position, that's all. Burney's a founding member of Normal Marriage for Normal People. He wouldn't like it at all if he knew I'd been invited to a lesbian wedding."

"So don't tell him. If you want to go, just tell him the new neighbors have invited you to an open house on Sunday, and you know for a fact that we're going to be there."

Lucille smiled. Burney hated Geoff almost as much as Geoff hated Burney. "It's a thought," she said. "Are you going?"

"I don't see why not. Who knows? I might learn something."

The Sunday of the wedding, I took forever to dress. Kim thought it was funny, but Geoff was impatient. "It's a lesbian wedding, for pity's sake. It's going to be full of middle-aged dykes with ugly haircuts. Nobody's going to care what you look like."

"I care," said Kim. "And I think that jacket is wicked cool."

I'd bought the jacket at a little Indian store in the Square and not worn it since. When I got it away from the Square's atmosphere of collegiate funk it looked, I don't know, too sixties, too artsy, too bright for a forty-something suburban matron. It was basically purple, with teal blue and gold and fuchsia flowers all over it and brass buttons shaped like parrots. Shaking my head, I started to unfasten the parrots.

Geoff exploded. "I swear to God, Evie, if you change again, that's it. It's not like I want to go. I've got papers to correct; I don't have time for this"—he glanced at Kim—"nonsense. Either we go or we stay. But we do it now."

Kim touched my arm. "It's *you,* Mom. Come *on.*"

So I came on, feeling like a tropical floral display.

"Great," said Geoff when we hit the sidewalk. "Not a car in sight. If we're the only ones here, I'm leaving."

"I don't think that's going to be a problem."

Beyond the copper beech, I saw a colorful crowd milling around as purposefully as bees, bearing chairs and flowers and ribbons. As we came closer, it became clear that Geoff couldn't have been more wrong about the wedding guests. There wasn't an ugly haircut in sight, although there were some pretty startling dye jobs. The dress code could best be described as eclectic, with a slight bias toward floating fabrics and rich, bright colors. My jacket felt right at home.

Geoff was muttering about not knowing anybody when Lucille appeared, looking festive in Laura Ashley chintz.

"Isn't this fun?" she said, with every sign of sincerity. "I've never met such interesting people. And friendly! They make me feel right at home. Come over here and join the gang."

She dragged us toward the long side-yard, which sloped down to a lavishly blooming double-flowering cherry underplanted with peonies. Which shouldn't have been in bloom at the same time as the cherry, but I was growing resigned to the vagaries of Ophelia's garden. A willowy young person in chartreuse lace claimed Lucille's attention, and they went off together. The three of us stood in a slightly awkward knot at the edge of the crowd, which occasionally threw out a few guests who eddied around us briefly before retreating.

"How are those spells of yours, dear? Any better?" inquired a solicitous voice in my ear, and, "Oh!" when I jumped. "You're not Elvira, are you? Sorry."

Geoff's grip cut off the circulation above my elbow. "This was not one of your better ideas, Evie. We're surrounded by weirdoes. Did you see that guy in the skirt? I think we should take Kimmy home."

A tall black man with a flattop and a diamond in his left ear appeared, pried Geoff's hand from my arm, and shook it warmly. "Dr. Gordon? Ophelia told me to be looking out for you. I've read *The Anarchists,* you see, and I can't tell you how much I admired it."

Geoff actually blushed. Before the subject got too painful to talk about, he used to say that for a history of anarchism, his one book had had a remarkably hierarchical readership: three members of the tenure review committee, two reviewers for scholarly journals, and his wife. "Thanks," he said.

Geoff's fan grinned, clearly delighted. "Maybe we can talk at the reception," he said. "Right now, I need to find you a place to sit. They look like they're just about ready to roll."

It was a lovely wedding.

I don't know exactly what I was expecting, but I was mildly surprised to see a rabbi and a wedding canopy. Ophelia was an enormous rose in crimson draperies. Rachel was a calla lily in cream linen. Their heads were tastefully wreathed in oak and ivy leaves. There were the usual prayers and promises and tears; when the rabbi pronounced them married, they kissed and horns sounded a triumphant fanfare.

Kim poked me in the side. "Mom? Who's playing those horns?"

"I don't know. Maybe it's a recording."

"I don't think so," Kim said. "I think it's the tree. Isn't this just about the coolest thing ever?"

Before I could think of an answer, we were on our feet again, the chairs had disappeared, and people were dancing. A cheerful bearded man grabbed Kim's hand to pull her into the line. Geoff grabbed her and pulled her back.

"*Dad!*" Kim wailed. "I want to dance!"

"I've got a pile of papers to correct before class tomorrow," Geoff said. "And if I know you, there's homework you've put off until tonight. We have to go home now."

"We can't leave yet," I objected. "We haven't congratulated the brides."

Geoff's jaw tensed. "So go congratulate them," he said. "Kim and I will wait for you here."

Kim looked mutinous. I gave her the eye. This wasn't the time or the place to object. Like Geoff, Kim had no inhibitions about airing the family linen in public, but I had enough for all three of us.

"Dr. Gordon. There you are." *The Anarchists* fan popped up between us. "I've been looking all over for you. Come have a drink and let me tell you how brilliant you are."

Geoff smiled modestly. "You're being way too generous," he said. "Did you read Peterson's piece in *The Review*?"

"Asshole," said the man dismissively. Geoff slapped him on the back, and a minute later, they were halfway to the house, laughing as if they'd known each other for years. Thank heaven for the male ego.

"Dance?" said Kim.

"Go for it," I said. "I'm going to get some champagne and kiss the brides."

The brides were nowhere to be found, but the champagne, a young girl informed me, was in the kitchen. So I entered Number 400 for the first time, coming through the mudroom into a large, oak-paneled hall. To my left a staircase with an ornately carved oak banister rose to an art-glass window. Straight ahead was a semi-circular fireplace flanked by a carved bench and a door that probably led to the kitchen. Between me and the door was an assortment of brightly dressed strangers, talking and laughing.

As I edged around them, puzzle-fragments of conversation rose out of the general buzz:

"My pearls? Thank you, my dear, but you know they're only stimulated."

"And *then* it just went 'poof'! A perfectly good frog, and it just went poof!"

". . . and Tallulah says to the bishop, she says, 'Love your drag, darling, but your *purse* is on fire.' Don't you love it? 'Your *purse* is on fire!'"

The kitchen itself was blessedly empty except for a stout gentleman in a tuxedo and a striking woman in a peach silk pantsuit, who was tending an array of champagne bottles and a cut-glass bowl full of bright blue punch. Curious, I picked up a cup of punch and sniffed at it. The woman smiled up at me through a caterpillery fringe of false lashes.

"Pure witch's brew," she said in one of those Lauren Bacall come-hither voices I've always envied. "But what can you do? It's the *specialité de la maison.*"

The tuxedoed man laughed. "Don't mind Silver, Mrs. Gordon. He just likes to tease. Ophelia's punch is wonderful."

"Only if you like Ty-D Bol," said Silver, tipping a sapphire stream into another cup. "You know, honey, you shouldn't stand around with your mouth open like that. Think of the flies."

Several guests entered in plenty of time to catch this exchange. Determined to preserve my cool, I took a gulp of the punch. It tasted fruity and made my mouth prickle before hitting my stomach like a firecracker. So much for cool. I choked and gasped.

"I tried to warn you," Silver said. "You'd better switch to champagne."

Now I knew Silver was a man, I could see that his hands and wrists were big for the rest of her—him. I could feel my face burning with punch and mortification. "No, thank you," I said faintly. "Maybe some water?"

The stout man handed me a glass. I sipped gratefully. "You're Ophelia and Rachel's neighbor, aren't you?" he said. "Lovely garden. You must be proud of that asparagus bed."

"I was, until I saw Ophelia's."

"Ooh, listen to the green-eyed monster," Silver cooed. "Don't be jealous, honey. Ophelia's the best. Nobody understands plants like Ophelia."

"I'm not jealous," I said with dignity. "I'm wistful. There's a difference."

Then, just when I thought it couldn't possibly get any worse, Geoff appeared, looking stunningly unprofessorial, with one side of his shirt collar turned up and his dark hair flopped over his eyes.

"Hey, Evie. Who knew a couple of dykes would know how to throw a wedding?"

You'd think after sixteen years of living with Geoff, I'd know whether or not he was an alcoholic. But I don't. He doesn't go on binges, he doesn't get drunk at every party we go to, and I'm pretty sure he doesn't drink on the sly. What I do know is that drinking doesn't make him more fun to be around.

I took his arm. "I'm glad you're enjoying yourself," I said brightly. "Too bad we have to leave."

"Leave? Who said anything about leaving? We just got here."

"Your papers," I said. "Remember?"

"Screw my papers," said Geoff and held out his empty cup to Silver. "This punch is dy-no-mite."

"What about your students?"

"I'll tell 'em I didn't feel like reading their stupid essays. That'll fix their little red wagons. Boring as hell anyway. Fill 'er up, beautiful," he told Silver.

Silver considered him gravely. "Geoff, darling," he said. "A little bird tells me that there's an absolutely delicious argument going on in the smoking room. They'll never forgive you if you don't come play."

Geoff favored Silver with a leer that made me wish I were somewhere else. "Only if you play too," he said. "What's it about?"

Silver waved a pink-tipped hand. "Something about theoretical versus practical anarchy. Right, Rodney?"

"I believe so," said the stout gentleman agreeably.

A martial gleam rose in Geoff's eye. "Let me at 'em."

Silver's pale eyes turned to me, solemn and concerned. "You don't mind, do you, honey?"

I shrugged. With luck, the smoking-room crowd would be drunk too, and nobody would remember who said what. I just hoped none of the anarchists had a violent temper.

"We'll return him intact," Silver said. "I promise." And they were gone, Silver trailing fragrantly from Geoff's arm.

While I was wondering whether I'd said that thing about the anarchists or only thought it, I felt a tap on my shoulder—the stout gentleman, Rodney.

"Mrs. Gordon, Rachel and Ophelia would like to see you and young Kimberly in the study. If you'll please step this way?"

The shift in manner from wedding guest to old-fashioned butler was oddly intimidating. Without argument, I trailed him to the front hall—empty now, except for Lucille and the young person in chartreuse lace, who were huddled together on the bench by the fireplace. The young person was talking earnestly and Lucille was listening and nodding and sipping punch. Neither of them paid any attention to us or to the music coming from goodness knew where. At the foot of the stairs Kim was examining the newel post.

It was well worth examining: a screaming griffin with every feather and every curl beautifully articulated and its head polished smooth and black as ebony. Rodney gave it a brief, seemingly unconscious caress as he started up the steps. When Kim followed suit, I thought I saw the carved eye blink.

I must have made a noise, because Rodney halted his slow ascent and gazed down at me, standing openmouthed below. "Lovely piece of work, isn't it? We call it the house guardian. A joke, of course."

"Of course," I echoed. "Cute."

It seemed to me that the house had more rooms than it ought to. Through open doors, I glimpsed libraries, salons, parlors, bedrooms. We passed through a stone cloister where discouraged-looking ficuses in tubs shed their leaves on the cracked pavement and into a green-scummed pool. I don't know what shocked me more: the cloister or the state of the ficuses. Maybe Ophelia's green thumb didn't extend to houseplants.

As far as I could tell, Kim took all this completely in stride. She bounded along like a dog in the woods, peeking in an open door here, pausing to look at a picture there, and pelting Rodney with questions I wouldn't have dreamed of asking, like "Are there kids here?"; "What about pets?"; "How many people live here, anyway?"

"It depends," was Rodney's unvarying answer. "Step this way, please."

Our trek ended in a wall covered by a huge South American tapestry of three women making pots. Rodney pulled the tapestry aside, revealing an iron-banded oak door that would have done a medieval castle proud. "The study," he said, and opened the door on a flight of ladder-like steps rising steeply into the shadows.

His voice and gesture reminded me irresistibly of one of those horror movies in which a laconic butler leads the hapless heroine to a forbidding door and invites her to step inside. I didn't know which of three impulses was stronger: to laugh, to run, or, like the heroine, to forge on and see what happened next. It's some indication of the state I was in that Kim got by me and through the door before I could stop her.

I don't like feeling helpless and I don't like feeling pressured. I really don't like being tricked, manipulated, and herded. Left to myself, I'd probably have turned around and taken my chances on finding my way out of the maze of corridors. But I wasn't going to leave without my daughter, so I hitched up my wedding-appropriate long skirt and started up the steps.

The stairs were every bit as steep as they looked. I floundered up gracelessly, emerging into a huge space sparsely furnished with a beat-up rolltop desk, a wingback chair and a swan-neck rocker at one end and some cluttered door-on-sawhorse tables on the other. Ophelia and Rachel, still dressed in their bridal finery, were sitting in the chair and the rocker respectively, holding steaming mugs and talking to Kim, who was incandescent with excitement.

"Oh, there you are," said Ophelia as I stumbled up the last step. "Would you like some tea?"

"No, thank you," I said stiffly. "Kim, I think it's time to go home now."

Kim protested vigorously. Rachel cast Ophelia an unreadable look.

"It'll be fine, love," Ophelia said soothingly. "Mrs. Gordon's upset, and who could blame her? Evie, I don't believe you've actually met Rachel."

Where I come from, social niceties trump everything. Without actually meaning to, I found I was shaking Rachel's hand and congratulating her on her marriage. Close up, she was a handsome woman, with a decided nose, deep lines around her mouth, and the measuring gaze of a gardener examining an unfamiliar insect on her tomato leaves. I didn't ask her to call me Evie.

Ophelia touched my hand. "Never mind," she said soothingly. "Have some tea. You'll feel better."

Next thing I knew, I was sitting on a chair that hadn't been there a moment before, eating a lemon cookie from a plate I didn't see arrive, and drinking Lapsang Souchong from a cup that appeared when Ophelia reached for it. Just for the record, I didn't feel better at all. I felt as if I'd taken a step that wasn't there, or perhaps failed to take one that was: out of balance, out of place, out of control.

Kim, restless as a cat, was snooping around among the long tables.

"What's with the flying fish?" she asked.

"They're for Rachel's new experiment," said Ophelia. "She thinks she can bring the dead to life again."

"You better let me tell it, Ophie," Rachel said. "I don't want Mrs. Gordon thinking I'm some kind of mad scientist."

In fact, I wasn't thinking at all, except that I was in way over my head.

"I'm working on animating extinct species," Rachel said. "I'm particularly interested in dodos and passenger pigeons, but eventually, I'd like to work up to bison and maybe woolly mammoths."

"Won't that create ecological problems?" Kim objected. "I mean, they're way big, and we don't know much about their habits or what they ate or anything."

There was a silence while Rachel and Ophelia traded family-joke smiles. "That's why we need you," Rachel said.

Kim looked as though she'd been given the pony she'd been agitating for since fourth grade. Her jaw dropped. Her eyes sparkled. And I lost it.

"Will somebody please tell me what the hell you're talking about?" I said. "I've been patient. I followed your pal Rodney through more rooms than Versailles and I didn't run screaming, and believe me when I tell you I wanted to. I've drunk your tea and listened to your so-called explanations, and I still don't know what's going on around here."

Kim turned to me with a look of blank astonishment. "Come on, Mom. I can't believe you don't know that Ophelia and Rachel are witches. It's perfectly obvious."

"We prefer not to use the W word," Rachel said. "Like most labels, it's misleading and inaccurate. We're just people with natural scientific ability who have been trained to ask the right questions."

Ophelia nodded. "We learn to ask the things themselves. They always know. Do you see?"

"No," I said. "All I see is a roomful of junk and a garden that doesn't care what season it is."

"Very well," said Rachel, and rose from her chair. "If you'll just come over here, Mrs. Gordon, I'll try to clear everything up."

At the table of the flying fish, Ophelia arranged Kim and me on one side while Rachel took up a teacherly position beside the exhibits. These seemed to be A) the fish; and B) one of those Japanese good-luck cats with one paw curled up by its ear and a bright enameled bib.

"As you know," Rachel said, "my field is artificial intelligence. What that means, in this context, is that I can animate the inanimate. Observe." She caressed the porcelain cat between its ears. For two breaths, nothing happened. Then the cat lowered its paw and stretched itself luxuriously. The light glinted off its bulging sides; its curly red mouth and wide painted eyes were expressionless.

"Sweet," Kim breathed.

"It's not really alive," Rachel said, stroking the cat's shiny back. "It's still porcelain. If it jumps off the table, it'll break."

"Can I pet it?" Kim asked.

"No!" Rachel and I said in firm and perfect unison.

"Why not?"

"Because I'd like you to help me with an experiment." Rachel looked me straight in the eye. "I'm not really comfortable with words," she said. "I prefer demonstrations. What I'm going to do is hold Kim's hand and touch the fish. That's all."

"And what happens then?" Kim asked eagerly.

Rachel smiled at her. "Well, we'll see, won't we? Are you okay with this, Mrs. Gordon?"

It sounded harmless enough, and Kim was already reaching for Rachel's hand. "Go ahead," I said.

Their hands met, palm to palm. Rachel closed her eyes. She frowned in concentration and the atmosphere tightened around us. I yawned to unblock my ears.

Rachel laid her free hand on one of the fish.

It twitched, head jerking galvanically; its wings fanned open and shut.

Kim gave a little grunt, which snapped my attention away from the fish. She was pale and sweating a little.

I started to go to her, but I couldn't. Someone was holding me back.

"It's okay, Evie," Ophelia said soothingly. "Kim's fine, really. Rachel knows what she's doing."

"Kim's pale," I said, calm as the eye of a storm. "She looks like she's going to throw up. She's not fine. Let me go to my daughter, Ophelia, or I swear you'll regret it."

"Believe me, it's not safe for you to touch them right now. You have to trust us."

My Great-Aunt Fanny I'll trust you, I thought, and willed myself to relax in her grip. "OK," I said shakily. "I believe you. It's just, I wish you'd warned me."

"We wanted to tell you," Ophelia said. "But we were afraid you wouldn't believe us. We were afraid you would think we were a couple of nuts. You see, Kim has the potential to be an important zoologist—if she has the proper training. Rachel's a wonderful teacher, and you can see for yourself how complementary their disciplines are. Working together, they. . . ."

I don't know what she thought Kim and Rachel could accomplish, because the second she was more interested in what she was saying than in holding onto me, I was out of her hands and pulling Kim away from the witch who, as far as I could tell, was draining her dry.

That was the plan, anyway.

As soon as I touched Kim, the room came alive.

It started with the flying fish leaping off the table and buzzing past us on Saran Wrap wings. The porcelain cat thumped down from the table and, far from breaking, twined itself around Kim's ankles, purring hollowly. An iron plied itself over a pile of papers, smoothing out the creases. The teddy bear growled at it and ran to hide behind a toaster.

If that wasn't enough, my jacket burst into bloom.

It's kind of hard to describe what it's like to wear a tropical forest. Damp, for one thing. Bright. Loud. Uncomfortable. Very, very uncomfortable. Overstimulating. There were flowers and parrots screeching (yes, the flowers, too—or maybe that was me). It seemed to go on for a long time, kind of like giving birth. At first, I was overwhelmed by the chaos of growth and sound, unsure whether I was the forest or the forest was me. Slowly I realized that it didn't have to be a chaos, and that if I just pulled myself together, I could make sense of it. That flower went there, for instance, and the teal one went there. That parrot belonged on that vine and everything needed to be smaller and stiller and less extravagantly colored. Like that.

Gradually, the forest receded. I was still holding Kim, who promptly bent over and threw up on the floor.

"There," I said hoarsely. "I told you she was going to be sick."

Ophelia picked up Rachel and carried her back to her wingchair. "You be quiet, you," she said over her shoulder. "Heaven knows what you've done to Rachel. I *told* you not to touch them."

Ignoring my own nausea, I supported Kim over to the rocker and deposited her in it. "You might have told me why," I snapped. "I don't know why people can't just explain things instead of making me guess. It's not like I can read minds, you know. Now, are you going to conjure us up a glass of water, or do I have to go find the kitchen?"

Rachel had recovered herself enough to give a shaky laugh. "Hell, you could conjure it yourself, with a little practice. Ophie, darling, calm down. I'm fine."

Ophelia stopped fussing over her wife along enough to snatch a glass of cool mint tea from the air and hand it to me. She wouldn't meet my eyes, and she was scowling. "I told you she was going to be difficult. Of all the damn-fool, pig-headed. . ."

"Hush, love," Rachel said. "There's no harm done, and now we know just where we stand. I'd rather have a nice cup of tea than listen to you cursing out Mrs. Gordon for just trying to be a good mother." She turned her head to look at me. "Very impressive, by the way. We knew you had to be like Ophie, because of the garden, but we didn't know the half of it. You've got a kick like a mule, Mrs. Gordon. "

I must have been staring at her like one of the flying fish. Here I thought I'd half-killed her, and she was giving me a smile that looked perfectly genuine.

I smiled cautiously in return. "Thank you," I said.

Kim pulled at the sleeve of my jacket. "Hey, Mom, that was awesome. I guess you're a witch, huh?"

I wanted to deny it, but I couldn't. The fact was that the pattern of flowers on my jacket was different and the colors were muted, the flowers more English garden than tropical paradise. There were only three buttons, and they were larks, not parrots. And I felt different. Clearer? More whole? I don't know—different. Even though I didn't know how the magic worked or how to control it, I couldn't ignore the fact—the palpable, provable fact—that it was there.

"Yeah," I said. "I guess I am."

"Me, too," my daughter said. "What's Dad going to say?"

I thought for a minute. "Nothing, honey. Because we're not going to tell him."

We didn't, either. And we're not going to. There's no useful purpose served by telling people truths they aren't equipped to accept. Geoff's pretty oblivious, anyway. It's true that in the hungover aftermath of Ophelia's blue punch, he announced that he thought the new neighbors might be a bad influence, but he couldn't actually forbid Kim and me to hang out with them because it would look sexist, racist, and homophobic.

Kim's over at Number 400 most Saturday afternoons, learning how to be a zoologist. She's making good progress. There was an episode with zombie mice I don't like to think about, and a crisis when the porcelain cat broke falling out of a tree. But she's learning patience, control, and discipline, which are all excellent things for a girl of fourteen to learn. She and Rachel have reanimated a pair of passenger pigeons, but they haven't had any luck in breeding them yet.

Lucille's the biggest surprise. It turns out that all her nosy-parkerism was a case of ingrown witchiness. Now she's studying with Silver, of all people, to be a psychologist. But that's not the surprise. The surprise is that she left Burney and moved into Number 400, where she has a room draped with chintz and a grey cat named Jezebel and is as happy as a clam at high tide.

I'm over there a lot, too, learning to be a horticulturist. Ophelia says I'm a quick study, but I have to learn to trust my instincts. Who knew I had instincts? I thought I was just good at looking things up.

I'm working on my own garden now. I'm the only one who can find it without being invited in. It's an English kind of garden, like the gardens in books I loved as a child. It has a stone wall with a low door in it, a little central lawn, and a perennial border full of foxgloves and Sweet William and Michaelmas daisies. Veronica blooms in the cracks of the wall, and periwinkle carpets the beds where old-fashioned fragrant roses nod heavily to every passing breeze. There's a small wilderness of rowan trees, and a neat shrubbery embracing a pond stocked with fish as bright as copper pennies. Among the dusty-smelling boxwood, I've put a statue of a woman holding a basket planted with stonecrop. She's dressed in a jacket incised with flowers and vines and closed with three buttons shaped like parrots. The fourth button sits on her shoulder, clacking its beak companionably and preening its brazen feathers. I'm thinking of adding a duck pond next, or maybe a wilderness for Kim's menagerie.

Witches don't have to worry about zoning laws.

LAND'S END

The Land's End Light flashed out into the pale gray dawn. Forty-second beam. Twenty-second eclipse.

Aboard the clipper *White Goddess,* the lookout shouted, "Land ho!" and the men of the watch raised a hoarse cheer. It did not penetrate to the cockpit, where Joshua Saltree dozed and woke and dozed again.

The sleeping was better than the waking, for the pain wasn't so troublesome when he was asleep, nor the dead weight of his leg, wrapped and tied like a broken spar. He groaned in protest when the ship's surgeon woke him to give him a dose of laudanum and the news that land was in sight.

"We'll make port by noon. Captain's going to look after you." Dr. Coffin's voice was dry as a ship's biscuit. "He's that grateful. See you're grateful back, Joshua Saltree; that's all I have to say."

Grateful? Saltree couldn't think why. The laudanum eased the pain some, but slowed his mind and his tongue terribly. He wanted to tell Dr. Coffin that Joshua Saltree wasn't dependent on any man, that he had a place to go and a few dollars laid by. But all he could get out was, "Rooming house."

Dr. Coffin laughed. "Mrs. Peabody's a sight too busy to nurse a man hurt bad as you are," he said. "Drink up."

"Don't hurt," Saltree protested, but he drank the bitter stuff down, and a moment, or maybe half a day later, he opened his eyes to find Captain Mayne and Dr. Coffin hanging over him.

"Well, lad," said the captain heartily. "Time to go ashore."

Saltree tried to sit up, found himself prevented by Dr. Coffin's hand on his shoulder. "Damn young fool," the surgeon snapped. "Bones're near sticking out your shin, and you want to walk ashore. Try it and be damned to you, but don't be surprised if you wake up one morning with no leg at all."

"It's splintered; no, s-splinted, devil take it."

Captain Mayne sighed louder than he needed to. "You'll be carried on a litter from here to my house. . . ."

A woman's voice finished the sentence: "And that is an order, Mister."

"Mary!" Captain Mayne's teeth flashed through his beard, and he turned away from the berth as fast as his bulk and the narrow space would let him.

"Seth." A woman's white hands slid around the captain's neck and pulled down his head. Saltree closed his eyes in shame and almost drifted off again, but a cool touch on his forehead brought him around.

Mrs. Mayne was bending over him, smiling. "Well, Mr. Saltree," she said. "This is a fine state for a sailor to be in."

Saltree frowned at her and feebly twitched his hand away from the tickling fringe of her shawl. He should be looking down at her, not up, should be saluting her from the rigging or standing by while the bo'sun piped her aboard, not lying here useless as a torn sail. She was a pretty woman—or had been, twenty years ago. Saltree smiled. A very pretty woman.

Most of the crew hadn't the first notion that the *White Goddess*'s figurehead was the spitting image of the captain's lady. Oh, the carver had given the figurehead greeny brown hair and draped a fancy white sheet under her round, high breasts. But anyone looking close at her face would see Mrs. Mayne's straight nose and dark, long-lidded eyes. Stuck out under the bowsprit as she was, hardly anyone'd notice. But he'd noticed right away. He was a noticing sort of man, was Joshua Saltree.

On calm days he used to scramble out the jib guys and stare out over the sea with one arm around the *Goddess*'s sun-warm shoulders. He liked listening to the thutter of the bow over the swell, and watching the water glitter and foam under the keel. Ahead, always ahead, were ocean, weather, unknown shores, and he liked the way she breasted them with her carved lips parted and smiling. Why was she frowning now? Saltree moaned and closed his eyes.

Time passed in a blur of pain, heat, fear, and strange dreams. Occasionally, Saltree was dimly aware of lying propped in a wide bed in a large room fitted with windows and curtains and gentle hands that brought him water and tended to his needs. But mostly he swam a pathless ocean, buffeted by storm. Lightning pulsed; sharks looked at him hungrily out of the eyes of dead sailors and rolled to snap at his feet. Saltwater clogged the air, crushed his chest so that he gasped and flailed. A ship loomed—at her prow, the *White Goddess,* decked out in seaweed. Her face was shadowed; her naked breasts rose and fell with the ship's breathing; her eyes streamed salt tears.

"Man overboard!" Saltree shouted; and she reached down her carven arms to him. Sometimes he caught her fingers—slick and cool as varnished wood—and sometimes he did not, but in either case he always woke wheezing and coughing and retching like a man hauled in from drowning.

It was deep night when finally he opened his eyes to see a fire burning in the grate, and a woman sewing by a shaded lamp. He felt light-headed and all his limbs were limp as rope yarn. A glass and a pitcher stood on a table nearby, with a brown bottle, a spoon, and a tin basin.

"Thirsty," he said, and was startled to hear how rusty his voice sounded.

The woman got up and came to the bed, her skirts hushing. "I'm not surprised to hear it, Joshua Saltree, for you've been sweating like a pig all night." She touched her hand against his forehead before pouring a glass of water and holding it to his lips. "The fever's nearly gone. You'll sleep quieter now."

When Saltree had swallowed the water, the woman busied herself plumping the pillows and smoothing the sheets. As she moved around the bed, the firelight fell on her face: dark, long-lidded eyes above a straight nose. His heart began to race.

"Goddess?"

"Don't try to talk now. You've had pneumonia and ship fever and I don't know what all else, and very nearly died. You're in Captain Mayne's house, and I'm Mrs. Mayne, as you'll remember just fine when you're feeling better. Go to sleep now. That's right. Sleep."

The next time Saltree woke, Captain Mayne sat by the bed, sucking on an empty pipe and regarding him gravely. "Glad to see you back with us, my lad," he said.

"The *Goddess?*"

She's up in dry dock, getting overhauled as good as new, if not better. A new mainmast's the heaviest expense, but eight members of the Pioneer Mining Association of Auburn're taking passage to San Francisco at fifty dollars a head, so she'll pay for her repairs and more soon enough. Owner's glad we brought her home at all, and he's real grateful to you in particular, as well he should be."

Saltree frowned. That's not what he meant. A broad hand gripped his arm, lying helpless on the white counterpane. "Don't you remember the storm?" asked Captain Mayne kindly. "Well, well, that's no loss to you. Never you worry, lad; the *Goddess* is safe and sound. You sleep now."

Once the fever was gone, Saltree was not long mending. The *White Goddess* had made port on the second of May. By the end of the month, Saltree could hobble from the bed to the window to the fireplace and back again; in the second week of June, he asked respectfully whether he better not be moving on.

"You've been dreadful kind—kinder than there's any call for," he said awkwardly, fearing to seem ungrateful.

"Nonsense," said Captain Mayne. "We're glad to have you, Mrs. Mayne and I. You mayn't remember going aloft with Tom Harris when the mainmast started to crack, but I do. The pair of you saved my ship, lad, for which I'm grateful; and my hide, for which Mrs. Mayne is grateful. Now Tom's dead and gone: we can't show him our gratitude. So let's hear no more of you leaving, at least not until you've got someplace better'n Mrs. Peabody's rooming house to leave to."

What could Saltree do but thank him and work out his restlessness in learning to walk again. His leg had healed twisted and gaunt. It bore him, with the help of two sticks, and Dr. Coffin promised he'd be able to dispense with at least one of them in time. But it would keep him off a ship, except perhaps as purser or ship's cook—a comedown in the world, and no mistake.

As the spring days passed, despair gathered over Saltree like a thunderhead. To be a cripple, only twenty-five years old and condemned to live ashore like an old man--it hardly bore thinking on. Mornings, when he pulled his pants over his twisted leg and his shirt over arms wasted by fever, Saltree ground his teeth and envied Tom Harris from the bottom of his heart.

Mrs. Mayne did her best to amuse him, and Saltree knew she meant it kindly. But whenever he saw her approaching with her hands folded around a fat black Bible, such rage swelled his breast that he liked to have burst from the force of it. Her motherly smile, her knitting, the hint of a double chin overlapping her lace collar—all were wormwood and gall to him.

He didn't know why he should have taken so strongly against the captain's wife, who'd nursed him like a mother. All he knew was that he didn't like being beholden, and he didn't know how he could stop being beholden, and what with one thing and another, he began to look near as peaked as he had when he was knocking at death's door.

Mary Mayne told her husband she feared Mr. Saltree might be sickening again.

Captain Mayne shook his head. "I doubt it's his body, my dear. It's hard on the lad, being land-bound at his age with no prospect of shipping out again."

"You'd think he'd be glad to be safe ashore and quit of storms."

"Saltree, well, Saltree's a queer bird. A fine seaman, but a queer bird nonetheless. He likes climbing masts, and he fair loves storms. The higher the sea, the better he's pleased; and the nearer he comes to death, the more he laughs. Tom Harris and he were a fine pair of fools, racing up the mainmast when anybody with an eye in his head could see she was cracked. But if they hadn't managed to cut loose the topgallant and trim the storm sails, we'd've run slap bingo into Bermuda Island." Seth Mayne sighed. "A fine seaman. It won't be easy to find him a living won't be the death of him. I'll have to stir my stumps."

And stir his stumps the captain did. One fine June morning, he drove all the way to Portland to see a friend he thought might have some pull with the Lighthouse Board down Washington way. Two days later he returned like a cheerful gale, blowing down Main Street and into the garden where Saltree was hobbling back and forth between two fruit trees.

"Ahoy there, Mr. Saltree," shouted the captain. "Double grog for all hands and plum duff for dinner." He took the astonished

Saltree by the hand and pumped vigorously. "I've news for you—the best. It seems Elisha Tully, who keeps the Land's End Light, is wanting an assistant. I told my old shipmate Captain Drinkwater about you, leg and all, and the long and short of it is that you've the job if you want it. Nobody's saying it's a ship, but it's the sea and plenty to do in a storm." Captain Mayne clasped his hands behind him, very pleased with himself. "It's a good life by all accounts—time to think and time to work and a dry place to lay your head off-watch. When my sailing days are over, we might like to keep a light ourselves, Mrs. Mayne and I."

No more than a week later, Saltree sat on his sea chest on the public pier, waiting for Elisha Tully to row in from Land's End Rock to fetch him. Piled around him were boxes of provisions, a keg of rum, and a small wooden crate marked "Chimneys: Fragile." Round about midmorning, a fat, red-faced man in a torn navy blouse clambered up onto the pier. He stared at Saltree, his sea chest, his groceries, and his "Chimneys: Fragile," and tongued a wad of tobacco from one cheek to the other. "Name of Saltree?"

"Ayuh."

"Elisha Tully. Lighthouse keeper." Tully bent and heaved Saltree's sea chest onto his shoulder. "Dory's below."

They loaded the dory, Tully handing down crates and Saltree disposing them neatly along the gunwales. When all were stowed, Saltree sat himself down on the rower's bench.

Tully, still on dock, spat thoughtfully into the gray water. "Thought you'd had 'newmony."

"Ayuh," said Saltree, and unshipped the oars.

Tully coiled the bow line and climbed down into the stern. "Not much of a hand at nursemaiding," he remarked.

"No call for it."

"Sure?" Tully squinted doubtfully at him.

"Sure." Saltree pushed off from the pilings and turned the dory around with two economical strokes, then set off slow and steady. He was blown before he'd gone a hundred yards, and by the time they made Land's End Rock, he felt like he'd been flogged. But when they landed, he hoisted the "Chimneys: Fragile" onto his shoulder and carried it over the rocks, steadying himself with his stick. Twisted leg or no, he'd be damned before he gave reason to say that Joshua Saltree was a helpless cripple.

"Keepers used to live in the Light," said Tully. "There was a room below the watch room, all right and tight. But the new revolving gear took up the watch room, so two, three years back, they built the house." Tully glared for a second at the comfortable shingle house and the horse weather vane trotting bravely on the roof. "Good nor'easter'll snap it into matchsticks one day. Matchsticks!"

Tully lugged Saltree's sea chest inside and led him up a wooded ladder to the assistant keeper's room. Its window looked out onto the light tower and headland beyond. Saltree could see sky in plenty, but no water. He shrugged. He was a landsman now, not a sailor, and he'd best get used to the sight of land.

Downstairs again, Tully led Saltree through a short, roofed passage to the iron-bound door of the light itself. There were windows cut in the walls, but they were sealed tight with wooden shutters, and the tower was black as a ship's hold. Groping in the gloom for the rail, Saltree laid his hand on the pitted wall and brought it away chilled and glistening with damp.

Tully's boots clanged upward, and his voice echoed flatly between iron and stone.

"This here's the old tank, and this here above it's the watch room." Tully opened a manhole into a wilderness of tables and boxes and tools piled higgledy-piggledy on every flat surface. The watch room reeked as strongly as the forecastle of a bad ship, with an unfamiliar metallic tang mixed in with a general stink of sweat, wet wool, and neglect. Saltree frowned.

Tully spat in the direction of a spattered, stinking bucket. "It ain't so bad, really," he said defensively. "Needs a bit of tidying, is all. Man can't keep everything shipshape when he's all on his own like I been. I can put my hand on what I need when I need it." Poking through the flotsam, he found a bull's-eye lantern, lit it, and hung it from a hook on the wall, where it smoked sullenly.

"Extry chimneys're there and there. Wicks, scissors, tool case for the clockwork, clock oil, tripoli, spirits of wine, chamois cloths, brushes, oil carriers." His grubby forefinger stabbed into the shadows, seemingly at random. Saltree stood and watched until at last Tully said, "What the hell. You'll find all that when you need it. Light's up here."

Slowly, for his leg was aching fiercely, Saltree followed Tully's ample rump up another steep stair to a door leading onto a circular gallery. Tully slapped the inner wall. "Lantern base."

They mounted a last, flimsy curl of steps.

Remembering how the sun dazzled on the water, Saltree squinted cautiously before stepping into a warm, golden fog. He blinked. The whole dome was swathed in cloth: yellow shades blinded the windows; a linen cover shrouded the lens. With a professional twitch, Tully unveiled a thing like a glass cage, tiers of long, louver-like prisms held in place with iron clips. Even in the dim light, it sparkled.

"Sunlight's not good for her," instructed Tully, "So we keep her covered, days. She's all ready to go. Lighting her's nothing. Real work's in the morning. You'll see."

Saltree did see, the next morning and every morning after. Tully's idea of training was to have his assistant do all the cleaning, polishing, oiling, and adjusting while he, Tully, sat on a crate with his feet on another and nursed a mug of strong coffee laced with rum.

"Not a speck of dust, now," he'd say. "Dust is hell on clockwork. Dust'll throw off a fly-governor faster'n rust, and that's saying something. Have you oiled the carriage rollers yet? Well, hop to it, boy. It's gone twelve noon, and you ain't even drained the oil cistern."

Unless there was a storm, Tully insisted on keeping the night watch alone. He'd light the lantern in the evening and eat a plate of hardtack and boiled beef in the kitchen. Come about nine o'clock, he'd get up, scratch in his thick beard, and take the bull's-eye down from the chimney piece. "There's a wreck, I'll wake you," he'd say, and disappear aloft.

Alone, Saltree would smoke a pipe, maybe put an extra polish on a brass oilcan, darn a sock, look at a newspaper if they had one, and then go to his attic room and watch the light pulsing its forty-second beam, twenty-second eclipse. The light, gathered and refracted by those hundred carefully ground prisms, cut through the night like lightning—its illumination self-contained, unrevealing. Beam. Eclipse. Beam. Here are rocks, it seemed to say. Here is harbor. Beam. Eclipse. Beam. Here. Am. I.

Compared to being second mate on a clipper, it was an easy berth. No long watches, no standing perched on an icy yardarm hauling at wet canvas with numb and swollen hands. No captain to curse at him, no first mate to lord it over him, no seamen to get uppity. No yarns, no songs, no jigs amidships. An easy berth. But a lonely one.

In October a carrier pigeon brought the news that the *White Goddess* had been cleared for San Francisco, and that Captain Mayne sent his kind regards and was counting on seeing Mr. Saltree and his light again sometime before midsummer. Though as a rule he wasn't a drinking man, Saltree locked himself in his attic that night with a blanket thrown over the window and dined on Tully's rum. He drank until his head spun and his leg no longer pained him. He drank until he liked to have drowned, but the liquor, whistling in his ears like wind in the rigging, could not drown the pain of the *Goddess* skimming the wave crests without him.

By November, Saltree had polished every oil carrier, honed every knife and scissors blade, arranged all the tools and glass chimneys in gleaming ordered rows, and generally overhauled the watch room until everything about it was entirely shipshape and Bristol fashion. The days were dull, though they went by quickly enough. Lighthouses take a good deal of keeping, what with swabbing the lens with spirits of wine, greasing the clockwork of the turning mechanism, dusting and trimming and winding all the gears and wicks, rollers and fittings of brass and iron that together create the forty-second beam and twenty-second eclipse.

But the nights were long and filled with dreams.

No sooner did Saltree lay his head on his pillow than he was aloft on the rigging of the *White Goddess* or striding down her deck. His legs were strong, and under his bare brown feet, the timbers shone clean and white as flax. His watch—the larboard watch—set up rigging, tarred down spars. The sun was warm on his shoulders. Gulls and terns wheeled in the wide sky, blue, then gray, then black with clouds foaming and churning like the black water that licked at the crosstrees. Rope between his hands, saltwater to his waist, clutching his feet, chilling his bones, his heart pounding fast and hard, Tom Harris beside him, grinning wider and wider until his whole face was teeth and bone and wisps of rotted hair.

Other dreams rang with cries of "Man overboard!" and Captain Mayne at the leeward rail, pointing down at the heaving waves. "For God's sake, man. He saved your life!" Making for the rail, laboring on one leg, lurching. Tom below, laughing, and in his arms the Goddess, carved lips parted and smiling. Wood and living flesh entwined, they rolled upon the swell like sleeping birds, then she drew Tom down, down below the black water.

Saltree awoke from these dreams half strangled with unuttered shouts. He'd rub the sweat from his face, then sit at the edge of his bed and watch the light's signal pattern. beam. Eclipse. Beam. Eclipse. Forty seconds' light. Twenty seconds' dark. Steady, sure as a heartbeat. The Land's End Light.

The first day of the New Year, Tully went ashore to buy provisions. The sky threatened snow, but they were down to their last mouthful of salt beef and moldy bread, so off he sculled. He left just after daybreak, in plenty of time to buy what was needful, raise a tankard or three at the Mermaid's Tale, and row back to the Rock again before dark.

Midafternoon, the wind rose and the sea with it. It grew bitter cold and Saltree stopped puttering with the clockwork to climb out on the parapet and rub the windows with glycerin and spirits of wine to keep them from icing over. Before he was half done, heavy flakes of snow began to slap at his cheeks. Tully'd be a fool to row back in this, when there was beer and company and a warm bed at the Tale.

Tully always kept a hammock rigged in the watchroom, and about midnight, Saltree climbed into it. The storm had settled into a steady blow, nothing that should give any trouble to a captain worth his brandy. He couldn't sleep, of course, but he had to rest his leg, which was aching like billy hell from the cold. In an hour or so, he'd get up and rewind the fog bell.

Within the granite tower, the sound of the storm was muted to a whistle and a far grumble of breaking waves. Saltree climbed the mainmast in a brisk wind with all the canvas shown. Saint Elmo's fire danced ghostly on the crosstrees, and a flight of petrels canted and mewed above the skysail. Tom Harris clung one-handed to the topgallant yard.

"Land ho!" he cried, and pointed into the gathering clouds. A cheer below, and all the sails bellied full as the *Goddess* rose above the swell and flew over the wave-crest like a skipped stone. It was snowing now, with rocks ahead, and nothing to say exactly where. Perched among the shrouds, Saltree squinted into the blizzard. Where were the lights? Every coast had lights. Did the snow hide them? Where were the fog bells? And why was Captain Mayne running blind before a gale into land?

A crash and a shudder spilled Saltree from his hammock, dazed and half convinced he was still aboard the *Goddess* and she was breaking up on the rocks of some unknown coast. The waves made a deafening roar, and a cold wind flooded down the turret stairs. He shivered like a beaten dog and blinked. Was that snow, coming down inside the tower? And what was that hullabaloo?

A good sailor leaps to what needs doing, and Saltree leaped now, swarming up the stairs like rigging. Wind and snow eddied in the dome, blinding white, then ghostly as the lens turned slowly on its carriage. It took Saltree a full two cycles of beam and eclipse to see the broken pane of glass and the bird that had broken it flapping through the shards.

"Bloody stupid bird," Saltree muttered, and lunged. The bird was farther away than he'd thought, but his hand closed on one powerfully flailing wing. It whipped its head around to peck at him with a bill like a marlinespike, and he ducked. Big gull, he thought. Looks like—the wing jerked from his grasp—an albatross.

"Devil take it!" It was almost a prayer. There were tales of shipwreck and sudden death caused by killing the bird that brought fair winds and guided ships blown off course to safe harbors. Saltree knew that the greater part of theses tales were nothing but so much rope yarn spun on the off-watch by bored seamen, but there was no denying that albatross were uncanny birds. He had seen them asleep on the water off Cape Horn, riding the swells from crest to trough. He had seen them perched on the masthead, so white in the sun that they seemed lit from within. The sight of this one, bedraggled and blood-splattered, frightened him more than a twenty-foot wave.

While Saltree hung fire, the albatross flapped and heaved its way inside the glass cage of the lens and up onto the lantern base. Briefly, it mantled with the light behind it, and the lens distorted it into a giant thing with wings like sails and an eye like the moon in eclipse.

Gears ground. The carriage, slowed, strained; and the albatross, screaming, battered its wings. A chimney broke. One wick went out; the others flickered wildly. Saltree found the trimming knife and crawled toward the bird. He was a lighthouse keeper now, he told himself, and his light was threatened. It didn't matter whether a gull or an albatross or a mermaid or King Neptune himself was sitting in that lantern. It didn't belong there, and it was up to him, Saltree, to get it out.

Saltree crooked one arm across his face to protect his eyes, and wormed his way into the lens.

Inside was a second storm of feathers and blood. The albatross's feet were entangled in the turning mechanism, and it attacked the clockwork with wings and darting beak. Shadows and light bewildered Saltree's eyes until he could have sworn that a thousand albatross were trapped in the prisms. He thrust blindly with the knife. A final scream, a convulsive flutter. The light flared, and a thousand albatrosses scattered into the snowy darkness.

The last wick went out.

Moving painfully, Saltree crawled out of the lantern and toward the door, cursing himself for not bringing up the extra lamp. It should have been instinctive, like carrying rope up the rigging. Crews were counting on him: it took no time at all for a ship to run aground.

Downstairs at last, Saltree snatched up an extra lantern, lit it with trembling hands, settled the chimney on it, and pulled himself up the stairs again, hop-and-heave as fast as he could go. It was only a small flame under a glass chimney, hardly bright enough to reach across the dome. But when he slid it into the empty holder, a clear, strong beam leaped into the darkness.

Saltree sighed in relief and turned his attention to the dead albatross. Its wings were singed and bloody, tattered as an old shawl. Carefully, so as not to endanger the lamp, he disentangled the yellow legs from the clockwork. They were thoroughly caught in the gears, and his sweater and hands were slimy with blood before he worked the bird free. He dragged it out of the lens, hoisted it up into his arms, and limped to the window with its feathers trailing against his knees. Under his cold fingers, the body was warm and yielding. Saltree shuddered and threw it from him, out the broken window and into the treacherous wind.

Clearing blood and feathers from the clockwork and the lens took him the rest of the night. Just before dawn, the wind dropped to nothing, but the snow continued heavy and the seas rough. Tully'd not come back today.

Alone, Saltree tacked in a temporary window, cleaned as much of the apparatus as he could without dismounting the frame, and oiled the carriage so it could turn again. He drove himself to wrench the heavy gears apart, strained his back and his legs manhandling wooden boards up the narrow stair. If he hadn't fallen asleep, if he'd killed the albatross right off, then the light wouldn't have gone out. Sure, there was no harm done this time. But what if the *Goddess* had been out there? What if other keepers were as careless, as unfit, as he?

By nightfall, Saltree was wet through and more dog-tired than he'd ever been on ship. He knew he'd have to spend another night in the watch room, but he thought he'd get himself a dry shirt. Then, once he got to his attic room, he thought he'd change his socks. He took a pair from the sea chest, sat on the edge of the bed to put them on, leaned wearily against the wall. He frowned. What if the *Goddess* had been out there?

He woke after moonset, feeling oddly peaceful. From the sound of the waves on the rocks, it was ebb tide, with a light sea running. He was lying on the bed, fully clothed. "Son of a bitch," he said. But his guilt was as dead as the albatross. His stolen sleep had been deep and dreamless.

A scrape, like a heavy object being dragged over the roof, brought Saltree upright. Silence. The window was luminous with the snow light and the lantern's intermittent dazzle. He shrugged. Maybe, as long as he was awake, he'd best get to the tower. He swung his legs to the floor. Between one flash and the next, he caught an odd shadow drifting down the window.

Saltree blinked. Too slow for a gull—and even an albatross wasn't that big. Another—a strange shape. Long, heavy, with strange knots and bulges. Another.

As a fourth shadow swam across the window, Saltree limped painfully across the rough planks. His hands met and clutched the window frame; his face approached the glass. Eclipse: he saw his own reflection staring back at him out of shadowed eyes. Beam: his gaze focused on the dome.

Figureheads: dripping seaweed, some far gone in decay, others still bright with paint. They clustered around the lantern like wingless and awkward moths, yearning toward the light. Some were headless, and stretched only their long necks, questing eyelessly for comfort. Some were snapped off at the waist. Most pathetic of all were the ones that retained their faces, for they were openmouthed, drowned, and their wooden eyes stared at the light with a dreadful and accusing intelligence.

One of these figureheads was not so sea-changed as the rest. She hovered between Saltree and the lantern so that at first he saw only her back and the dirty front of her clothes. Then she drifted outside the crowding school of figureheads and showed Saltree her profile. Straight nose; high, round, naked breasts: the *White Goddess.*

There was a swath of seaweed draped around her shoulders and tossed across her throat like a bedraggled feather boa, which gave her a rakish look, like a dockside whore. Saltree's hands tightened on the window frame. The *Goddess* drifted farther around, and he saw that half her wooden head had been sheared away, one breast and shoulder splintered.

Saltree threw open the sash and leaned far out the window. "Goddess!" he shouted, and held out his hand to her.

The *White Goddess* floated nearer, bobbing with a long swell. Dark water dripped from her like blood. Her eye glittered wetly. Her hand that had held back the carved folds of her drapery released them and reached for him.

Beautiful. She was so beautiful, and as she drew near Saltree, she brought with her the smells of salt and sun-warmed tar and varnish and newly scrubbed decks. His breath came fast; his fingers trembled.

The revolving lens flickered slowly. Forty-second beam: twenty-second eclipse. The figurehead hovered just out of his reach, stretching her fingers to him.

Saltree flung his good leg over the sill, braced the other against his sea chest, and hung from the sash by the length of his arm.

Beam. Eclipse. Beam.

An inch, no more, separated their hands. Eclipse. In the brief darkness, Saltree touched the slick coolness of varnished wood. Beam. His fingers closed on hers, and his muscles strained to pull her into his arms.

Eclipse. Beam. Eclipse.

She was his now, wild sea smell, smooth breasts and all, clinging to his neck like kelp and smiling into his eyes. He felt her body yield to his hands like flesh, but cold, so cold. Entwined, buoyant as gulls, they rolled upon the waves, sliding from crest to trough out to the open sea. They sailed beyond the breakers to black water, and then she drew him down with her, gently down to her cold ocean bed.

THE PARWAT RUBY

Whether the disaster of the Parwat Ruby would have taken place if Sir Alvord Basingstoke had not married Margaret Kennedy is a matter of conjecture. Given his character, Sir Alvord would undoubtedly have married a woman like Margaret even if Margaret herself had never been born. He was a gentle man, slow to talk, devoted to solitude—in short, the natural mate of a woman who talked a great deal and loved society.

Margaret Kennedy had been much courted in her youth, being not only mistress of three thousand pounds a year, but lively and clever and very well dressed as well. Over time she grew domineering and unpleasant, but as Sir Alvord spent the best part of the next thirty years exploring uncharted wildernesses, it is likely that he did not notice. When ebbing vital forces put a period to his travels, Lady Glencora Palliser prophesied a speedy separation. But months passed, and still the reunited couple showed every sign of mutual affection, demonstrating that even the most skillfull hunters of human weakness must sometimes draw a blank.

A certain coolness having arisen between Mrs. Mildmay and Lady Basingstoke, Mrs. Mildmay had seen little of her brother since his last journey abroad. Consequently, she was much astonished, one evening as the Season began, to hear her maid announce the name of Sir Alvord Basingstoke. Althought it was time to be thinking of changing for supper, she had him shown into her sitting room, and received him with a sisterly embrace.

"So here you are, Alvord," she said. "Handsome as ever, I see." It had been a schoolroom joke that they looked very alike, although the heavy jaw and pronounced nose that made the brother a handsome man kept the sister from being considered anything but plain.

He pressed her hands and put her from him. "I have something very particular to say to you, Caroline. You are my only sister—indeed, my only living blood relation—and I am an old man."

Somewhat distressed by this greeting, Mrs. Mildmay bade her brother sit and indicated her readiness to hear what he had to tell her, but he only sighed heavily and rubbed his forehead with his right hand, which was decorated with a ring set with a large cabochon ruby. The ring was familiar to her, as much a part of Sir Alvord as his pale blue eyes and his indifferently tailored coats. He had brought the stone back from a journey to Ceylon in his youth and it had never left his hand since. Massy as it was, it had always looked perfectly at home on his broad hand, but now it hung and turned loosely on his finger.

The white star that lived in its depths slid and winked, capturing Mrs. Mildmay's eye and attention so fully that when Sir Alvord spoke, she was forced to beg him to repeat his words.

"It's this ring of mine, Caroline," said Sir Alvord patiently. "It's more than a trinket."

"Indeed it is, Brother. I've never seen such a fine stone."

"A fine stone indeed. Your true, clear star is very rare and very precious in a ruby of this size. But that is not what I meant. There is a history attached to this ring, and a responsibility."

He seemed to experience some difficulty in continuing, a difficulty not remarkable in a man who all his life had been accustomed to let first his mother and then his wife speak for him. Mrs. Mildmay sat quietly until he should find words.

"This is unexpectedly difficult," he said at length.

Mrs. Mildmay looked down at her hands. "I have often wished us better friends," she said.

"I have wished the same. But my wife had a claim upon my loyalty."

Mrs. Mildmay flushed and would have retorted that she hoped that his sister had at least an equal claim, but he held up his hand to forestall her, his ruby glowing as the star caught the afternoon sun.

He continued, "I have not come to quarrel with you. Margaret has been a good wife to me. However, I don't mean for her to have this ring. I had hoped to leave it to a son of mine"—here he sighed once again—"but that was not to be. I have it in my mind to put in my Will that you're to have it when I die, and that it must pass to Wilson after you." Wilson was Mrs. Mildmay's oldest son, a likely young man of four-and-twenty.

Mrs. Mildmay, much moved, reached out and patted her brother's hand. "There's no need to be talking of wills and dying, Brother. I've no doubt you'll see out your century with ease."

He shook his head heavily. "I will not see out the year. No, Caroline, don't argue with me. The ring must stay in the family." He rose slowly and tottered as he stood and Mrs. Mildmay sprang to her feet to steady him. Once more he kissed her cheek. "God bless you, Caroline. I don't suppose I'll see you again."

After this conversation, Mrs. Mildmay was not much amazed when, not three days later, she received word that Sir Alvord had suffered an apoplectic fit. At first, his life was despaired of, and even when it seemed sure he would live, he could no longer move his arms or legs, but must be fed and turned and bathed like an infant. In this great exigency, Lady Basingstoke displayed all the careful tenderness that could be hoped from a loving wife and, although she was herself not a young woman, undertook the entire burden of his nursing. To be sure, there were nurses hired to tend him, but as Lady Basingstoke considered them all worthless baggages, she would not leave any of them alone with him for more than a few moments. So it was that when Mrs. Mildmay called to inquire after her brother's health, Lady Basingstoke did not come down to her, but received her in Sir Alvord's dressing room with the communicating door ajar.

She was seated in a shabby wing-chair, her head inclined upon her hand in an attitude eloquent of the most complete dejection, but she lifted her head at Mrs. Mildmay's entrance and waved her to a chair. "Please forgive me not rising to greet you, dear Caroline," she said. "I am utterly prostrate, as you see. He had a very bad night, and this morning was discovered to be unable to speak. Sir Omicron Pie has warned me to prepare myself for the worst."

Mrs. Mildmay may have considered her brother's wife a harpy, but it would be a harder heart than hers to have denied Lady Basingstoke a sister's comfort at such a time. "My dear Margaret," she said. "I am so very sorry. You must let me know if there is anything I may do to help you. Sit with Alvord, perhaps, so that you can take some rest?"

"No, no. You are too kind, Caroline, but no. Dear Alvord will suffer no one about him but me." Her voice faltered and she raised her hand to her eyes, as though to hide springing tears. The gesture reminded Mrs. Mildmay irresistibly of her brother's when he had come to call, the more so that it displayed Lady Basingstoke's hand, well kept and very large for a woman, just now made to look delicate by a great gold ring set with a single large, red stone: the Parwat Ruby.

"I beg your pardon, Margaret," said Mrs. Mildmay, "but is that not Alvord's ring?"

The question caused Lady Basingstoke to have recourse to her handkerchief, and it was not until she had composed herself that she said, "He gave it to me last night. It was as though he knew he'd soon be beyond speech, for he took it from his finger and put it upon mine, saying that it was the dearest wish of his heart to see it always upon my hand. It is, of course, far too big; but I have tied it on with a bit of cotton, which I trust will hold it until I can bear to be parted with it long enough to have it made to fit."

"How very touching," said Mrs. Mildmay. There was nothing so very exceptionable in her tone, but Lady Basingstoke absolutely frowned at her and requested her to explain what she meant.

"Only that dear Alvord was not commonly so fluent in his speech."

"I think, dear Mrs. Mildmay, that you are hardly qualified to have an opinion," said Lady Basingstoke, "considering that you have hardly spoken to him twice in twenty years. I assure you it took place just as I have told you."

"No doubt," answered Mrs. Mildmay, and took her leave not many minutes afterwards. It is perhaps not necessary to say that Mrs. Mildmay had every doubt as to the accuracy of Lady Basingstoke's recollection, but she could hardly say so. An evening call is not a Will, after all, and her brother had every right to change his mind as to the distribution of his own property.

Now Lady Basingstoke was even more indispensable to Sir Alvord than when he had been merely bed-bound, for she was the only one who could make shift to understand his gruntings and gesturings and bring him a little ease. In fact, she dispensed with the nurses altogether and snatched her rest when she might upon a trundle bed, for in her absence he would become unbearably agitated. Sir Omicron Pie continued to call each morning, but he could do nothing above prescribing a calming draught. Given the tenor of her last visit, Mrs. Mildmay was not surprised when the butler turned her from the door when next she came to call. But she was much astonished the following morning, when she read the notice of Sir Alvord Basingstoke's death in *The Times.*

"It's a bad business," she exclaimed to her husband, who was enjoying the text of Mr. Gresham's latest speech. "It's a bad business when a sister must read of her brother's passing in the public press."

"Not at all, my dear. Devoted wife, prostrate widow. Likely it slipped her mind. Here's Gresham rabbitting on about the poor again, as if he could do anything, with his party feeling as it does about taxes. It's a crime, that's what it is. A crime and a sin."

"I daresay, Quintus, but do pay attention. When I called yesterday afternoon, the curtains were not drawn, there was no crepe on the knocker, and the butler said only that his mistress was not at home to visitors."

"Man wasn't dead yet," said Mr. Mildmay reasonably.

"Nonsense," said his wife. "I defy even the most energetic widow to get a notice of death in *The Times* in anything under a day, and if he were alive when I called, she could have had only a few hours. I call it a bad business."

"Odd, anyway," said Mr. Mildmay. "Wonder if he left you anything?"

"As if I cared about that! He did mention his ruby ring to me when last I saw him, but I doubt that anything will come of it."

Mr. Mildmay put down his paper. "His ruby, eh? Worth a good few hundred pounds, I'd think. The ruby would be worth having indeed."

"The ring may be worth what it will, Quintus. My point is that Alvord expressed the wish that it remain in the family, and yet I saw it upon Lady Basingstoke's hand."

"Woman's his wife, Caroline. A wife is part of a man's family, I hope."

"Not when she's a widow, Quintus, for she may then marry again and take her husband's property into another man's family."

"Then we must hope that your brother put the thing down in his Will." Mr. Mildmay took up his paper again to show that the subject was closed, firing as he did so a warning shot around its crackling edges: "Won't look well to make a fuss, Caroline."

Mrs. Mildmay so far agreed with her husband that she was able to pay her condolence call and support the grieving widow at Sir Alvord's funeral without adverting to the subject of Sir Alvord's last visit. Yet as she stood next to Lady Basingstoke at the graveside, she could not suppress a shudder at the sight of the Parwat Ruby glowing balefully against the deep black of the widow's wash-leather gloves. She could not think it well done of Margaret to have worn it, hoping only that her grief had blinded her to the impropriety of flaunting a ruby at a funeral. Yet, as the first shovelfuls of dirt fell upon the casket, Mrs. Mildmay could have sworn that the widow was smiling.

"But she was heavily veiled," exclaimed her bosom friend Lady Fitzaskerly when Mrs. Mildmay had unburdened herself of her righteous anger.

"Nonetheless," said Mrs. Mildmay. "You know what she looks like."

"A horse in a flaxen wig," replied Lady Fitzaskerly, who disliked Lady Basingstoke as heartily as the most exacting friend could wish.

"Precisely. And the heaviest veil to be purchased at Liberty's would be insufficient to hide the most subtle of her expressions. The woman was grinning like an ape. And there was no mention of the ring in the Will—not a single word, though many of his collections are dispersed and the entire contents of his library are to be given to his club."

"Perhaps he fell ill before the lawyer might be called."

"Perhaps. And perhaps he didn't. I thought Mr. Chess wished to speak to me when the document had been read, but Lady Basingstoke entirely engaged his attention. And now here is a note from Mr. Chess in the first mail this morning, begging me to receive him at four this very afternoon. What do you think of that?"

Lady Fitzaskerly did not know what to think, but she found the whole matter so very interesting that she could not forbear mentioning it to Lady Glencora Palliser when next she had occasion to call upon her. Lady Glen was sitting, as she often was, with Madam Max Goesler of Park Lane.

"Why, it's just like the Eustace diamonds!" Lady Glencora exclaimed when Lady Fitzaskerly had done. "You remember the fuss, when that silly girl Lizzie Eustace stole her own diamonds to keep them from her husband's family?"

"It's not so very much like it, not to my mind," said Madam Max. "No one has stolen anything, so far as I can tell. A gentleman in his dotage has changed his mind about the disposition of his personal property and created an unpleasantness."

"Well, I think Mrs. Mildmay is hardly used in the matter."

"Consider, my dear. Lady Basingstoke is his widow. She cared for him in his last illness and shared his interests."

"His interests!" Lady Glencora was scornful. "We best not inquire too closely into his interests, if all I hear be true."

"Surely, Lady Glen, you can't believe he was a wizard," exclaimed Lady Fitzaskerly. "Why, he wasn't even interested in politics."

"Well, he was a member of the Magus," said Lady Glen. "And he left all his books to his club. What else am I to believe?"

"If he was a wizard," said Lady Fitzaskerly, "he was a decidedly odd one."

"Perhaps he wasn't, then," Lady Glen said. "Wizards like nothing better than talking, and they seldom travel. Well, how could they, being subject to seasickness as they are? Sir Alvord barely said a word in company, and he was forever in some foreign land or another."

"Be that as it may," said Madam Max. "If he was a wizard, it is foolhardy at best for Lady Basingstoke to keep his ring if he wished it to go elsewhere."

"No doubt," said Lady Fitzaskerly dryly. "But I knew Margaret Kennedy at school. She was the sort of girl who always ate too many cream buns, even though she was invariably sick after."

So Mrs. Mildmay had her partisans among the most highly placed persons in the land—a fact that might have brought her some comfort as she sat listening to her brother's lawyer set forth his dilemma in her drawing room. Mr. Chess was a man of substance, silver-haired and solid as an Irish hound, with something of a hound's roughness of coat and honesty of spirit, which had brought him to confess to Mrs. Mildmay that he had misplaced the most recent codicil to her brother's Will.

"It was the day he was taken ill, you know, or perhaps a day or two before that. He came by my chambers without the least notice, and insisted upon having it drawn up then and there and witnessed by two clerks. It described the ring most particularly—'The stone called the Parwat Ruby, and the Ring in which it is set, the bezel two Wings of gold tapering into the Shank'—and gave it to you for your lifetime and to your son Wilson on your death, with the testator's recommendation that neither ring nor stone be allowed to pass out of the hands of his descendants. He insisted on the exact wording."

"And you said that the codicil was not in the document box when you removed the Will to read it?"

"The document box was quite empty, Mrs. Mildmay, save for the Will itself, some few papers pertaining to his investments, and a quantity of fine dust. Nevertheless, knowing his wishes in the matter, I did not think it wise to drop the matter without consulting Lady Basingstoke."

"And Lady Basingstoke laughed in your face," said Mrs. Mildmay.

"I only wish she had done something so relatively predictable." Mr. Chess extracted his handkerchief from his pocket and wiped his forehead with it. "She heard me out quietly, then gave me to understand that the ring would have to be cut from her hand before she'd give it up. Furthermore, she impugned my memory, my competence as a lawyer, even my motives in coming to see her, and all in such a tone of voice as I hope never in my life to hear again."

"It was doubtless very rude of her," said Mrs. Mildmay soothingly.

"Rude!" Mr. Chess gave his neck a surreptitious dab. "She was most intemperate. If she were not very recently widowed, I would question her sanity."

"And the ring?"

"Unless the codicil should come to light, the ring is hers, along with all her husband's chattels and possessions not otherwise disposed of. We might file a case in Chancery on the basis of my recollection of the afternoon call, supported by affidavits from my two clerks who witnessed the document, but it would almost certainly cost more than the ring is worth, and success is by no means sure."

Mrs. Mildmay thought for a moment, than gave a decided nod. "I'll let it go, then. It's only a ring, after all. May she have joy of it, poor woman."

And there the matter would have rested had it not been for Lady Basingstoke herself, who, some two weeks after her husband's death, wrote to Caroline Mildmay requiring her attendance in Grosvenor Square. *You know I would come to you if I might,* she wrote, *but I am grown so ill that I cannot stir a foot abroad.*

"I shouldn't go," said Mr. Mildmay when his wife showed him Lady Basingstoke's letter. "You owe her nothing and she'll only be unpleasant."

"I owe her kindness as my brother's widow, and if she is unpleasant, I need not prolong my visit."

Mr. Mildmay smiled knowingly upon his wife. "I know how it is, Caroline. You're eaten up with curiosity what she could have to say to you. Wild horses would not keep you from her, were she five times worse than she is."

"I don't expect to find her so ill as all that," said Mrs. Mildmay provokingly. But she did not deny her husband's allegation, nor, in good conscience, could she. Indeed, she did not think Lady Basingstoke likely to be ill at all. But when she was shown into the parlor where Lady Basingstoke was laid down upon a sofa with a blanket over her feet, Mrs. Mildmay observed that she looked withered and drawn, with the bones of her cheeks staring out through her skin and great dark smudges beneath her eyes, which seemed to have retreated under her brows. The Parwat Ruby glowed like a live coal on her hand.

She was attended by ferrety person with a wealth of black hair, who was introduced to Mrs. Mildmay as Dr. Drago, an Italian gentleman learned in the study of medicine and the arcane arts.

"Dr. Drago has been invaluable to me," said Lady Basingstoke, and held out her hand, which he kissed with great grace; though it seemed to Mrs. Mildmay, looking on with some disgust, that the salute was bestowed rather upon the Parwat Ruby than on the gaunt hand that bore it. "It is at his suggestion, in fact, that I called you here, Caroline. You know, of course, that dear Alvord was a great wizard?"

Mrs. Mildmay drew off her gloves to cover her confusion. "A wizard, Margaret?"

"I think I spoke clearly. Are you going to pretend that you don't believe in wizards when the country is ruled by them? Why, half the members of the House of Lords, two-thirds of the Cabinet, and the Prime Minister himself are members of the Magus!"

"I hardly know what I do believe, Margaret."

"There was never wizard living as powerful as Alvord, and it was all the ruby, Caroline, the ruby."

"The ruby?" Mrs. Mildmay faltered, convinced that Lady Basingstoke's complaint was more serious than a mere perturbation of the spirit. Alvord a wizard! What would the woman say next?

Lady Basingstoke plucked angrily at the fringe of her shawl. "Why do you mock me, Caroline? You must know what I mean. Alvord must have spoken to you. Why else would he have called on you so soon before he fell ill?"

"I assure you, Margaret, that Alvord told me nothing. Only . . . ."

Lady Basingstoke leaned forward, a horrid avidity suffusing her countenance. "Only what, dear Caroline? It is of the utmost importance that you tell me every word."

"I'm afraid it must cause you some distress."

The Italian gentleman added his voice to Lady Basingstoke's, and reluctantly Mrs. Mildmay recounted her conversation with Sir Alvord substantially as it has been recorded here, noting Lady Basingstoke's almost comical expression of malicious triumph when Caroline mentioned her brother's intention to change his will. When she had made an end, Lady Basingstoke turned to the Italian gentleman and burst out, "Is there anything there, Drago? Is she telling the truth?"

"As to that, gracious lady, I cannot say without subjecting the lady to certain tests."

He smiled beguilingly at Mrs. Mildmay as he spoke, as if proposing a rare treat. Mrs. Mildmay was not to be beguiled. "Tests!" she exclaimed. "Are you both mad?"

Both Lady Basingstoke and the Italian gentleman ignored her. "Your husband certainly meant his sister to have the ring, lady, and I do not think he told her why."

"Well, I think he did. I think he told her all about it, and she's come here to frighten me out of it. Well, I won't frighten, do you hear? I won't frighten and I won't give up the Parwat Ruby. It's going to make me great, isn't it, Abbadelli? Greater than Mr. Gresham, greater than the Queen herself, and once I learn its secret, the first thing I shall do is destroy you, Caroline Mildmay!"

With every word of this extraordinary speech, Lady Basingstoke's voice rose, until at last she was all but screaming at her hapless sister-in-law, at the same time rising from her sofa and menacing her with such energy that Mrs. Mildmay thought it best to take her leave.

After such an interview, Mrs. Mildmay did not, of course, call in Grosvenor Place again. Nor did she ever tell a soul, saving only her husband, what had passed between her and her sister-in-law. She did, however, hear what the world had to say concerning Lady Basingstoke's subsequent behavior. For that lady, far from hiding herself in the seclusion expected of a widow, began to go abroad in the world.

"I saw her in Hyde Park, my dear, astride her horse, if you please. I would not have credited it had I not seen it with my own eyes. And looking quite brown and dried-up, for all the world like a farm wife, and so hideously plain you'd think that horrid Darwin justified in declaring us all the grandchildren of apes."

"Lady Glencora!" Madam Max admonished her, with a glance at Mrs. Mildmay.

Lady Glencora was at once contrite. "Oh, Mrs. Mildmay, I beg your pardon to speak so of a close connection, but surely the woman is not mistress of herself, to be riding astride in the company of a gentleman in the most appalling hat."

"Dr. Drago," murmured Mrs. Mildmay.

"He might be the Grand Cham of Arabia if he chose; it still wouldn't be proper. And it is common knowledge that her servants have left her without notice, and Lizzie Berry says her new bootboy tells such blood-curdling stories of Lady Basingstoke's household that the servants all suffer from nightmares."

Feeling Lady Glencora's curious eyes upon her, Mrs. Mildmay schooled her features to gentle dismay. "How difficult for Lady Berry," was all she said, but her heart burned within her, and she thought of Lady Basingstoke's astonishing remark, that England was governed by wizards. Lady Glencora's husband, Plantagenet Palliser, was said to be performing miracles as Chancellor of the Exchequer. Were they miracles indeed? Did Lady Glencora think she knew, or was she deriving amusement from her ignorance? Prey to melancholy reflections, Mrs. Mildmay brought her visit to an end as soon as she might do so without betraying the agitation the conversation had caused her, and went home again wishing that Alvord had seen fit to take her more fully into his confidence.

A month passed. The Season's round of balls and card parties was enlivened by stories of Lady Basingstoke's eccentricities, which grew wilder with each telling. Lady Basingstoke had thrown scones at the waiter at Liberty's Tea Room; Lady Basingstoke had snatched a fruit-woman's basket of apples and run away with it; Lady Basingstoke had bitten a policeman on the arm. Mrs. Mildmay was privately mortified by her sister-in-law's behavior, and took full advantage of her own state of mourning to regret all invitations that might bring her into Lady Basingstoke's erratic orbit. But she could not avoid the morning-calls of ladies eager to commiserate and analyze, nor the occasional glimpse of her brother's widow, gaunt, unkempt, and draped in black, dragging on Dr. Drago's arm as if it were all that kept her upright.

Then, as suddenly as she'd emerged, Lady Basingstoke disappeared once again into Grosvenor Place. Society looked elsewhere for its amusement, and as the Season wore on, Mrs. Mildmay ventured to hope that she had heard the end of the matter. In mid July, her hope was frustrated by Mr. Chess, who called upon her once again, this time accompanied by one of his clerks.

"I don't know how sufficiently to beg your pardon," Mr. Chess told her, his honest hound's eyes dark with distress.

"It wasn't Mr. Chess's fault, madam," his clerk said. "It was all mine. If you intend to go to law with someone, it'll have to be me, and I won't contest the charge, indeed I won't."

"Let us have no talk of going to law," said Mrs. Mildmay. "Please, tell me what has happened."

And so the unhappy story came out. Apparently, the afternoon of the day upon which Sir Alvord had changed his Will, he had returned to Mr. Chess's chambers and left in the possession of the clerk (whose name was Mr. Rattler) a thick packet, with instructions that it be conveyed to Mrs. Mildmay as soon as possible.

"But it wasn't possible, not if it were ever so, not with the Queen vs. Phineas Finn coming up to trial, and me run clear off my feet until ten of the clock. So I took it home so as to be sure and deliver it next morning on my way to Chambers, and my old mother was taken ill in the night, and that's the last I thought of the packet until I was sorting through things yesterday—for she died of her illness, I grieve to say, and the house is to be sold—and found it, dropped behind the bootrack."

The poor man looked so close to tears that Mrs. Mildmay was moved to give him her full forgiveness. "I have the packet in my hand now, after all, and we must hope that there's not too much harm done. Why don't you wait in the library while I read it, Mr. Chess, in case there is something in it I don't understand?"

"Certainly, Mrs. Mildmay," said Mr. Chess, and withdrew, herding the wretched clerk before him.

Now, if the reader be tempted, like Mrs. Mildmay, to pity Mr. Rattler, the reader may put his mind at ease. Mr. Rattler, less honest than provident, was not to be pitied; for upon discovering Sir Alvord's packet behind the bootrack, he had lifted its seal with the aid of a heated knife, read it through, whistled thoughtfully, and immediately set himself to copy it all over. It was a long document, and the task took him the better part of the night, but his labor was well paid, for he sold the copy to one of the more sensational papers for a sum sufficient to buy passage to America, where we may only hope he found honest employment. Mr. Rattler's industry, in the meantime, has relieved the present writer of reproducing the whole text of Sir Alvord's letter to his sister, as the document was published in full soon after the Grosvenor Place Affair became public, and may be read by anyone who cares to ask for the July ___ edition of *The People's Banner.*

In brief, the letter recounted how, not long after his marriage to Margaret Kennedy, Sir Alvord Basingstoke had taken himself off to Ceylon, where he had wandered, lost in impenetrable forests, for nearly two years. His adventures in this period were numerous, but in the letter, he restricted himself to the month he spent with a tribe whose god was an idol in the shape of a great ape carved of wood and inlaid with gold and precious stones.

> *Its teeth were pearls, perfectly matched, the largest I have ever seen, and it was crowned with beaten gold set, in the Eastern manner, with rough-cut sapphires, emeralds, and rubies. But its chiefest glory were its eyes, that were perfectly matched cabochon rubies of great size, each imprisoning a perfect, clear, bright star that gave the creature an air of malevolent intelligence. I chaffered with the king of those people, who was a wise and far-sighted woman, and brought her to understand that it would be much to her advantage to accept from me half the arms and ammunition I had brought with me, along with certain cantrips I had learned of a warrior-wizard in Katmandu. In exchange for all this, which would almost certainly ensure her victory over some two or three neighboring tribes, I would receive the left eye of the ape-god.*
>
> *The gift came hedged around with warnings and restrictions, the greater part of which I have been able to circumvent or neutralize. I could do little, however, with the fundamental nature of the stone, which is likely to manifest itself in the form of a dreadful curse. I am exempt from this curse, as are all persons related to me by blood. But anyone else who wears it upon his finger, be it the Queen of England or Mr. Gresham or His Grace the Archbishop of Canterbury, will most assuredly and inevitably regret it. If you do not feel equal to the role of caretaker, dear Caroline, or harbor any doubts as to the fitness of young Wilson to undertake this responsibility, I enjoin you to send to* (mentioning the name and direction of a gentleman whose position in Society *commands our complete discretion) and tell him how the land lies. He'll know what to do. You'll need to call upon him in any case, to initiate you and your boy into the uses and rituals of the stone.*

In the course of reading this extraordinary document, Mrs. Mildmay was forced to ring for brandy, and when she had finished, sat for a few minutes with the sheets of her brother's narrative spread on her knees. Poor Alvord, she thought. And poor Margaret. She rang again for Mr. Chess and his clerk and her hat and cloak and her carriage to take them all to Grosvenor Place.

"For I'll certainly want you for witnesses or help, or both," she told them. "And there's not a moment to be lost, not that it probably isn't too late already."

When the carriage pulled up to Lady Basingstoke's house, all seemed as it should be, save that the steps clearly had not been swept nor the door brass polished in some time.

"There, you see?" said Mrs. Mildmay. "Something is dreadfully amiss. It is unlike Margaret not to have hired new servants."

"Perhaps she couldn't find any to hire," Mr. Chess suggested.

"Servants are always to be had in London," said Mrs. Mildmay, "unemployment being what it is."

A distant crash within put an end to idle conversation and inspired Mr. Chess to try the door, which was locked. A thin, inhuman screech from an upper floor sent him backing hastily down the steps, drawing Mrs. Mildmay, protesting, by the arm. "This is a matter for the police, dear lady, or perhaps a mad doctor. Rattler, find a constable."

While Rattler was searching out a member of the constabulary, Mr. Chess suggested that some tale be agreed on to explain the necessity of breaking into the town residence of a respectable baronet's widow, but in the event, no explanation was needed, for such a screeching and crashing greeted the constable's advent as to lend considerable weight to Mrs. Mildmay's plea that the door be forced at once.

With a blow of the constable's truncheon, the lock was broken. He set his broad shoulder to the door, and, with the help of Mr. Chess and Mr. Rattler, thrust it open upon a scene of chaos. The rugs had been tumbled about and smeared with filth. Furniture had been overturned, paintings ripped from the walls, draperies torn, and a display of native weapons cast down from the wall. The noise had ceased upon their entrance, and a deathly, listening silence brooded over the ruined hall.

Mrs. Mildmay was the first of the quartet to regain her presence of mind. She stepped forward to the foot of the stairs and called: "Margaret, are you there? It is Caroline Mildmay, with Mr. Chess and a constable. Answer us if you can."

At the sound of her voice, the noise began again, a wild gibbering and screeching like a soul in torment, and a figure appeared upon the gallery above the hall, wrapped in a voluminous pale dressing gown. The figure tore off the gown, threw it down upon the pale faces turned up to it, and swung itself from the gallery high over their heads to the great central chandelier, where it crouched, chattering angrily.

"It's an ape," said Mr. Chess unneccessarily.

"And a bleedin' 'uge un," said the constable, "beggin' the lady's parding."

But Mrs. Mildmay hardly noticed, for she was examining the creature—which was indeed one of the great apes that make their homes in the remoter reaches of the East—with more dismay than fear. "Why, it's Margaret," she exclaimed. "I'd know that chin anywhere. Oh, Mr. Chess!"

"Pray calm yourself, Mrs. Mildmay. Mr. Rattler shall alert this rude fellow's superiors of our predicament so that he may have help in subduing the creature, after which we may search the house for news of Lady Basingstoke."

"But we have news of Lady Basingstoke, I tell you! Look at her!" Mrs. Mildmay indicated the ape in the chandelier, whereupon the creature burst into a frenzy of hooting and bounced furiously up and down.

"Pray, Mrs. Mildmay, don't agitate it, or you'll have it down upon our heads. This is no place for a lady. Perhaps you'd best step outside until it is disposed of. Let the official gentlemen do their jobs and we'll sort it all out later."

But Mrs. Mildmay would not have it so, not unless Mr. Chess were to carry her bodily from the house. They were still arguing the point when the ape gave an almost human scream of rage and leapt from the chandelier.

Its intention was clearly to land upon Mrs. Mildmay's head, which, given the height of the chandelier and the weight of the ape, would certainly have snapped her neck. Fortunately, the constable, who had in the interval snatched a wicked-looking spear from the pile of weapons, cast it at the ape, catching it squarely in the chest. The ape screamed again and fell to the marble floor with a terrible thud.

In a moment, Mrs. Mildmay was kneeling beside it, careless of the spreading pool of blood, examining its leathery paws while Mr. Chess wrung his hands and begged her for heaven's sake to come away and leave the filthy thing to the authorities.

"Do be silent, Mr. Chess," said Mrs. Mildmay abstractedly. "I can't find the ring. We must find it—don't you see?—before it does further harm. I made sure it would be upon her finger, but it is not."

As she commenced gently to feel over the inert body, the ape groaned and opened its eyes. Mrs. Mildmay's hand flew to her mouth, and at this last extremity, she was at some trouble to stifle a scream. For the ape's right eye was grey and filled with pain and fear. And the ape's left eye—the ape's left eye was red as fire, smooth and clouded save for a clear star winking and sliding in its depths: the Parwat Ruby.

"Poor Margaret," said Mrs. Mildmay, and plucked the stone from the creature's head. As soon as the ruby was in her hand, the ape was an ape no more, but the corpse of an elderly woman with a spear in her breast.

As to the aftermath of this terrible story, there is little to say. Mr. Chess and the constable together searched the house in Grosvenor Place. Of Dr. Drago, no trace was found, saving a quantity of bloody water in a copper hip-bath and some well-chewed bones in my lady's bedchamber. In the ruins of Sir Alvord's study, Mr. Chess discovered some papers that suggested that Lady Basingstoke had extracted the codicil from the document box in Mr. Chess's chambers by means into which he thought it best not to delve too deeply. He thought it likely, also, that Lady Basingstoke had been instrumental in her husband's death, an opinion shared by Mrs. Mildmay and her husband, when she told him the story. Yet all were agreed that Lady Basingstoke, having suffered the most extreme punishment for her crimes, should not go to her grave with the stigma of murder upon her name. There was a brief period when no London jeweler could sell any kind of ruby, even at discounted prices, and no fashionable gathering was complete without a thorough discussion of the curse, its composition, and effect. But then came August and grouse-shooting, with houseparties in the country and cubbing to look forward to, and the nine-days' wonder came to an end.

As for the ruby itself, Mrs. Mildmay wore it on her finger. It was perhaps a coincidence that Mr. Mildmay's always lively interest in politics soon became more active, and that he successfully stood for the seat of the borough of Lessingham Parva for the Liberals. After he became Minister of Home Affairs, he introduced and forced through the House the famous Poor Law of 18__, which guaranteed employment to all able-bodied men and women, and a stipend for the old and helpless. In all his efforts, he was ably seconded by his wife, who became in her later years a great political hostess and promoter of young and idealistic Liberal MPs. After her husband's death, at an age when most women are thinking of retiring to the country, Mrs. Caroline Mildmay mounted an expedition to the impenetrable forests of Ceylon, from which journey neither she nor the Parwat Ruby ever returned.

THE FAERIE CONY-CATCHER

In London town, in the reign of good Queen Bess that was called Gloriana, there lived a young man named Nicholas Cantier. Now it came to pass that this Nick Cantier served out his term as apprentice jeweler and goldsmith under one Master Spilman, jeweler by appointment to the Queen's Grace herself, and was made journeyman of his guild. For that Nick was a clever young man, his master would have been glad for him to continue on where he was; yet Nick was not fain thereof, Master Spilman being as ill a master of men as he was skilled master of his trade. And Nick bethought him thus besides: that London was like unto the boundless sea where Leviathan may dwell unnoted, save by such small fish as he may snap up to stay his mighty hunger: such small fish as Nicholas Cantier. Better he seek out some backwater in the provinces where, puffed up by city ways, he might perchance pass for a pike and snap up spratlings on his own account.

So thought Nick. And on a bright May morning, he packed up such tools as he might call his own—as a pitch block and a mallet, and some small steel chisels and punches and saw blades and blank rings of copper—that he might make shift to earn his way to Oxford. Nick put his tools in a pack, with clean hosen and a shirt and a pair of soft leather shoon, and that was all his worldly wealth strapped upon his back, saving only a jewel that he had designed and made himself to be his passport. This jewel was in the shape of a maid, her breasts and belly all one lucent pearl, her skirt and open jacket of bright enamel, and her fair face of silver burnished with gold. On her fantastic hair perched a tiny golden crown, and Nick had meant her for the Faerie Queene of Master Spenser's poem, fair Gloriana.

Upon this precious Gloriana did Nick's life and livelihood depend. Being a prudent lad in the main, and bethinking him of London's traps and dangers, Nick considered where he might bestow it that he fall not prey to those foists and rufflers who might take it from him by stealth or by force. The safest place, thought he, would be his codpiece, where no man nor woman might meddle without his yard raise the alarm. Yet the jewel was large and cold and hard against those softer jewels that dwelt more commonly therein, and so Nick bound it across his belly with a band of linen and took leave of his fellows and set out northward to seek his fortune.

Now this Nick Cantier was a lusty youth of nearly twenty, with a fine, open face and curls of nut-brown hair that sprang from his brow; yet notwithstanding his comely form, he was as much a virgin on that May morning as the Queen herself. For Master Spilman was the hardest of taskmasters, and between his eagle eye and his adder cane and his arch-episcopal piety, his apprentices perforce lived out the terms of their bonds as chaste as Popish monks. On this the first day of his freedom, young Nick's eye roved hither and thither, touching here a slender waist and there a dimpled cheek, wondering what delights might not lie beneath this petticoat or that snowy kerchief. And so it was that a Setter came upon him unaware and sought to persuade him to drink a pot of ale together, having just found xii pence in a gutter and it being ill luck to keep found money and Nick's face putting him in mind of his father's youngest son, dead of an ague this two year and more. Nick let him run on, through this excuse for scraping acquaintance and that, and when the hopeful Cony-catcher had rolled to a stop, like a cart at the foot of a hill, he said unto him:

"I see I must have a care to the cut of my coat, if rogues, taking me for a country cony, think me meet for skinning. Nay, I'll not drink with ye, nor play with ye neither, lest ye so ferret-claw me at cards that ye leave me as bare of coin as an ape of a tail."

Upon hearing which, the Setter called down a murrain upon milk-fed pups who imagined themselves sly dogs, and withdrew into the company of two men appareled like honest and substantial citizens, whom Nicholas took to be the Setter's Verser and Barnacle, all ready to play their parts in cozening honest men out of all they carried, and a little more beside. And he bit his thumb at them and laughed and made his way through the streets of London, from Lombard Street to Clerkenwell in the northern liberties of the city, where the houses were set back from the road in gardens and fields and the taverns spilled out of doors in benches and stools, so that toss-pots might air their drunken heads.

'Twas coming on for noon by this time, and Nick's steps were slower than they had been, and his mind dwelt more on bread and ale than on cony-catchers and villains.

In this hungry, drowsy frame of mind, he passed an alehouse where his eye chanced to light upon a woman tricked up like a lady in a rich-guarded gown and a deep starched ruff. Catching his glance, she sent it back again saucily, with a wink and a roll of her shoulders that lifted her white breasts like ships on a wave. She plucked him by the sleeve and said, "How now, my friend, you look wondrous down i' the mouth. What want you? Wine? Company?"—all with such a meaning look, such a waving of her skirts and a hoisting of her breasts that Nick's yard, fain to salute her, flew its scarlet colors in his cheeks.

"The truth is, mistress, that I've walked far this day, and am sorely hungered."

"Hungered, is it?" She flirted her eyes at him, giving the word a dozen meanings not writ in any grammar. "Shall feed thy hunger then, aye, and sate thy thirst, too, and that right speedily." And she led him in at the alehouse door to a little room within, where she closed the door and, thrusting herself close up against him, busied her hands about his body and her lips about his mouth. As luck would have it, her breath was foul, and it blew upon Nick's heat, cooling him enough to recognize that her hands sought not his pleasure, but his purse, upon which he thrust her from him.

"Nay, mistress," he said, all flushed and panting. "Thy meat and drink are dear, if they cost me my purse."

Knowing by his words that she was discovered, she spent no time in denying her trade, but set up a caterwauling would wake the dead, calling upon one John to help her. But Nick, if not altogether wise, was quick and strong, and bolted from the vixen's den 'ere the dog-fox answered her call.

So running, Nick came shortly to the last few houses that clung to the outskirts of the city and stopped at a tavern to refresh him with honest meat and drink. And as he drank his ale and pondered his late escape, the image of his own foolishness dimmed and the image of the doxy's beauty grew more bright, until the one eclipsed the other quite, persuading him that any young man in whom the blood ran hot would have fallen into her trap, aye and been skinned, drawn, and roasted to a turn, as 'twere in very sooth a long-eared cony. It was his own cleverness, he thought, led him to smoke her out. So Nick, having persuaded himself that he was a sly dog after all, rose from the tavern and went to Hampstead Heath, which was the end of the world to him. And as he stepped over the world's edge and onto the northward road, his heart lifted for joy, and he sang right merrily as he strode along, as pleased with himself as the cock that imagineth his crowing bring the sun from the sea.

And so he walked and so he sang until by and by he came upon a country lass sitting on a stone. Heedful of his late lesson, he quickly cast his eye about him for signs of some high lawyer or ruffler lurking ready to spring the trap. But the lass sought noways to lure him, nor did she accost him, nor lift her dark head from contemplating her foot that was cocked up on her knee. Her gown of gray kersey was hiked up to her thigh and her sleeves rolled to her elbows, so that Nick could see her naked arms, sinewy and lean and nut-brown with sun, and her leg like muddy ivory.

"Gie ye good-den, fair maid," said he, and then could say no more, for when she raised her face to him, his breath stopped in his throat. It was not, perhaps, the fairest he'd seen, being gypsy-dark, with cheeks and nose that showed the bone. But her black eyes were wide and soft as a hind's and the curve of her mouth made as sweet a bow as Cupid's own.

"Good-den to thee," she answered him, low-voiced as a throstle. "Ye come at a good hour to my aid. For here is a thorn in my foot and I, for want of a pin, unable to have it out."

The next moment he knelt at her side; the moment after, her foot was in his hand. He found the thorn and winkled it out with the point of his knife while the lass clutched at his shoulder, hissing between her teeth as the thorn yielded, sighing as he wiped away the single ruby of blood with his kerchief and bound it round her foot.

"I thank thee, good youth," she said, leaning closer. "An thou wilt, I'll give thee such a reward for thy kindness as will give thee cause to thank me anon." She turned her hand to his neck, and stroked the bare flesh there, smiling in his face the while, her breath as sweet as an orchard in spring.

Nick felt his cheek burn hot above her hand and his heart grow large in his chest. This were luck indeed, and better than all the trulls in London. "Fair maid," he said, "I would not kiss thee beside the common way."

She laughed. "Lift me then and carry me to the hollow, hard by yonder hill, where we may embrace, if it pleaseth thee, without fear of meddling eye."

Nick's manhood then informed him that it would please him well, observing the which, the maiden smiled and held up her arms to him, and he lifted her, light as a faggot of sticks but soft and supple as Spanish leather withal, and bore her to a hollow under a hill that was round and green and warm in the May sun. And he lay her down and did off his pack and set it by her head, that he might keep it close to hand, rejoicing that his jewel was not in his codpiece, and then he fell to kissing her lips and stroking her soft, soft throat. Her breasts were small as a child's under her gown; yet she moaned most womanly when he pressed them, and writhed against him like a snake, and he made bold to pull up her petticoats to discover the treasure they hid. Coyly, she slapped his hand away once and again, yet never ceased to kiss and toy with open lip, the while her tongue like a darting fish urged him to unlace his codpiece that was grown wondrous tight. Seeing what he was about, she put her hand down to help him, so that he was like to perish e'er he achieved the gates of Heaven. Then, when he was all but sped, she pulled him headlong on top of her.

He was not home, though very near it as he thrust at her skirts bunched up between her thighs. Though his plunging breached not her cunny-burrow, it did breach the hill itself, and he and his gypsy-lass tumbled arse-over-neck to lie broken-breathed in the midst of a great candle-lit hall upon a Turkey carpet, with skirts and legs and slippered feet standing in ranks upon it to his right hand and his left, and a gentle air stroking warm fingers across his naked arse. Nick shut his eyes, praying that this vision were merely the lively exhalation of his lust. And then a laugh like a golden bell fell upon his ear, and was hunted through a hundred mocking changes in a ring of melodious laughter, and he knew this to be sober reality, or something enough like it that he'd best ope his eyes and lace up his hose.

All this filled no more than the space of a breath, though it seemed to Nick an age of the world had passed before he'd succeeded in packing up his yard and scrambling to his feet to confront the owners of the skirts and the slippered feet and the bell-like laughter that yet pealed over his head. And in that age, the thought was planted and nurtured and harvested in full ripeness, that his hosts were of faerie-kind. He knew they were too fair to be human men and women, their skins white nacre, their hair spun sunlight or moonlight or fire bound back from their wide brows by fillets of precious stones no less hard and bright than their emerald or sapphire eyes. The women went bare-bosomed as Amazons, the living jewels of their perfect breasts coffered in open gowns of bright silk. The men wore jewels in their ears, and at their forks, fantastic codpieces in the shapes of cockerels and wolves and rams with curling horns. They were splendid beyond imagining, a masque to put the Queen's most magnificent Revels to shame.

As Nick stood in amaze, he heard the voice of his coy mistress say, "'Twere well, Nicholas Cantier, if thou wouldst turn and make thy bow."

With a glare for she who had brought him to this pass, Nick turned him to face a woman sat upon a throne. Even were she seated upon a joint-stool, he must have known her, for her breasts and face were more lucent and fair than pearl, her open jacket and skirt a glory of gemstones, and upon her fantastic hair perched a gold crown, as like to the jewel in his bosom as twopence to a groat. Nick gaped like that same small fish his fancy had painted him erewhile, hooked and pulled gasping to land. Then his knees, wiser than his head, gave way to prostrate him at the royal feet of Elfland.

"Well, friend Nicholas," said the Faerie Queen. "Heartily are you welcome to our court. Raise him, Peasecod, and let him approach our throne."

Nick felt a tug on his elbow, and wrenched his dazzled eyes from the figure of the Faerie Queen to see his wanton lass bending over him. "To thy feet, my heart," she murmured. "And, as thou holdest dear thy soul, see that neither meat nor drink pass thy lips."

"Well, Peasecod?" asked the Queen, and there was that in her musical voice that propelled Nick to his feet and down the Turkey carpet to stand trembling before her.

"Be welcome," said the Queen again, "and take your ease. Peasecod, bring a stool and a cup for our guest, and let the musicians play and our court dance for his pleasure."

There followed an hour as strange as any madman might imagine or poet sing, wherein Nicholas Cantier sat upon a gilded stool at the knees of the Queen of Elfland and watched her court pace through their faerie measures. In his hand he held a golden cup crusted with gems, and the liquor within sent forth a savor of roses and apples that promised an immortal vintage. But as oft as he, half fainting, lifted the cup, so often did a pair of fingers pinch him at the ankle, and so often did he look down to see the faerie lass Peasecod crouching at his feet with her skirts spread out to hide the motions of her hand. One she glanced up at him, her soft eyes drowned in tears like pansies in rain, and he knew that she was sorry for her part in luring him here.

When the dancing was over and done, the Queen of Elfland turned to Nick and said, "Good friend Nicholas, we would crave a boon of thee in return for this our fair entertainment."

At which Nick replied, "I am at your pleasure, madam. Yet have I not taken any thing from you save words and laughter."

"'Tis true, friend Nicholas, that thou hast scorned to drink our Faerie wine. And yet hast thou seen our faerie revels, that is a sight any poet in London would give his last breath to see."

"I am no poet, madam, but a humble journeyman goldsmith."

"That too, is true. And for that thou art something better than humble at thy trade, I will do thee the honor of accepting that jewel in my image thou bearest bound against thy breast."

Then it seemed to Nick that the Lady might have his last breath after all, for his heart suspended himself in his throat. Wildly looked he upon Gloriana's face, fair and cold and eager as the trull's he had escaped erewhile, and then upon the court of Elfland that watched him as he were a monkey or a dancing bear. At his feet, he saw the dark-haired lass Peasecod, set apart from the rest by her mean garments and her dusky skin, the only comfortable thing in all that discomfortable splendor. She smiled into his eyes, and made a little motion with her hand, like a fishwife who must chaffer by signs against the crowd's commotion. And Nicholas took courage at her sign, and fetched up a deep breath, and said:

"Fair Majesty, the jewel is but a shadow or counterfeit of your radiant beauty. And yet 'tis all my stock in trade. I cannot render all my wares to you, were I never so fain to do you pleasure."

The Queen of Elfland drew her delicate brows like kissing moths over her nose. "Beware, young Nicholas, how thou triest our good will. Were we minded, we might turn thee into a lizard or a slow-worm, and take thy jewel resistless."

"Pardon, dread Queen, but if you might take my jewel by force, you might have taken it ere now. I think I must give it you—or sell it you—by mine own unforced will."

A silence fell, ominous and dark as a thundercloud. All Elfland held its breath, awaiting the royal storm. Then the sun broke through again, the Faerie Queen smiled, and her watchful court murmured to one another, as those who watch a bout at swords will murmur when the less skilled fencer maketh a lucky hit.

"Thou hast the right of it, friend Nicholas: we do confess it. Come, then. The Queen of Elfland will turn huswife, and chaffer with thee."

Nick clasped his arms about his knee and addressed the lady thus: "I will be frank with you, Serenity. My master, when he saw the jewel, advised me that I should not part withal for less than fifty golden crowns, and that not until I'd bought with it a master goldsmith's good opinion and a place at his shop. Fifty-five crowns, then, will buy the jewel from me, and not a farthing less."

The Lady tapped her white hand on her knee. "Then thy master is a fool, or thou a rogue and liar. The bauble is worth no more than fifteen golden crowns. But for that we are a compassionate prince, and thy complaint being just, we will give thee twenty, and not a farthing more."

"Forty-five," said Nick. "I might sell it to Master Spenser for twice the sum, as a fair portrait of Gloriana, with a description of the faerie court, should he wish to write another book."

"Twenty-five," said the Queen. "Ungrateful wretch. 'Twas I sent the dream inspired the jewel."

"All the more reason to pay a fair price for it," said Nick. "Forty."

This shot struck in the gold. The Queen frowned and sighed and shook her head and said, "Thirty. And a warrant, signed by our own royal hand, naming thee jeweler by appointment to Gloriana, by cause of a pendant thou didst make at her behest."

It was a fair offer. Nick pondered a moment, saw Peasecod grinning up at him with open joy, her cheeks dusky red and her eyes alight, and said: "Done, my Queen, if only you will add thereto your attendant nymph, Peasecod, to be my companion, if she will."

At this Gloriana laughed aloud, and all the court of Elfland laughed with her, peal upon peal at the mortal's presumption. Peasecod alone of the bright throng did not laugh, but rose to stand by Nicholas' side and pressed his hand in hers. She was brown and wild as a young deer, and it seemed to Nick that the Queen of Elfland herself, in all her glory of moony breasts and arching neck, was not so fair as this one slender, black-browed faerie maid.

When Gloriana had somewhat recovered her power of speech, she said: "Friend Nicholas, I thank thee; for I have not laughed so heartily this many a long day. Take thy faerie lover and thy faerie gold and thy faerie warrant and depart unharmed from hence. But for that thou hast dared to rob the Faerie Queen of this her servant, we lay this weird on thee, that if thou say thy Peasecod nay, at bed or at board for the space of four-and-twenty mortal hours, then thy gold shall turn to leaves, thy warrant to filth, and thy lover to dumb stone."

At this, Peasecod's smile grew dim, and up spoke she and said, "Madam, this is too hard."

"Peace," said Gloriana, and Peasecod bowed her head. "Nicholas," said the Queen, "we commence to grow weary of this play. Give us the jewel and take thy price and go thy ways."

So Nick did off his doublet and his shirt and unwound the band of linen from about his waist and fetched out a little leathern purse and loosed its strings and tipped out into his hand the precious thing upon which he had expended all his love and his art. And loathe was he to part withal, the first-fruits of his labor.

"Thou shalt make another, my heart, and fairer yet than this," whispered Peasecod in his ear, and so he laid it into Elfland's royal hand, and bowed, and in that moment he was back in the hollow under the green hill, his pack at his feet, half naked, shocked as by a lightning bolt, and alone. Before he could draw breath to make his moan, Peasecod appeared beside him with his shirt and doublet on her arm, a pack at her back, and a heavy purse at her waist, that she detached and gave to him with his clothes. Fain would he have sealed his bargain then and there, but Peasecod begging prettily that they might seek more comfort than might be found on a tussock of grass, he could not say her nay. Nor did he regret his weird that gave her the whip hand in this, for the night drew on apace, and he found himself sore hungered and athirst, as though he'd sojurned beneath the hill for longer than the hour he thought. And indeed 'twas a day and a night and a day again since he'd seen the faerie girl upon the heath, for time doth gallop with the faerie kind, who heed not its passing. And so Peasecod told him as they trudged northward in the gloaming, and picked him early berries to stay his present hunger, and found him clear water to stay his thirst, so that he was inclined to think very well of his bargain, and of his own cleverness that had made it.

And so they walked until they came to a tavern, where Nick called for dinner and a chamber, all of the best, and pressed a golden noble into the host's palm, whereat the goodman stared and said such a coin would buy his whole house and all his ale, and still he'd not have coin to change it. And Nick, flushed with gold and lust, told him to keep all as a gift upon the giver's wedding day. Whereat Peasecod blushed and cast down her eyes as any decent bride, though the goodman saw she wore no ring and her legs and feet were bare and mired from the road. Yet he gave them of his best, both meat and drink, and put them to bed in his finest chamber, with a fire in the grate because gold is gold, and a rose upon the pillow because he remembered what it was to be young.

The door being closed and latched, Nicholas took Peasecod in his arms and drank of her mouth as 'twere a well and he dying of thirst. And then he bore her to the bed and laid her down and began to unlace her gown that he might see her naked. But she said unto him, "Stay, Nicholas Cantier, and leave me my modesty yet a while. But do thou off thy clothes, and I vow thou shalt not lack for pleasure."

Then young Nick gnawed his lip and pondered in himself whether taking off her clothes by force would be saying her nay—some part of which showed in his face, for she took his hand to her mouth and tickled the palm with her tongue, all the while looking roguishly upon him, so that he smiled upon her and let her do her will, which was to strip his doublet and shirt from him, to run her fingers and her tongue across his chest, to lap and pinch at his nipples until he gasped, to stroke and tease him, and finally to release his rod and take it in her hand and then into her mouth. Poor Nick, who had never dreamed of such tricks, was like to die of ecstasy. He twisted his hands in her long hair as pleasure came upon him like an annealing fire, and then he lay spent, with Peasecod's head upon his bosom, and all her dark hair spread across his belly like a blanket of silk.

After a while she raised herself, and with great tenderness kissed him upon the mouth and said, "I have no regret of this bargain, my heart, whatever follows after."

And from his drowsy state he answered her, "Why, what should follow after but joy and content and perchance a babe to dandle upon my knee?"

She smiled and said, "What indeed? Come, discover me," and lay back upon the pillow and opened her arms to him.

For a little while, he was content to kiss and toy with lips and neck, and let her body be. But soon he tired of this game, the need once again growing upon him to uncover her secret places and to plumb their mysteries. He put his hand beneath her skirts, stroking her thigh that was smooth as pearl and quivered under his touch as it drew near to that mossy dell he had long dreamed of. With quickening breath, he felt springing hair, and then his fingers encountered an obstruction, a wand or rod, smooth as the thigh, but rigid, and burning hot. In his shock, he squeezed it, and Peasecod gave a moan, whereupon Nick would have withdrawn his hand, and that right speedily, had not his faerie lover gasped, "Wilt thou now nay-say me?"

Nick groaned and squeezed again. The rod he held pulsed, and his own yard stirred in ready sympathy. Nick raised himself on his elbow and looked down into Peasecod's face—wherein warred lust and fear, man and woman—and thought, not altogether clearly, upon his answer. Words might turn like snakes to bite their tails, and Nick was of no mind to be misunderstood. For answer then, he tightened his grip upon those fair and ruddy jewels that Peasecod brought to his marriage-portion, and so wrought with them that the eyes rolled back in his lover's head, and he expired upon a sigh. Yet rose he again at Nick's insistent kissing, and threw off his skirts and stays and his smock of fine linen to show his body, slender and hard as Nick's own, yet smooth and fair as any lady's that bathes in ass's milk and honey. And so they sported night-long until the rising sun blew pure gold leaf upon their tumbled bed, where they lay entwined and, for the moment, spent.

"I were well served if thou shouldst cast me out, once the four-and-twenty hours are past," said Peasecod mournfully.

"And what would be the good of that?" asked Nick.

"More good than if I stayed with thee, a thing nor man nor woman, nor human nor faerie kind."

"As to the latter, I cannot tell, but as to the former, I say that thou art both, and I the richer for thy doubleness. Wait," said Nick, and scrambled from the bed and opened his pack and took out a blank ring of copper and his block of pitch and his small steel tools. And he worked the ring into the pitch and, within a brace of minutes, had incised upon it a pea-vine from which you might pick peas in season, so like nature was the work. And returning to the bed where Peasecod lay watching, slipped it upon his left hand.

Peasecod turned the ring upon his finger, wondering. "Thou dost not hate me, then, for that I tricked and cozened thee?"

Nick smiled and drew his hand down his lover's flank, taut ivory to his touch, and said, "There are some hours yet left, I think, to the term of my bond. Art thou so eager, love, to become dumb stone that thou must be asking me questions that beg to be answered 'No?' Know then, that I rejoice in being thy cony, and only wish that thou mayst catch me as often as may be, if all thy practices be as pleasant as this by which thou hast bound me to thee."

And so they rose and made their ways to Oxford town, where Nicholas made such wise use of his faerie gold and his faerie commission as to keep his faerie lover in comfort all the days of their lives.

SACRED HARP

The first time I heard shape-note singing, I thought I'd died and gone to heaven. It was in an old church in Cambridge, Presbyterian, I think, during a rainstorm. In a moment of weakness, I'd promised a friend I'd go hold her hand—she was trying to get out more—and didn't feel I could let her stick. But I was feeling pretty crabby about sloshing my car through Harvard Square and finding a place to park and listening to a bunch of old folkies pretending they were Psalmodists. I was not being a lady about it, and Harriet had just told me she wished she'd never asked me to come. Then the singing started. I didn't understand quite what I was hearing, but when the music started to rise, I rose with it, and stayed there for two solid hours.

Harriet decided she liked Cajun dancing better, but I went back to that church every week until I was leading hymns regularly. When I moved away from Boston, I sat in on every choir I could find, all types, all styles. And when I fetched up here, I finally did what I'd wanted to do since the first time I'd led a hymn. I started a choir of my own.

A choir of my own. Listen to me. You'd think it was the Robert Shaw Chorale instead of a bunch of enthusiastic amateurs barely able to tell Fa from Sol. Still, it's mine. I founded it, and I'm the chairman. Our weekly singing is Monday night at seven sharp. People with kids complain that it's a little late for them, but I can't get here from work any earlier, not and get set up, so I just tell them that they'll have to come early. This isn't a social club, it's a Sacred Harp choir, and all I really want out of life is for it to be a decent one. A better job and a steady relationship would be nice, too, but I'll settle for a decent choir.

This Monday night is typical. I show up at 6:45, wishing that I'd had more time to work out my list of hymns. I like singings to have a shape to them, to build musically and even thematically. Since it's traditional to let other people lead hymns of their choosing, I don't have complete control, but I do what I can.

So I've hardly gotten my coat off and taken out the Xeroxed hymns I've found in a nineteenth century hymnal when Morton comes up to me, looking sheepish. Morton's a sweet guy, if not very interesting—fortyish, scraggly, given to red plaid flannel shirts and playing with his beard.

"Um," he says. "I brought a friend. Hope you don't mind. Jess, this is Gretchen, who started all this. She's our, um, chairman."

What an idiot. He knows he's supposed to call me the night before if he wants to bring someone along so I can tell him no. Now there's a woman I've never seen before standing in front of me with her hand held out, expecting me to smile and welcome her to our happy little family. I ostentatiously juggle my hymnal and my Xeroxes and she lets her hand drop.

Whoever she is, she isn't Morton's girlfriend. She's short and chunky and plain—not homely, plain, like whole wheat bread. She's wearing denim overalls and a cracked brown leather bomber jacket and her hair is cut really, really short. It's a bad haircut—well, mine is too; you can't get a good haircut around here—but this is a particular kind of bad haircut I haven't seen since I left Cambridge. There aren't many wommyn living in this neck of the woods, if you know what I mean.

"What do you sing?" I ask, praying she won't say alto. We're overburdened with altos.

"Morton tells me I'm a treble."

It's not a voice you'd expect to come out of a face like hers: a real girl's voice, light and sweet. She grins at me.

"Yeah. I've always wanted to sound like Tallulah Bankhead, but I hate the taste of scotch, and cigarettes make me sick."

I'm replaying her last comment. "Morton tells you? Haven't you done this before?"

"Nope," she says cheerfully. "Sacred Harp Virgin, that's me. Ignorant but willing, all the way up to high 'C.'"

"Great," I say. Morton winces—he's a sensitive soul. "Listen. I'm not in the business of teaching shape-note singing. It's taken me years to get these people marginally up to scratch, and I don't want them thrown off by someone who doesn't know the music." I turn to Morton, who is looking more and more like a Suffering Christ in plaid flannel. "You know the rules, Morton. Since she's here, she can sit and follow in the hymnal, but she can't sing."

"She reads music," Morton says.

"I've taken solfeggio classes," the woman says helpfully.

The clock on the wall tells me it's 6:55. Out of the corner of my eye, I see April and Ben and the Barnabys waiting to get my attention. "I don't have time for this," I say. "Get Melissa to explain shape notes to you—she's in the back row, braids, Fair Isle sweater. First sour note I hear, you shut up for the rest of the evening. Capisce?"

For some reason, this makes her grin like a five-year-old. Her teeth are very even. "Capisco," she says, and heads off toward Melissa, Morton gloomily in tow.

April and Ben hand me a wad of hymn slips. It's a system I've invented. Everyone who wants to lead a hymn writes its number and their name on a piece of paper for me to call out. It cuts down on arguments and bad programming.

"OK, people, listen up." Everybody pipes down. "Last call for slips. I've got two left over from last week. Rebecca, the third hymn's yours. When you're all in your places, we'll warm up."

In two, three minutes, they're all seated with their hymnals in their laps and their eyes on me; all except Morton's friend, who's whispering with Melissa.

"Jess," I say sweetly, pulling her name from random access memory. "We're going to do a couple of scales, and then 'The Young Convert' on page twenty-four. The way this works, we sing the notes together first—Fa, Sol, La, Mi and so forth—and then the words to the verses. Until you learn the names of the shapes, sing la la la." Melissa rolls her eyes, but Jess just looks extra interested. Bitch, I think, and raise the pitch-pipe to my lips.

"From Fa," I say, and we're off, ragged on the first two notes, melding into a solid unison by the end of the scale. They rise with me from Fa to Sol to La to Fa, climbing steps of shape and sound, seeing the notes as we sing them, just as B. F. White and E. J. King intended, triangle to oval to square to triangle. The sound doesn't stink for cold voices in a cold church hall. I lead them through a few simple exercises. I've got a good voice for leading, if I say so myself. It's got a pretty limited range—sometimes the alto line gets too high for me, and I have to double whatever part is below it for a note or two. But it's strong and clear and well-supported. We finish up "The Young Convert's" "wonder, wonder, wonder" exactly on key.

"Not bad," I say. "Albion, fifty-two. 'Come, ye that love the Lord.'"

I always start with a simple, quiet piece, not too high in the treble, not too low in the bass. Five minutes of scales isn't really adequate warm-up for any kind of singing, but we've only got the damn hall for two and a half hours, a half hour of which is wasted on juice and cookies and sweeping up afterwards. It's astonishing how much mess forty people can make in two hours.

Anyway. The purpose of the first piece is to tell me what color the chorus is going to be tonight. I have this theory, see, that voices are like colors. You know how a single color can have a bunch of hues or tints? Yellow, for instance, can be pale and acid, or soft and buttery, or bright and clear, or rich and golden. So can voices. That's why a chorus is like a painting. As every discrete voice blends with the voices around it, note by note, brushstroke by brushstroke, they build up layers of color into a coherent picture, a recognizable melody. Some choruses I've heard paint Rembrandts; some paint Titians or Turners or Monets. Mine paints Warhols. On bad nights, it's more like finger-painting, and even on good nights, they tend toward acid greens and neon yellows, Pepto-Bismol pinks and electric blues. I'm trying to bring us up to Grandma Moses.

Tonight, we're almost there. They drag the tempo, of course: all choruses drag slow pieces. But the sound I'm part of is deeper and wider than I've heard before, as if someone's added burnt umber to everything. When we come to the end, everyone looks at each other and smiles.

"One hundred and ninety-six," I say, and lead them through the notes. "Alabama" is a simple fuging tune, with one lonely staggered entrance. The singers start out fine and strong on "Angels in shining order stand," and then things fall apart. The basses muff "Those happy spirits," and the trebles straggle after, throwing off the tenors and completely flummoxing the altos, who come in strong and pure at entirely the wrong moment. Everybody flounders on for a measure or so, then falls apart into nervous giggles.

"You," I say. "Jess. That's it."

Melissa frowns. "That's not fair, Gretchen. It wasn't her fault. We all miscounted it. She's holding up the pitch."

The treble section nods vigorously. "Please let her sing, Gretchen," says Alice. "She's really good."

"Listen," says Jess, "I don't want to make trouble. Gretchen's the chairman. She says I shut up, I shut up. No problem." Closing her hymnal, she folds her hands on top of it. Superior bitch. I'm damned if I'm going to let her take the moral high ground on me.

"That's right," I say. "When I say shut up, you shut up. Did anyone hear me say shut up?"

Melissa glares at me; April and Betsy, embarrassed, stare at the floor; Mary and Gwen exchange looks; Jess simply opens her book. I ignore them all and call the next hymn.

"Gretchen? Gretchen." Rebecca's waving over in the altos. "You said the third hymn was mine. I didn't get to lead last week."

She's pouting—she's got that kind of face—and the pout deepens as I explain that we need to do one that works before I let anyone else lead. "Before break, I promise, Rebecca. But you want it to sound good, don't you, not like the hash we just made of 'Alabama'?" She nods unhappily, and during "Mission" single-voicedly pulls the altos down a quarter-tone. The next two hymns aren't much better. The singers manage to stay pretty much on-pitch, but the sound remains muddy and off-focus. I finally let Rebecca lead "New Lebanon" just before break, by which time she's so twitchy she can hardly keep the parts together, and brings in the tenors a full measure early on a perfectly straightforward fugue. At this point, she bursts into tears and runs off toward the bathroom, leaving everyone a choice between stopping and limping through the rest of the hymn the best they can. They choose to limp, which shows guts if not good judgment, and then it's over at last and they all make a grand rush for the stage, where April and Morton have set out cartons of O.J. and packages of Oreos, with hard candy and Fisherman's Friends for those whose throats need soothing. The usual break-time buzz of conversation is muted tonight, and nobody hangs around to ask me if I'm going to any concerts this weekend or whether I've heard the new Hilliard CD. I can't really blame them. I'm not exactly Miss Congeniality, even when I'm in a good mood.

I'm busy axing all the complicated hymns from my program when someone taps me on the shoulder. It's Melissa, looking as determined and grim as a middle-aged woman with pink plastic rabbits on her braids is capable of looking.

"Listen, Gretchen. Rebecca's in the bathroom crying her eyes out and saying she's going to quit. Joshua's beside himself, and Zach says the stress is beginning to get to him. We're amateurs, Gretchen—we're in this because we want to get together and have fun once a week, not because we want a recording contract."

She delivers this speech all in one breath, as if she's afraid she'll forget a point if she slows down. When she's done, she glares at me, daring me to lose my temper. Which I can't do, no matter how much I want to, because a bad choir is better than no choir, and no choir is what I'll have if my singers all decide to take up a less demanding hobby. So I swallow all the things that come to my mind about amateurs in general and oversensitive crybabies and New-Age wimps in particular, and I say, "You want me to talk to Rebecca?"

"No," says Melissa. "I think I've got her calmed down. Just lighten up, will you? And try to remember that I'm on your side."

"Yeah," I say. "Thanks."

Melissa sighs; the pink plastic rabbits bob and disappear. A moment later, I catch sight of her in a knot of trebles: April, Gwen, and Morton's friend. Jess. Troublemaker. The straw that breaks the camel's back. The feather that unbalances the scale. She isn't really doing anything wrong, but I can feel her in every piece we sing, coloring it with her uncertainty. I frown at her through the straggle of bodies returning to their seats. Catching my eye, she smiles back. I want to kill her.

Henry leads the first hymn after break, and April and Ben the two after that. I'm not stupid. I know they're all out there hating me right now, like a bunch of teenagers who've been told that they're not working up to their potential.

They work really hard to show me that it's all my fault, and they make a pretty good job of it. I mean, they're almost on pitch, and their entrances are reasonably solid, and since break, they seem to have learned how to count. Maybe it's the O.J. or the hard candy. Or maybe they're right, and I'm a bad musician and a worse leader. Maybe they'd be better off if I just walked out of here and never came back, took up clog-dancing or something where I could make a fool only of myself. They seem to like that Jess woman; maybe they'll elect her chairman, once she's learned the names of the notes.

I wish they'd all go to hell.

I've set "The Weary Pilgrim" as the next hymn, but I change my mind and call "Melancholy Day."

The words to shape-note hymns come in four main flavors: praise, resignation, entreaty, and admonition. By secular humanist standards, they're pretty unenlightened, and "Melancholy Day" is one of the most unenlightened of the lot: "Death, 'tis a melancholy day to those who have no God, When the poor soul is forced away to seek her last abode. In vain to heav'n she lifts her eyes, for guilt, a heavy chain, Still drags her downward from the skies, to darkness, fire and pain." It has a good, rousing melody, too, and a bitch of a running fugue.

Nobody's cutting anybody any slack. I beat out a brisk pace and they leap after my hand like hungry dogs. They're mad and on their mettle and all warmed up, and by God, they're singing the hell out of "Melancholy Day." The basses roar deep in the shadows; the trebles, brightened by a clear, full-throated voice that has to be Jess, highlight each curve of the fugue with high Gs and B-flats. Everyone's looking more cheerful. As I release the final note, I catch sight of Jess. Her cheeks are red, her eyes are unnaturally bright, her bad haircut is standing straight up in front, and she's grinning like the village idiot. I feel the corners of my mouth twitch. What the hell, I think, and say, "Want to try one, Jess?"

Melissa, who has gone back to her usual cow-like placidity, bristles up again. Behind me, in the tenor section, I hear Morton go, "Oh, shit." I get mad again.

"I don't know what you guys want from me," I say. "I'm making an offer here, in good faith, and you act like I've come out for shooting baby ducks. If Jess wants to lead the next hymn, she can. If Morton wants to lead it, or Melissa, or Fred or Ben or April, they can. They'll have to. Because that was my last hymn. You guys give me a swift pain. You don't care about the music or how hard I've worked or anything but your Tuesday night get-togethers. Well, now you can get together all you want and talk about what a bitch I am. Have fun. I'm quitting."

I close my hymnal and snatch up my coat and my boots and my scarf and my clipboard and my Xeroxed sheets and stalk out of the hall to the church porch, where I dump everything on a bench. Outside, the wind herds sleet noisily around the corner of the building. I may be mad enough to cut my own social throat, but I'm not mad enough to walk out into a winter storm without a coat. It's cold in the porch, and I'm shivering as I pull on my boots, cram my watch-cap down over my eyebrows, wrap my muffler up over my mouth, and button myself into my gray down coat that makes me look like the Michelin Tire man. I tamp my papers even and go to put them in my backpack.

No backpack. Not on the bench, not on the floor. I've left it in the church hall, and if I don't want to trudge out to my car in blowing snow with my arms full of loose papers and risk the cover of my hymnal bleeding all over my gray down coat, I'm going to have to go inside and get it.

I wish I was dead.

And I go on wishing it as I open the door and stalk back into the hall I left so melodramatically five minutes ago. Nobody's moved except Melissa, who is standing in the middle of the square with her hymnal in her hand. On my side, my ass.

I step into the square. My backpack is under my chair, grinning a gap-zippered and mocking grin. "Gretchen," says Melissa slowly. "We were about to sing 'Rose of Sharon.' Will you lead it?"

"Nope," I say. "I just quit."

"It's your favorite hymn," she says.

"I know it's my favorite hymn. That's why I don't want to hear it tortured to death."

"If you're quitting, what do you care?"

I can't read her tone, and I can't read the choir. They look solemn, almost grim, but I'm damned if I can tell what they're thinking. Probably that I look like an idiot standing there sweating in my Michelin Man coat and my watch-cap and my muffler, and that I'll look like an idiot whether I take Melissa at her word or walk out again. A lose-lose situation. I'm used to those. The trick is to do the thing they really don't want you to do, which, in this case, is to stay.

"OK," I say. "'Rose of Sharon' it is. 'I am the Rose of Sharon and the Lily of the Valley.'"

Silence. Silence while I shed my winter-proofing; silence while I find my place and my pitch-pipe; silence while I raise my hand. On the downbeat the trebles come in on Sol, round and clear as a Raphael madonna. Five measures later, the altos join them on the upbeat, Sol and Fa. Our voices blend, tone on tone, layer on layer, shivering with overtones like heat lightning in the desert. We're one big instrument, an organ piped through forty throats, sending our hymn to heaven. The music swells to bursting, and then it does burst, and the air trembles and explodes into an angel.

Although I've never seen an angel before and I'm not what you'd call a religious person, it never crosses my mind to question what I'm seeing. It's more beautiful then I could have imagined, with eyes like suns and hair like glory and wings like a thousand rainbows flickering all around it. Still singing, I gawk up at it; our eyes meet, the world inverts, and suddenly I'm suspended between heaven and earth, floating in music.

The first thing I notice is that I'm happy. Happy? Ecstatic. Blissful. Joy runs through me like blood, burning in my cheeks and pulsing in the soft feathers of my wings. Joy informs my vision, sharpens it so that I can see every scratch in the heavy beams upholding the church tower, every tiny insect living in its cracks and corners, every prayer that has been prayed here. I can see the choir, mouths and throats working, a fourfold unity every bit as mysterious as Divinity. I see each pore of their skin, each hair of their heads, each nail, each eyelash in all their fleshly presence. And beyond and behind that, I can see their souls, their complex, eternal selves.

I could understand them in a myriad ways, but the clearest to me is paintings and music. Melissa is a mastiff painted by Frida Kahlo and scored by Aaron Copland. Morton is a Monet garden set to Wagner. Jess is a Dürer engraving of a hare twitching its nose to Philip Glass. Each holds one shape for a moment and then drifts as I watch into another form, another mode, another composition of line and spirit different from the one preceding it, but allied. Secure in eternity, I contemplate the multiplicity of the souls and the singleness of the purpose that have called and created me.

In the center of the choral square a single figure stands islanded. She's the horse from Picasso's *Guernica,* angular and agonized, and the horse from *Guernica* she remains, petrified in terrified fury. The music that defines her is a shape-note hymn, repeated endlessly. As I focus on her, the melody drops away and leaves only the words, chanted in a voiceless howl: "And must I be to judgment brought and answer in that day / For every vain and idle thought and every word I say?"

That's not right, I think. She's got it all wrong. And I reach down and brush her cheek with one of my thousand wings. "Rejoice," I sing. "Rise, my soul, and stretch thy wings, thy better portion trace. Rise from all terrestrial things toward heaven, thy native place."

Below me, "Rose of Sharon" paces slowly to its end. We end up in a perfect chord, La, Sol, Fa, Fa, so absolutely on pitch that harmonics sound the octaves above and below it, as if the whole heavenly choir were singing with us. The figure in the square—a woman atomized, a Picasso or a Braque—closes her mouth, brings down her hand and the tower is empty, the singers silent, and I'm standing among them, my cheek tingling.

"Wow," says someone, breaking the mood of exaltation, or at least making it bearable. People start to breathe and move again, fold their chairs, clean up the stage, put on their coats, and drift slowly toward the door. Nobody's talking a lot, but everybody's smiling, and there's a lot of spontaneous hugging. They're like that around here, even without angels.

The hall is almost empty when I finally pull myself together. Melissa's still there, and Morton and Jess, putting on their coats. As I collect my belongings from the middle of the empty floor, Melissa comes up to me. Her plastic rabbits are tucked away under a huge purple knitted tam with a bright green bobble. She shakes my hand.

"A great singing, Gretchen," she says. "I look forward to next week."

"Yeah," I say. "Me too. You want to warm us up?"

Melissa smiles, and I think I hear an echo of *Appalachian Spring*. "Sure," she says. "Bye."

Jess gives my arm a punch in passing. "Thanks," I say, and she nods. "Nice music. I'll be back."

"Good," I say.

Morton holds out his arms, offering an embrace. I intercept his right hand and shake it firmly, vaguely relieved that seeing an angel hasn't turned me into an indiscriminate hugger.

Outside, the wind has let up and the sleet has softened into snow. Everything's white-feathered—the gray stone church, the parking lot, the markers in the old graveyard. The ground is cold and slick and treacherous underfoot. But as I pick my way carefully towards my car, I'm humming "Rose of Sharon," and my face is warm with the touch of an angel's wing.

THE PRINTER'S DAUGHTER

On the morning of All Hallow's Eve, Hal Spurtle sat at the window of his shop and watched the children play. They were ragged children, as it was a ragged street, their faces and caps smudged with dirt and their petticoats and breeches tattered as old paper. Grave as judges, they linked hands and danced sunwise, chanting the while in their bird-shrill voices.

Thread the needle, thread the needle,
Eye, eye, eye.
Thread the needle, thread the needle,
Eye, eye, eye.
The tailor's blind and he can't see,
So we must thread the needle.

Hal remembered singing that rhyme himself. He'd taught it to his young sisters as they played on a Shoreditch street that differed from this not so much as milk from cream. As he watched little Rose and Ned Ashcroft, Anne and Katty and Jane Dunne winding up and down the cobbles, he told the rhyme over to himself, very soft.

Hal sighed and turned his eyes back to the trays of type, the compositor's stick, and the manuscript pages stacked alongside. The collected sermons of the good Dr. Beswick, passed by the Queen's censor and writ down in the Register of the Company of Stationers. Dull as an old knife, but legal to print and to sell, making a change from the bawdy broadsides, the saucy quartos, the unblushingly filthy octavos that made up the greater part of his stock-in-trade. The great pornographer Arentino himself might have turned color at *The Cuckold's Mery Iest* and expired of shame at *In Praise of Pudding-Pricks*. But it had been a matter of Necessity the son riding before Caution the father, for on being made free of the Company of Stationers, Hal must needs set up shop for himself, though he could scarce afford a press and its furniture. To pay for which, Hal must needs converse with scarcity and rogues, until by chance a country clergyman approached him with a manuscript of sermons and a purse to pay for their printing.

Hal's old master, John Day, would have done the job in a week, but John Day had two 'prentices to ink, cut pages, and distribute type, as well as compositors, pressmen, gatherers, folders, and binders to do the other work. Hal, working man-alone, had been at the business two weeks already, with Dr. Beswick threatening to take his sermons and his ten pounds elsewhere, God take the thought from him; for his ten pounds were even now scattered like grain among Hal's creditors.

Furthermore, Hal himself was weak and weary with poor feeding, and as like to drop a line of type as bring it whole to the imposing-table. On All Hallow's Eve, he did that once or twice, and then he transposed two lines of type, the which cost him fifty sheets of best French Imperial, and over-inked a plate with so free a hand that he must pour the piss-pot over it to cleanse it. Not three impressions later, he did the same again, whereupon Hal consigned Dr. Beswick and his sermons to the most noisesome deep of Hell; viz, Satan's arse-hole. For over-inking was such a monkey's trick as he'd not been guilty of for fifteen years or more.

An apprentice would serve the present need, he thought; a likely, lively lad content to live upon pulp and printer's ink, a lad who never reversed lines nor set them arsy-versy. But Hal well knew that were there such a 'prentice in London, he'd never bind himself to a press where half the texts were unlicensed and the other half unlicensable. His eyes falling upon the twists of paper from *In Praise of Pudding-Pricks* and Dr. Beswick's sermons, equally damned by their ill-printing, piled in the corner where an apprentice might sleep, Hal gathered up divers sheets and twisted them into skinny arms and legs, wrapped scraps and wads into a lumpy head and carcass, and bound the whole with thread into human shape. When it was done, he shook his head over the poor, blind face, and taking up ink and pen, carefully limned features: a button nose, doe's eyes, and a Cupid's mouth. He thought it favored his small sister Kate.

The wind, having risen with the moon, came hunting down the narrow street for mischief, the which it found in the shape of Hal's window shutter. Howling, it pounced upon the latch and tore it open and slapped the wood to and fro against the glass. Hal laid his poppet upon a nest of paper and ran out-a-doors to catch it. He had just put the shutter up and was going in again when a small, straddling fellow clawed him by the elbow and would not be put by.

"I seek Hal Spurtle the printer's," he said.

"I am Hal Spurtle," said Hal. "What would you with me?"

"To go within," said the man. "My business is not for the common street."

Loath was Hal to oblige him, the hour being late and none save rogues likely to be abroad. Yet rogues were the chiefest part of his custom; and so he brought the stranger into the shop. In the lamplight the man proved a veritable Methuselah, with a face like a shelled walnut and a back like the hoop of a cart. His hands and stump-trimmed beard were vilely stained, and there hung a stink about him of sulphur and brimstone. By which signs Hal understood the stranger to be an alchemist, the which he further understood to be a filthy trade and unlawful. So it was with faint courtesy that he demanded of the old man once again why he sought Hal Spurtle the printer?

"To give him a job of work," answered the alchemist, and poked and patted in his gown until he found a thick sheaf of vellum tied with tape, the which he handed to Hal, who took it as gingerly as may be.

"Untie it. 'Twill not eat thee," said the man.

Slowly, Hal did so, uncovering a page writ margin to margin in secretary hand, damnably crabbed. Forty pages in quarto, or perhaps fifty, say two weeks to set and print if the edition were not large. He squinted at the tiny, curling letters.

Liquor conioynyth male with female wife,
And causith dede thingis to resorte to lyfe.

Hal dropped the manuscript hastily. "Your job of work could bring me to my neck verse, granddad."

"*In Praise of Pudding-Pricks* could lose thee thy right hand, or any of the bawdry thou dost use to print. This goose is only more highly spiced, and lays golden eggs besides. An edition of thirteen copies, printed as accurate as may be, sewn for binding. Shall we say twenty crowns?"

Hal's teeth watered at the sum. Twenty crowns would rid him of his debts and buy him a new font of type, an apprentice, even a pressman who knew a platen from a frisket. Before he could gather his wits to say yea or nay, the old man said, "It must be done by Sunday moonrise, mind, or 'tis no good to me."

"Sunday moonrise! Why did you not come to me earlier, pray? I cannot set, proof, print, and sew thirteen copies in two days, not if I worked without stop or let from dawn to dawn. The thing's impossible. As well ask a cat to pull a cart."

"You have no apprentice?"

"I have not, sir. An had I the two apprentices the law allows, yea, and twenty journeymen, too, still the job would take a week or more. And I've another book promised and owing must take precedence."

The old man peered shortsightedly into the shadows. "Yet I thought I saw an apprentice as I came in—a lad sleeping on a pallet, there in the corner."

Hall followed the goodman's gaze to the poppet he'd made. It did look uncommonly like a sleeping child. "'Tis naught," he said shortly. "A pile of paper."

The old man heaved himself upright, took up the lamp, and hobbled over to see for himself. "An homunculus, as I am a man! You'd not said you dabbled in the Art, Master Spurtle."

Hall crossed himself. "God forbid, sir."

The old man's crow-bright eye pierced Hal's skull from brow to bald spot. "Art lonely, lad?"

"Aye," said Hal, surprised into honesty.

"And no sister or wife to keep thy house or warm thy bed?"

"My sisters will not forgive me my learning, an it not go hand-in-hand with wealth. As for a wife, I've no stomach for the wooing, nor coin for the keeping when she's won."

"No matter," said the old man. "See here, Hal Spurtle. Should I find thee a 'prentice fit for the work, wilt undertake to print my book by Sunday moonrise?"

"He needs must be a prodigy of nature."

"As prodigious as thou wilt. 'Tis a bargain, then. Thy hand on it, Hal Spurtle. This purse will stay thy present need."

The purse contained five pounds in silver: a goodly earnest. Hal weighed it in his palm. "Why, if I'm a madman, you're another, and there's a pair on us. My hand on it, then."

They shook hands solemnly, and then the old gentleman took up his carven stick, hobbled to the door, and, without another word, was gone like the devil in the old play.

St. Martin's tolled midnight. Hal rubbed his cheeks wearily and picked up the lamp to light him to bed. Catching a movement in the corner of his eye—*a rat,* he thought, and had turned him away when a voice arrested him: a small, dry voice, like the rustling of pages.

"Sinner," it said, "look thou to thine end."

The hair crept upon Hal's skin like lice. What had the old rogue left behind him?

"To each thing must thou pay heed," said the voice. "To thy comings-in and thy goings-out, to thy pleasures and thy pains, that they be pleasing unto the Lord."

Surely a demon would not prate as from a pulpit; though 'twas said the devil could quote scripture to the soul's confusion. "Back to Hell with thee, demon," said Hal sternly. "I've no wish to look upon thy hideous countenance."

There was a faint rustling from the corner. "The kingdom of God is of a fairness beyond the measure of man, and the tidings thereof are comfortable." The voice was sad and something fearful, like Hal's sister Kate begging grace for some roguery. The memory softening his heart, he turned and beheld no horned devil, but a girl-child of six years' growth, sitting mother-naked in a nest of paper.

"Hallelujah, saith the angel, and the sons of man rejoice," she said firmly.

Hal squatted down before her and reached out one hand to touch her head. It was not bald, but covered with an uneven pelt, white mottled with black, like blurred print. Her face was likewise piebald and soft as old rags, her cheeks round as peaches, like Kate's or Ann's or any of the small sisters whom Hal had dandled. Like them, she was as bony as a cur-pup, and as hollow-eyed. Only her mouth was fair, a pure and innocent bow.

The fair mouth opened and she spoke. "A groat will buy my hand, good sir, and a penny my cunt. But 'tis three pennies for my mouth, for washing the taste out after."

"Out upon thee for a forward wench," cried Hal, and struck her with his open hand so that she wailed aloud. As shocked as he'd been by her bawdry, still more was Hal grieved by her piteous cries. He caught up a clout from a chair, bundled it around her naked, flailing arms and legs, and gathered her, howling, to his breast.

"There, now," he crooned over the piebald head. "Hush thee, do. Thou'rt not so hurt as astonished, the which may be said of me as well."

The child quietened at his voice and sniffled and settled against him. "His yoke is easy and his burden is light," she said tearfully. "Wherefore dost thou grieve him with thy sins?"

Hal rocked her silently for a moment, then asked, "Art hungered, sweeting? Shall I fetch thee a sop of milk and bread?"

"Flesh and ale's good meat to my belly, and swiving thereafter."

Hal looked stonily upon the lass; she showed him small, crooked teeth in an imp's smile. "Thou shalt cry, 'Pardon, Pardon,' and it will avail thee naught. For sin is stamped upon thy soul from thy mother's womb; thou art cast and molded of it."

"'As prodigious as thou wilt,'" murmured Hal. "I begin to apprehend." He loosed his arms, and the girl-child stood upright on paper-twist limbs and made her ways to the composing-table, where she began to distribute the scattered type into the cases, her arms spinning like flywheels so that the clout dropped from her shoulders and she stood naked on the floor.

Hal slipped into the inner room, where he hunted out hose and a shirt only a little torn and a rope to belt it. These he carried into the shop and tossed upon the table where she could not choose but to see them.

She straightway fetched up the clothing and held it this way and that against her body until Hal began to laugh, whereat she cocked her head, aggrieved. "So ask not, saying, how shall we eat, or how shall we drink, or wherewithal shall we be clothed; for after all these things do the Gentiles seek."

"Do them on nonetheless; the wind will not temper itself to a shorn lamb, and thou'rt prodigy enough in a clothed state. Thou'lt need a name, too. Textura? Roman? Bastarda?" The child blew a fart with her lips. Hal grinned. "Not Bastarda. Demy. Broadside." Gazing here and there in search of inspiration, his eye chanced to light upon the press, the frisket unfolded, the tympan empty. "Frisket," he said decidedly.

The child smiled at that, and uttered not a word, neither of bawdry or scripture, by which Hal understood that she was much moved, as, in truth, was Hal himself.

"'Gie thee good den, Frisket," said Hal. "Now to bed, under the press, as snug as a mouse. We'll up betimes and begin work."

Upon entering his shop at cock-crow next morning, Hal half thought he'd wandered in his sleep to his master's printing shop at Alder's Gate. The composing and imposing tables were scrubbed clean of ink stains, the floor swept and garnished, the ink-balls washed and hung to dry. The piebald child was bent over the press, industriously greasing the tracks. She'd shot up in the night, mushroom-like, to a gawky girl of twelve or thereabouts, with her hair grown to rat's tails strewn across the back of Hal's shirt and her bony arms black to the elbow with ink.

"Frisket," said Hal. "Is't thou in very sooth, lass?"

"When I was a child, I understood as a child; now I am become a man, I put away childish things."

"Thou'rt nigher Heaven than thou wast, and something stouter." He glanced suspiciously at the cupboard. "Has left me a sup?"

"Man doth not live by bread alone," said Frisket smugly. "Come kiss me, sweet chuck, and clip me close." And she gestured to the hearth, where ale was warming, and a half-loaf of bread and a crust of cheese laid ready on a plate, to which Hal applied himself right heartily.

"There is a wanton will not want one, if place and person were agreeable to his desires."

Hal swallowed hard. "Before we make a start, I would say a word. Sermonizing I can bear. Bawdry ill befits thy tender years. Cleave to Dr. Beswick, an it pleaseth thee, and let *In Praise of Pudding-Pricks* be."

Frisket looked dumpish. "As the goose is sauced, so is the gander," she said.

"I'd think shame to read the knavery my poverty beds me withal," Hal said.

"Out upon thee, old juggler! Thy sparrow is dead 'i the nest, and will not rise up and sing, squeeze and kiss I never so cleverly."

Hal yielded the field blushing, nor sought to engage again; but as they worked that day composing and printing the sheets, he made note that Frisket's tongue wagged less, and more upon a pedantical breeze than a bawdy. The morning flowed into day and the evening into night like streams into a river, quiet and unmarked. But when St. Anthony's bell came tolling midnight, there were only three sheets made perfect, twenty-four pages out of fifty-two. Despairing, Hal sat him down for a brace of minutes to rest his aching back.

He woke to broad daylight and Frisket mixing ink.

"Wake thee, wake thee, sinner, for the bridegroom cometh," she caroled.

Hal started to his feet. Ten stacks of perfect sheets stood ranged upon the composing-table. He took one up and checked it, back and front. The inking was dark and even, the lines prettily justified, the text as sensible as such a text might be.

"So thou shalt ask of thyself: am I a sinner, or am I a righteous man?"

Hal looked up at Frisket's ink-blotched face in wonder. "A righteous man, beyond all doubt. In fact," he continued, "there's a question which of us is master and which 'prentice."

Frisket smiled to show her teeth—piebald as her skin and hair—and then he and she turned to collating the sheets, to folding and cutting them into books and sewing the signatures together. They worked in quiet amity, with the ease of long use and custom, the one handing the other knife or thread at need, without a word exchanged. Now and again he'd glance from the sewing-frame to see her ink-drop eyes upon him, whereat they'd smile at one another and bend to their tasks again.

Hope came to Hal, that long had been a stranger to his heart. His mind began to wander in uncharted seas of poems and plays and philosophical tracts that might be registered and put for public sale in St. Paul's churchyard, and a little house in St. Martin's Lane, with a shop at the back and two journeymen to run the press, and Frisket, of course, properly bound and entered in the Rolls of Apprentices. She'd need a better name than Frisket. Mary, he thought—the mother of Our Lord. Mary Spurtle, his elder brother's child, if any were to ask. But he and she would know she was Hal's own Frisket, the daughter of his heart.

Come moonrise, Hal and Frisket were grinning at one another across the hearth, with thirteen quarto alchemical ordinals stacked neatly on the composing-table behind them. The door latch rattled and Frisket ran to open it.

"Behold, the bridegroom cometh, and upon his brow is righteousness," she said, flourishing a bow.

The alchemist beetled his brows at her and at Hal, who sat laughing by the fire. "Thou art pleased to take thine ease," he said testily. "The silver I gave thee cost me something in the making. I trust thou hast not squandered it in liquor."

"Nay, nay, good Master Alchemist, I have not, nor so much as a moment in sleep or sup. There is your book as you required it, printed as fine, though I say it, as Caxton in his prime."

The alchemist took up the topmost book and leafed through its pages, hemming here and hawing there, looking up at last and nodding to Hal almost with courtesy. "Excellent," he said. "Excellent good in very sooth. Thou hast labored mightily, thou and thy 'prentice, in bringing forth this text. And so I will ask thee, Hal Spurtle, whether thou wouldst take a copy in payment, that is the only true receipt for the making of gold and silver, or content thee only with the twenty crowns I promised thee."

Hal laughed aloud. "I cry you pardon, granddad, but I'd leifer have ink upon my hands than quicksilver. Twenty crowns, wisely spent, will bring me to twenty more as well as thy receipt, and with more surety. We'll do well enough, my 'prentice and I."

The alchemist shrugged his shoulders, and having dealt the books here and there about his person, took out a purse and gave it over to Hal's hand and prepared to go his ways. Upon reaching the door, a thought stopped him. "Thy apprentice," he said. "How dost thou like him?"

Hal, feeling Frisket shadowy at his side, drew her forward into his arm. "I like her very well," he said.

"Her," said the old man. "Curious."

When he was alone, Hal tossed the heavy purse aloft, jingling. "Here's a weighty matter, poppet, must be lightened ere it burst. We've need of meat and ale and bread and women's weeds to clothe thee withal."

"Smock climb apace, that I may see my joys."

"Aye, a smock, and petticoats and a woolen skirt and a shawl against the winter wind, and leathern shoes." He kissed her lightly upon the head. "I'll warrant thee to make a bonny wench. We'll to market at daylight."

Overwatched, Hal slept almost until noon, by which time Frisket had finished printing Dr. Beswick's sermons, aye, and cut and sewn them, too. Hal crowed with joy, swung her under the arms, bundled the books with binding thread, and carried them to Dr. Beswick's lodgings, where he gave them into the gentleman's hand, full of apologies for the delay and thanks for his patience.

"Patience," piped Frisket, "is of the Virtues the most cardinal; for all things come to him who waiteth upon the word of God."

Hal looked sharp to see whether the reverend gentleman be offended or no. "My new apprentice, sir, my brother's child. Touched by the finger of God, sir, but quick and good-hearted as may be."

"So I perceive," said Dr. Beswick. "My own words upon patience, pat as I writ 'em. 'Tis pity he's so ill-marked. Stay, now, here's another sovereign. I'd not thought to see my books this sennight."

Hal took the sovereign and thanked the reverend gentleman, and bore Frisket off to the old-clothes market at Cornhill. He bought a woolen gown and a shawl, two smocks, a pair of stays, and after some hesitation, a petticoat of fine scarlet—lifted, no doubt, from some merchant's drying-yard—and a linen cap. Home again, he pinned and laced her into her new array as tenderly as a mother, even to braiding her magpie hair down her back and tying her cap over it.

"Thou'rt a proper lass now," he told her, "and the apple of mine eye. I'm off now to St. Paul's to hear the news, see perhaps may I come by a pamphlet or a book of ABC to print and sell. No more Merry Jests, my Frisket, or Valentines or Harlot's Tricks for us. From this moment, the bishop of London himself will have no cause to blush for our work."

"Here lieth an alehouse, with chambers above and beds in the chambers. Pray you, love, walk in with me."

"Nay, child, I'll take thee another time. Take thou thine ease, but see thou stray not, and, as thou lovest me, temper thy tongue as thou mayst; for not all have the trick of thy speech. If any ask, thou art my brother's child, called Mary, Mary Spurtle, come to keep my house and learn my trade." He took his purse then, and finding therein some coppers and a silver piece, wrapped them in a clout and bade her tie them underneath her petticoat.

She looked at the little bundle with bemusement. "I swive for love, and not for base coin," she said doubtfully.

"The daughter of the house must have coin when she ventures abroad. And thou art the only daughter I am like to have. So take thy purse. Thou has earned it."

So Hal went whistling towards St. Paul's and Frisket watched him down the street, her eyes bright and shy as a mouse's.

"Hey there, wench." A boy's sharp treble hailed her from Mistress Dunne's front window. "What makest thou at Hal Printer's?"

Frisket stepped out in the street and smiled, which brought Jane and Ann and Katty forth across the cobbled street to sniff about her skirts in the manner of pet dogs: cautious, but more apt to fawn than to bite.

"What's thy name?" inquired Ann, who was the eldest.

Frisket opened her mouth and closed it again. "Frisket" was nowhere printed on her body. Yet Hal had given her another name, a name found in both sermon and bawdry. "Mary," she said. "Come, play with me."

"What wouldst thou play?" asked Katty, ever generous. "Wildflowers and Old Roger and Thread the Needle's our favorites, but we'll play a new if thou'lt learn it us."

Frisket had knowledge of many plays, all of them new to Katty and all of them from that part of her mind Hal disapproved of her speaking. Accordingly, she hoisted one skinny shoulder as one who defers to her hosts, and Jane said, "Let it be Lazy Mary, then. Dost know it?"

Frisket shook her head.

"Hath the cat a-hold of thy tongue, Mary?" taunted Jane; in response to which Frisket exhibited hers, catless, but mottled pink and black, whereat Jane laughed 'til Ann cuffed her ear and bade her mend her manners. Jane subsiding, Ann told Frisket the words to the game, that were *Lazy Mary will you get up, will you get up today?*

"And then thou shalt answer," interrupted Jane, "that thou wilt not, whatever dainties we offer, until that we offer thee a nice young man."

So they laid Frisket down among them, with her apron over her face, and turned about her, singing. And when it was time for her to answer, Frisket frowned under her apron, opened her mouth, and sang:

My mistress is a cunny fine
And of the finest skin.
And if you care to open her,
The best part lies within.
Yet in her cunny burrow may
Two tumblers and a ferret play.

Jane giggled; Ann blushed rose.

"Nay, now, Mary, prithee do not mock us," said Katty.

"The devils of Hell mock the blessed," said Frisket, "for those very joys they are blest withal."

"Art mad?" asked Ann. "We are not let to play with mad folk."

"Sing again," said Jane, and Frisket sang again, by bad fortune just when Mistress Dunne was out at her door to see her children play. Now, Mistress Dunne was a God-fearing woman, a great enemy to oaths and tobacco and all manner of loose living; so that hearing Frisket's song, she screeched like unto a scalded cat and pounced upon the girl and boxed her ears until they rang like St. Paul's at noon.

Frisket put her hands to her ears wonderingly, as though she hardly understood the smart. "Well mayst thou look sullen," scolded Mistress Dunne. "Thou'rt overripe for a beating. Filthy girl. Dost not know so much as wash thy face?"

Frisket spat upon her hand and rubbed her cheek, then held her hand to Mistress Dunne to show it neither more black nor more white, but mottled as before, like the coat of a brindle dog. Mistress Dunne looked at the hand and the face and the thick, piebald plait lying over Frisket's shoulder, and made the sign of the Cross in the air between them. "Devil's mark," she cried, and spat, and gathering her children to her, chivvied them within, Frisket trailing after, saying:

"May not a sinner, being penitent, enter into the Kingdom of Heaven?"

"God save us, the child is mad," cried Mistress Dunne, and clapped to the door against Frisket's nose, whereat Frisket, showing a perfect devil's countenance of red and black, cast a flood of Bilingsgate upon the unyielding wood, drenching it with such verbs, nouns, and adverbs that would have stunk, had they been incarnate, like unto three-days' fish. And then she turned and ran heedless among the lanes and alleys of East Cheape.

The force that drove her no man could tell, nor could Frisket neither. She did not think as men thought, did not feel or know or hope as a child begotten of man and born of woman. The highest and most base exhalations of man's soul had gone into her making, and the words they gave her were all she knew. Neither piety nor bawdry taught her to say, "there is no place for me here; I must return to that I was."

Hal came again unto his house when the bells of St. Martin's were ringing for Evensong. His feet spurned the mud and his eyes dwelt on the wonders of being able to command a font of print and then buy the right of a pamphlet upon the making of cheese and enter it upon the Register and still have money and enough in his purse to do the same again.

"Frisket," he called as he lifted the latch. "Frisket, heart of my heart, come hither, and thou shalt partake of roast fowl and sack at the Doublet and Hose as 'twere any lady. Frisket? Frisket, I say! Beshrew me, where is the wench?" And receiving no answer, Hal peered and pried through his two small chambers where a mouse could not lie hid, searching in rising panic for his paper 'prentice.

Presently did Hal go out into the streets around, calling for Frisket up and down, and then, weary and sick with worry, to Mistress Dunne to entreat her whether she had seen his niece or no.

"His niece, quotha!" she exclaimed. "His trull, more like, and a good riddance to her and her slattern's tongue."

Hal, hoping for news, kept firm hold upon his temper. "She knows no better, God forgive my brother that it should be so," he said humbly. "I've hopes of teaching her better ways in time. She's a good lass at heart."

"A good lass would disdain to know such oaths, nor profane the purity of her lips with bawdry."

"She is an innocent of offense as of the true meaning of what she says."

Mistress Dunne patted Hal on the shoulder. "Thou'rt a kind man, Hal Spurtle, and simple as a newborn lamb. Never doubt thy self-called niece hath cozened thee finely. She's off with thy purse or thy linen, or some costly matter of thy trade, depend on't." And from this opinion she could not be turned.

So Hal took him home again to his empty shop, emptier now of one piebald, cheeky wench, and soon came out again, determined as Jason to find that moth-eaten golden fleece the ancient alchemist, to beg of him news of Frisket.

The while Hal was seeking her up and down, Frisket had won through the alleys of Cheape Ward to Fish Street, that was a broad street of fair houses, very busy with horses and men in furred gowns and velvet caps and women in farthingales and hooded cloaks. They jostled her as she stood, heeding her no more than the lean dogs nosing at the fish heads in the road, save for one young girl with a feathered hat perched on her bright hair, who pressed a penny in Frisket's hand and smiled pityingly upon her. For want of a better direction, Frisket followed her, losing her almost at once in the bustle that bore her will-she, nil-she across a bridge cobbled like a street and lined with rich houses. On the further bank, Frisket turned aside from the high way to walk along the river, flowing grey and brown as porridge between slick, pewter banks. The sky was pewter too, tarnished and pitted with clouds, and the houses along the wharf leaned between them like beggars at an almshouse board.

One in three of those houses were marked like taverns, with signs painted bright above their doors, as the Cardinal's Cap, the Bird in the Bush, the Silent Woman, the Snake and Apple. Outside this last, a weaseling, minching fellow accosted Frisket, who gazed thoughtfully at the one-eyed snake of the blazon, that curled from Adam's loins toward the Apple held between Eve's plump thighs.

"Hey, thou ninny," he said. "What maketh thou here, walking so bold in Southwark?"

Frisket's ado with Mistress Dunne had taught her to stick to scripture. So she bethought her a moment and said, "The ways of the Lord are surpassing strange and beyond the wit of man to tell them."

The man drew closer, darted out his hand like Adam's snake and, clipping her by the wrist, held her fast. "A prating Puritan maid, by Cock," he snarled. "Marked like the Devil's own, and comely as a succubus withal. What are thy parents?"

"We have no father nor mother, save that Heavenly Parent is Father and Mother to us all."

The man's eyes gleamed in his sharp face. "Art meat for my feeding, then."

Frisket, finding no apt response recorded in the tablets of her mind, met his eyes gravely, glanced at his fingers about her wrist, and back into his eyes, whereupon he dropped her arm to shield him from her gaze. "Go thy ways," he said. "Thou'rt safe from me. Yet the Southwark bawdy-houses are an ill place for a maid to wander, even a maid touched by God."

Frisket nodded. "The way of righteousness is the way of truth, and much beset with thorns." Then she turned her about and made away from the river, leaving the bawd muttering and scratching his head.

Some things she did that afternoon and evening of her flight, who can say why or wherefore. She bought a loaf with the young girl's penny and divided it among a man in the stocks, three beggars, and a starve-boned dog; she slipped into the Bear Garden to watch the baiting with ink-drop eyes, and when 'twas done, crept back to where the bears were kept tied in the straw, undid their muzzles with quick fingers, picked apart the heavy knots about their feet, and slipped away again, leaving the gate a little ajar behind her.

Just at dusk, she passed a tall wooden building with cressets burning by the door, and a noise within like a giant's roaring, and bills without proclaiming that Mr. William Shak-spere, his *Tragedie of Cymbeline* was this day to be played. The bills were hastily run-up, and the inking over-heavy, so that the letters were spread and blurred; Frisket frowned ere she turned away.

Some little time later, she came to a tavern and passed it not, but entered under its sign of The Swan and Cygnet. Within was noise and heat enough for a liberty of Hell, from trollops and cony-catchers and 'prentices and clerks and wharfmen, all calling for ale while tavern-maids and potboys scurried among them with tankards and trays and wooden bowls.

Frisket made like a hunting dog for the back of the house, where sat a young man all among the kegs and barrels. He, like the man in the stocks, the bears, and the beggar, was in difficulties. The host stood glaring whilst he expostulated, pale as a ghost, showing a pair of strings across his palm that might have borne a purse, before they'd been cut.

"I'll leave the jewel from my ear in surety," he was saying. "An I come not again to pay you, it will bring you twenty times the price of the ale and meat."

"For all I know, 'tis base metal overlaid with brass, and worth no more than thy word. I'm minded to take thy two shillings out of thy hide, and set thee up for an exemplum of a liar and a thieving knave."

The host raised one hand like a haunch of beef and the young man sprang to his feet, caught between pride and fear whether he would flee the host or close with him. Frisket slipped between them and laid her hand upon the host's uplifted arm, and said, "I'll pay thy price, though it be an hundred pound."

The host shaking her away, she took her pocket and jingled it in his ear that would hear no other plea, and it spoke to him and calmed him, and by and by he took the monies owed him, and a little over to buy a pottle of wine to soothe the young man's nerves, and left them there together amongst the kegs and barrels in the quiet back of the tavern.

The young man smoothed his doublet that was worn and frayed at the cuffs, and then his beard, and having set himself to rights, handed Frisket onto a joint-stool as it had been a chair of state and she the Queen's own Grace.

"Robert Blanke the poet thanks thee, fair maid," said he. "Whithout thy silver physic, I had been as dead as Lazarus, without hope of resurrection. How may I call thee?"

"Mary, sir, and withal the merriest Mary thou has melled withal."

The young man eyed her in the uncertain light. "A harlot? Sure, I grow old, that jades look like fillies to me, and trollops like young maids."

"For I am thy savior, saith the Lord, and a present help in all thy trouble."

"Now the Lord help me indeed, for I bandy words with a madwoman. Yet the mad are touched by God, they say, and own a wisdom beyond the understanding of the wise." He reached out long fingers and, taking her by the chin, tilted her head gently to catch the light. What he saw was a girl on womanhood's threshold, her brow serene, her nose straight and fine, her eyes large and smooth-lidded, her lips clear-carved in a perfect Cupid's bow, her expression open and grave. Thus might an angel look, he thought, or a spirit of antiquity dressed in flesh and a patched woolen gown, were an angel's skin marred and mottled everywhere with flecks of black like blurred print. He released her chin and caressed his beard. "What are you?" he asked.

"I am," said Frisket, "none of your plain or garden whores; I can read and play the virginals. We are children of God, each one, and His angels have the keeping of the least of us no less than of the greatest."

"A very sensible nonsense, as I live. I well can believe that you, like the phoenix, are alone of your kind, and I accept you mean no harm. I am your debtor for your mere acquaintance, the more for your saving of me. And therefore I ask of you what you would of me?"

Blanke was a quick-witted man, and eager to unriddle her cypher. Still it took Frisket long and long to make him understand what she was and what she wanted, by which time the tavern was empty and the host hovering by with a broom and a scowl.

"Hark ye," said the poet. "'Tis dawn, or very nigh, and my head is a tennis ball betwixt your sermons and your bawdries. Company me to my lodging and rest you there, and we'll take counsel of a new day."

So they went their ways through the waking streets, and when they reached the tenement where the poet lodged, he bowed her reverently through the door, saying, "I serve you in all honor, Mistress Mary; in token of which I give you my bed to rest upon and will sleep myself upon the floor."

For the first time Frisket smiled at him, showing him her mottled teeth. "For the eye of God sleepeth not," she said, "but watcheth ever over thy slumbers and wakings."

So Robert Blanke slept and Frisket watched, and Hal Spurtle came at last to the goal he had pursued throughout the long, sad night: the shop of the old alchemist, on Pardoner's Lane in Cripplegate, outside London Wall.

When the old man opened the door, he knit his brows. "Too late," he said. "The offer once refused will not be made again. Thou hast thy twenty crowns. Go thy ways."

Hal stuck his foot betwixt door and jamb. "And right content I am with them, I assure you. 'Tis my 'prentice, sir, the child you made from my poppet of paper."

"Hist," said the alchemist, and bundled Hal into the shop as quick as he'd been minded to bundle him out. "Hast no sense, man, to quack hidden things abroad in the public street? Thou'lt be the death of us both."

"And she's less sense than I, poor unbegotten mite, three days old, knows printing and naught else, not even her name, nor the skill to ask her way home again. Here are ten crowns, the half of your fee, to inquire of your demons where she may be and how she may be faring."

And Hal pressed his purse into the alchemist's greasy hand, who put it by, saying gruffly, "Nay. I'll help thee for kindness' sake, or not at all. Now," he said when Hal had put the purse into his bosom again, "now. The tale of the paper 'prentice. Calmly and simply as may be." He listened, his sharp eyes hooded and his stained hands laced before his long nose, while Hal told him of Frisket's cleverness and her goodness and her speaking in phrases either from Dr. Beswick's sermons or from one of the bawdy pamphlets whose spoiled sheets he'd used in her making. And when Hal was done, the alchemist lipped at his fingers, and hemmed once or twice, and nosed out a great clasped book, and found a page in it, and ran his finger down the page, and hemmed again, and peered out another that was small and black and powdery with age, and consulted that, and shut it, and closed his eyes, and munched his jaws. And just as Hal had decided that the old gentleman had fallen asleep, he sat himself upright, saying,"Thine apprentice, called by thee Frisket, was lent thee for a space, to answer thy present need. Give thanks for the loan, and grieve not the loss. For she is not of this earth, nor is there a place for her therein."

The tears started to Hal's eyes, nor was he too proud to let them fall, but wept for the daughter of his heart. And the alchemist rose from his chair and laid his hand upon his shoulder and pressed it. "Be of good cheer, man. The joy thou hadst of her is real. Consider that all children grow and leave their father's house, and 'prentices become journeymen at last."

"Yea," said Hal. "And yet may their fathers mourn them."

And Hal went from the alchemist to St. Paul's church, and knelt within, and prayed a space, and from thence among the bookstalls, inquiring for a journeyman to hire.

And it came to pass that Robert Blanke the poet woke to the sun's golden fingers laid upon his face and Frisket seated in the peaked window of his chamber, that was small and damp and high in the house.

Blanke sat up, scrubbed his hands in his eyes, and raked his hair seemy with his fingers. "Art up, old snorter?" Frisket inquired. "Or shall I lend a hand to raise thee?"

"Peace, good Mistress Mary; I prithee, peace. I am up, as thou see'st, but in no wise awake. Give me an hour to learn to believe in thee again, and to think what I may do with thee."

So Frisket accompanied Blanke to a cookshop, where she bought him a mutton pie, and to a tavern, where she bought him a tankard of small beer, and watched him eat and drink the same, and then into St. George's church, where she sat in a bench while he took to his knees, and so back to his lodging again as dusk drew her mantle across the sky.

"'Twas less magic than desire birthed thee," Blanke said to her, "the printer's desire for company; the alchemist's desire for his grimoire. So logic would argue 'tis desire must send thee back to thy papery womb. And there, dear Mistress Mary, is the rub. For my desire is rather to keep thee whole and sensible than to see thee senseless rubbish."

"Beware the Last Days, when all men are come to Judgment, and the inmost secret thoughts of their hearts laid bare."

For a space each pled his case, to and fro like lawyers, until at last Blanke threw up his hands and declared himself desirous, at least, of pleasing her who desired no other thing than to put off her dress of flesh, that chafed her as it had been a dress of fire.

"I have considered and I have prayed and I have invented a rite seems to answer your purpose." And he opened his mind and said what he purposed, whereat Frisket nodded and did off her clothes and laid her down upon his table, that he had cleared of his writing and his candle and his pens. The which persuaded him above all else that she was not of mankind.

"The Lord giveth," he said solemnly, "and the Lord taketh away. Even as it pleaseth the Lord, so cometh things to pass: blessed be the name of the Lord." And he took his quill pen into his hand and pressed the inky tip of it to her breastbone, that fanned apart as he touched it into leaves of paper, close-woven and white as snow, printed small and even, the margins wide and straight. Thus he unfolded Frisket and sorted her, praying over her all the while the Service of the Burial of the Dead, and when he'd made an end, he folded the great bundle of pages into her scarlet petticoat, that became a binding of scarlet leather stamped with gold on the cover and on the spine. And he lit a candle, for it had grown full dark, and turned the book to the light, and opened it.

The title page was plain and bare of ornament, bearing only the name of the book—*The Philosophy of the Senses: A Novel in Five Parts*—and the name of the author—Mary Spurtle. Blanke turned the page, crisp and white as a communion host, and read there, printed sharp and clear beyond all common type: "This book is dedicated to my father, Henry Spurtle, printer of East Cheape, and to Robert Blanke, poet and friend."

On the instant, Blanke started up from his chair and hied him to East Cheape, where he inquired high and low of the printer Henry Spurtle, where his shop lay. By and by he came to the lane behind St. Martin's church, and a low house that leaked out light and the heavy, wooden clacking of a printing press. Blanke knocked at the door, which was opened by a tall, sad-eyed man with a grandfather's lined cheeks under his nut-brown hair.

"I deal no more in curiosities," he said, and made to close the door.

"Stay, Henry Spurtle, an you would hear news of your daughter Mary."

A light came into Hal's dull eye and he drew Blanke into his shop, that was all a-bustle with activity. A man sat at the composing-table, selecting and sliding type into a composing stick with the steady rhythm of a new-wound clock. A boy stood at the press, an inking-ball in each hand, ready to apply them to the form when his master should be pleased to return to the press.

Hal wiped inky hands on his leathern apron. "A pamphlet on cheese making," he said and, bidding his new apprentice and his journeyman make all tidy 'gainst the morning's work, he gestured Blanke into the inner chamber, where the poet told him of Mistress Mary and all that had befallen her that he knew or guessed. And when he had done, he gave Hal the book bound in red leather and said, "Here is the book. I read the title and the letter dedicatory, and not one word more. For the book is yours, and no man else hath the right to read it."

Hal wiped his hands clean upon a clout, and took the book, and ran his thumb along the spine and along the gilded edges, and opened it, and gazed long and long upon the dedication to the author's father, Henry Spurtle, printer of East Cheape. As one who leaves a mourner to his grief, Blanke crept to the door; but when he lifted the latch, Hal raised his eyes saying, "I thank you, Robert Blanke, poet and friend. I'd repay you, an I could."

"Your thanks suffice, and Mistress Mary's tale, more wonderful than any of Master Boccacio's. And yet am I bold to beg the boon of you to read the book and learn what she became."

"Beyond question shall you read her, aye, and dine with me before, if you will. So much would any father do for the man who returned his daughter to him. Further, I had in mind to print an edition of your poems, had you enough to make two perfect sheets or three, cut into octavo and bound in boards, the profit to be split between us."

Blanke laughed aloud and clasped Hal's hand and pumped it as he'd pump water out from his mouth. "Now am I fallen deeply in thy debt," he cried. "Yet why speak of debt betwixt close kin? For if thou art her father, then am I her godfather, and we two bound together by love of her who has no like on earth. Now, thou hast a great work here in hand, must be pursued i' the heat. Come Sunday next, I'll be your man, and we'll drink to Mistress Mary in good sack. In the meantime, I'll look out my poems and copy them fair."

Hal pressed his hand and took him to the door and latched it behind him and smiled at his journeyman, who was making his bed under the press, and at his new 'prentice, asleep already in the shadowed corner by the fire, and at the sheets of the pamphlet on cheese-making, all hung out neat to dry. And he went into his inner chamber and closed the door, and took *The Philosophy of the Senses* in his hands, and opened it, and began to read.

NANNY PETERS AND THE FEATHERY BRIDE

Nanny Peters? You ain't never heard of old Nanny Peters? My land, if that don't beat all! Well, you set yourself down right here on the porch swing, and I'll tell you about her.

Nanny Peters was half ox, half prairie dog, with just a touch of the Rio Grande to leaven the mixture. She could hoe forty acres of beans, birth twenty calves, *and* set a good dinner on the table by noon, all without breakin' into a sweat. She had good, strong horse sense, and could tell a skunk from a woodchuck even on a dark night.

And cool! That woman was so cool, she didn't need an icehouse—she just put the milk jug under her bed and it'd keep a week or more. Why, she didn't even turn a hair when a big, sandy-white snake slithered in the front door one day, bold as brass. Nanny, she was scourin' the pots after a bean supper, and that snake sashayed right on up to her with his mouth wide open, showin' fangs like the horns on a Texas longhorn.

Nanny hears him slidin' along on the floor (on account of the scales on his belly, see). So she waits for him to get real close, and then she jest grabs that snake ahind the jawbone and wraps him three times around her fist and commences to scour her good cast-iron pot her mama give her. She scrubs and scrubs with that snake until there warn't a lick of crust left in the pot and the snake didn't have no more scales on his back than a baby has on her bottom. What's more, he was madder'n a wet hen and drippin' pizen and leavin' burnt marks on the floor and all.

So Nanny lets go the end of his tail and cleans the chimney with it, the snake givin' her considerable help by whoppin' around against the bricks. By the time the chimney's clean, the snake's feelin' mighty humble. So Nanny tells him to expect more of the same should he think to call again and takes and heaves him out the back door.

Now, old Nanny Peters bein' pretty strong in the arm from hoein' and scrubbin' and such, that snake sailed smack-dab across the state and landed five miles west of Abuquerque, New Mexico. He was half bald down the back and all covered with ashes and his tail was cut to shreds from frailin' it on the chimney bricks and his skull was all flatted out on account of he'd landed on his head. By and by he got better, but he warn't the same snake after—no, ma'am. His head stayed flatter'n a hotcake and his new scales grew in patchy. What's worser yet, his tail healed in hard ridges that clattered together and kep him awake at night.

And that, jest in case you wondered, is why there's rattlesnakes, and why they're so dad-burned tetchy.

But that's not what I set down to tell you about. Now, this here's the story, so you listen close.

Nanny Peters was a great quilter. In fact, some say she invented quiltin'. She could piece a double-size "Road to Texas" or "Tippecanoe" while the bread was risin', tack the top and the battin' and the back together while the oven heated, and quilt it solid before the crust turned brown. Something elegantifferously complicated, like "Grandmother's Flower Garden" or "Double Wedding Ring," might take her a mite longer. Her seams was so straight that people came from far away as Houston to check their yardsticks by 'em, and her stitches was so tiny you couldn't hardly see 'em, not even with a magnifying glass. And strong! My land, when the calico and battin' wore out, there's still be little white chains of stitches left, like a skellerton, and you could use it for a fancy bed throw or maybe a pair of lace curtains.

Nanny's specialty was weddin' quilts, and this was the reason for that. Let a couple spend their weddin' night under one of Nanny's quilts, and they was set for life. Whatever kind of rip-staver a man had been before his weddin' night, he was a changed man ever after. If he'd been a boozer, he'd take the pledge—and keep it, too. If he'd been a gambler, he'd clean forget the difference between a deuce and a three-spot, and he wouldn't care. A brawler'd get religion, a spendthrift'd pinch pennies till they squealed, a layabout'd bounce to work like a cougar, and as for a ladies' man! Why, he'd rather crawl into a nest o' wildcats, heels foremost, than think of lookin' at a woman other than his wife.

This being the case, it won't come as no surprise that girls got in the way of asking Nanny Peters if she'd kindly make them a weddin' quilt. Why, it got to be that a girl wouldn't walk down the aisle until she had Nanny's quilt safely folded in brown paper and laid in her linen chest. Some Saturdays the girls'd be lined up from Nanny's front door clear to Amarillo, beggin' her for a quilt—nothing fancy, mind you, just "Log Cabin" or "Round the World" or "Drunkard's Path" and they'd wait for it, if 'twas convenient, seein' as the weddin' was next week. And Nanny almost always obliged 'em, providin' they was willin' to help with the cuttin' out.

But ever once in a while, Nanny'd look at a girl, all bright and shy and eager to get hitched, and Nanny'd shake her head and say, "No."

Sometimes she'd say it sad, with a pat on the girl's shoulder or a cup of fresh coffee to make the "No" go down easier, and sometimes like she was too busy countin' clouds jest now and would be so long as that girl was askin'. Some of those girls Nanny said "No" to married their men anyway, and every last one of them ended up plum ramsquaddled: dead, or so put about by their menfolk's bodaciousness that they might as well be dead and save theirselves the shame. It got so that Nanny's "No" was enough to break off an engagement, even if the couple'd been courtin' twenty year.

More than one girl tried to talk Nanny into changin' her mind, but when Nanny Peters said "No," it stayed said. Argufyin', cryin', shoutin,' and bullyraggin'—none of it budged her an inch. Only one time Nanny Peters ever came a country mile near to changin' her "No" to a "Yes," and that's the story I want to tell you.

But first I got to tell you about Cora Mae Roberts.

Cora Mae Roberts, now, she was one winsome girl. Pretty as a picture, with eyes like Texas bluebonnets and curls so yaller that if her bonnet fell off while she was feedin' the chickens, you'd go plum blind lookin' at her. But only if the sun was shinin'—they weren't as yaller as all that when the sun was ahind a cloud. Her biscuits was like buckshot, her stitchin' like a picket fence, she could outscream a catamount, and she didn't have the sense God gave an armadillo, but every single man in the county was after her, from the widderman who owned the feed store to the deputy sheriff who hadn't nowhere to sleep but the jailhouse. By the time Cora Mae was sixteen years old, they was lined up five-deep around her daddy's ranch house, offering her everything from the moon to dresses from Pittsburgh if only she'd marry them.

Now, some of Cora Mae's suitors was good men, but some of them was more like coyotes on two legs. The worst varmint of them all was one of her daddy's cowhands, a rip-tail roarer could whip his weight in wildcats and ride straight through a crab apple orchard on a flash of lightning. He was so hard he could kick fire out of a flint rock with his bare toes, and he had a thirst for whiskey would put a catfish to shame. His name was Jim Cleering, and he was the man of all men that Cora Mae Roberts wanted to marry.

Jim warn't long on patience or temperance or even on readin' or writin', but his worst enemy'd admit he was a pretty critter. He was so tall he didn't know when his feet was cold. There warn't no bunk long enough for him, but that didn't matter, 'cause his shoulders was so wide he couldn't get in the bunkhouse door anyhow, so he just slep in the barn and scairt away the rats. His jaw was square as the jailhouse cornerstone and twice as hard. He was hairy as a bear and proud as an unbroken stallion, the yaller flower of the Texas plains. And if he warn't, there warn't a man alive dared to say so.

Nanny Peters said so, though, and said it so loud you could hear it through three counties. "That man's no durn good," she told Cora Mae. "He's got more stalls than a good-sized stable and if you can't see that, you'd miss a buzzard settin' on a dead cow. He'll spend your daddy's money and whup your tail until it's tough as saddle hide. It'd take more than a quilt to reform that man, and that's a gospel fact."

Then she held open the door for Cora Mae to leave and the next girl to come in and say her piece.

Well. Cora Mae, she didn't think *her* piece was said yet. She wanted that man and she wanted that quilt to tuck him up in, and she warn't going to leave until she had it.

First she cries, whoopin' and hollerin' and pourin' saltwater out her eyes until you couldn't tell the difference between Cora Mae Roberts and a four-star Texas thunderstorm. But Nanny jest fetches her bucket and a couple of yards of petticoat flannel for a nose rag and leaves her to it.

Then Cora Mae screams and, as I said before, she could outscream a catamount. On this occasion, she extends herself some. Her screaming's louder than two catamounts and an entire pack of coyotes howling at the full moon. But Nanny jest rocks in her rockin' chair, sayin' less than nothin'.

Then Cora Mae cusses, and I most teetotaciously hopes you never hears the like of Cora Mae Roberts's cussin'. The words she said'd burn the ears right off your head and singe your eyeballs naked, for she'd learnt 'em off her sweetheart, and Jim Cleering, he had a gift for profanity. Well, Nanny sets and listens until Cora Mae says a word makes Nanny's hair jump straight out behind her, scatterin' hairpins ever which way.

"Gal," says Nanny, real pleasant-like. "Gal, that ain't no way to address your elders." And quickern' a mocking bird after a fly, she takes the bucket Cora Mae's cried into and douses Cora Mae with saltwater, takin' the starch right out of her yaller curls and sendin' up clouds of steam where the cold water met the air she'd heated up with her cussin'. And while Cora Mae's drippin' and gaspin' like a landed catfish, Nanny takes her broom and sweeps her right on out the door.

But that's not the end of the story, not quite.

One thing you have to give Cora Mae, she warn't no quitter—no, ma'am. She'd set her heart on tamin' Jim Cleering with one o' Nanny's quilts and she wouldn't rest until she was sure that colt was broke to the saddle and a quiet ride for a lady. She'd do it by fair means if she could, but she wouldn't stick at foul.

So Cora Mae thought and thought until her pore brain was smokin' like a prairie fire, and then she come up with what she thought was one bodaciously smart trick. She'd wait for a full moon and then strip herself stark naked and roll around in the hog waller until she was all caked with sticky, smelly, sandy-brown Texas mud. Then she'd stick chicken feathers in the mud, and possum teeth and rattlesnake rattles and such, and she'd creep up to the foot of old Nanny's Peters's bed and plumb *scare* a quilt out of her.

Come the full moon, and Cora Mae Roberts was ready. She rolled in that waller and rolled in the hen litter, stuck possum teeth on her buttocks and a rattlesnake rattle in her navel, caught some glowworms and stuck 'em in her hair, and she crep through the winder of Nanny's shack and commenced to wail and moan.

"Nanny Peters! Nanny Peters! This is the magic speakin' to you," she says.

Nanny sets up in bed and reaches for her spectacles. "Hmm?" she says. "That so?"

Put out that Nanny ain't quiverin' and beggin' for mercy, Cora Mae wails and moans a mite louder. "You made a mistake, Nanny

Peters, a terrible mistake, and if you don't make it right, I'll haunt you and haunt you until the day you die."

"That so?"

"That's so. And I'll give you a taste of that hauntin' beginnin' right now." And Cora Mae commences to shake mud and feathers and chicken dirt—not to mention possum teeth and rattlesnake rattles—all over Nanny's bed and Nanny's clean floor.

And what does Nanny do? Does she squeeze that girl into jelly or knock out five teeth and one of her eyes, or tie her fingers up in twenty-three separate knots? No, ma'am. Nanny takes a double-size blue-and-red "Rob Peter to Pay Paul" from the chest at the foot of her bed, wraps it in brown papers, and hands it to Cora Mae Roberts.

"Here you are, Cora Mae," she says. "I hope this here quilt breaks Jim Cleering for you, 'cause he's in powerful need o' breakin', and that's a gospel fact."

Two weeks later, give or take a day, Cora Mae Roberts married Jim Cleering and went to bed with him under the blue-and-red quilt pieced in the pattern called "Rob Peter to Pay Paul." Three weeks later Jim Cleering was in the Silver Garter, twenty dollars in the hole to Wildcard Pete the gambler and too drunk to find his gun when the shootin' started. Cora Mae was home nursin' a broken jaw, which didn't stop her screamin' fit to be tied when they brought Jim home on a board with a bullet through his lung.

It was mighty tragic. Cora Mae never got over it. Of course she married lots of men after Jim: marryin' was one of her weaknesses, along with whiskey and cussin'. But she took the quilt back to Nanny right away after Jim's funeral, and she wouldn't take another, not even though Nanny swore up hill and down dale that quilt hadn't had nothin' to do with him breakin' her jaw and getting himself killed in the Silver Garter.

And I believe Nanny. I do indeed.

MISS CARSTAIRS AND THE MERMAN

The night Miss Carstairs first saw the merman, there was a great storm along the Massachusetts coast. Down in the harbor town, old men sat in taverns drinking hot rum and cocking their ears at the wind whining and whistling in the chimneys. A proper nor'easter, they said, a real widow-maker, and huddled closer to the acrid fires while the storm ripped shingles from roofs and flung small boats against the piers, leaping across the dunes to set the tall white house on the bluffs above the town surging and creaking like a great ship.

In that house, Miss Carstairs sat by the uncurtained window of her study, peering through a long telescope. Her square hands steady upon the barrel, she watched the lightning dazzle on the water and the wind-blown sand and rain scour her garden. She saw a capsized dinghy scud past her beach in kinetoscopic bursts, and a gull beaten across the dunes. She saw a long, dark, seal-sleek figure cast upon the rocky beach, flounder for a moment in the retreating surf, and then lie still.

The shallow tidal pool where the figure lay was, Miss Carstairs calculated, not more two hundred yards from her aerie. Putting aside the telescope, she reached for the bell pull.

The peculiarities of both ocean storms and seals had been familiar to Miss Carstairs since earliest childhood. Whenever she could slip away from her nurse, she would explore the beach or the salt marshes behind her father's house, returning from these expeditions disheveled: her pinafore pockets stuffed with shells, her stockings torn and sodden, her whole small person reeking, her mother used to say, like the flats at low tide. On these occasions, Mrs. Carstairs would scold her daughter and send her supperless to bed. But her father usually contrived to slip into her room—bearing a bit of cranberry bread, perhaps—and would read to her from Linnaeus or Hans Andersen's fairy tales or Lyell's *Natural History*.

Mr. Carstairs, himself an amateur ichthyologist, delighted in his daughter's intelligence. He kept the crabs and mussels she collected in the stone pond he had built in the conservatory for his exotic oriental fish. For her fifteenth birthday, he presented her with a copy of Charles Darwin's *The Origin of Species*. He would not hear of her attending the village school with the children of the local fishermen, but taught her mathematics and Latin and logic himself, telling her mother that he would have no prissy governess stuffing the head of his little scientist with a load of womanish nonsense.

By the time Mr. Carstairs died, his daughter had turned up her hair and let down her skirts, but she still loved to tramp all day along the beaches. In hopes of turning her daughter's mind to more important matters, her mother drained the pond in the conservatory and lectured her daily on the joys of the married state. Miss Carstairs was sorry about the pond, but she knew she had only to endure and eventually she would be able to please herself. For five years, endure she did, saying, "Yes, Mama" and "No, Mama" until the day when Mrs. Carstairs followed her husband to the grave, a disappointed woman.

On her return from her mother's funeral, Miss Carstairs promptly ordered a proper collecting case, a set of scalpels, and an anatomy text from Codman and Shurtleff in Boston. From then on, she lived very much alone, despising the merchants' and fish-brokers' wives who formed the society of the town. They, in turn, despised her. It was a crying and a shame, they whispered over cups of Indian tea, that the finest house in town be wasted on a woman who would all too obviously never marry, being not only homely as a haddock, but a bluestocking as well.

A bluestocking Miss Carstairs may have been, but her looks were more primate than piscine. She had a broad, low brow, a long jaw, and her Scottish father's high, flat cheekbones. Over the years, sun and wind and cold had creased and tanned her skin, and her thin hair was as silver-gray as the weathered shingles on the buildings along the wharf. She was tall and sturdy and fit as a man from long tramps in the marshes. She was patient, as a scientist must be, and had taught herself classification and embryology and enough about conventional scientific practices to write articles acceptable to *The American Naturalist* and the Boston Society of Natural History. By the time she was forty-nine, "E. Monroe Carstairs" had earned the reputation of being very sound on the *Mollusca* of the New England coast.

In the course of preparing these articles, Miss Carstairs had collected hundreds of specimens, and little jars containing pickled *Cephalopoda* and *Gastropoda* lined her study shelves in grim profusion. But she had living barnacles and sea slugs as well, housed in the conservatory pool, where they kept company with lobsters and crabs and feathery sea worms in a kind of miniature ocean. In shape the pond was a wide oval, built up at the sides with a mortared stone coping, nestled in an Eden of Boston ferns and sweet-smelling mint geraniums. Miss Carstairs had fitted it out with a series of pumps and filters to bring seawater up from the bay and keep it clean and fresh.

She was very proud of it, and of the collection of marine life it housed. Stocking it with healthy specimens was the chief pleasure of her life. Summer and winter she spent much of her time out stalking the tidal flats after a neap tide or exploring the small brackish pools of the salt marshes. But nothing was as productive of unusual specimens as a roaring gale, which, in beating the ocean to a froth, swept up rare fauna from its very floor.

As Miss Carstairs stood now with her hand upon the bell pull, her wide experience of such storms told her that she must either bring in the seal immediately, or watch it wash away with the tide. She pulled sharply, and when the maid Sarah sleepily answered it, ordered her to rouse Stephen and John without delay and have them meet her in the kitchen passage. "Tell them to bring the lantern, and the stretcher we used for the shark last spring," she said. "And bring me my sou'wester and my boots."

Soon two oil-clothed men, yawning behind their hands, awaited Miss Carstairs in the dark kitchen. They were proud of the forthright eccentricity of their mistress, who kept lobsters in a fancy pool instead of eating them, and traipsed manfully over the mud flats in all weather. If Miss Carstairs wanted to go out into the worst nor'easter in ten years to collect some rare grampus or other, they were perfectly willing to go with her. Besides, she paid them well.

Miss Carstairs leading the way with the lantern, the little company groped its way down the slippery wooden stairs to the beach. The lantern illuminated glimpses of scattered flotsam: gouts of seaweed and beached fish, broken seagulls and strange shells. But Miss Carstairs, untempted, ran straight before the wind to the tidal pool where lay her quarry.

Whatever the creature was, it was not a seal. The dim yellow lantern gave only the most imperfect outline of its shape, but Miss Carstairs could see that it was more slender than a seal, and lacked a pelt. Its front flippers were peculiarly long and flexible, and it seemed to have a crest of bony spines down its back. There was something familiar about its shape, about the configuration of its upper body and head.

Miss Carstairs was just bending to take a closer look when Stephen's impatient "Well, miss?" drew her guiltily upright. The wind was picking up; it was more than time to be getting back to the house. She stood out of the way while the men unfolded a bundle of canvas and sticks into a stretcher like a sailor's hammock suspended between two long poles. They bundled their find into this contrivance and, in case it might still be alive, covered it with a blanket soaked in seawater. Clumsily, because of the wind and the swaying weight of their burden, the men crossed the beach and labored up the wooden stairs, wound through the garden and up two shallow stone steps to a large glass conservatory built daringly onto the sea side of the house.

When Miss Carstairs opened the door, the wind extinguished most of the gaslights Sarah had thoughtfully lit in the conservatory. So it was in a poor half-light that the men hoisted their burden to the edge of the pool and tipped the creature out onto the long boulder that had once served as a sunning place for Mr. Carstairs's terrapins. The lax body rolled heavily onto the rock; Miss Carstairs eyed it doubtfully while the men panted and wiped at their streaming faces.

"I don't think we should submerge it entirely," she said. "If it's still alive, being out of the water a little longer shouldn't hurt it, and if it is not, I don't want the lobsters getting it before I do."

The men went off to their beds, and Miss Carstairs stood for some while, biting thoughtfully at her forefinger as she contemplated her new specimen. Spiky and naked, it did not look like anything she had ever seen or read about in Allen, Grey, or von Haast. She dismissed the temptation to turn up the gas and examine it more closely with the reflection that the night was far advanced and she herself wet and tired. The specimen would still be there in the morning, and she in a better state to attend to it. But when she ascended the stairs, her footsteps led her not to her bedroom but to her study, where she spent the rest of the night in restless perusal of True's *Catalogue of Aquatic Mammals.*

At six o'clock, Miss Carstairs rang for Sarah to bring her rolls and coffee. By 6:30 she had eaten, bathed, and dressed herself, and was on her way to the conservatory. Her find lay as she had left it, half in and half out of the water. By the light of day, she could see that its muscular tail grew into a powerful torso, scaleless and furless and furnished with what looked like arms, jointed like a human's and roped with long, smooth muscles under a protective layer of fat. Its head was spherical, and flanked by a pair of ears shaped and webbed like fins.

At first, Miss Carstairs refused to believe the evidence of her eyes. Perhaps, she thought, she was overtired from reading all night. The creature, whatever it was, would soon yield its secrets to her scalpel and prove to be nothing more wonderful than a deformed porpoise or a freak manatee.

She took its head in her hands. Its skin was cool and pliant and slimy, very unpleasant to touch, as though a fish had sloughed its scales but not its protective mucus. She lifted its thick, lashless lids to reveal pearly eyes, rolled upward. She had never touched nor seen the like. A new species, perhaps? A new genus?

With a rising excitement, Miss Carstairs palpated its skull, which was hairless and smooth except for the spiny ridge bisecting it, and fingered the slight protrusion between its eyes and lipless mouth. The protrusion was both fleshy and cartilaginous, like a human nose, and as Miss Carstairs acknowledged the similarity, the specimen's features resolved into an unmistakably anthropoid arrangement of eyes, nose, mouth, and chin. The creature was, in fact, neither deformed nor freakish but, in its own way, harmoniously formed and perfectly adapted to its environment as an elephant or a chimpanzee. A certain engraving in a long-forgotten book of fairy tales came to her mind, of a wistful child with a human body and a fish's tail.

Miss Carstairs plumped heavily into her wicker chair. Here, lying on a rock in her father's goldfish pond, was a species never examined by Mr. Darwin or classified by Linnaeus. Here was a biological anomaly, a scientific impossibility. Here, in short, was a mermaid, and she, Edith Carstairs, had collected it.

Shyly, almost reverently, Miss Carstairs approached the creature anew. She turned the lax head toward her, then prodded at its wide, lipless mouth to get a look at its teeth. A faint, cool air fanned her fingers, and she snatched them back as though the creature had bitten her. Could it be alive? Miss Carstairs laid her hand flat against its chest and felt nothing; hesitated, laid her ear where her hand had been, and heard a faint thumping, slower than a human heartbeat.

In terror lest the creature awake before she could examine it properly, Miss Carstairs snatched up her calipers and her sketchbook and began to make detailed notes of its anatomy. She measured its cranium, which she found to be as commodious as most men's, and traced its webbed, four-fingered hands. She sketched it full-length from all angles, then made piecemeal studies of its head and finny ears, its curiously muscled torso and its horny claws. From the absence of external genitalia and the sleek roundness of its limbs and body, she thought her specimen to be female, even though it lacked the melon breasts and streaming golden hair of legend. But breasts and streaming hair would drag terribly, Miss Carstairs thought: a real mermaid would be better off without them. By the same token, a real merman would be better off without the drag of external genitals. On the question of the creature's sex, Miss Carstairs decided to reserve judgment.

Promptly at one o'clock, Sarah brought her luncheon—a cutlet and a glass of barley water—and still the creature lay unconscious. Miss Carstairs swallowed the cutlet hastily between taking wax impressions of its claws and scraping slime from its skin to examine under her microscope. She drew a small measure of its thin scarlet blood and poked curiously at the complexity of tissue fringing the apparent opening of its ears, which had no parallel in any lunged aquatic animal she knew. It might, she thought, be gills.

By seven o'clock, Miss Carstairs had abandoned hope. She leaned over her mermaid, pinched the verdigris forearm between her nails, and looked closely at the face for some sign of pain. The wide mouth remained slack; the webbed ears lay flat and unmoving against the skull. It must be dead after all. It seemed that she would have to content herself with dissecting the creature's cadaver, and now was not too early to begin. So she laid out her scalpels and her bone saw and rang for the men to hoist the specimen out of the pool and onto the potting table.

"Carefully, carefully, now." Miss Carstairs hovered anxiously as Stephen and John struggled with the slippery bulk and sighed as it slipped out of their hands. As it landed belly-down across the stone coping, the creature gave a great huff and twitched as though it had been electrified. Then it flopped backward, twisted eel-quick under the water, and peered up at Miss Carstairs from the bottom of the pool, fanning its webbed ears and gaping.

The men fled, stumbling and slipping in their haste.

Fairly trembling with excitement, Miss Carstairs leaned over the water and stared at her acquisition. The mer-creature, mouthing the water, stared back. The tissue in front of its ears fluttered rhythmically, and Miss Carstairs knew a moment of pure scientific gratification. Her hypothesis was proved correct; it did indeed have gills as well as lungs.

The mer undulated gently from crest to tail-tip, then darted from one extremity of the pool to the other, sending water slopping into Miss Carstairs's lap. She recoiled, shook out her skirts, and looked up to see the mer peering over the coping, its eyes deep-set, milk-blue, and as intelligently mournful as a whipped dog's.

Miss Carstairs grinned, then hastily schooled her lips into a solemn line. Had not Mr. Darwin suggested that to most lower animals, a smile is a sign of challenge? If the creature was the oceanic ape it appeared to be, then might it not, as apes do, find her involuntary smile as terrifying as a shark's grinning maw? Was a mer a mammal at all, or was an amphibian? Did it properly belong to a genus, or was it, like the platypus, *sui generis*? She resolved to reread Mr. Gunther's *The Study of Fishes* and J. E. Grey on seals.

While Miss Carstairs was pondering its origins, the mer seemed to be pondering Miss Carstairs. It held her eyes steadily with its pearly gaze, and Miss Carstairs began to fancy that she heard—no, it was rather that she sensed—a reverberant, rhythmic hushing like a swift tide withdrawing over the sand of a sea cave.

The light shimmered before her eyes. She shook her head and recalled that she had not eaten since lunch. A glance at the watch pinned to her breast told her that it was now past nine o'clock. Little wonder she was giddy, what with having had no sleep the night before and working over the mer-creature all day. Her eyes turned again to her specimen. She had intended ringing for fish and feeding it from her own hand, but now thought she would retire to her own belated supper and leave its feeding to the servants.

The next morning, much refreshed by her slumbers, Miss Carstairs returned to the conservatory armored with a bibbed denim apron and rubber boots. The mer was sitting perched on the highest point of the rock with its long fish's tail curled around it, looking out over the rose beds to the sea.

It never moved when Miss Carstairs entered the conservatory, but gazed steadily out at the bright vista of water and rocky beach. It sat extremely upright, as if disdaining the unaccustomed weight of gravity on its spine, and its spiky crest was fully erect. One clawed hand maintained its balance on the rock; the other was poised on what Miss Carstairs was obliged to call its thigh. The wide flukes of its yellow-bronze tail draped behind and around it like a train and trailed on one side down to the water. This attitude was to become exceedingly familiar to Miss Carstairs in the weeks that followed; but on this first morning, it struck her as being at once human and alien, pathetic and comic, like a trousered chimpanzee riding a bicycle in a circus.

Having already sketched it from all angles, what Miss Carstairs chiefly wanted was for the mer to *do* something. Now that it was awake, she was hesitant to touch it, for its naked skin and high forehead made it look oddly human and its attitude forbade familiarity. Would it hear her, she wondered, if she tried to get its attention? Or were those ear-like fans merely appendages to its gills?

Standing near the edge of the pool, Miss Carstairs clapped her hands sharply. One fluke stirred in the water, but that might have been coincidence. She cleared her throat. Nothing. She climbed upon a low stool, stood squarely in the creature's field of vision, and said quite firmly, "How d'ye do?" Again, nothing, if she excepted an infinitesimal shivering of its skin that she might have imagined. "Boo!" cried Miss Carstairs then, waving her arms in the air and feeling more than a little foolish. "Boo! Boo!"

Without haste, the mer brought its eyes to her face and seemed to study her with a grave, incurious attention. Miss Carstairs climbed down and clasped her hands behind her back. Now that she had its attention, what would she do with it?

Conquering a most unscientific shrinking, Miss Carstairs unclasped her hands and reached one of them out to the creature, palm upward, as if it had been a strange dog. The mer immediately dropped from its upright seat to a sprawling crouch, and to Miss Carstairs's horrified fascination, the movement released from a pouch beneath its belly a boneless, fleshy ocher member that could only be its—unmistakably male—genitalia.

Miss Carstairs hid her confusion in a Boston fern, praying that the merman would withdraw his nakedness, or at least hide it in the water. But when she turned back, he was still stretched at full length along the stone, his outsized privates boldly—Miss Carstairs could only think defiantly—displayed.

He was smiling.

There was nothing pleasant, welcoming, friendly, or even tangentially human about the merman's smile. His gaping mouth was full of needle teeth. Behind them, his gorge was pale rose and palpitating. He had no tongue.

Although she might be fifty years old and a virgin, Miss Carstairs was no delicate maiden lady. Before she was a spinster or even a woman, she was a naturalist, and she immediately forgot the merman's formidable sexual display in wonder at his formidable dentition. Orally, at least, the merman was all fish. His grin displayed to advantage the tooth plate lining his lower jaw, the respiratory lamellae flanking his pharynx, the inner gill septa. Miss Carstairs seized her notebook, licked the point of her pencil, and began to sketch diligently. Once she glanced up to verify the double row of teeth in the lower jaw. The merman was still grinning at her. A moment later she looked again; he had disappeared. Hurriedly, Miss Carstairs laid aside her book and searched the pool. Yes, there he was at the deep end, belly-down against the pebbled bottom.

Miss Carstairs seated herself upon the coping to think. Had the merman acted from instinct or intelligence? If he had noted her shock at the sight of his genitals, then his flourishing them might be interpreted as a deliberate attempt to discomfit her. On the other hand, the entire display could have been a simple example of instinctive aggression, like a male mandrill presenting his crimson posterior to an intruder.

Miss Carstairs mounted to her study and picked up her pen to record her observations. As she inscribed the incident, she became increasingly convinced that the merman's action must be the result of deliberate intention. No predator—and the merman's teeth left no doubt that he was a predator—would instinctively bare rather than protect the most vulnerable portion of his anatomy. He must, therefore, have exposed himself in a gesture of defiance and contempt. But such a line of reasoning, however theoretically sound, did not go far in proving that her merman was capable of reasoned behavior. She must find a way to test his intelligence empirically.

Miss Carstairs looked blindly out over the autumn-bright ocean glittering below her. The duke of Argyll had written that Man was unique among animals in being a tool user. Yet Mr. Darwin had argued persuasively that chimpanzees and orangutans commonly use sticks and stones to open hard nuts or knock down fruit. Surely no animal lower than an ape would think to procure his food using anything beyond his own well-adapted natural equipment.

Since he was immured in a kind of free-swimming larder, Miss Carstairs could not count upon the merman's being hungry enough to spring her trap for the bait alone. The test must engage his interest as well. Trap: now there was an idea. What if she were to use one of the patent wire rattraps stacked in the garden shed? She could put a fish in a rattrap—a live fish, she thought, would prove more attractive than a dressed one—and offer the merman an array of tools with which to open it—a crowbar, perhaps a pair of wire snips. Yes, thought Miss Carstairs, she would put the fish in a rattrap and throw it into the pool to see what the merman would make of it.

Next morning the merman had resumed his station on the rock looking, if anything, more woebegone than he had the day before. Somewhat nervously, Miss Carstairs entered the conservatory carrying a bucket of water with a live mackerel in it. She was followed by Stephen, who was laden with the rattrap, a crowbar, a pair of wire snips, and a small hacksaw. With his help, Miss Carstairs introduced the mackerel into the trap and lowered it into the deep end of the pool. Then she dismissed Stephen, positioned herself in the wicker chair, pulled *Descent of Man* from her pocket, and pretended to read.

The tableau held for a quarter of an hour or so. Miss Carstairs sat, the merman sat, the rattrap with its mackerel rested on the bottom of the pool, and the tools lay on the coping as on a workbench, with the handles neatly turned toward their projected user. Finally, Miss Carstairs slapped over the page and humphed disgustedly; the merman slithered off the rock into the pool.

A great rolling and slopping of briny water ensued. When the tumult ceased, the merman's head popped up, grinning ferociously.

He was clearly incensed, and although his attitude was comic, Miss Carstairs was not tempted to laugh.

With an audible snap, the merman shut his gaping mouth, lifted the rattrap onto the rock, hauled himself up beside it, and carefully examined the tools set out before him. The wire snips he passed over without hesitation. The hacksaw he felt with one finger, which he hastily withdrew when he caught it upon the ragged teeth; Miss Carstairs was interested to observe that he carried the injured member to his mouth to suck just as a man or a monkey would. Then he grasped the crowbar and brought it whistling down upon the trap, distorting it enough for him to see that one end was not made all of a piece with the rest. He steadied the trap with one hand and, thrusting the crowbar through the flap, pried it free with a single mighty heave. Swiftly, he reached inside and grabbed the wildly flapping mackerel.

For a time the merman held the fish before him as if debating what to do with it. He looked from the fish to Miss Carstairs and from Miss Carstairs to the fish, and she heard a sound like a sigh, accompanied by a slight fluttering of his gill flaps. This sigh, combined with his habitual expression of settled melancholy, made his attitude so like that of an elderly gentleman confronted with unfamiliar provender that Miss Carstairs smiled a little in spite of herself. The merman stiffened and gazed at her intently. A long moment passed, and Miss Carstairs heard—or thought she heard—a noise of water rushing over sand; saw—or thought she heard—a glimmer as of sun filtered through clear water.

Now, Miss Carstairs was not a woman given either to the vapors or to lurid imaginings. Thunderstorms that set more delicate nerves quivering merely stimulated her; bones and entrails left her unmoved. Furthermore, she was never ill and had never been subject to sick headaches. So, when her head began to throb and her eyes to dazzle with sourceless pinwheels of light, Miss Carstairs simply closed her eyes to discover whether the effect would disappear. The sound of rushing waters receded; the throb subsided to a dull ache. She opened her eyes to the merman's pearly stare, and sound and pain and glitter returned.

At this point she thought it would be only sensible to avert her eyes. But being sensible would not teach her why the merman sought to mesmerize her or why his stare caused her head to ache so. Deliberately, she abandoned herself to his gaze.

All at once, Miss Carstairs found herself at sea. Chilly green-gray depths extended above and below her, fishy shadows darted past the edges of her vision. She was swimming in a strong and unfamiliar current. The ocean around her tasted of storm and rocks and fear. She knew beyond doubt that she was being swept ever closer to a strange shore, and although she was strong, she was afraid. Her tail scraped sand; the current crossed with windblown waves and conspired to toss her ashore. Bruised, torn, gasping for breath in the thin air, Miss Carstairs fainted.

She came to herself some little time later, her eyes throbbing viciously and her ears ringing. The merman was nowhere to be seen. Slowly, Miss Carstairs dragged herself to her chair and rang for Sarah. She would need tea, perhaps even a small brandy, before she could think of mounting the stairs. She felt slightly seasick.

Sarah exclaimed in shock at her mistress's appearance. "I've had a bit of a turn," said Miss Carstairs shortly. "No doubt I stayed up too late last night reading. If you would bring me some brandy and turn down my bed, I think I should like to lie down. No,"—in answer to Sarah's inquiring look—"you must not call Dr. Bland. I have a slight headache; that is all."

Some little time later, Miss Carstairs lay in her darkened bedroom with a handkerchief soaked in eau de cologne pressed to her aching forehead. She did not know whether to exult or to despair. If her recent vision had been caused by the feverish overexcitement of an unbridled imagination, she feared that excessive study, coupled with spinsterhood, had finally driven her mad as her mother had always warned her it would.

But if the vision had been caused by the merman's deliberate attempt to "speak" to her, she had made a discovery of considerable scientific importance.

Miss Carstairs stirred impatiently against her pillows. Suppose, for the sake of argument, that the experience was genuine. That would suggest that somewhere in the unexplored deeps of the ocean was a race of mermen who could cast images, emotion, even sounds, from mind to mind. Fantastic as the thing sounded, it could be so. In the first edition of the *Origin*, Mr. Darwin had written that over the ages a bear might develop baleen and flippers, evolving finally into a kind of furry whale, if living upon plankton had become necessary to the species' survival. The general mechanism of evolution might, given the right circumstances, produce anthropoid creatures adapted for life in the sea. Why should not some ambitious prehistoric fish develop arms and a large, complex brain, or some island-dwelling ape take to the sea and evolve gills and a tail?

Evolution could also account for a telepathic method of communication, just as it accounted for a verbal one. To Miss Carstairs's mind, the greater mystery was how she could have received and understood a psychic message. Presumably, some highly evolved organ or cerebral fold peculiar to mermen transmitted their thoughts; how could she, poor clawless, gill-less, forked creature that she was, share such an organ?

An exquisitely stabbing pain caused Miss Carstairs to clutch the handkerchief to her brow. She must rest, she thought. So she measured herself a small dose of laudanum, swallowed it, and slept.

Next morning, armed with smelling salts and a pair of smoked glasses that had belonged to her mother, Miss Carstairs approached the conservatory in no very confident mood. Her brain felt sore and bruised, almost stiff, like a long-immobilized limb that had been suddenly and violently exercised. Hesitantly, she peered through the French doors; the merman was back on his rock, staring out to sea.

Determined that she would not allow him to overcome her with visions, she averted her gaze, then marched across the conservatory, seated herself, and perched the smoked glasses on her nose before daring to look up.

Whether it was the smoked glasses or Miss Carstairs's inward shrinking that weakened the effect of the merman's stare, this second communion was less intimate than the first. Miss Carstairs saw a coral reef and jewel-like fish darting and hovering over the sea floor like images painted on thin silk, accompanied by a distant chorus of squeaks, whistles, and random grunts. She did not, however, feel the press of the ocean upon her or any emotion other than her own curiosity and wonder.

"Is that your home?" she asked absurdly, and the images stopped. The merman's face did not, apparently could not, change its expression, but he advanced his sloping chin and fluttered his webbed fingers helplessly in front of his chest. "You're puzzled," said Miss Carstairs softly. "I don't wonder. But if you're as intelligent as I hope, you will deduce that I am trying to speak to you in my way as you are trying to speak to me in yours."

This speech was answered by a pause, then a strong burst of images: a long-faced grouper goggling through huge, smoky eyes; a merman neatly skewered on a harpoon; clouds of dark blood drifting down a swift current. Gasping in pain, Miss Carstairs reeled as she sat and, knocking off the useless smoked spectacles, pressed her hands to her eyes. The pain subsided to a dull ache.

"I see that I shall have to find a way of talking to you," she said aloud. Fluttering claws signed the merman's incomprehension. "When you shout at me, it is painful." Her eye caught the hacksaw still lying by the pool. She retrieved it, offered it to the merman blade-first. He recoiled and sucked his finger reminiscently. Miss Carstairs touched her own finger to the blade, tore the skin, then gasped as she had when he had "shouted" at her and, clutching her bleeding finger dramatically, closed her eyes and lay back in her chair.

A moment passed. Miss Carstairs sat slowly upright as a sign that the performance was over. The merman covered his face with his fingers, webs spread wide to veil his eyes.

It was clearly a gesture of submission and apology, and Miss Carstairs was oddly moved by it. Cautiously, she leaned over the coping, and grasped him lightly by the wrist. He stiffened, but did not pull away. "I accept your apology, merman," she said, keeping her face as impassive as his. "I think we've had enough for one day. Tomorrow we'll talk again."

Over the course of the next few weeks, Miss Carstairs learned to communicate with her merman by working out a series of dumb shows signifying various simple commands: "Too loud!" and "Yes" and "No." For more complex communications, she spoke to him as he spoke to her: by means of images.

The first day, she showed him an engraving of the Sirens that she had found in an illustrated edition of *The Odyssey*. It showed three fishtailed women, rather heavy about the breasts and belly, disposed gracefully on a rocky outcropping, combing their long falls of hair. The merman studied this engraving attentively. Then he fluttered his claws and sighed.

"I don't blame you," said Miss Carstairs. "They look too stupid to sit on the rocks and sing at the same time, much less swim." She laid aside *The Odyssey* and took up a tinted engraving of a parrotfish. The merman advanced his head and sniffed, then snatched the sheet from Miss Carstairs's fingers and turned it this way and that. Catching her eyes, he sent her a vision of that same fish, shining vermilion and electric blue through clear tropical waters, its hard beak patiently scraping polyps out of coral dotted with the waving fronds of sea worms. Suddenly one of the coral's thornier parasites revealed itself as a merman's hand by grabbing the parrotfish and sweeping it into the predator's jaws. "Oh," said Miss Carstairs involuntarily as she became aware of an exciting, coppery smell and an altogether unfamiliar taste in her mouth. "Oh my."

She closed her eyes and the vision dispersed. Her mouth watering slightly and her hands trembling, she picked up her pen to describe the experience. Something of her confusion must have communicated itself to the merman, for when she next sought his eyes, he gave her a gossamer vision of a school of tiny fish flashing brilliant fins. Over time, she came to recognize that this image served him for a smile, and that other seemingly random pictures signified other common emotions: sunlight through clear water was laughter; a moray eel, heavy, hideous, and sharply toothed, was grief.

Autumn wore on to winter, and Miss Carstairs became increasingly adept at eliciting and reading the merman's images. Every morning she would go to the conservatory bearing engravings or sepia photographs and, with their help, wrestle some part of the merman's knowledge from him. Every afternoon, weather permitting, she would pace the marshes or the beach, sorting and digesting. Then, after an early dinner, she would settle herself at her desk and work on "A Preliminary Study of the Species *Homo Oceanus Telepathicans,* With Some Observations on His Society."

This document, which she was confident would assure E. Monroe Carstairs a chapter of his own in the annals of marine biology, began with a detailed description of the merman and the little she had been able to learn about his anatomy. The next section dealt with his psychic abilities; the next was headed "Communication and Society":

> As we have seen (*Miss Carstairs wrote*), quite a sophisticated level of communication can be achieved by an intelligent merman. Concrete as they necessarily are, his visions can, when properly read and interpreted, convey abstract ideas of some subtlety. But they can convey them only to one other mer.

Chemical exudations (*vide supra*) signal only the simplest mer emotions: distress, lust, fear, anger, avoidance; booms and whistles attract a companion's attention or guide cooperative hunting maneuvers. All fine shades of meaning, all philosophy, all poetry, can pass from one mer to another only by direct and lengthy mutual gazing.

This fact, coupled with an instinctive preference for solitude similar to that of the harlequin bass (*S. tigrinus*) and the reef shark (*C. melanopterus*), has prevented *H. oceanus* from evolving anything that *H. sapiens* would recognize as a civilized society. From the time they can safely fend for themselves at about the age of six, mer-children desert their parents to swim and hunt alone, often faring from one ocean to another in their wanderings. When one of these mer-children meets with another of approximately its own age, it will generally pair with that mer-child, whether it be of the same or of the opposite sex. Such a pairing, which seems to be instinctive, is the merman's only means of social intercourse. It may last from a season or two to several years, but a couple with an infant commonly stays together until the child is ready to swim free. Legends exist of couples who swam faithfully together for decades, but as a rule, the enforced and extreme intimacy of telepathic communication comes to wear more and more heavily on one or both members of a pair until they are forced to part. Each mer then swims alone for whatever period of time fate and preference may dictate, until he meets with another receptive mer, when the cycle begins again.

Because of this peculiar behavioral pattern, the merfolk can have no government, no religion, no community; in short, no possibility of developing a civilization even as primitive as that of a tribe of savages. Some legends they do have (*vide* Appendix A), some image-poems of transcendent

> beauty remembered and transmitted from pair to pair over the ages. But any new discovery made by a merman or a merwoman swimming alone may all too easily die with its maker or become garbled in transmission between pair and pair. For, except within the pair-bond, the mer's instinct for cooperation is not strong.

The more she learned about the customs of the mer-folk, the more conscious Miss Carstairs became of how fortunate she was that the merman had consented to speak to her at all. Mermen swimming solitary were a cantankerous lot, as likely to attack a chance-met pair or single mer as to flee it.

Though Miss Carstairs realized that the merman must look upon her as his companion for the duration of his cycle of sociability, she did not fully understand the implications such a companionship had for him. When she thought of his feelings at all, she imagined that he viewed her with the same benevolent curiosity with which she viewed him, never considering that their relationship might seem different from his side of the equation.

The crisis came in early December, when Miss Carstairs determined that it was time to tackle the subject of mer reproductive biology. She knew that an examination of the rituals of courtship and mating was central to the study of any new species, and no scientist, however embarrassing he might find the subject, was justified in shirking it. So Miss Carstairs gathered together her family album and a porcelain baby doll exhumed from a trunk in the attic, and used them, along with an anatomy text, to give the merman a basic lesson in human reproduction.

At first, it seemed to Miss Carstairs that the merman was being particularly inattentive. But close observation having taught her to recognize his moods, she realized at length that his tapping fingers, gently twitching crest, and reluctance to meet her eyes, all signaled acute embarrassment.

Miss Carstairs found this most interesting. She tapped on his wrist to get his attention, then shook her head and briefly covered her eyes. "I'm sorry," she told him, then held out a sepia photograph of herself as a stout and solemn infant propped between her frowning parents on a horsehair sofa. "But you must tell me what I want to know."

In response, the merman erected his crest, gaped fiercely, then dove into the deepest cranny of the pool, where he wantonly dismembered Miss Carstairs's largest lobster. In disgust, she threw the baby doll into the pool after him and stalked from the room. She was furious. Without this section, her article must remain unfinished, and she was anxious to send it off. After having exposed himself on the occasion of their first meeting, after having allowed her to rummage almost at will through his memories and his mind, why would he so suddenly turn coy?

All that afternoon, Miss Carstairs pondered the merman's reaction to her question, and by evening had concluded that mer-folk had some incomprehensible taboo concerning the facts of reproduction. Perhaps reflection would show him that there was no shame in revealing them to her, who could have only an objective and scientific interest in them. It never occurred to her that it might bewilder or upset the merman to speak of mating to a female to whom he was bonded, but with whom he could never hope to mate.

The next morning, Miss Carstairs entered the conservatory to see the merman sitting on his rock, his face turned sternly from the ocean and toward the door. Clearly, he was waiting for her, and when she took her seat and lifted her eyes to his, she felt absurdly like a girl caught out in some childish peccadillo and called into her mother's sitting room to be chastised.

Without preamble, the merman sent a series of images breaking over her. Two mer—one male, one female—swam together, hunted, coupled. Soon they parted, one to the warm coral reefs, the other to arctic seas. The merwoman swam, hunted, explored. A time passed: not long, although Miss Carstairs could not have told how she knew. The merwoman met a merwoman, drove her away, met a merman, flung herself upon him amorously. This exchange was more complex than the earlier couplings; the merman resisted and fled when it was accomplished.

The merman began to eat prodigiously. He sought a companion and came upon a merman, with whom he mated, and who hunted for him when he could no longer easily hunt for himself. As the merman became heavier, he seemed to become greedier, stuffing his pouch with slivers of fish as if to hoard them. *How ridiculous,* thought Miss Carstairs. Then, all at once, the scales covering the pouch gave a writhing heave and a tiny crested head popped out. Tiny gills fluttered; tiny arms worked their way out of their confinement. Claiming its wandering gaze with iridescent eyes, the merman's companion coaxed the infant from its living cradle and took it tenderly into his arms.

Three days later, Miss Carstairs sent John to the village to mail the completed manuscript of her article, and then she put it out of her mind as firmly as she could. Brooding, she told herself, would not speed it any faster to the editor's desk or influence him to look more kindly upon it once it got there. In the meanwhile, she must not waste time. There was much more the merman could tell her, much more for her to learn. Her stacks of notes and manuscript pages grew higher.

In late January, "Preliminary Study of the Species *Homo Oceanus Telepathicans*" was returned with a polite letter of thanks. As always, the editor of *The American Naturalist* admired Mr. Carstairs's graceful prose style and clear exposition, but feared that this particular essay was more a work of imagination than of scientific observation. Perhaps it could find a more appropriate place in a literary journal.

Miss Carstairs tore the note into small pieces. Then she went down to the conservatory. The merman met her eyes when she entered, recoiled, and grinned angrily at her; Miss Carstairs grinned angrily back. She felt that her humiliation was his fault, that he had misled or lied to her. She wanted to dissect his brain and send it pickled to the editor of *The American Naturalist*; she wanted him to know exactly what had happened and how he had been the cause of it all. But since she had no way to tell him this, Miss Carstairs fled the house for the windy marshes, where she squelched through the matted beach grass until she was exhausted. Humanity had always bored her and now scholarship had betrayed her. She had nothing else.

Standing ankle-deep in a brackish pool, Miss Carstairs looked back across the marshes to her house. The sun rode low in a mackerel sky; its light danced on the calm water around her and glanced off the conservatory glazing. The merman would be sitting on his rock like the Little Mermaid in the tale her father had read her, gazing out over the ocean he could not reach. She had a sudden vision of a group of learned men standing around him, shaking their heads, stroking their whiskers, and debating whether or not this so-called merman had an immortal soul. Perhaps it was just as well the editor of *The American Naturalist* had rejected the article. Miss Carstairs could imagine sharing her knowledge of the merman with the world, but she could not share the merman himself. He had become necessary to her, her one comfort and her sole companion.

Next morning she was back in the conservatory, and on each morning succeeding. Day after day she gazed through the merman's eyes as if he were a living bathysphere, watching damselfish and barracuda stitch silver through the greenish antlers of elkhorn coral, observing the languorous unfurling of the manta ray's wings and the pale groping fingers of hungry anemones. As she opened herself to the merman's visions, Miss Carstairs began not only to see and hear, but also to feel, to smell, even to taste, the merman's homesick memories.

She became familiar with the complex symphony of the ocean, the screeching scrape of parrotfish beaks over coral, the tiny, amatory grunts of frillfins. In the shape of palpable odors present everywhere in the water, she learned the distinct tastes of fear, of love, of blood, of anger. Sometimes, after a day of vicarious exploration, she would lie in her bed at night and weep for the thinness of the air around her, the silent flatness of terrestrial night.

The snow fell without Miss Carstairs's noticing, melted and turned to rain, which froze again, then warmed and gentled toward spring. In her abandoned study, the ink dried in the well and the books and papers lay strewn around the desk like old wrecks. Swimming with the merman in the open sea, Miss Carstairs despised the land. When she walked abroad, she avoided the marshes and clambered over the weed-slick rocks to the end of the spit, where she would stand shivering in the wind and spray, staring into the waves breaking at her feet. Most days, however, she spent in the conservatory, gazing hungrily into the merman's pearly eyes.

The merman's visions were becoming delirious with the need for freedom as, in his own way, he pleaded with Miss Carstairs to release him. He showed her mermen caught in fishermen's nets, torn beyond recognition by their struggles to escape the ropes. He showed her companions turning on each other, mate devouring mate when the social cycle of one had outlasted the patience of the other. Blinded by her own hunger, Miss Carstairs viewed these horrific images simply as dramatic incidents in his submarine narrative, like sharks feeding or grouper nibbling at the eyes of drowned sailors.

When at last the merman took to sulking under the rock, Miss Carstairs sat in her wicker chair like a squid lurking among the coral, waiting patiently for him to emerge. She knew the pond was small; she sensed that the ocean's limitless freedom was more real to him when he shared his memories of it. She reasoned that no matter how distasteful the process had become, he must eventually rise and feed her the visions she craved. If, from time to time, she imagined that he might end her tyranny by tearing out her throat, she dismissed the fear. Was he not wholly in her power? When she knew the ocean as well as he, when she could name each fish with its own song, then she would let him swim free.

One spring morning, Miss Carstairs came down to the conservatory to find the rock empty. At first she thought the merman was hiding; only when she moved toward the pool did she notice that the floor of the conservatory was awash with water and the door was ajar. Against all odds, her merman had found a way to escape her.

Miss Carstairs groped for her wicker chair and sat, bereaved and betrayed as she had not been since her father's death. Her eye fell on the open door; she saw blood and water smeared over the steps. Rising hurriedly, she followed the trail through the garden to where the merman lay unconscious at the head of the beach stairs. With anxious, delicate fingers, she caressed his mouth and chest to feel the thin breath coming from his lips and the faint rhythmic beat under his ribs. His tail was scored and tattered where the gravel garden path had torn away the scales.

Somewhere in her soul, Miss Carstairs felt dismay and tenderness and horror. But in the forefront of her brain, she was conscious only of anger. She had fed him, she thought; she had befriended him; she had opened her mind to his visions. How dare he abandon her? Grasping him by the shoulders, she shook him violently. "Wake up and look at me!" she shouted.

Obediently, the merman opened his opalescent eyes and conjured a vision: the face of a middle-aged human woman. It was a simian face, slope-jawed and snub-nosed, wrinkled and brown.

The ape-woman opened her mouth, showing large, flat teeth. Grimacing fearfully, she stooped toward Miss Carstairs and seized her shoulders with stubby fingers that stung and burned her like anemones. Harsh noises scraped over Miss Carstairs's ears, bearing with them the taint of hunger and need and envy as sweat bears the taint of fear. Miss Carstairs tore herself from the ape-woman's poisonous grasp and covered her face with her hands.

A claw gripped her wrist, shook it to get her attention. Reluctantly, Miss Carstairs removed her hands and saw the merman, immovably melancholy, peering up at her. How could he bear to look at her? she wondered miserably. He shook his head, a gesture he had learned from her, and answered her with a kind of child's sketch: an angular impression of a woman's face, inhumanly beautiful in its severity. Expressions of curiosity, wonder, joy, discovery darted across the woman's features like a swarm of minnows, and she tasted as strongly of solitude as a free-swimming mer.

Through her grief and remorse, Miss Carstairs recognized the justice of each of these portraits. "Beast and angel," she murmured, remembering old lessons, and again the merman nodded. "No, I'm not a mer, am I, however much I have longed for the sea. And it isn't you I want, but what you know, what you have seen."

The merman showed her a coral reef, bright and various, which seemed to grow as she watched, becoming more complex, more brilliant with each addition; then an image of herself standing knee-deep in the sea, watching the merman swim away from her. She smelled of acceptance, resignation, inwardness—the taste of a mer parting from a loved companion.

Wearily, Miss Carstairs rubbed her forehead, which throbbed with multiplying thoughts. Her notebooks, her scholarship, her long-neglected study, all called to her through the merman's vision. At the same time, she noted that he was responding directly to her. Had she suddenly learned to speak visions? Had he learned to see words? Beyond these thoughts, Miss Carstairs was conscious of the fierce warmth of the spring sun, the rich smell of the damp soil, and the faint green rustle of growing leaves. She didn't know if they were the merman's perceptions or her own.

Miss Carstairs pulled herself heavily to her feet and brushed down her skirts with a shaking hand. "It's high time for you to be off," she said. "I'll just ring for Stephen and John to fetch the sling." Unconsciously, she sought the savor of disapproval and rum that was John's signal odor; it lingered near the kitchen door. At the same time, she had a clear vision of Stephen, wrapped in a disreputable jacket, plodding with bucket and fishing pole across the garden to the seawall. She saw him from above, as she had seen him from her bedroom window early that morning. So it was her vision, not the merman's. The scientist in her noted the fact, and also that the throbbing in her head had settled down to a gentle pulse, discernible, like the beating of her heart, only if she concentrated on it.

A laughing school of fish flashed through the ordered currents of her thoughts, and Miss Carstairs understood that the merman found her new consciousness amusing. Then a searing sense of heat and a tight, itching pain under her skin sent her running into the house shouting for John. When he appeared—from the kitchen, she noted—she said, "Get a bucket and a blanket and wet down the merman. You'll find him in the garden, near the sundial. Then bring the stretcher." He gaped at her uncomprehendingly. "Hurry!" she snapped, and strode off toward the seawall in search of Stephen.

Following his scent, she found him hunched over his fishing pole and his pipe. He tasted of wet wool, tobacco, and solitude. "Stephen, I have learned everything from the merman that he is able to tell me. I have decided to release him."

Stephen began to pull in his line. "Yes, miss," he said. "About time."

The tide was going out, and the men had to carry their burden far past the tidal pool where the merman had first washed ashore. It was heavy going, for the wet sand was soft and the merman was heavy. When they came to water at last, Miss Carstairs stood by as they released the merman into the shallows, then waded out up to her knees to stand beside him. The sun splintered the water into blinding prisms; she turned her eyes inshore, away from the glare. Behind her, Stephen and John were trudging back toward the beach, the conservatory glittering above them like a crystal jewel box. Sharp tastes of old seaweed and salt-crusted rocks stung her nose. Squinting down, Miss Carstairs saw the merman floating quietly against the pull of the sea, one webbed hand grasping the sodden fabric of her skirt. His crest was erect, his mouth a little open. Miss Carstairs read joy in his pearly eyes, and something like regret.

"I shall not forget what you have shown me," she said, although she knew the words to be superfluous. Mentally, she called up the ape-woman and the scientist and fused them into a composite portrait of a human woman, beast and angel, heart and mind, need and reason; and she offered that portrait to the merman as a gift, an explanation, a farewell. Then he was gone, and Miss Carstairs began to wade back to shore.

THE MAID ON THE SHORE

I live on a rocky coast at the easternmost tip of Newfoundland, in a cottage huddled under a cliff at the beach's edge. Its tumbled stones suggested poverty, a reeking seaweed fire, and a dirt floor, but that was just my father's caution. We did burn seaweed, but cleanly, in a well-vented hearth, and our floors were laid with polished stone flags softened with wool rugs of my mother's weaving. The two bedrooms behind the kitchen were furnished with finely carved beds and chairs of walrus bone. The windowless walls of the inmost room were lined with rows of books.

I cannot remember a time when I did not read. Sheltered by my family's isolation, I learned of mankind and magic from the volumes on my father's shelves. On winter nights, we would sit by the salt-smelling fire—Mother, Father, me—each absorbed in worlds that touched but did not disturb each other. Mother would card the wool from her sheep and spin the fluffy rolags into yarn that she would thread upon her handloom and weave into fine cloth. She sang as she worked, the cloth inspiring the song and the song the cloth, for her magic was wordless and deep and strange: the inhuman, sifting magic of the sea.

Father sat at the other side of the hearth, a lap-desk of fine teak upon his knee, scratching-scratching with a gray goose quill on the thin pages of his notebook. His magic was all words. Spells, formulas, observations of the stars and moon, charms, cantrips, and incantations—he played with them through the winter evenings, muttering constantly under his breath.

Sometimes I could coax Father out of his wizardly fog by begging him for a tale of his life upon the Continent and in the fabled East, where magicians were still held in honor. His favorite story, and mine, was of the one time when he had found himself without words: the soft May night when he had seen my mother dancing naked on the shore.

Under the moon she had danced and sung with her sisters, her body white and fluid as sea-foam, her hair black as a starless night. Knowing that she was a seal-maiden, knowing that he must hide her sealskin if he wished to possess her, knowing she would not return until next May Eve, my father cast aside his knowledge and his clothing together and walked naked down to the strand to meet her and the seal-maidens took him into their dance as the sea takes a swimmer.

When the dawn-star rose and her sisters drew on their pelts to slide into the ocean, my mother held my father's hand and watched them go. Next morning she was with him still. Of her own will, she lived with him and loved him; of her own will, she bore him a maid-child: me.

Like my parentage, my person and magic were strange, mixed things. My human and selkie blood mingled to give me a subtle, elusive magic that would seep away if I were to lose my virginity—a fate that seemed more distant than the ever-receding horizon. On the winter evenings of my childhood, I would sit between Mother and Father on a sealskin rug, reading to myself and humming in counterpoint to Father's mutterings and Mother's singing. I understood and loved both their magics: Mother's songs and patterns spoke to me as though tongued; Father's words seeped into my bones like music. I was, I know now, content.

Although I had heard tales of mortal men, I never saw one until the autumn of my eighteenth year, when an unlucky fisherman ran aground in a sudden squall on the rocks at the mouth of our bay and my mother swam out and hauled him to shore, bruised, half frozen, terrified. Father insisting that she bring him into the cottage, she dragged him through the door and dropped him beside the kitchen fire, where he lay panting and staring about him.

In that fisherman's wondering eyes, I saw my family anew. My father—small and spindle-shanked; a reader by the squint of his ice-blue eyes; a thinker by the animation of his dark, thin face. My mother—plump and white-skinned; strong, smooth muscles mounding her arms; hair and whiteless eyes black-brown and glowing like a healthy animal's. Me—plump and white-skinned like my mother, small like my father; black-haired, blue-eyed, seal-toothed. The fisherman drank our broth and reluctantly accepted Father's offer of a pallet beside our hearth. When dawn came, he was gone, and one of Father's books, left carelessly on a side table, went with him, and the finely woven cloth under it as well.

Mother roared her rage at the theft and Father talked of moving. But as the days and weeks went by, our fear ebbed. The fisherman might have died making his way overland, or lost the book or the weaving; perhaps no one believed his story of a wizard and a selkie and their witch-daughter living alone in a distant bay. We did not move.

Winter came. We folded our sheep, stored the potatoes and dried the beans from Mother's garden, salted the last of the fish she had caught for us with her sharp seal's teeth, and settled in gratefully to our usual winter pursuits.

At midwinter, in the dark aftermath of a heavy snow, men came to hunt us out. Even now, I wake whimpering and bleating like a seal cub from dreams of the fishermen breaking in upon us and clubbing my father until his blood pooled on the kitchen floor. Three of them came after Mother and me, their clubs uplifted and their eyes shiny with fear and lust. We roared and hurled ourselves at them. There was nothing in me of my father that night. We tore the throats from four of them, my mother and I, while the rest fled yammering from our cottage.

When all was quiet, we bundled the torn bodies out of the kitchen and down to the ocean, where the tide took them out to sea for the fish to eat. We scrubbed the blood from the polished flags with melted snow and fine sand, and then my mother stripped off her shawl and her linen bodice, her woolen skirt and her petticoats, took the sealskin rug from the study floor, and wrapped it around her naked shoulders.

I had always known that the rug upon which I sat and drowsed on winter days was Mother's sealskin, for the pelt smelled of her and never wore thin or lost its living gloss. From time to time, it and she would disappear together to lie upon the ice floes, and I would spread an ordinary sealskin before the study fire to support the fiction of my father's ignorance. But never before that day had I seen her go from woman to seal. One moment she was standing before the kitchen fire, a plump woman draped in a sealskin cloak. The next, she melted into the floor like candle wax and became a sad-eyed seal, sleek and whiskered. She whistled to me urgently and I helped her drag my father's body across the rocky beach to the water, where she towed him out to sea under the solemn moon. When I saw her after, it was only as a brown seal swimming out in the bay. At high tide she might come near and leave a fish on the rocky beach, but she never came ashore again. After a few years she stopped coming altogether. I think the sealers must have taken her.

I suppose the fishermen reckoned me dead or swum out to sea with my selkie mother, or were too afraid to check. In any case, they never returned. Suns rose and set, moons waxed and waned, snows fell and melted, and still I lived a maid on the shore, tending my mother's sheep and garden, reading my father's books, fishing for salmon and hunting for partridge and wild goose when I tired of shellfish and mutton. Sometimes I longed for some reason to use my power to an end other than charming fish to my hook—to call up a tempest or call down a storm, just to show that I could do it. But my father's books had taught me what can come of power used for power's sake, and I refrained.

Time runs oddly for a wizard's child who does not age like a human woman, so I do not know how long I lived alone. But it was many and many a long year before men came again to break my solitude and my peace.

Again it was late autumn, the time of the worst storms, and a northeasterly gale hunted early snow across the uplands. The gale blew for three days, whipping the ocean to a terrible frenzy of freezing water and stinging foam, scouring the gulls from the sky and driving both me and my sheep into shelter. On the third day the wind turned northwest, as it always does in these latitudes, bringing to my bay high tides, floating islands of kelp, and an intruder.

I had been gathering a harvest of seaweed to cover my garden, and near sundown was laboring back with it over the rocks. Although I am almost as strong as a selkie, the sodden bundle of kelp dragged heavily at my shoulders. As I set it down and stretched, my hands to the small of my back, I looked out over the bay and saw a ship—a clipper by her proud sleekness—three-masted, many-sailed, and badly maimed by the storm. Her mainmast was down, her mizzen was splintered, and only a few rags of canvas flew from her foremast. Wearily she rocked at anchor, and sailors swarmed over her like rats, cutting free the useless rigging and clearing the decks of debris.

Among the bustle, one still figure stood aft by the taffrail and held a glass to his eye, transfixing me in its sights, arms akimbo, breasts thrust forward with unintended boldness. I felt his gaze, and its touch, even at that distance, was intimate and unwelcome. Shuddering, I bent to my bundle, hurried back to my cottage, and barred the door behind me.

By nightfall I had fretted myself into a rage. Was I not the daughter of a magician and a skin-changer, a sorceress in my own right, mistress of word and song and woven pattern? Why should I fear a crippled ship and her exhausted crew? But memory mocked me with visions of a helpless fisherman and blood upon the kitchen floor, and I tossed between revenge and retreat, hatred and fear, until at last I fell asleep.

Early next morning, I was started awake by a rapping at the door. The hair at my neck rose and prickled. Whoever it was knocked again, shy and soft, as though unsure of a welcome. Would a ravager, a pirate tap so mannerly? A third knock, weaker yet. Curious, I put on my shawl, drew the bolt, and opened. Before me stood a young man in a blue coat and a handful of ragged sailors with buckets.

"Aye?" I said, folding my shaking hands under my apron.

"Ma'am." The young man bowed awkwardly. He was a full head taller than I, with a sailor's blue eyes and a pale beard like a gosling's down blurring his cheeks. "Captain Pelican's compliments, ma'am, and may we please draw water from your stream? We've been a mortal long time at sea, and never a dipperful of clean water do we have aboard."

He was respectful, afraid only of frightening me, and my terror faded before his downcast gaze. Mistress of myself once more, I made a shooing movement with my hand as though he were a gosling indeed. "Help 'eeself, boy. Water's free."

I was careful to speak the common coast dialect, as though I were an ordinary fishwife with nothing strange or wonderful about me that must be feared or spoiled. Still, the sailors eyed me as they dipped the water from my stream into small barrels, and I was grateful that the young man lingered by my door.

"I am Thomas Fletcher, ma'am, first mate of the clipper *Cape Town Maid*. We sail from China, around the Cape of Good Hope to

Salem with a cargo of gold, porcelain, spices, and silks. Our captain is Elias Pelican." He faltered, reddened, continued. "He asks, ma'am, for grain if you can spare it, and news of forests with trees suitable for a jury mast, for we will never make Salem in this state." Timidly, he smiled down at me, and I found that I was smiling in return.

"There do be fir above, and pine. It be up along the moor and not easy found. I'll lead 'ee," I said.

The shadows were short by the time we had trekked over the moorland to a respectable stand of fir, and had lengthened almost to dusk before we returned, for the seamen bickered over the choice of a tree, then bickered over the best way of felling and stripping it. My father had told me how seamen must work together, each individual becoming a part of a human mechanism called "crew," harmonious in action as canvas and wind, capstan and rope. As I listened to the sailors curse and pick at each other, I thought that this particular crew was no more harmonious, either in action or in voice, than a beach of bull seals in rut.

"Damn your eyes," shouted Mr. Fletcher at last when two of them had nearly come to blows over the angle and height of the cut they were to make. "Do you want the captain ashore?"

His words fell on the crew like a fog. Faces greyed; eyes dulled; voiced fell utterly silent. Working quickly now, the men felled the tree, stripped it, and hauled it across the moor to the beach. Only their bodies and hands spoke to me, who knew from my mother how to understand the wordless speech of wind and fish and sheep, and told me that they were afraid.

Watching them stumble and fumble, I could not imagine how they had survived the passage of the Horn without hanging themselves on the rigging or tumbling from the crosstrees. Indeed some of them night have recently fallen from a lesser height, so stiffly did they move. One young man, with a bruised face and an angry eye, wore a shirt marked across the back with rusty stains that darkened and gleamed wetly as he worked.

That night I dreamed of my mother standing by the shore, ankle-deep in the tide, changing. The strange thing was that she never became wholly seal or woman, but remained mutable: a woman's face and torso might end in a seal's hind flippers; a sleek, whiskered head might dart above a woman's full white breasts. I dreamed, too, of the bulls roaring on the beaches, of the remembered salt of human blood on my lips, the jar of human bones between my teeth. More than once, I woke sweating and trembling, only to slip again into uneasy dreaming. But when morning came, I opened the door to Mr. Fletcher's knock and asked him in most civilly to take a cup of chamomile tea.

He sat by the fire in my father's chair, nursing the thick brown mug between his hands and casting curious glances at the polished wooden furniture, the woven cloths, the pewter and china ranked on the heavy oak dresser.

"This puts me in mind of my mother's kitchen," he said at last. "You live here alone?"

"Aye." He was a lovely man, strong and clean-limbed. His sun-burnished face warmed my dark kitchen, and I wanted him to stay. "Our mam and dad drowned," I went on. "It be three winters since, now."

His pity was quick and sweet to hear. "Poor girl, so young to be left alone," he said gently, not knowing that I was far older than he. "Why did you not leave this lonely place? There are fishing villages up and down this coast would welcome you."

"Here I were born, and here 'tis fitty I stay," I said shortly. "Tell I, Mr. Fletcher, where be your mother's kitchen and what set 'ee to sailing?"

So he told me of the snug clapboard house in Gloucester, of his father who had followed the whales until his ship was lost, of his mother who had listened dry-eyed to her son's decision to serve the same harsh mistress. He had been a cabin boy on a whaler, an apprentice on a merchantman, a boatswain, and a mate. "I've turned my hand to most things, and know how a ship should be run. My last captain advanced me when his first mate washed overboard, and it was as first mate I came aboard *The Cape Town Maid,* two years ago."

"Two years be a mortal long time afloat," I said. "Hast a sweetheart?"

He nodded, fumbled in his waistcoat and brought out a tarnished locket, which he opened and held out to me. "Nancy Bride," he said, low and earnest. "The sweetest girl in Gloucester."

Being a black paper silhouette, the portrait cold have been of any young girl with a straight nose and ringlets, but I read in the angle of his head and the trembling of his broad hand that he saw his Nancy's loving face and no other smiling from that anonymous snippet. Suddenly, I was out of patience, even angry.

"Her be a clean-featured maid," I said. "Does 'ee think her'll have waited on 'ee all this long time?"

Mr. Fletcher flushed, snapped the locket shut, and restored it to his bosom. "She's as true as death, ma'am," he said stiffly. "I'd stake my soul on her."

I hastened to make up the ground I'd lost. "I'm thinking her be a lucky maid. So ye'll be a married man as soon as ever the banns can be called?"

"No."

There was a long and uncomfortable pause. What ailed the man? He was stirring now in the chair as if preparing to leave. To keep him, I said, "'Tis an odd thing the captain's not come ashore."

Mr. Fletcher mumbled something into his waistcoat that I asked him to repeat. "I said, 'it's not the oddest thing about him,' ma'am." He hesitated with the air of a sheep at a gate—afraid to move, eager to be on the other side—then began to speak.

"Although he's a merchant, he refuses to take passengers on board. He doesn't seem to care how many seasoned sailors there are among the crews he buys from the crimps, providing they come cheap enough.

Why, there's hardly four men knew a belaying pin from a capstan spar when they shipped aboard, though they found out soon enough which falls the hardest on a man's back." He was through the gate now, and trotting. "Two years is a long time at sea, as you've said, ma'am, and it's longer yet if you're sailing under a captain like Pelican. He's one who likes to put the cat among the pigeons just to see the feathers fly—never mind if the cat scratches or the pigeons peck. He'll order the scuppers cleaned by the dawn watch if the fancy takes him, or the deck holystoned at midnight, and it's twenty lashes for any sailor who might be slow at leaping to obey. He's too free with the lash and too free with his fists and his knife. Flogging's been against the law for thirty years and more, yet he's ordered ten strokes for a dirty shirt, though the men have no place to wash their linen except the scuppers, and he's filthy as bilge water himself."

Once Mr. Fletcher had begun, there was no more hope of stopping him than of turning a starving sheep from rich pasture. He was angry now, fairly flaming with it, and his sparkling eyes and flushed cheeks were a pleasure to see.

"Round the Horn's a hard passage, and you expect to lose a dozen men or so to sickness and accident, but we've buried that many from dysentery and lash weals gone septic, and lost as many again overboard. He tied Carbone high in the mainmast rigging once when a fever kept him from coming up with his watch. 'The sea air'll cure him,' he said, and left him there all night. Next morning, Carbone was all but dead. Two days later, he died." Mr. Fletcher shook his head.

"Could'ee not have cut him down and bade Captain Bucko go whistle?" I asked curiously.

Mr. Fletcher stretched his eyes wide. "But ma'am, that would be mutiny! It's no part of a first mate's job to countermand his captain's orders."

I doubted it was part of a first mate's job to flog his shipmates for no reason but the captain's fancy. Though I said nothing, my scorn must have shown in my face, for before I knew it, he was on his feet, thanking me for the tea, and out the door.

My father always said that confession was a relief to the soul, but telling me of the horrors aboard *The Cape Town Maid* did not relieve Mr. Fletcher. After that morning's confidences, he stayed well away from my door. He was certainly nowhere to be found when six of my sheep were stolen from the fold and slaughtered on the beach. "Captain's orders," one squint-eyed runt told me when I stormed out to confront the butchers. "Ye mun tak' it up wi' he."

I glared out at the *Maid,* rocking quietly in the swell. A tall figure stood in the stern, the sun winking from the barrel of his glass. Outraged, I shook my fist at the brazen eye, went back to my cottage, and barred the door.

The next day they were finished at last. The mast had been trimmed, banded with iron, floated out to *The Cape Town Maid,* stepped, and rigged. There was much going back and forth from shore with barrels and game and strings of fish. By sundown the strand was empty at last, and I ventured out to care for my remaining sheep.

The clipper lay at anchor, her masts rerigged and proud against the rosy sky. Across the quiet bay came the boom of Captain Pelican's harsh voice haranguing his men. Though I rejoiced that they'd be gone by morning so that I could sleep easy again, as the night fell I found myself staring out my window at the *Maid*'s moon-touched shadow, restless and angry and sure that my anger would not simply sail with the clipper out of the bay.

Here, I told myself, was a reason to use my powers at last. Perhaps I would send lightning to strike down the cruel captain as he strutted on the poop; perhaps I would simply call up a storm and sink *The Cape Town Maid* with all her thieving hands aboard. I was still debating alternatives when Mr. Fletcher knocked once more on my door.

He was cold, still, correct, as though his indiscretion and my scorn still rankled in his mind. "Seeing as you've been so kind, ma'am, and so generous with the water and the sheep and all, the captain asks you to come on board to view the cargo, take a glass of sherry wine, and be properly thanked. He will not take 'no' for an answer."

I looked past Mr. Fletcher at the faces of the men who accompanied him. They looked uneasy, but some looked eager as well, their eyes bright and flat like the eyes of those fishermen so many years ago.

"Nay, sir, no need for thanks," I said. "Water's free, I told 'ee, and help is too. Though the captain could pay for they sheep, come 'pon that."

"The captain wishes to convey his thanks himself, ma'am," Mr. Fletcher repeated stubbornly. "He'll settle the matter of the sheep with you on the *Maid*." And he began to extoll the value and beauty of the cargo as if to dazzle me with the prospect of some rare and unnamed reward for my kindness.

Was the man daft, or did he think I was? A glass of sherry wine, indeed. If I went out to that ship, I would never return to the shore. A woman is not bad luck while a ship is at anchor, and no doubt the captain intended me to be dead and overboard long before the *Maid* sailed on the dawn tide.

So I listened, or seemed to, and made no response. Mr. Fletcher began to sweat and his voice took on a pleading note. He seemed to have settled with himself that he would not force me out to the ship. If he could persuade me, well, then, I would get what I deserved. But if he had to pick me up and carry me, protesting, his conscience might prick him to defiance.

Briefly I considered pressing Mr. Fletcher into making a choice between the two sides of his sense of propriety. But I had a curiosity to meet this Captain Pelican, so, "Thank'ee kindly sir," I said as his eloquence began to run dry. "I'll be pleased to take sherry wine with your captain." And I set briskly off down the strand, trailed by Mr. Fletcher and the sailors.

They helped me into the stern of the longboat and rowed out to the ship. As we approached, I could see her figurehead clearly: a naked woman supporting her massive breasts in her hands and leering out at the innocent sea. Then we were alongside the ship, a ladder was lowered, and dozens of hard, eager hands pulled me onto the deck.

Captain Pelican was on the bridge, and Mr. Fletcher led me up to him ceremoniously. The captain was an imposing man, over six feet tall, fleshy in a salt-stained frock coat. Above his high collar and frayed cravat, his face was dark, craggy, pitted like granite; his iron-colored hair hung lank around his ears. "Pleased to meet you," he said and spat a brown stream of tobacco juice at my feet.

I dropped a curtsy, my eyes downcast, trying very hard not to laugh. He was so ridiculous after all, whipping his sailors to show them that he was as fearless and lawless as the ocean he sailed upon. But his swanking could not fool me. Under his sour odor of sweat, tobacco, and stale gin, I could smell the fear upon him sharp as a knife.

Captain Pelican hitched up my chin with his finger and leered down into my face. His pale eyes were rheumy. "Mr. Fletcher has pumped you some bilge about sherry wine and thanks, but I intend you no such courtesy. You'll spend a watch or two in my bunk, doing what a woman does best, and then I've promised my crew they'll get what's left."

He showed me his tobacco-stained teeth, waiting, I suppose for some sign of revulsion or terror. I thought of tearing out his throat or singing such a sea-spell that he would face the world with a walrus's head upon his shoulders and clapped my hands together like a child.

"O, thankee, sir, thankee," I cried. "Thee has no notion what weary company a maidenhead be, and no proper man for to lighten me of un."

Captain Pelican looked taken aback by this speech, and not so happy as one might expect. "Well," he said, and cleared his throat. "Always glad to be of service to a lady. Some sherry wine?"

I clasped my hands over the greasy arm of his jacket and smiled. "Come, my dear, thee ben't shy?"

"There's no hurry," he said hoarsely. Without taking his eyes from me, he shouted for Mr. Fletcher to bring the wine and two glasses and led me to the wooden bench that ran along the stern of the ship.

By this time, I could all but taste the captain's blood on my lips. I sank onto the bench and into his arms. He bent to kiss me, his massive head and shoulders black against the silver moonlight, his breath rank in the clean, salt air. Eagerly, I raised my face to him.

"Captain Pelican, sir," came Mr. Fletcher's prim voice. "Your sherry wine, sir."

The captain released me unkissed and, damning Mr. Fletcher for a fish-buggering old woman, poured and handed me a glass of wine.

Sipping the sherry gave me time to reflect. The moonlight glittered at me from the watchful, rat-bright eyes of the crew. While they might stand by and cheer while I tore out their captain's throat, they were unlikely to set me safely ashore when I was done. Lust for my body or lust for my blood, both were alike to them. If I killed their captain, they were apt simply to skewer me where I sat and throw my body overboard with his.

When Captain Pelican finished his wine, he laid aside his glass and began to fumble at my bosom. I smiled, took a deep breath, and began to sing. Startled, he drew back his hands, lifted them to muzzle me, hesitated, and then, as the spell caught him, let them drop to his knees.

My song was the lament that the heart of every seaport woman sings when her man sets sail. Its notes were love and longing and the dark night watches when a woman's spirit is at low tide and every breeze seems to sigh with the last prayers of downing sailors. My seal's voice, low-pitched and resonant, carried its plaint to each crewman's bones. Not only the captain, but every man on that ship heard my song, and in my wordless melody, heard the ceaseless calling of his wife, sweetheart, sister, mother. From the foredeck came the sound of weeping.

The captain glared at me, tearless, stiff, and resistant.

I wove into my song the slow, sleepy brush of waves over sand. The captain's lids drooped, and he began to slip sideways on the bench, the hilt of his sword poking into his ribs. Wind breathed in the rigging and sent small waves shushing gently against the hull. *The Cape Town Maid* slept.

Now, I thought, and turned to the silent figure slumped against the stern railing. I rolled his heavy body off the bench and tore open his coat and his shirt. Shadow caught in the folds of his untanned throat as if already it ran with blood. He's a monster, I thought as I crouched over him; I have wanted to kill him since I first saw his ship in my bay, and I *will* kill him. Now.

I lowered my mouth to his throat. His skin against my tongue was foul and slick as rotting fish. I recoiled and spat and scrubbed my mouth with my skirt. Thoughts chased one another through my mind, cold and bright and quick: to murder will make me human; to flee will make me animal; there are more kinds of virginity than one.

The moon was slipping down the mainmast, barring the deck with black shadows, silvering the hair on Captain Pelican's bared chest. I brushed my fingers over the thatch. It gave under my touch, springy as uncarded wool. Although his pelt was thick, there was not enough hair to weave a mat. But it might be worked into a larger pattern. Humming thoughtfully, I gave the hair a little tug. It came easily free from his skin.

Singing as I worked, I opened and laid back the wings of his coat and linen shirt and plucked the hair from his chest. Under my busy hands, his naked skin shone almost luminous in the moonglow, its pale expanse broken only by the faint shadows of his nipples. I cupped them in my palms; the flesh beneath them stretched, softened, swelled.

Song welled up within me, flowed from my lips and fingers, guiding and guided by the movement of my hands. I caressed the knot from his throat, stroked the stubble from his cheeks. Wherever my hands passed, the texture of his skin became finer, denser. When I had done with his face, my fingers wandered down across the heavy, round breasts to unclasp the captain's belt and rest on his belly. As my witch-song sank into his flesh, the world narrowed to the beating of my blood and his and the echo of the tide flowing in the notes of my song.

Captain Pelican gave a great cry that flew from his altered throat like a sea gull's plaintive scream and died away to a whimper. So, too, died my song.

I knelt shivering on the deck until my limbs unknotted, then rose and went to the captain's cabin. I found there a sea chest, from which I took six pieces of gold as payment for my slaughtered sheep, a brick of black tea, and a length of sea-green silk. When I came up again, I searched for Mr. Fletcher among the coiled ropes and the snoring sailors and found him folded like a sleeping sheep at the foot of a companionway. From him I took the tarnished locket that held the silhouette of Nancy Bride and his clasp knife. I stove in five of the ship's longboats and, freighting the sixth with my booty, lowered it to the sea.

The moon had long since sunk behind the cliffs and set. By the time I pushed off, dead night shrouded *The Cape Town Maid* and her slumbering crew. In a little while the sky would lighten, the tide would turn, and the crew would wake and sail the *Maid* out of my bay. With luck, they'd be well away to Salem before they had attention to spare for their captain, asleep on the wooden boards at the stern of the ship. As I paddled the longboat back to the shore, I wondered what they would make of what they found.

ACKNOWLEDGMENTS

"The Maid on the Shore" was written in 1986. "The Ghost of Cwmlech Manor" was written in 2011. That's twenty-five years. I cannot hope to remember everyone who helped me with criticism, encouragement, advice, research, and occasional stern talkings-to (especially at the beginning), but I do have some very particular thanks to render.

To all the librarians, docents, guides, and chance-met acquaintances, for answering searching questions about seals, Darwin, tropical fish, the Siege of Paris, ghosts, Cajun patois, 16th century jewelry-making, lighthouses, Texas tall tales, and Impressionist painting with patience and humor.

To Greer Gilman, for reading endless drafts of "The Maid on the Shore," "Nanny Peters," "Miss Carstairs and the Merman," and "Land's End."

To Terri Windling and Ellen Datlow, for inspiring me to write "The Fiddler of Bayou Teche," "La Fée Verte," "The Red Piano," "The Printer's Daughter," and "The Fairy Cony-Catcher."

To Kelly Link and Gavin J. Grant, for being not only the best publishers a writer could hope for, but excellent critique partners and even better friends.

To Ellen Kushner, for everything.

ABOUT THE AUTHOR

Delia Sherman was born in Japan and raised in New York City. Her work has appeared most recently in the anthologies *Naked City, Steampunk!,* and *Queen Victoria's Book of Spells.* She is the author of six novels including *The Porcelain Dove* (a *New York Times* Notable Book), *The Freedom Maze,* and *Changeling,* and has received the Mythopoeic and Norton awards. She lives in New York City.